MW00613075

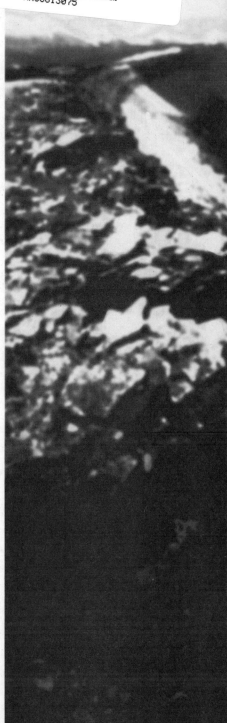

the CARDINAL DIVIDE

A COLE BLACKWATER MYSTERY

NeWest Press

the CARDINAL DIVIDE

STEPHEN LEGAULT

Library and Archives Canada Cataloguing in Publication
Legault, Stephen, 1971-
The Cardinal Divide / Stephen Legault.
(Nunatak fiction)
ISBN 978-1-897126-32-5
I. Title. II. Series.
PS8623.E46633C37 2008
C813'.6
C2008-902313-7

Editor for the Board: Don Kerr
Cover and interior design: Natalie Olsen
Cover image: Stephen Legault
Author photo: Dan Anthon

Canadian Heritage   Patrimoine canadien

Alberta Foundation for the Arts

Canada Council for the Arts   Conseil des Arts du Canada

edmonton arts council

NeWest Press acknowledges the support of the Canada Council for the Arts, the Alberta Foundation for the Arts, and the Edmonton Arts Council for our publishing program. We also acknowledge the financial support of the Government of Canada through the Book Publishing Industry Development Program (BPIDP).

NeWest Press

#201 8540–109 Street
Edmonton, Alberta T6G 1E6
780.432.9427
newestpress.com

No bison were harmed in the making of this book. We are committed to protecting the environment and to the responsible use of natural resources. This book is printed on 100% recycled, ancient forest-friendly paper.

1 2 3 4 5 11 10 09 08

printed and bound in Canada

This book is for the future:
for Rio Bergen and Silas Morgen Legault
for Jenn

The Cardinal Divide is a work of fiction. While the Cardinal Divide is a real place, the Buffalo Anthracite Mine, the town of Oracle, and the characters who populate it are fictional, and any resemblance to actual localities and people is purely coincidental.

Prologue

Mike Barnes stood at the window of his fourth-floor office and looked out at the sweep of emerald forest stretching beyond the Buffalo Anthracite Mine's fenced compound. The last fingertips of daylight tipped the dark spruce and fir forests with light the colour of smouldering embers and then were eclipsed by darkness. Barnes watched for another five minutes as the colour was sucked from the scene before him by the encroaching night. He looked at his watch: it was after nine. He was weary. The day had started early and was ending late, and he still had to drive the long, winding dirt road back to Oracle to his rental house on a hill overlooking town. It would be midnight before he crawled into bed. Alone.

He craned his neck and looked south into the darkness, beyond the existing mine, toward the Cardinal Divide's jagged back. In his mind's eye he saw the reef of stone rising abruptly from the rolling foothills that broke against the implacable wall of the Rocky Mountains. Though the Divide was beyond his line of sight, Mike Barnes knew it was there. Could not forget it was there. So much angst over a hill.

He stretched and turned from the window, the woods now completely dark, the mountains beyond pale shapes in the darkening sky. Barnes sat down at his desk and tidied up a few papers he had shown to his last guest. He filed them neatly in the hanging files in his desk drawer and cleared away his pens. Except for a portrait of his family, and his Day-Timer, the surface was pleasingly empty. His secretary, Tracey, urged him to track his appointments in Outlook, so she could have easy access to them from her own computer. But while Barnes was not opposed to technology, in fact embraced it, he preferred the old-fashioned full-sized calendar book that could be spread open each morning for a panoramic view of the day. It appealed to his sense of aesthetics and to his nostalgia. Barnes recalled his father's Day-Timer, how each January he had given Mike the previous year's to play with. Barnes had spent hours with those Day-Timers, colouring in his father's doodling that adorned the margins of the book and carrying it around in a worn satchel that he pretended was a briefcase.

And now, with his computer sitting at Oracle's only PC repair shop, Mike Barnes was glad for this outdated method.

Barnes took a deep breath, closed the calendar, and stood to clear away the glasses and water pitcher that sat on the low, round table at the centre of his spacious office. He collected two of the dirty glasses along with the pitcher and placed them on Tracey's desk. She'd take care of them in the morning.

Mike Barnes' final appointment of that long day hadn't been interested in the glass of water he'd put out for him, though it might have cooled the flames of their heated discussion. Barnes had managed to keep his composure. His final guest had descended into red-faced shouting and livid finger pointing by the end of their two-hour meeting.

All this over a mine. All this over a chunk of stone called the Cardinal Divide. Barnes shook his head.

As he passed her desk again, Barnes thought about Tracey. She had taken it hard when he'd called it off between them, but that was necessary. In a week his wife and two children would arrive in Oracle to live with him for the summer. If he wasn't done this job by the fall they would head back to Toronto on their own. If he finished, the family could head back together.

It was fun while it lasted with Tracey, and he didn't relish sleeping alone, but all good things must come to an end.

He felt the water he'd consumed over the course of the last two-hour marathon meeting sluice in his gut. Time to tap a kidney, then retrieve his things and head for home.

He made his way down the corridor to the washroom at the far end of the hall, passing now empty offices as he went. When he had arrived six months before, most of these offices had been occupied, but slowly he was seeing to that. The operation was top heavy and he had a job to do. And while it wasn't unusual for mining operations to lay off administrative staff, after a steady six months of cutbacks, some people inside and outside the operation were obviously getting wise to what Mike Barnes' true purpose was in Oracle.

He opened the door to the bathroom and stepped in, flipping on the light as he did. He glanced at himself in the mirror, pushed a hand through his wavy blonde hair, pinched his nose where his wire-rimmed glasses rested, and then stood at a urinal to relieve himself.

His last two meetings of the night played out in his mind. He was surprised to find that he had actually enjoyed the meeting with Cole Blackwater. It was entertaining to see through Blackwater's sketchy attempt at covering his environmentalist tracks by pretending to be a reporter. Wonders never cease, he thought. But his last meeting? That left a bad taste in his mouth.

But what did he expect? The cat was out of the bag.

He finished and stepped to the sink to wash his hands. Then he turned the water off and pulled a few paper towels from the dispenser to dry his hands. Mike Barnes heard footsteps in the hall. JP, the night watchman, had just made his rounds. Did he forget something? The footsteps stopped outside the door. Mike suddenly felt a chill rush through his body. He stood still, watching the door, and without knowing why, held his breath. When the door to the washroom opened, Barnes let his breath out through his teeth with a hissing sound. He turned back to the mirror and regarded himself as he spoke. "I told you there is nothing more to say on the subject," he said as he removed a piece of dry skin from the bridge of his nose, stepping back from the mirror. Alberta is dryer than the desert, he thought.

The blow caught him entirely by surprise. The back of his head exploded with bone-crushing force, sending a thick rope of blood splashing against the bathroom's tiled walls. Barnes pitched forward, his forehead connecting with the edge of the wash basin, blood spraying in a fine mist beneath the counter and across the walls. He collapsed in a heap on the floor, his eyes blank and staring into nothing, into a darkness as black as the hole in the earth called the Buffalo Anthracite Mine.

1 Cole Blackwater heard the phone ring as he locked the door to his eighth-floor office in Vancouver's Dominion Building. He stood with his hand on the chrome doorknob worn smooth and glossy with decades of use. The key was still inserted in the door as he listened to one ring, then a second, and a third. He looked at his watch. It was nearly 6:30 PM. Friday.

He let his head fall forward heavily in a gesture of weariness and stared blankly at his scuffed and dirty black boots.

The phone rang a fourth time and then stopped. His voicemail would pick up and the caller would hear Mary's voice ask if they wanted to leave a message. Until two hours ago Mary had been his assistant and sole employee. Now Mary no longer worked for him. He'd had to let her go.

He stared at his boots, his hand rested lightly on the door handle. He was dreadfully tired. More tired, he thought, than he'd ever been in his life. Whoever was calling could wait until Monday. If Monday came. Cole failed to see how he would make it through the weekend. He had no intention of throwing himself off Lion's Gate Bridge or hurling himself in front of the B-Line bus on Broadway. It was simply that he could not imagine going on as he was, his only client almost a year behind on payments, no prospects for new work in sight, and a litany of personal problems that would give an advice columnist work for a year. Something had to give.

He locked the door and slipped his keys into a crowded pocket. On the etched glass window of the door simple black letters read, "Blackwater Strategies." He turned and walked to the elevator and pushed the "down" button.

Three years ago he'd signed a lease on this office in the historic Dominion Building and pledged to take the stairs up to his office every morning and down to street level every night. Daily comings and goings, he imagined, would require the use of the elevator—rushing out to a press conference, or dashing to respond to a client's urgent need. But at least once each day he planned to walk up and down the spiral stairs that climbed dizzily through the centre of the building. He peered over the railing—too short by modern standards – down the five, six, seven, eight stories to the bottom floor and imagined himself inside an M.C. Escher print.

But that was three years ago. It had been more than a year since he'd last run up those stairs to work in the morning, and probably six months since he'd jogged down them in the evening. It wasn't because he'd grown too busy to spare the few minutes required for the trip. It was the exact opposite.

He stood in front of the elevator as it climbed from street level toward the eighth floor. He tried to see himself through to the other side of the weekend, going on as he was. Now without Mary. He sighed heavily, his shoulders hunched forward, his back slouched.

Of course, there were options available to him. There were always options. He hadn't fallen so far that he couldn't claw and scramble his way back out of the hole. But to take advantage of those options meant defeat to Cole Blackwater. And Blackwater did not take defeat — or even retreat — well at all. He had suffered the humiliation of retreat and defeat in the past, and he had sworn never to suffer their indignity again.

The elevator chimed to signal that its ancient door would soon slide open.

Then he heard the phone in his office ring again. He must remember to call-forward his office phone to his cellphone now that Mary was gone.

The phone rang again. Intuitively he guessed that it must be the same caller that had rung a few minutes ago. He looked at the elevator door open in front of him and his body shifted toward it.

The phone rang again.

The elevator waited.

Blackwater muttered under his breath. He turned away from the elevator and walked quickly toward his office door, his right hand searching in his pocket for his keys.

He reached the door in time to hear the phone ring a fourth time. He rummaged in his pocket, grumbled under his breath, and finally resorted to pulling the pocket's entire contents out in his fist. Loose change, receipts, two shopping lists, a to-do list, SkyTrain receipts, gum wrappers, and an alarming amount of pocket lint came forth, along with a heavy ring of keys. Coins and wads of paper fell to the ground — one coin rolled toward the open banister that surrounded the spiral staircase and rolled over the

Stephen Legault

precipice — while Blackwater found the right key and forced it into the lock. The door opened. The phone stopped ringing.

"Sweet Jesus," Blackwater grumbled, looking at the phone on Mary's reception desk, and then chided himself because he'd promised Sarah that he would watch his language.

The red light blinked, indicating at least one message. He closed the door behind him, ignoring the pocket detritus on the floor, and stepped into the office.

Immediately he felt sad. For the last three years Cole Blackwater had occupied this space, and for nearly two of those years, Mary Patterson had been there with him. Most often she was there when he arrived in the morning, and most evenings she was there when he left. She had been stalwart in her service, and dignified that very afternoon when he had told her that there simply wasn't any money left to pay for her services, regardless of how underpaid she was, and for how few days of the week she accepted pay.

Mary Patterson, of course, knew this. She had known it before Blackwater himself. After all, Mary kept the books for this two-person shop, and had more financial sense in her little toe than Blackwater had in his whole, ever-increasing-in-size torso. Months ago she had presented him with a financial forecast that predicted dark days ahead unless their fortunes should change. Two months ago Blackwater cut his own salary in half, and Mary trimmed her work week to three days. Last month Blackwater didn't write himself a cheque. Finally, on the last working day of April, he told Mary that he simply could not pay her for May.

Mary smiled her sweet smile and said that it was OK. Then she said she would call him next week to check in and see how things were progressing. He saw in her eyes no malice or ill will, just the same kindness and resolute confidence she radiated when he interviewed her for the position of Executive Assistant. Like most of the women in Cole's life, he had done nothing to deserve her kindness or loyalty. And like all the women in his life except one, he'd finally lost her.

He sat down behind her desk in the high-ceilinged room that formed the reception area and lunch room of his two-room office. The telephone's red light flashed and Cole decided to wait a minute or two so that the caller, whoever it was, would have time to leave a message before he dialled into the voicemail service to retrieve it.

He looked around the space. The clear light of April filtered through the tall windows on the western wall. He had chosen the office not just for the lovely staircase, but for the deep sense of history that the Dominion Building radiated. Once the tallest building in the British Empire, its copper roof and irregular shape, along with its central location on the edge of Vancouver's Gastown, made it a regional landmark. The social and environmental justice organizations housed in it had dubbed it the Tower of Lost Causes, just as 1 Nicholas Street, his former office in Ottawa, had been known as The Green Building.

The whitewashed walls of this outer office were tastefully decorated with framed prints and posters of west coast landscapes and environmental campaigns. A large potted fern occupied one corner, and a used but well-maintained loveseat and club chair another. It was all in perfect order, clean and tidy.

His own office, however, suffered the same lack of order that afflicted his pants' pockets.

Blackwater leaned back in the office chair behind Mary's empty desk, sighed heavily, leaned an elbow on the desk, and looked at the phone. Maybe he should go and she should stay? It almost made sense to lay off the boss. Mary Patterson had learned a lot in the two years they worked together, and more often than not he sought and valued her advice on his few remaining projects. But he hadn't taken on a new client in months. Blackwater's one remaining client, a small First Nations band council from the north end of Vancouver Island who looked to him for advice on how to stop the spread of salmon farms, hadn't paid him in a year. He'd stopped asking. He knew it was bad business, but they were good friends, and so he continued to help where he could. They had their own troubles.

I wonder if there are any things I do, Blackwater thought cynically, that Mary cannot?

He picked the phone from its cradle and dialled *98 and then, without listening, punched in his four-digit pass code and pressed 1 for new messages. Two messages waited.

He listened. "Hi, this is a message for Cole Blackwater. It's Peggy McSorlie calling. From Oracle, Alberta. I don't know if you remember me, but we worked together on a Jasper Park issue when

15   Stephen Legault

you were still in Ottawa. That was a while ago. Anyway, the reason that I'm calling is that the group I'm working with now, we're called the East Slope Conservation Group, could really use some help with a big issue that's popped up with the local mine here in Oracle. It's the Cardinal Divide, Cole. They want to dig a mine right below it and we need help figuring out how to stop them. I understand that you do that sort of work and we'd like to talk with you about it. Could you give me a call tonight? I'm tied up most of the weekend, so please call this evening if you can. Thanks, Cole. Hope to hear from you soon." Cole jotted down the number that she finished the message with.

He used the speaker phone so he could jot a few notes on a scrap of paper from Mary's recycling bin. He was about to hang up and quickly call Peggy McSorlie back, but decided to hear the second message.

"Hi Cole, it's Peggy again. Listen, I have to run out to pick up the kids at basketball, and then we're going to get some dinner in town. Pick up some groceries. I'll be home around ten Alberta time, I guess that's nine yours. I hope to talk to you then." She left her number again.

Cole hung up. He sat back in Mary's chair and looked at the scrap of paper with Peggy McSorlie's name on it, and her phone number.

It must have been six or seven years since he'd heard from Peggy McSorlie. At the time he had been working for a national conservation group as its young and enthusiastic National Parks Conservation Director. Jasper National Park's Management Plan was up for its mandated five-year review when Peggy McSorlie contacted his Ottawa office to ask for help thwarting a proposed plan for increased white-water rafting on the fragile Maligne River. Harlequin ducks, endangered in some parts of Canada, nested on that river in the spring, and raised their young there before migrating to the west coast in the fall.

With McSorlie and a coalition of other conservation groups, Blackwater managed to put the kybosh on the rafting proposal. They argued successfully that white-water rafting had no business on the narrow Maligne River whatsoever, given that waterway's value to the secretive harlequin ducks.

Cole Blackwater remembered Peggy McSorlie as a feisty and

competent biologist who studied the Maligne and other National Park rivers to assess their value for harlequin ducks. She was middle-aged, with a Master's degree in something or other and, as he recalled, the mother of two school-aged boys. She lived on a farm on the eastern edge of Alberta's foothills near Oracle, Alberta, with her cabinet-maker husband who ran a small woodlot.

Like many before her, McSorlie had worked diligently on contract to Parks Canada, helping the federal agency understand the complex resources that they were legally mandated to protect, only to watch her years of study and labour collect dust on a shelf while the Park Superintendent and Chief Park Warden ushered in plans from the local business community to expand development, use, access, and ultimately, corporate profits in the National Park.

But McSorlie, Blackwater recalled, wasn't one to sit on her hands. When the Jasper Park Management Plan review called for more rafting on the Maligne, she went to the media, and was "fired" for her action. Nobody had actually written her a pink slip. No, she was simply informed that her contract was complete, and was asked to hand in the keys to the rusty 1980 Dodge Ram that served as her research vehicle. That's when she called Blackwater.

He looked at the number again, and at his watch. It was 6:45. An hour later in the Mountain Time Zone. He stood up, heard his knee pop and felt his back creak, pushed the slip of paper with the number into his pocket, and walked to the door. His keys still hung in the lock. He closed the door behind him, locked it, and stooped to scoop up the litter at his feet, jamming it, along with his keys, in with the note. He had a couple of hours to kill before he could call Peggy back. He walked to the elevator, stopped to peer down the long spiral of stairs, and then punched the "down" button. Blackwater had become good at killing time of late. He knew just what to do.

He stepped from the Dominion Building onto West Hastings Street and walked west to the lights where he waited with a dozen others to cross the road. It was a cool evening, and clear. He turned the collar of his coat up against the chill. The Dominion Building sat on the very edge of Canada's poorest postal code, the area of Vancouver known to the world as the Downtown Eastside. Looking east along West Hastings, Cole Blackwater saw the shops and storefronts fade and deteriorate. Looking west, toward the downtown business core, he viewed glitter and flash. Cole Blackwater stood at the intersection of two worlds.

Cole's best friend — his only real friend, not just a drinking buddy — Denman Scott spent night and day advocating for the rights of the people on the streets of the Downtown Eastside. But powerful interests opposed him.

Waterfront property along English Bay and False Creek was quickly being bought up by American, Asian, and European investors, and twenty-, thirty-, and forty-storey high-rise luxury condominiums were being built over the rubble of some of Vancouver's poorer neighbourhoods. Handfuls of the million-dollar condominiums were being bought by wealthy Americans as safe havens for themselves and draft-aged sons who could be conscripted for American's new war — the same old war with a new name, thought Cole. More and more dilapidated Eastside hotels, flop houses, and ancient warehouses were being bought and renovated or razed and rebuilt as flats and condominiums for the upper-middle class.

The light turned green and Blackwater stepped into the street. The consequence of this gentrification was evident: more people on the streets. Now that their $30 a week hotel rooms were converted to one room apartments for Vancouver's chic business and arts community, with rent starting at $1,500 a month, more and more people were forced into alleys and doorways. And not just on the streets of the Downtown Eastside, where the problem could be contained and "managed" by police and what social service providers remained after deep provincial cuts to mental health facilities and services for those living in squalid poverty. Now the Downtown Eastside's drug, prostitution, and crime problems had spread throughout the city as the most desperate people sought shelter, food, and a fix elsewhere.

Blackwater stopped on the corner of Cambie and West Hastings to drop a quarter into the hat of a man he recognized.

"God bless," muttered the man, looking into his greasy ballcap at his take. Blackwater said nothing, but turned down Cambie toward the water.

Many of Cole's acquaintances, those who had lived in Vancouver longer than six months, learned to look right through the homeless, the vagrants, dope dealers, and the beggars in the Downtown Eastside. Not Blackwater. Not yet. He was deeply cynical about many — most — aspects of the human condition, but so far he hadn't formed a callous over the part of his heart that encouraged him to drop a quarter (and sometimes in the winter a dollar) into the hand, cap, or cup of someone who desperately needed it.

He understood why people turned away. "There but for the grace of God go I," he thought many times as he strolled through the neighbourhood between his office and the Stadium SkyTrain station just a few blocks away. When faced with such terrible human suffering, when confronted with such a staggering waste of human life and potential, how could you not eventually turn away?

Cole paced off the short walk to his favourite tavern and remembered a man named Sam, who three years ago had panhandled outside the Dominion Building. Sam had taught Cole about the bond that existed between people no matter how different their lives were.

Sam approached Cole each evening for spare change, and one cold, rainy night in November Cole gave Sam fifty cents, reached the street corner, turned, walked back, and gave him five dollars. Sam's face lit up even as the rain poured from his eyebrows onto his cheeks, over his nose, and down his unshaven chin.

Cole said nothing and was about to turn and walk away when Sam tugged at his coat. "I can sing and dance," said Sam in a voice that was at once happy and terribly sad. "I'd like to bring a smile to your face."

Cole stopped and looked at Sam. Cole guessed that like many on the street, Sam was plagued with mental illness and possibly addiction troubles. But through the rain and the hardness of his life, he was beaming at Cole Blackwater.

"You already have," said Cole, smiling for the first time in a week.

He didn't care if they used the money he gave them for booze or drugs or food. Who am I to argue with a good stiff drink, he thought, as he turned into the Cambie Hotel to wet his whistle and while away a few hours before calling Peggy McSorlie.

He pushed his way through a clutch of young people on the sidewalk hunched over cigarettes puffing furiously, and stepped into the bar. Rock and roll and the excited voices of the crowd settling in for a night of enthusiastic drinking broke over him like a warm wave on the beach, and he pushed through the people toward the familiar draft counter. Luck was with him and he found an empty stool. Elbows up on the bar and wearing his heavy black leather jacket, worn and weathered from many seasons of use, Blackwater looked more like a menacing hoodlum than a sophisticated political and environmental strategist. His dark hair fell in shaggy curls around his forehead and ears, and his eyes — not blue, not grey, not green — darted up and down the bar in search of friend or foe. When he wasn't slouching, Cole stood just over six feet tall, and while he had been willowy with corded muscles as a young man, he had gone soft of late.

A male bartender stepped in front of him. No uniform for this chap, barely out of high school, just a loose-fitting T-shirt and a pair of factory faded blue jeans. The bartender was new to the Cambie and Cole did not recognize him. He would be gone in another few weeks. Cole wouldn't much care.

"What'll it be?"

Cole looked up and down the bar. He hated being served by a male bartender. If he wanted to be served a drink by a man he'd drink alone at home. What his bones and joints ached for right now was a beautiful woman to ask him what he would like. To drink.

"Pint of Kick Ass," he said sombrely.

The young bartender pulled back on the handle and dispensed a pint of golden ale. He flipped a coaster under the pint before setting the frothing glass before Blackwater, who handed him a five dollar bill and left the quarter change in the runner along the edge of the bar. A woman would have warranted digging into his pocket for another quarter or two. A quarter was all a boy in a T-shirt could expect from Cole.

It would be easy to mistake Cole's trajectory to the bar for a single-minded desire to obtain ale. But nothing could be farther from the truth. Cole Blackwater turned his back on the bartender and looked out over the plank tables of the Cambie and through the tall windows to the night beyond, and began his careful assessment of the raucous and familiar crowd.

It was spring again and the city was coming alive. University students, under pressure to finish assignments and prepare for exams, were also obviously under the influence of spring fever and the nearly irresistible mammalian urge to prowl for food and frisky fun after a long winter's nap. Cole too sensed the energy of the city change as the damp winter winds were replaced by warm rains and the occasional blue sky. Winter's rubbish washed away into False Creek, English Bay, and Burrard Inlet, and new life blossomed everywhere.

Blackwater drank deeply, then stood to survey the room. Before he strode purposefully through the front doors, Cole had done a quick visual sweep of the room to determine any initial threats. Now he made a careful assessment of each table, scanning for faces he might know, friendly, or more importantly, otherwise.

Cole Blackwater had his reasons: in more than fifteen years of activism, he had made his fair share of enemies. He prided himself on being aggressive and uncompromising in his approach to conservation. And while he wasn't troubled by the politicians and corporate executives that he'd taken to the mat over their plans to clearcut some swath of ancient forest or to bore into the side of a sacred mountain in search of precious metal, he did worry from time to time about the unstable sorts.

Though he'd been called every name in the book by yahoos and goons in the newspapers, on television, and face-to-face at blockades and rallies, he worried more about the quiet powder kegs waiting to explode, and that he might be the match it took to ignite them. He worried about the disgruntled and possibly mentally unstable mill worker, longshoreman, or miner angry that radical environmentalists had stolen his job to save some "itty bitty spotted owl."

Blackwater didn't buy that bunk; he saw it for what it was. It was tough to explain his point of view: that corporations who raped the land and the seas cut and run when the profit margins grew thin, leaving entire communities in the lurch. For every hundred honest fellows who toiled in the mill or the mine or on a boat week after week and year after year to put food on the table for their families, there were always a few angry, frustrated sods who looked for an excuse to mash someone's nose or stomp their face.

So Blackwater had got in the habit of scanning the crowd whenever he entered a public house, looking for likely candidates for trouble. Cole knew he was recognizable — for fifteen years his face had been on the evening news. His enemy wasn't. In the last couple of years he had begun to regard nearly every stranger as a potential foe. In the grocery store, standing in line, he regarded his fellow shoppers with suspicion. On the SkyTrain an innocent jostle made Cole Blackwater's six-foot frame stiffen and prepare for a blow.

Cole Blackwater was growing paranoid.

But Cole's surveillance wasn't driven purely by fear. He was an opportunist as well as deeply suspicious. Cole also scanned rooms like the rocking Cambie for a little sport. While all men were potential adversaries to Cole, he regarded all women as potential conquests.

At thirty-seven Blackwater wasn't the catch that he once was. His nose, broken twice in high school, was bent awkwardly to the left, the result of too many right roundhouse punches. His once slender and well-muscled body had grown soft over the last ten years. Truth be told, thought Cole, while Ottawa's pace had been gruelling, it was Vancouver that had put the nail in his once limber and lithe corporeal coffin. It wasn't for lack of opportunity for fitness, Vancouver having one of the most active populations in the country. No, it was a lack of will. Cole Blackwater had lost his resolve to keep himself up.

Scanning the room and feeling fleshy, a Paul Simon song played in Cole's head: "Why am I soft in the middle now, the rest of my life is so hard?"

Cole grimaced. Even if he did face trouble with a few thugs or, more optimistically with a skirt, he wasn't sure he was up to the challenge anymore.

It wasn't only the lack of time on the trail, in the mountains, or on the rivers that had softened Cole Blackwater. It wasn't the years that he'd been away from the gym. It wasn't the time. It was the miles. It was the many, many miles that had turned Cole soft. He finished his ale, disgusted with himself.

He shook his head a little to slough off the feeling. Straightening, he took comfort that it wasn't all for rot and ruin. Allowing his gaze to troll the sea of churning humanity before him, he found solace in the fact that he still had most of his hair, and his face, never a candidate for an Oil of Olay commercial, was yet ruggedly good looking, though by no means handsome. Years and years of Alberta sun and wind, a lifetime of riding the range herding his family's cattle, weeks in the mountains skiing and climbing, and months in the backcountry paddling wild rivers, had etched Blackwater's face into a maze of lines. Even after three years on the wet coast, when months passed without the sun showing its rosy face, Blackwater still wore the appearance of a tan, though it was more from wear and tear than basking.

Then there was the boxing. Nothing puts years on a man's face like being hit, again and again, with a leather glove, every day and night for nearly two decades.

He finished his sweep of the room, elbows resting on the bar, one leg cocked back and jammed against the boot-worn wood. The room was getting busier, the decibel level rising with the frenzied excitement of young people on a Friday night. Blackwater spotted a solid dozen women who fit his description of beautiful, but nearly each one was guarded by a man ten years younger than he was, and perceptibly more good looking. He would be content to let his fantasies play out from afar.

Cole Blackwater's third reason for making a careful assessment of this bar was to see if any of his cronies had taken up residence to hoist a few without him. Gregarious by nature, Blackwater loved any chance to swap a week's worth of political gossip with his acquaintances. Also, he hated the thought of being left out. Of being left behind. He feared nothing more than missing something. Some decision might be made without him. Some plan hatched in his absence. He had spent his professional life scrambling to be in on all the big opportunities. Cole Blackwater knew that those opportunities were often conceived over a beer-stained tablecloth, or across a cocktail table littered with tumblers and highball glasses.

Where had those years of scrambling got him? Drinking alone on a Friday night after laying off his only employee, not knowing where the next paycheque would come from. Then he thought of Peggy McSorlie and, out of habit, checked his watch. Desperation will make a man do funny things, thought Cole Blackwater.

He saw nobody he knew in the bar, which saddened him more than his unfulfilled search for potential adversaries or conquests. He was lonely. He reached to plunk his pint glass on the bar behind him without taking his eyes from the room.

"Another?" asked the boy bartender.

"Please," he answered over the din.

He took stock of himself: he was paranoid, lonely, and fighting so far below his weight class it embarrassed him.

"Bottoms up," said the bartender, and Cole fished another five from the garbage in his pockets to pay for the beer.

The note with Peggy McSorlie's phone number fell out and landed on the floor. He reached to pick it up. He looked at his watch again. It wasn't yet eight o'clock.

He tipped the beaded pint glass toward his lips and drank half of the ale before returning it to the coaster. He blew out through pursed lips and felt the beer settle into his belly. That's better, he mused, the pints doing their work to loosen his limbs and calm his frenzied thoughts. Cole settled into a familiar funk, assessing what he considered to be the ruined landscape of his life. Maybe his critics were right: he was a failure as a consultant. Maybe it was time for a change. Take a job. Stop trying to save the world single-handedly. He let his gaze fall on one of the TVs in the corner of the bar, and became absorbed by his next pint and the silent hockey game on the Sports Network, and let half an hour pass this way.

A heavy hand on Cole's shoulder startled him, and he tipped his fourth beer, spilling a trickle of it down the front of his shirt. "What the!..." he growled, turning on the man next to him.

He was greeted by the grinning face of Dusty Stevens. "Easy, champ."

"Didn't see you come in," grumbled Cole, using a handful of paper napkins to mop the beer from his shirt.

"You were in your own little world, as usual," said Dusty, peering over his glasses at Cole. Martin Middlemarch stood behind his friend, looking thoughtful. "Little jumpy tonight, Blackwater?"

Cole grimaced and nodded and dumped the sodden napkins on the bar while Martin and Dusty ordered beers. "Let me get you a refill, Cole," said Dusty, taking Cole's glass from his hand. Stevens was in his mid-forties, but looked much older. He was a short, round man with closely cropped hair that had silvered long ago. He wore a green golf shirt under a shiny leather jacket. He sported tiny rectangular glasses and had a habit of looking over them when he spoke to people, as though the spectacles were meant only for reading.

"Rough week, Cole?" Martin asked.

Cole recounted the story of Mary's last day on the job.

"You'll be answering your own phone then for a while," said Dusty Stevens sympathetically.

"For a while. Until things pick up," sighed Blackwater, sipping his pint.

"What do the prospects look like for that happening?" Middlemarch was younger than Stevens by a decade, taller by half a foot, and lighter by fifty pounds. He spoke in a mild, measured tone despite the din of the bar. He had the build of the long-distance runner that he was, and wore his sandy hair neatly parted to one side. He took a satisfying sip of his glass of beer. No pint glasses for Martin Middlemarch: he was here mostly for the company.

Cole just shook his head. Martin looked at Dusty. "You could always take a J-O-B," he said, sipping from his glass.

Cole looked around the room and then at the two men who were standing beside him. He simply shrugged. The three men had known each other for a decade or more, but had become friends only since Cole Blackwater moved to Vancouver three years earlier. When Cole had been working for the Canadian Conservation Association, Dusty and Martin had worked in the Vancouver office of Greenpeace. Dusty's specialty was the media. He had been employed as a communications officer in the provincial NDP government in the early 1990s, and took the post with Greenpeace after Glen Clark became premier.

Martin Middlemarch was a campaigner, who had come to Greenpeace by way of the social justice movement. They had recruited Cole and the CCA to help them stop a US nuclear submarine from docking at the Canadian Forces Base at Esquimalt, just outside of Victoria. For Cole and the CCA it was tit-for-tat: Greenpeace would help them with the federal Endangered Species Act.

Cole had used his contacts with sympathetic Members of Parliament to create a lengthy and acrimonious debate in the House of Commons over Canada's tacit support of nuclear weapons on the high seas while Greenpeace activists in rubber Zodiac boats got between the submarine and the port. After that, whenever Cole visited Vancouver for work he had been a welcome guest at the Greenpeace office, and the three men drank beer and swapped stories in the pubs and bars along Commercial Drive.

But around the time that Cole was being ushered out of Ottawa, both Dusty and Martin had been lured away from Greenpeace to work for industry-supported consulting firms. Dusty and Martin couldn't say no to the opportunity to work inside the corporations, media, and government relations firms they'd been fighting. The pay was too good and the jobs secure, and they were able to justify their moves by saying that they could now change the system from within. Cole Blackwater didn't buy it.

"Worse things in the world, Cole," said Dusty, his eyes fixed on Cole over his glasses. "We can't all be holy crusaders. Some of us have to roll up our sleeves up and try to work from inside the belly of the beast to change things. We don't get the spotlight, we don't get any glory. We just slog away, trying to change things one step at a time."

Cole drank deeply from his glass, his shaggy curls dropping in front of his eyes.

"Did you happen to get a call from Wild Rose?" asked Martin.

Cole looked up. "Yeah."

"Good. What did you think?"

"Jeremy Moon just left a message."

"Did you call him back, Cole?" asked Martin.

"Not yet."

"Not yet," echoed Dusty Stevens. "It's a good job, Cole. It starts at like 70K a year."

Cole shrugged again.

"I know, I know. It's not about the money. It's about changing the world. Well, there are more ways than one to change the world, sonny boy. You think it's easy sitting in a room full of corporate suits and telling them that they are doing things wrong, and trying to convince them that what's good for the earth is good for business too?"

Cole looked around the bar, appraising recent entrants.

"Look," Stevens said, peering over his glasses. "If real change is going to happen in this world, someone is going to have to show these corporations how to do things differently. And who do you think they are going to listen to? You? Out there waving your arms in the air and shouting your fucking head off? Do you think they're going to listen to the vw-driving hippies protesting the wto and the World Bank and the imf? Jesus, Cole. They aren't going to listen to those people."

Martin cleared his throat. "Cole, it's like this: you and your clients are out in the public focusing in on these businesses that Dusty and I work for. So what do they do? Well, they do what every good cowboy would do. They circle their wagons, hunker down, and shoot back. But eventually somebody has to show these people how to drive those wagons through a little opening that you and your folks leave for them so that they can save face, and save some of the natural world that we three all believe in."

"Take Wild Rose for example," said Dusty, ordering another round from the boy behind the bar. "You should call them. We all know Jeremy. He's good people. They've got a bunch of new clients, mostly mining and coal bed methane, and they're looking for someone who knows the biz. You could help them. You could hold their feet to the fire. Make sure they do things right. Help them talk to the locals. Make sure they consult with Aboriginal communities. That's right up your alley, Cole. "

"Cole, there's more than one way to save the world."

Cole was watching a young woman stand up and brush something from her jeans. He shook his head.

"What, Cole. Not pure enough for you?"

Cole looked at Dusty and smiled.

"We can't all be white knights, Cole," he said again.

Cole sluiced the beer in his glass and focused on the golden suds. "I really think you guys believe this bullshit you're spouting," he finally said with only a trace of a smile. "I do. But I think those corporations that you're working for are just using you to show them how to drive their wagons through *whatever* hole they can find. Oh, there's lots of talk about sustainability, and giving back to communities and all, but at the end of the day, little is changing in a real, meaningful way. And the reason is that guys like you two aren't able to push hard enough from the inside, and guys like me can't get any traction to push from the outside as long as the companies can point to guys like you and say, look, we've got respected environmentalists on staff showing us the way."

Dusty Stevens opened his mouth to talk but Cole silenced him with a grimace.

"Save it, Dusty," he said. "I'll call Jeremy, but I'm telling you right now, I'd rather work for the little Aboriginal band or the community of ranchers that the coal bed methane or mining company is going to screw over than try to make sure Wild Rose uses the world 'sustainability' enough times in the Environmental Assessment."

The three men stood awkwardly a moment. Then Martin said earnestly, "We've got to try, Cole."

"I know," said Cole. "God, don't I know it? And I don't blame you guys, really. Maybe I'm just jealous."

"Look, Cole," said Stevens, "we do what we can. Hell, if it wasn't Marty and me doing this, some bastard who comes straight out of the Forest Products Association would be doing it."

"Is that what you tell yourself so you can sleep at night?" asked Cole.

"No, that's the way it is," said Stevens.

"What about Sarah?" asked Middlemarch more seriously. "You've got to think of her."

Cole Blackwater sighed and his shoulders slouched noticeably. "There is that," he admitted.

"Look on the bright side," said Martin, draining his glass and setting it on the bar. "There is no shortage of work in this biz, only a shortage of work as a holy crusader. Sooner or later even the great Cole Blackwater will have to cozy up to a corporate client."

"Or the fucking Liberal government," grinned Stevens.

That set the three of them laughing. Finally, his face still pressed into a grin, Blackwater said, "I've no illusions, boys. My white knight days are long passed. But today marks the beginning of a new era, though which era I'm not quite certain."

The bartender set up a new round of ale for Dusty and Cole, with Martin opting for a soda water, explaining that he had a race on Sunday. The three men hoisted their glasses.

"To the good fight," said Martin. "May there always be one!"

"For the sake of my mortgage, let there always be lost souls to wage them," agreed Dusty Stevens.

Cole Blackwater drank deeply from his pint, but said nothing. He was thinking about the slip of paper stuck in his pocket with the phone number of one lost soul he needed to telephone.

It was just after ten o'clock when Cole stepped out of the elevator and slouched to his office door. He found his keys and tried in vain to poke them in the lock. Finally the keys found their mark, the tumblers turned, and he pushed the door open, stumbled, and groped for the light.

He flopped onto Mary's chair, his head spinning. From his littered pocket he extracted the phone number and focused, then snatched the receiver from its cradle and punched in the numbers.

It rang. Rang again. Rang again. He was preparing his message in his head when a female voice answered: "Hello."

"I'm looking for Peggy McSorlie," said Cole.

"This is she."

"It's Cole Blackwater calling, Peggy."

Her voice was just as Cole Blackwater remembered it. They had met face to face only once, on a lobbying trip she had made to Ottawa, but they had talked dozens of times on the telephone. He knew her phone voice far better than he knew her in person. In a big country you developed that sort of relationship – the conference call friendship, he called it.

"Hi, Cole, thanks for calling. I've just got the boys home from basketball. They're having a snack. I can chat now."

"I'm sorry to call so late," he said.

"It's fine. Like I said, it's good timing. He heard her shuffling something, likely groceries or bags of sweaty teenage laundry.

"What was it that you thought I might be able to help with?"

"Where to start?"

"The Reader's Digest version is fine for now," he said.

"Well, it's the same old thing, really." Peggy McSorlie spoke in an even-toned voice that Blackwater figured she must have perfected for dealing with mining executives, Parks officials, and the media. "You remember a few years ago, even before the whole Jasper thing that you and I worked on together, there were plans for an open-pit mine south of the town of Oracle, along the eastern boundary of Jasper?"

"I remember it," answered Blackwater. "Some sort of coal operation on the north side of Cardinal Divide."

"That's right, metallurgical coal, the stuff they use to make steel. Well, that mine didn't play out. The market was in the sewer, and the company who owned the operation couldn't get their act together and wrote a rotten environmental assessment. They forgot really to make any mention of the mine's impact on any of the wildlife in the area."

"Convenient," said Blackwater.

"Yup, convenient. They likely thought that the assessment would just sail through with a rubber stamp from the province. You know, the good old boys in Edmonton would make some sounds about protecting wildlife and sustaining the local economy and the mine would be off to the races. But it didn't happen like that."

"It got bumped to the feds, as I recall."

"Right. I wasn't doing this sort of thing then. I was still doing contract work for Jasper. But some concerned locals made the argument that the mine would impact the National Park. The folks at Parks Canada agreed and that got the Federal Environmental Assessment Office involved. The EcoDefence Fund threatened to sue the federal government, saying that because the mine would come within a few kilometres of Jasper and would destroy fish habitat and impact endangered species, that both Environment Canada and Fisheries and Oceans had obligations to protect."

"Did they win the suit?"

"It never went to court. But the feds did get involved, and the whole thing went to a hearing, and that's where the coal company's assessment basically fell apart. It wasn't even so much that they were planning on dumping mine waste in streams full of bull trout and harlequin ducks, but that their economic arguments were pretty weak. Full of holes, really."

"Ducks, eh?"

"What's that?"

"Harlequin ducks?"

"Yeah, there are nesting sites on the streams they want to use as a dumping ground for waste rock."

"Who found the nesting sites?"

Peggy McSorlie laughed. "Me, of course. On my days off, of course."

"Of course."

"But listen, Cole, the ducks weren't the point. That proposal wasn't worth the paper it was written on. And I might add that it was written on a lot of paper. The thing was a thousand pages long! I could hardly lift it—a thousand pages of bull crap. Shameful. Written by a former Park Superintendent turned environmental consultant, no less. It was a disgrace. He should have known better. Or if he did, he chose to look the other way.

Lot of that going around, thought Cole Blackwater.

"Anyway, the review board sent the company back to the drawing board. They didn't say no —"

"They never do in Alberta."

"No, they never do, but it was enough to delay the project, and the company ended up selling out."

"Not the end of the story," said Cole.

"Nope. Not end of story. A big Toronto-based company bought up the whole operation a year ago, including the two mines that currently operate in the region and the rights to coal, maybe even coal bed methane in the area. It's hard to say with coal bed methane. Anyway, this all happened in the last year. Now they've brought in a new hotshot area manager named Mike Barnes and he's making the rounds saying the company is going to bring forward a new proposal for a mine. They're dancing in the street in Oracle."

Cole was silent. When it came to conservation, those on the side of nature had to win every time. Those on the side of reckless exploitation needed to win only once.

"What's different this time?" asked Cole.

"Well, we're not sure yet. We suspect two things. First, they likely read the report by the Environmental Assessment Agency and plugged up some of the holes in their report. And second, we understand that they might be taking a new tack this time around."

"What tack would that be?"

"Breaking the project up into little pieces and doing mini-assessments on each piece so it doesn't trigger a full environmental review panel hearing, where they're sure to lose."

"That's illegal."

"Maybe so, but lots of folks get away with it. They just say that they're building an exploratory road, or digging a test pit, or some such baloney. Before you know it you've got a full-scale operation on your hands."

"So, what do you need me for?"

"We need you to help us stop it. We need you to help us work up a strategy to kill this thing dead so it stays dead. Once and for all."

"What's the timing on this?

"Not much time, as usual."

"As usual," he muttered.

"Barnes came by the house last week and told me they plan on bringing forward a preliminary proposal for the community to comment on in about a month. Then, based on the feedback from the locals, they'll redraft the environmental assessment and submit it to the province by the end of June."

"Less than two months from now."

"Don't I know it!"

"Not much time. Who's doing the assessment?"

"I can't remember the name, isn't that funny?" she laughed. "It's someone I've never heard of before. From Calgary. Wild Rose or some flower name like that."

Cole sighed. "I know them. I think they're new, but they have some good people working with them." Cole mentally crossed Wild Rose Consulting off his list of two options to put food on the table this month.

"Cole, that's why we need you."

"Right," he said, sounding cynical.

"No, really, Cole. Look, I know this is sort of, well, beneath you right now. I'm sure you've got all sorts of jobs for the big groups, but this is important."

Cole Blackwater was silent. He felt like laughing, sitting in Mary's empty chair, or maybe weeping. "Well," he finally said, "you're right to think you're not going to win this by challenging the environmental assessment, though that'll be part of the strategy we might use to delay things. We'll likely have to put together a strategy that takes this to the public and makes them think about those ducks, buried under all that overburden."

Peggy laughed. "Sounds like you're interested. I heard you say *we* twice."

Cole silently cursed his eagerness. Desperate to earn enough money to pay the rent on his office and his home, and to take care of Sarah. And his eagerness to put the screws to the jokers who wanted to cut a slice out of some of the greatest country in Canada. It weakened his negotiation power. But then he thought of something his old friend Sid Marty once wrote: "Hunger makes the hunter."

Finally he said, "Yeah, I'm interested. It would mean having to drop a few things here in Vancouver to take the job."

"We can pay for this one," said McSorlie.

"Good," Blackwater said matter-of-factly.

"The first thing I did when I heard that this had popped up again was call Papa Grizzly and he offered some money to develop a strategy."

"He's still alive?"

"And kicking. We can offer you $5,000 for a month's worth of on-the-ground work, plus some expenses."

Jesus, thought Blackwater. Middlemarch and Stevens could burn that in a week working against him on a project, and sleep at night thinking that they kept enough harlequins alive to breed and maintain a viable population.

"What do you think?" asked Peggy.

"Can you fly me out?"

"I think so. But just to Edmonton."

"I'll need to rent a car for the time I'm there."

There was a silence. "I don't know that we can cover that, Cole."

"I'll need to get around the community, get up to look at the proposed mine site. Talk to this Barnes character and all that rot."

"Can you drive out?"

Cole thought of his aging but eager 1988 Toyota SR5 with its rusted sideboards and cracked windshield, and its trusty but clearly taxed engine with half a million kilometres to its name. It was falling apart, but still roadworthy, and familiar and comfortable. "Yes," he said, "I can drive out."

"We'll need to get started soon," Peggy said. "There isn't much time."

"I know," said Cole. "I'll tie up a few loose ends over the weekend, drive out on Sunday night, maybe Monday morning at the latest. That OK?"

"That's great, Cole. I know that we can stop this thing, if only we can find the right lever."

"I know we can too, Peggy." But he really wasn't all that sure. He'd been up against Goliath before, and while he relished the image of David flinging stones at the enemy, he knew things rarely turned out as they did in the story, even if it was the Bible.

Sensing Cole's mood, Peggy added, "It will be good to work together again, Cole."

"Yes, it will," said Cole. And of that he was certain.

2 One of the loose ends showed up first thing Saturday morning. Suffering the miasma of a pounding hangover, Cole stood in the shower, one hand pressed against the tiled wall, and let the hot water drum the ache from his head and neck. When he stepped from the shower he heard the doorbell ringing, and could tell by its impatient tone that it was Jennifer Polson, there to drop Sarah off for the weekend. He went to the door in a robe, let Sarah in, and smiled crookedly at Jennifer.

"Looking sharp this morning, Cole," Jennifer said. "Tough night?"

"I'm not getting into it with you this morning," said Cole, his smile slipping from his face.

"You able to look after my daughter right now?"

"Our daughter."

"*Our* daughter," said Polson, gritting her teeth.

"See you Sunday," said Cole, closing the door and tousling Sarah's hair.

After his conversation with Peggy McSorlie, Cole had walked from the Dominion Building to the Stadium SkyTrain station and caught the train one stop to Main Street station. It was 11 PM, and the streets were quiet, the train almost empty. He transferred to the Number 3 bus and rode it twenty blocks up Main Street. His intent was to walk home and go to bed early, but as he ambled past the Coach and Horses Pub the raucous sound of merrymaking and the clamour of a live band roared out into the street. He was pulled toward it like a moth to a flame. "Why not?" he reasoned. He was celebrating. He had a new client. He had *a* client.

Inside the bar, people were in a celebratory mood. He pushed his way into the bar and scanned the crowd for friend or foe. Finding no familiar faces, and feeling the need for company to celebrate his success, he called Denman Scott.

"We're celebrating. Get your butt down here," yelled Cole over the ruckus in the bar.

"Cole, it's eleven-thirty."

"So? It's not a school night."

Cole liked to drink with Martin and Dusty just fine, but when he wanted someone who understood him, someone that he jived with in the same way, it was Denman he called on.

It was midnight when Scott showed up.

"What are we drinking to?" asked Denman, ordering a pint of John Courage at the bar. Cole was drinking Jameson Irish Whiskey.

"New client," said Cole, close to his ear. Cole had to lean down to make himself heard. While Cole stood six feet tall, Denman Scott was five eight. And where Cole had gone soft as he approached forty, Denman Scott had maintained the narrow, angular body he had enjoyed since youth. His Chinese-German heritage provided him with a timeless, handsome face, stout legs, and muscled arms.

Denman asked about the work and Cole filled him in on the details, Denman nodding. "Sounds like a good job, Cole," he finally said.

"You don't think I'm scraping the bottom of the barrel?"

"No, I think you can help these people."

"Just seems like I can't fall much farther," Cole said, shaking his head.

"You can, and you will if you keep thinking like that. I should know; I see it every day."

"Another tough case?" asked Cole, yelling over the din of the pub.

"Every case is a tough one," said Denman, finishing his pint of Courage and ordering another.

"I don't know how you do what you do," said Cole, shaking his head. He was leaning on the bar, looking into Denman's angular face, his dark eyes. Denman Scott had a clean-shaven head and a small, neat goatee. He wore a dark, patterned shirt, the top two buttons open, his small, muscular body pushing out of it in the shoulders and across the chest.

"We just do it," he finally said.

It was after 2 AM before Cole stumbled from the bar, leaning on Scott for balance. Then he wandered the five blocks to his second-storey apartment atop an aging character home on a tree-lined street. He always felt better after talking with Denman, so despite his stagger he had a bit of a bounce in his step. He capped off the night with a short pull from a bottle of Jameson, just to wash a couple of Advil down, and crawled into bed.

Morning had come so swiftly.

Cole closed and locked the door before Jennifer had turned to walk down the stairs. He went to the bedroom to change. Instead he fell back into bed. He woke and heard Sarah rattling around the kitchen. He moaned.

"Are you awake, Dad?"

"Unfortunately," he groaned.

"I've made coffee," she said.

"You are my angel." He slowly opened his eyes. He sat up in bed and rubbed a hand over his hair and his face. Despite the shower he still smelled like beer and whiskey.

"I'm coming in, Daddy," said the voice from the kitchen.

"You'd better have a cup of coffee in your hands!" he said.

The bedroom door opened. Sarah entered wearing a blue sweatshirt and jeans, her sandy blonde hair tied in two pigtails that swayed as she carried, with great concentration, a tray with cup of coffee, a plate of toast, and a jar of jam. "Breakfast in bed," she announced.

"Oh, my little girl," crooned Cole Blackwater.

Sarah placed the tray on the bed next to Cole, carefully removed the cup of steaming coffee, and handed it to her father. Then she climbed up beside him.

"You still smell." She turned up her nose.

"I took a shower," he grimaced, raising the coffee to his nose, then his lips.

"Mommy says you drink too much."

"Mommy has her own issues," said Blackwater, closing his eyes to savour the flavour of the coffee, and to suppress what he really wanted to say about Jennifer Polson. "This is really good, Sarah. Thank you, sweetheart."

"You're welcome."

"Where did you learn to do this? You're only seven years old."

"I'm almost eight," Sarah said, as if that explained every-thing.

She sat beside and watched him drink the coffee. He relished each taste. Then he looked at her.

They sat in silence for a while. Cole finished his coffee and Sarah twisted her pigtails and looked out the window at the twin peaks of the Lions across the bay, beyond the city.

"It's a really nice day today," said Cole, squinting into the sun. "What would you like to do?"

She thought for a minute, then exclaimed, "Let's go to Lighthouse Park!"

"Sounds great, sweetheart. Have you had breakfast?"

"Hours ago," said Sarah, rolling her eyes.

"Right."

"Eat your toast before it's cold."

"Where would I be without you?" he asked.

"Still asleep."

"Don't I know it," he smiled and tousled her hair, making a mess of the pigtails.

They drove to Lighthouse Park, over Lions Gate Bridge and through West Vancouver. It was a sunny day, full of the promise of spring. The parking lot was crowded, and as they strolled through the grove of ancient trees to the rocky shoreline they passed families with picnic hampers and young couples walking hand in hand. Cole pulled in long breaths of moist air and Sarah ran ahead of him and darted back through the trees. He marvelled at her energy. They found a place on the rocks to sit and look at the ocean, their backs toward the burgeoning city. The sky was a pale blue, the sun warm. Gulls wheeled overhead, and from the forest they heard ravens squabbling over a found treasure – a dead squirrel, or someone's picnic lunch, thought Cole.

"When are you going to get married again, Daddy?" Sarah asked, watching a young couple, each of them not more than twenty years old, hold each other on the rocks not far away.

Cole Blackwater stared out beyond the lighthouse at the inlet. He smiled, "I haven't found anybody that is good enough for you, my little girl." He leaned down and kissed her on the head.

"That's funny," she said.

"Funny ha-ha or funny peculiar?"

"Funny ha-ha," she answered. "Mommy is remarried."

"That's your mommy for you."

"I like Roger."

"Roger," he said mockingly. It still stung Cole to think that another man was playing father to his only child.

"He's nice."

"I'm sure he is, sweetheart."

"You don't like him?"

"I hardly know him. If you say he's OK, then he's OK."

"He's OK."

It had been such a long journey from Ottawa, where he and Jennifer Polson had fallen into a steamy romance in the power-hungry centre of the country, only to fall on the rocks amid rumours and realities of infidelity, recklessness, and careerism. He had nearly lost Sarah when Jennifer had picked up and moved to Vancouver. Jennifer's exodus preceded Cole's own forced march from the capital by a few months, and when he came to rest, finally, he found himself on the left coast. Battered and bruised, but still standing. So far.

And a father figure once again; no matter that Polson thought of his role as *father lite*. Maybe he deserved the moniker. But he tried. And he loved Sarah more than anything else in the world. More than everything else in the world all crammed together. Though he had a funny way of showing it, he mused. After this gig in Alberta, he would make more of an effort to be a real dad, rather than allow his daughter to be a mother to him.

They drove back into the city through Stanley Park, past the busy downtown core, and turned up Main Street. They parked the old Toyota in the backyard and then walked five blocks back to Main Street to eat dinner and rent a movie.

It was over dinner that he told her. "I've got to go away for a few weeks, Sarah." He ate a hamburger and she munched on chicken fingers in a classic mom-and-pop style diner run by an elderly Chinese couple.

She poked at her French fries. "Again?"

"I don't travel that much anymore, do I?"

"You were gone for two weeks just last month."

"That was in February."

"Seems like last month."

"I know it does, sweetheart," he said, taking a drink of Pepsi. "It feels that way to me, too. But my work involves some travel, you know that. That was the price of moving out here, away from Ottawa. I sometimes have to go and meet with people to do my work."

"Are you going to Ottawa?"

"Not this time, sweetheart. Alberta."

Her face brightened. "Will you see Grandma?"

"Maybe," he said, taking a bite of his burger. "I'm going to a place called Oracle, west of Red Deer. That's about six hours from Grandma's place, but I'll try to get down to see her."

"When can I go to visit Grandma?"

"When would you like to?"

"Soon."

"OK, we'll go soon. July is a better time than May or June to go and see Grandma," said Cole. "It's often really rainy in the foothills in June. Sometimes it snows. July is better. The hills are covered in wildflowers, and the cattle have been put to pasture. We can go riding."

"I like to ride horses," said Sarah matter-of-factly.

"I know you do. Let's plan on a trip there this summer. Deal?"

"I've never been to Grandma's ranch, you know," Sarah said, eating a French fry.

"Really?" asked Cole, though he knew it was the truth.

"Really."

"Well, I haven't been there in a while myself," said Cole, introspectively. "Three years. Since I moved out here."

"Really? Don't you like it there?"

"Sure I like it there, sweetheart, but I just never find the time or money to visit. Grandma comes here once a year to visit you."

"But it's not the same. I want to see the horses."

"Well, then we'll have to go."

"Promise?"

"I promise. We'll go this summer. Deal?" he repeated.

"Deal." The girl reached her hand across the table and Cole Blackwater shook it firmly.

On Sunday he changed the oil in the Toyota and did a quick tune-up, changed the spark plugs and cables and blew out the air filter. Sarah handed him tools. Then he packed. Along with his street clothes, he chucked outdoor gear into a duffle bag. At the last minute he added some riding gear: boots, his aged and worn chaps, and a dusty Stetson that had belonged to his father and which Cole had never worn. This he threw into the bed of the pickup. Then he packed his laptop and other technology into a shoulder bag along with some mostly clean clothes he herded from the floor, his closet, and the drawers of a dresser.

He spent Sunday afternoon with Sarah. They walked along False Creek and then downtown and had a late lunch at an outdoor café packed with Vancouverites basking in the sun. They caught the SkyTrain back as far as the Main Street Station and walked up Main Street.

"I'm tired," Sarah complained.

"Not as tired as I am," said Cole.

They stopped for gelato at a new trendy shop on Main and dogged it the rest of the way home.

"I'll drop you at your mom's on the way out of town, OK, sweetheart?"

"I'm going to miss you, Daddy," she said.

"Me too, angel."

Late in the afternoon they drove down Main, turned west on Broadway, and threaded their way through afternoon traffic to Kitsilano.

There was a scene. He saw it was coming.

"You can't keep expecting me to pick up your slack, Cole," Jennifer said when he told her that he couldn't take Sarah the following weekend.

"It's just one weekend, Jennifer."

"You always say that, and then it's two and three. Do you think I'm stupid?"

He refused to answer that question. "This is an important job, Jennifer."

"Who's it for?"

He told her.

"Sounds like you're sinking, Cole, taking work from back-woods yokels."

He didn't say anything. A thin smile came to his lips as he looked away down the tree-lined streets. All the cherry trees were in bloom, and the air smelled of blossoms. Finally he turned back and said, "It's an important issue."

They stood there in silence.

"Well, fine," she finally said. "What can I do? You go off and do this important job. I'll take care of our daughter."

He grinned again. Two stab wounds were all that he could take. His smile faded. "Someone still has to fight for what they believe in," he said, "and not just fight for a paycheque."

"That's tough talk, Cole. Tough talk."

"The truth hurts," he said.

"The truth is we're all fighting for a paycheque," she said.

He looked around the neighbourhood, up at the two-storey house, the lawn, the Lexus in the driveway. The whole scene was worth a cool mill, maybe more in the hot Vancouver market. "Some of us don't seem to have to work too hard," he said. "What's Roger pulling in?"

"Fuck you, Cole," she said.

The chitchat was interrupted by a tiny voice. "Please don't fight. I hate it when you fight." Sarah pushed past her mother and stood on the step between Jennifer and Cole.

"We're not fighting, munchkin," said Jennifer.

"Yes, we were," said her father. "I'm sorry."

"It's OK," said Sarah. "Be safe, OK Daddy?" she said brightly, beaming up at him.

"I will be. It's just a campaign plan. Nothing dangerous," he said, bending down. "Kisses?"

She put her arms around him and hugged him. "I love you, Daddy."

"I love you too, angel. I'll call you in a couple of days when I get settled."

He walked down the driveway and got into his truck. He waved and was gone.

3 He drove as far as Kamloops that night and checked himself into the Motel 6 after midnight. On Monday he rose early and by 7 AM turned north on Highway 5 and drove toward Clearwater, Valemont, and Jasper National Park. The day was clear and bright and Cole Blackwater felt good to be on the road with a stint of meaningful work ahead. By late afternoon he crossed the Columbia River and turned east again to climb up the western slope of the Rocky Mountains through Mount Robson Provincial Park. His timing was perfect, and he was rewarded with a view of the highest peak in the Canadian Rockies. In the crepuscular light the giant peak stood chiselled in white, stark against the indigo sky. It was good to be back in the Rocky Mountains. He slipped an old Blue Rodeo disk into the truck's after-factory CD player and listened to the band croon the same sentiment: *And I'd rather be back in the Rocky Mountains, than sitting in some bar on Queen Street.*

The Toyota laboured over the Yellowhead Pass and slipped into Alberta. The anticipated push and pull of his home province hit him. He was ready for it. At least he thought he was. Three years ago he swore he would never be back. He was on the run then from the ruins of his Ottawa life. His stopover in Alberta was a spur-of-the-moment decision; in a dilapidated state of mind he felt an urge to be in the comforting hills of his family's ranch. But he found no comfort there. His visit culminated in nothing short of calamity. That tragedy sent him skidding across British Columbia to come to rest on the wide Fraser River delta, in Vancouver, and he'd never looked back.

Until now.

As he crossed the Great Divide and drove down the long back slope of the continent, he was coming as close to home as he had been in a while. Panic gripped him by the throat. As he neared the town of Jasper, his breath quickened and his heart seemed to skip a beat. Keep it together, Cole, he thought. He gripped the wheel and struggled to focus his eyes. You haven't been in Alberta an hour and you're falling apart.

He stopped in the town of Jasper to stretch his legs and steady his nerves. From a phone booth he called Peggy McSorlie to tell her he'd be in Oracle that night. They arranged a 10 AM meeting at her house the next day, and he took directions to get to her spread a half hour outside of town.

Seeking some comfort in human company, he made a call to a friend he knew from his days at the Canadian Conservation Association. The phone rang three times and then he heard the familiar voice: "Jim Jones."

"Jim, Cole Blackwater here. How are you?"

"I'm well, Cole. Been a long time. Long time."

"It has. Say, I'm in town. How about a quick drink?"

"Sure thing. Why don't you come by the place, Cole?"

"OK, but I can't stay too long. I'm on my way to Oracle tonight."

"No trouble, Cole. Oracle's not more than an hour's drive. I'll have you on your way safe and sound."

"Fine, fine. Where you at?"

Jim gave him directions and Cole navigated through Jasper's back streets to the address.

Jim Jones met him at the door. The house was a cedar Panabode with a few additions since its original construction three decades before. The home was set in a yard strewn with monolithic boulders, piles of aggregate stone, slabs of limestone, and clusters of round and water-polished river rock in various states of arrangement. Some of the larger rocks had been ordered in clusters and erected as monuments, while others were simply piled, awaiting attention. There was no lawn. Instead, crushed gravel filled the spaces between the arrangements. The effect was pleasing, despite being a work in progress. It felt like a combination of Japanese Zen garden, quarry, and construction site.

"Doing a little landscaping?" Cole asked, walking up the pathway that wove through the stone.

Jim Jones was a geologist, though he'd spent most of his sixty years doing other things. But his passion for stone was obvious in his front yard.

"Just a little," Jones smiled, extending a large, rough hand with a few bandaged fingers for Cole to shake. "Good to see you, Cole," he said.

"Good to see you, Jim. What's it been? Five, six years?"

"About that, I'd say. I was in Ottawa when they reviewed the National Parks Act. That was an epoch ago now, it seems."

Cole stepped into the house. It was warm and smelled pleasingly of wood smoke. "Hang your coat behind the door there, Cole, or just toss it wherever you like. What will you have?"

"What have you got?"

"Most everything a road-weary body could want, I'd guess."

"A nice cold beer would be great," Cole said, mouth watering.

"Kokanee do you?"

"Fine."

They settled into the living room with their beer. Jim sat in an Ikea reclining chair in front of the wood stove. Cole walked around the room, beer in hand, drinking deeply and looking at the artwork on the walls and the books stacked on the shelves.

"So, Cole, are you still with the CCA?"

Cole smiled. He assumed that his departure from Ottawa was common knowledge in the enviro world. He was simultaneously pleased and disappointed that someone, even someone living near the edge of the universe as Jim Jones did, didn't hang on his every parry and thrust. Finally he said, "No. Not for more than three years."

"They quit you or you quit them?"

Cole took a drink of his beer. "Good question. I guess a little of both."

Jim's eyes twinkled. "Sounds like they quit you."

Cole kept his back to Jim, reading the spines of books in a floor-to-ceiling bookcase built into the wall. "I'd say I had a little help in my decision to go."

"Its no matter one way or another," said Jim, taking a sip of beer. "I've never had a job so good that I couldn't quit or get fired from it. Hell, I've been fired from half a dozen jobs, and quit far more 'n that. All that really matters is that you keep some pride and dignity and in the end, *walk* away, not run or get your ass booted out of town."

"Suppose so," said Cole, his lips on the beer bottle's mouth. His metaphorical ass still sore, he meditated on that while taking another deep pull of his beer.

"So what are you doing these days?" Jones asked.

"Freelance stuff," said Cole, happy to turn the conversion to the present, regardless of how dismal it seemed to him. "Consulting. Strategy. Communications."

"Hired gun, hey?"

"Suppose you could say that."

"So what brings you to Oracle, as if I can't guess?"

"I'm doing a little job for the Eastern Slopes folks."

"The McLeod River Mine down below the Cardinal Divide?"

"You got it."

"That's a fucking nightmare if I ever heard of one. And I've heard of a lot of them," said Jones, shaking his head and pulling at the label on his beer.

"What do you know about it?"

"About the mine, or the bunch of folks trying to stop it?"

"Both, I guess."

"Well, if you ask me, and I guess you just did," he smiled, "I'd say they were both a damned mess."

Cole sat down across from Jim on a long, worn couch. He looked at the man, inviting him to continue.

"The mine is being planned as your typical open-pit coal job. It's going to be just south of the headwaters of the McLeod River."

"That's right along the southern ridge of the Cardinal Divide, isn't it?" interrupted Blackwater.

"'Tis. The plan calls for them to dig straight back along the southwestern side of the divide toward the park boundary. Build an all-weather haul road over the divide, and then a railway line north to move the coal out to Oracle. The mine is going to be nearly twenty kilometres long," said Jones, shaking his head.

"Holy cow," said Blackwater under his breath, and Jones laughed.

"The rest of us just say holy fuck," chuckled Jones.

"I used to," said Cole, wistfully. "I loved to curse. I could make a sailor blush," he said, finishing his beer. "But it's a bad influence on my daughter, Sarah, so I try to substitute."

Jones nodded his agreement. "Good thinking. Anyway, the McLeod River job isn't all that much different than previous incarnations of nearby operations. You remember. Overburden into the valley below, killing bull trout and harlequin duck habitat, and a twenty-kilometre long hole in the ground that grizzly bears, cougars, and wolves won't be able to navigate around. Even if they did, they'd likely get plastered on the haul road by those monster dump trucks, or cut up on the rail line."

45   Stephen Legault

"Effectively cutting off another north-south migration route for wildlife," said Cole.

"That's right, and all the genetic diversity that goes with it. The mountain parks are already islands, with the animals trapped on them, unable to migrate into the surrounding country to breed, seek food, find shelter, or take refuge from fires, floods, and other natural disasters. What that means is that the populations of these critters are getting inbred. No diversity means no resilience to weather the storms of life. This isn't going to help."

"Sounds like a nail in the coffin, at least on Jasper's eastern slopes. Now I understand the urgency in Peggy McSorlie's call."

They sat in silence a moment.

"Another for the road?" Jim Jones asked.

"Couldn't hurt," said Blackwater, deep in thought.

Jones stood to get the beers, and Cole followed him through the house.

"Where's Betty?" he asked absentmindedly.

Jones fished a couple of bottles from the fridge and opened them on an opener affixed to the kitchen doorframe.

"She's at her mother's in Ontario."

"Everything OK?"

"With the mother? Yeah. But Betty and I are on the rocks, if you'll excuse the pun."

Cole nodded solemnly.

They touched bottles and drank again, standing in the kitchen. There were no obvious signs of domestic disarray: no pile of dishes, no half-eaten box of pizza on the counter. "You seem to be getting along," said Cole.

"I'm getting by. Would prefer that I didn't have to."

"Is it permanent?"

"Who knows?"

They nodded together, drinking.

"So you must know Wild Rose, out of Calgary. They're doing the EA."

Cole smiled.

"You know them?"

"Yeah," said Cole, nodding, his chin touching his chest. "I know them. I know one of the principals from a while back. We did some work together a long, long time ago in a galaxy far away. Jeremy Moon is a good man, but he's got some pretty rotten clients."

"Well, you can add Athabasca Coal to that list now."

"How far along are they on the environmental assessment?"

"Nearly done. As of last week they were just looking for someone to put the magic to the report. You know, the buzz words like *mitigation, ecological footprint, carrying capacity.* That sort of thing. Take a fucked-up project like this and make it seem like the whole landscape will flourish after the pit has been reclaimed. Add a few bighorn sheep grazing on the slopes of the mine so that the American big-game hunters have something to shoot at. Grizzly bears be damned."

"Sounds like they got it all worked out," said Cole.

"Maybe, but I'm not drinking the Kool-Aid."

"You sound familiar with the project," Cole wondered.

"They asked me to review it. Add the magic," Jim grinned.

"I got a note from Wild Rose last week too. Sounds like you said no."

"Sure did. What did you say?"

"I said yes. To Peggy McSorlie."

They touched bottles again and finished their second beer.

"Still, there might be something to keeping the door open with Wild Rose," said Cole, looking out the kitchen window at the rock garden beyond. "I think I'll call Jeremy tomorrow and see what I can learn."

Jim Jones was looking down at the kitchen floor. "You know, Cole. There's something funny about the project."

"How do you mean?"

"Well, they bring in this new hot-shot mine manager. He's been on the job for six months and suddenly they shift their whole focus from Mountain Park, where they tried to dig years ago, you remember? To the other side of the Divide, where nobody has done much preliminary work. I mean, there are hardly any core samples to show that coal exists there in the first place. Now they have the full-court press on, trying to set a speed record for completing an environmental assessment. They want to start work on the haul road this summer! They want tracks laid down for the rail line for the fall. It all seems so damn fast."

Cole was silent.

"And Cardinal Divide, I mean, the place is synonymous with trouble. People have been fighting over it for thirty years. In the last ten years we've made some progress, getting some protection for it. Now these guys want to skirt the little provincial park and dig a *huge*, and I mean huge, hole in the side of it. It seems like a recipe for disaster for the company. Are they looking for a fight? Doesn't make any sense to me.

"Anyway," said Jim, "it just seems a little strange. And asking *me* to review the assessment? And *you*? What's up with that?"

"That's more and more common. Find a known entity in the environmental movement to get some fingerprints on the report before it goes public, so they can say that the enviros are in support of the project."

"Slimy bastards."

"Yup."

"Is there anything I can do to help, Cole?"

Cole thought a moment. "There might be. I'm going to be a known player by Tuesday evening. It might be that a call to Wild Rose from me won't go over all that well. Maybe you could call them and say you're having second thoughts, and that you just want to have a look at what they've got, you know, time lines, preliminary reports, et cetera, to reassess if you should take the job."

"Could do. I didn't slam the door *too* hard on them."

"Then just give me a call on my cell if anything seems funny." Cole handed Jim his card.

"Cole, we can't lose this one, you know," said Jim as they stood on the road by Cole's pickup.

"Jim, I don't plan on losing," he said, looking his friend in the eye. "Hey listen, you said that they were both a mess. What did you mean?"

Jones shuffled a little. "Well, I guess that's a pretty harsh indictment of the little band of eco-warriors that Peggy McSorlie has assembled. I don't know. It's just that there isn't much bench strength there. Peggy is really the brains of the outfit. She's got this guy working with her named Dale van Stempvort."

"Van Stempvort?"

"A loose cannon. No other way of saying it: the man is trouble. He moved to the region, I don't know, ten years ago or so, and nobody really knows much about him, like where he came from or why he chose Oracle, but since he got there, funny business has been afoot."

"What do you mean, Jim?"

Standing on the road, Jones peeled the label from his empty bottle of beer. "Funny business. Like the local forestry company plans to log one of its cut blocks, and they get a note saying that the trees have been spiked. Sure enough, they go out with metal detectors and there they are, six-inch long nails in the trees. Too high to hurt the faller, but a little land mine for the mill. And that was just the start of it. There were explosives."

"I remember hearing about that. It made the national news. That was Dale?"

"Nobody knows for sure, but it's pretty strange that two gas wells got blown up within a few kilometres of his place. And Dale was in the paper a lot those days talking about the impacts of sour gas on his livestock. Still births, birth defects. He said some pretty vicious things to the media."

Cole shook his head.

Jim put the bottle down. "Need a traveller, Cole?" he asked.

"Better not," said Cole.

"Suit yourself," said Jones, looking up at the mountains. "Nobody has ever been charged with any of that stuff, but Dale has never denied that he had anything to do with it. It's odd that Peggy would let him in on this Cardinal Divide campaign. The guy is a wing nut."

I haven't even made it to Oracle yet, Cole thought, and already I want to turn around and head back home. It's one thing to fight a lost cause. It's another altogether to fight a lost cause and do damage control at the same time.

"I better hit the road, Jim," said Cole, looking at his watch.

"Well, give my best to Peggy, and let me know if there's anything else I can do. Happy to be errand boy."

"Thanks, Jim, and thanks for the beers. Just what the doctor ordered."

It was after 9 PM when Cole Blackwater turned his pickup east on Highway 16 and drove toward Oracle. He kept his speed down through the park, conscious of the herds of bighorn sheep that lurked along the shoulder of the highway east of the town.

Heading east on Highway 16, the Rocky Mountains came to

an abrupt end. The eastern slope thrust fault that had jostled the great slabs of limestone skyward also created a clean break between the rugged mountains to the west and the undulating foothills to the east. It took Cole less than an hour to reach Oracle. Cresting a small rise, the town was laid out below him along the banks of the Portsmith River, named for one of the first mining families in the region, a minor tributary of the Athabasca River. In the last wisps of daylight, Cole could see the town squared neatly along its streets and avenues, grid style. The highway cut across it to the north of the old downtown. There he could see the lights from gas stations and the Motel 6. On the north side of the highway ran the railway tracks, and then, below, in a deep dale, the river. Above the old main street and its neat lattice, on a small knoll, perched the new subdivisions, looking out toward the Rocky Mountains. Oracle, Alberta. Population 3,700 including dogs, guessed Cole. Home for the next two weeks.

Cole drove slowly down the highway, turned down Main Street, and looked for 2nd Avenue, which would lead him to his hotel, his bed, and sleep. It had been a long day, and the days ahead would be just as long. Maybe longer.

He found the street and turned to the south. The Rim Rock Motel and Suites was set back from the road, with a large parking lot in front filled nearly to capacity with pickup trucks. And not your rinky-dink Toyota SR5s. Ford F250 Diesels and Dodge Ram 2500s and Chevy Sierras bulked up the lot. Next to his Toyota, a cherry-red Dodge stood a good foot taller.

He made his way to the motel office. A light in the office and another beside the screen door welcomed weary travellers.

He opened the screen door and the wooden inner door to the Rim Rock and entered the lobby of the motel. A woman stepped out from the back office. She smiled at him and said in a friendly, sing-song voice, "Good evening."

Cole Blackwater guessed she was about forty, though he wasn't very good at placing a person's age, so she could be five years on either side of that. She wasn't the sort of beautiful that Cole Blackwater scoped in the Cambie on Friday nights. She could be the mother of one of the girls that flitted about that joint. But he was taken with her strong features, clear blue eyes, and sandy blonde hair that hung loosely to her shoulders in waves.

He signed in and she handed him a key. "You're in room 232," she said. He took the key and jammed it in his pocket. "Thanks," he said, and then, "What's your name?"

"It's Deborah, Deborah Cody. My husband and I own the motel," she said, extending a hand.

He shook it. "Well, it's a pleasure, Deborah," he said.

"Pleasure's all mine," she said with a sly smile. He watched her eyes, which for a moment locked on his.

"Is there a place to get a drink nearby?" he said as he turned toward the door.

"Right next door." She gave him directions to The Quarry. "You'll find George behind the bar."

"George?"

"My husband."

"Right," he said and stepped out into the night.

Cole found his room and dumped his bags on the bed, then felt his way to the bar. It was packed. Country music blared loudly and he made out the clack of pool cues striking balls over the din of mostly male voices. It's Monday night, he thought. Who are all these people? He gave himself a minute to adjust to the light, then had a look at the bar which ran along one long wall to his right. He made his way there, aware of the eyes on him, and the perceptible hush that fell over the conversations in the room.

He waited at the bar while George attended to the waitress' tray, piling on bottles of Molson's Canadian and tumblers of what looked like rum and coke. George was a large man, with broad shoulders, a thick neck, and arms that looked as though they could double as rock crushers. His hair, formerly red and likely curly, receded up toward the crown of his wide head and was cut short. Like his wife, he had blue eyes. George wore a trim moustache but otherwise was clean-shaven.

"Evening. What will you have?"

"Jameson, neat," said Cole.

"Coming up." George turned and Cole noticed his broad back beneath the shirt. Had he played football when he was younger? A body like that didn't come from heavy labour alone. A man had to work at a physique like the one George Cody lugged around.

George pulled a bottle from the back row on the counter behind the bar, eyeballed a healthy shot into a glass, and placed it before Blackwater.

"Looks like you could use a good belt," said George.

"Sorry?" said Cole, startled.

"A stiff drink. You look like you could use one," George smiled, showing his teeth.

"Right. Long day on the road," said Cole. He raised his glass, then took a hit from it.

George smiled again and turned to another customer. Cole took up his customary position at the bar. He scanned the crowd and ruled out two of his three motives: friends and companionship. That left foes. Trouble was, every man in this place looked as if he might just as soon crack Cole's head as give him the time of day, especially if he knew Cole Blackwater's purpose in town. That's how Cole figured it, anyway. It had been a long time since Cole had been in a room with this much plaid and denim. Every man in the bar looked to be employed by the mine, by the local lumber mill, or by a hauling company. Either that or he sold materials to the mine or was on contract to them. Cole decided that he'd better cook up a good story for his purpose in town. Shutting down the mine wasn't going to sit very well with his new drinking companions.

Cole Blackwater wasn't one to turn away from a fight. He knew how to handle himself, though he'd tried to steer clear of the rough stuff since becoming a father. He had boxed at the provincial level in high school, and had made it to the national championships one year. He'd gone more than a few rounds outside the ring too while in high school. The odd time some punk wanted to see if the kid with the golden gloves could throw a punch without the calfskins on. Cole had cleaned a few clocks in those days. But those days were long ago. And Cole knew how fisticuffs could escalate when they were ideologically motivated, as a round with one of the boys in this bar was likely to be. Cole Blackwater wasn't the man he used to be, he lamented, thinking about the stairs in the Dominion Building.

He finished his drink and ordered a second.

Boxing. He shook his head. How long since he'd stepped into a ring? He counted backward. Twenty years since he had gone to the national junior championships at seventeen? Then he'd trained on and off, just for fun, at the U of T, until he got his undergrad degree at twenty-two. Fifteen years: half a lifetime ago. Good God, he thought, where did the time go? He rubbed his middle. It seemed to be accumulating right there, he mused, not entirely pleased with the prospect. He sipped his drink. He had been a decent fighter, with a long, powerful reach, but he lacked something. His old man always ridiculed him. "You've got no fire in the belly, Cole," he chided him. "No fire! You got to punch with every black ounce of your heart, not just your hands! You've got to hate that man you're punching." Cole could never bring himself to hate any of the boys that he stepped into the ring with.

He reserved his hatred for one person alone.

Cole never felt passion in a fight, only fear. And the fear wasn't for what might happen while he was in the ring. Getting knocked out didn't bother Cole, though it happened only once, in his last fight. No, Cole felt fear of what would happen if he lost, after he climbed between the ropes.

"Need another?" asked George Cody from behind him, whisking away the empty glass.

"Always," said Cole, "but I need sleep more," he said, shaking off the memory.

"You staying here?"

Here it comes, thought Cole. "Yup."

"Want to run a tab?"

Cole breathed out, "Sure, that'll make it easy." Dodged the bullet until the morning.

"What room you in?"

"232."

"Done."

Cole thanked him and walked out of the bar on wooden legs. In his room he sat down on the bed to remove his boots and laid back, intending to rest only a moment before showering and turning in. He was fast asleep in seconds.

Stephen Legault

4 The morning was clear and crisp. Cole woke early and spent some time settling in. He jammed his clothes into the drawers of the dresser and hung a few things in the open closet next to the bathroom, where he set up his shaving kit. Then he opened his laptop, plugged in a phone line, and tried to access the internet. It was slow, painfully slow, but he was able to get connected and download some email and read a few online newspapers. He did some quick research on Athabasca Coal, the parent company of the Buffalo Anthracite Mine. Its 2004 Annual Report, available to download from its homepage, said the company grossed more than a billion dollars in sales, and made a tidy profit of fifty-five million. It wasn't a huge margin, but Cole suspected that most of the company's shareholders hadn't complained too loudly, given the volatility in the metals markets. He also Googled Peggy McSorlie, Dale van Stempvort, and the Eastern Slopes Conservation Group.

Then he drove back through town, and to his relief found a Tim Hortons on the highway. He bought a newspaper and stood in a long line, awaiting caffeine and carbohydrates. Coffee and doughnut in hand, he sat by the window, looked out over the highway, and revived himself. At half past eight he stood stiffly, stretched, felt his stomach pressing against his shirt, and with a second coffee in hand, walked to his truck. He double-checked that he had everything he needed for the day's meeting and piloted the Toyota west along the highway for a mile, then north along Highway 40. After a few miles he turned off 40 onto a gravel road that ran north and west into the Rocky Mountain foothills.

The woods through which he steered the Toyota were dark and close, the trunks of the spruce, pine, and fir growing nearly on top of each other, creating a tight ceiling that kept sunlight from reaching the forest floor except along the dirt road. There tangles of alder and willow clutched at the full, bright sunlight. It was a quarter after nine when he arrived. He intended to spend some time with Peggy to go over some of the details of his contract and to discuss the players on both sides of the equation.

He drove up the long, pine-bordered driveway. This track was rougher than the gravel road, which was maintained by the province of Alberta to keep the logging and oil companies happy.

He drove 250 metres or so on this roadway, then entered a large clearing where the main homestead was situated. Cole was underwhelmed. He had envisioned an older style ranch house like the ones he had grown up with in southern Alberta, with a long sprawling main floor, broad windows, dormers, and a wide front porch that looked great, but was almost never used by busy ranchers. Instead, the McSorlie place was a two-storey home, built, Cole guessed, shortly after World War II. It wasn't old enough to be attractive or new enough to be well-maintained. It was simply drab as far as farm houses went. A poured cement pad complete with a basketball net stood alongside the main house, and Cole remembered that Peggy had two teenage boys. Instead of a porch there was a stoop, where two ridiculously friendly border collies wagged their tails, backsides and whole bodies. Cole parked his pickup alongside the three other vehicles already there.

He noted them: a newish Ford F150, a grey four-door sedan that could have been made by nearly any car company, and an older, red Chevy pickup, with drooping running boards and a rusted tailgate. Cole figured all the vehicles could belong to the McSorlie family, but it could also mean that his hoped-for time alone with Peggy before the festivities got underway had been trumped.

He opened the truck door and the sounds of the morning filled his ears. *That* wasn't a disappointment. Birdsong like a symphony flooded his senses. He heard livestock too, goats, cattle, chickens, and a rooster, from out behind a large weathered barn that leaned to one side. Sunlight spilled into the clearing in thick streams, pollen suspended in the dancing light. A large plot was turned and awaited the summer's vegetables, and beyond that a fence, which prevented the McSorlie goats and chickens from wandering into the dense woods.

He closed his truck door and walked toward the main house. He greeted the dogs, climbed the steps, and rapped on the wooden door.

Peggy McSorlie answered after a few seconds. Cole remembered Peggy McSorlie as lighter, fairer, and younger than the woman who stood smiling before him now. But it had been five years since

55

they met face to face in Ottawa, and then only briefly. And, Cole thought, I was younger, fairer, and lighter then myself.

Peggy McSorlie invited Cole into the house. She was of average height, and Cole thought her solid frame made her appear that much more wholesome on this farm. She wore a pair of slacks, a bright sweater, and a scarf wrapped around her neck. Her hair was short, with enough grey to qualify as salt-and-pepper. Her handshake was firm, her smile broad, and when she said that it was so good of Cole to come, he felt real warmth.

They stepped into the kitchen, which was cozy, with lots of windows, and smelled of coffee and fresh baking. Any disappointment Cole felt about the exterior of the house was erased by the warmth and charm of the interior. The large kitchen had a generous island at its centre, and along one wall a couch and rocking chair gave it a welcoming touch. Large pots and frying pans hung from the ceiling over the island, and a wood cookstove accented the otherwise modern appliances with country charm. Cole felt the heat radiating from the woodstove and gravitated toward it.

"Care for coffee?"

"Yes, please."

"How do you take it?"

"With a little cream."

"No sugar?"

"I'm sweet enough already," he grinned and was rewarded with another warm smile.

Cole sat in the rocking chair, Peggy on the couch, and she offered him fresh cinnamon buns. They ate and sipped their coffee and chatted.

"Tell me what you're looking for, Peggy," he said, taking a bite of his bun.

She let out a breath and thought a moment. He liked that. She was careful with her words. "Cole," she finally said, "I'm looking for a miracle."

She told him about the previous attempts by the company to open a new open-pit mine to replace the two existing, depleted operations in the area. She told him about the local economy's unhealthy dependence on coal, and to a lesser extent timber. "This town is caught in a perpetual boom-and-bust cycle," she said, sipping her coffee. "We live and die with commodity prices. When there's high demand for the coking coal that the Buffalo Anthracite Mine produces, we live high on the hog. But only ten, fifteen years ago you couldn't give the stuff away, and lots of businesses closed. We can't go on like this, Cole. This town needs to make the leap into the twenty-first century, but as long as we're looking over our shoulders at yesterday's bonanza, at yesterday's dreams, we're going to slowly die. Another market slump like we had in the eighties and this town is done for, and then what? The forests have all been turned into pulp, the mountains have been levelled to make steel. Nobody is going to want to live here. If we're not careful, Oracle will be a ghost town." She shook her head.

Then she told him about the plans for the McLeod River Mine below the Cardinal Divide. Much of it he had heard from Jim Jones the night before, but he sat silently, sipping the excellent coffee, watching her face, more interested in how she presented the information than the information itself. Was she emotionally attached to the issue? What things set her off?

"Despite the fact that new technology exists that allows steel makers to ply their trade with much less coal, the company seems intent on pushing ahead with the McLeod River Mine. It's almost as if they are programmed to keep looking for more coal. As soon as one project starts to wind down, they move onto the next one. Do you think it's in their DNA?" She looked quizzically at Cole, who grinned.

"I just don't know," Peggy said, finishing her coffee and standing up.

"Tell me about the Eastern Slopes Conservation Group," he said as she walked to the oven to take out more cinnamon buns.

"You mean ESCOG?" She smiled at him.

"Right. What's the O stand for?"

"Nothing. But it didn't sound right without it."

He laughed. She told him about the history of the little band of eco-warriors. For more than a decade they had been battling to save Cardinal Divide, Mountain Park, and the surrounding meadows, ridges, rivers, and valleys. "We've mostly had to go it alone. We've had a lot of help from the provincial and national groups with our legal battles, but they don't live here, do they? They don't have to see these people at the post office. It's hard sometimes. It gets personal. And the provincial and national groups are tired, Cole.

It's been more than a decade. Every time we defeat one proposal, it goes underground for a few years, and then pop!" She snapped her fingers. "It comes right back at us. The big groups will support us, but if we're going to stop this thing, we're going to have to do it ourselves. We're pretty much alone this time."

"You're not alone," Cole said quietly.

"Thank you," she smiled. "I know."

"So what should I expect this morning?"

"How do you mean?"

"Who's going to be attending this meeting and what are the politics?"

"We're mostly just a ragtag bunch of farmers, ranchers, a few small-time loggers, and some small business people from town. There are a couple of young kids from the community who are idealistic and enthusiastic, but don't have much experience. There's a biologist from the University of Alberta who's been doing work on large carnivores in the area: bears, wolves, and cougars. None of us really has much experience with this sort of thing."

"Except you."

"Except me," she confirmed. "And Dale."

"And Dale."

"That's his red truck in the yard. He's out with Gord in the barn right now. Dale van Stempvort. He's been through this before."

Cole finished his coffee and put the cup on the kitchen counter. "Tell me about Dale."

"Well," sighed Peggy.

"Well, what?"

"Well, Dale is a bit of a renegade," said Peggy quietly, leaning forward, echoing Jim Jones. "He's kind of a radical element." She smiled.

"Radical means getting to the root," Cole reminded her.

"Well, not that kind of radical." Peggy sat back. "A few years ago Dale was under suspicion for blowing up a gas well."

Cole was silent.

"Actually, two," added Peggy.

Cole nodded solemnly.

"He had made some threatening statements about running the oil and gas companies off his land. A couple of weeks after he was quoted in the local paper, two well sites were blown up.

They weren't on Dale's land; they were a few miles away. Nobody was hurt, but there was a lot of damage to the equipment. Lots of time lost. The local community was in an uproar. Dale continued to inflame the situation by saying that he supported that sort of action, and was glad that someone else in the community felt as he did."

Cole shook his head.

"It went on for a year, and the RCMP did a pretty thorough investigation. The Mounties couldn't make anything stick. I think it was probably disgruntled employees who blew up those wells. But Dale sure didn't help his own case by talking to the newspapers the way he did."

They sat in silence. After a minute Cole said, "He's not an asset to your efforts, Peggy. He's a liability."

"What can I do?" She sounded defensive. "Tell him not to get involved? Kick him out of my house? He's going to get involved anyway. He's going to say things. With him on the inside, on our side, maybe we can manage him. Control him."

Cole shook his head again. "I don't think so, Peggy. I don't know this man, but I've seen others like him. British Columbia is full of crazies. People who are passionate about the places they live, but are motivated by other things – anger, jealousy, greed, ego, insecurity. Rage. They don't contribute much to the actual effort to protect nature. They just inflame the situation. Make a lot of noise. Polarize communities."

"Well," said Peggy, looking out the window over Cole's shoulder, "he's heading this way. Let's see how it goes today, and cut our losses later, if we can."

The back door opened and Dale van Stempvort called, "Hey Peggy, I'm coming in!" He had a loud voice with a thick Dutch accent.

There was the rustle of a coat being hung and the sound of boots being kicked off, and then Dale van Stempvort entered the kitchen.

Cole stood to greet the large man, powerfully built, who walked with confidence and ease. "I'm Dale van Stempvort," he said and extended a hand to Cole.

"Cole Blackwater," he said, shaking the hand, his own nearly disappearing to the wrist in the big man's paw.

"You've come to help us stop those bastards from digging another hole in the ground. That's good," grinned van Stempvort.

"I'm going to try," smiled Blackwater.

"From what Peggy has told us, you could do it singlehandedly! Like David and Goliath!" The big man roared and slapped Cole on the shoulder.

Cole just smiled. "Where will we meet?" he asked Peggy, and she showed him to the living room.

Within fifteen minutes another dozen people arrived, and Peggy made sure they all had coffee and cinnamon buns and were comfortable in the large living room. Cole greeted each person as they entered, shook hands, and chatted about their background and interest in the mine.

Finally they were all seated and Peggy asked for everyone's attention. Cole looked at the eager faces. The majority of the group were middle-aged women. There was a handful of older men and two younger women. Where *are* all the young people, he wondered? Two of the men wore jackets and ties and Cole figured they were the business people Peggy had mentioned. That didn't bother him. He'd worn his share of ties to kitchen table meetings in the past. One of the young women was decked out in Mountain Equipment Co-op hiking clothing from head to foot. She looked as if she could fend for herself for a month in the woods if she had to. She had long, straight hair and a shiny, fresh face that made Cole envious. The other young woman wore blue jeans and a loose-fitting flower print sweater. The whole spectrum, from suit to flower power, was in the room. Cole grinned.

"Folks, let's get started." Peggy McSorlie clapped her hands and the room fell silent. "We've asked Cole to help us develop a strategy to stop the McLeod River Mine. He's come a long way to do that."

Cole found himself tuning out Peggy's introduction. While she extolled his virtues as a campaign strategist, leaving out his humiliating and career-interrupting departure from the Nation's Capital, his attention drifted to considering how far he was from where he hoped to be.

By this time in his five-year career plan, formulated on the long drive from Ottawa to Calgary and then updated on his slide across BC to Vancouver, he hoped to be a senior advisor to a political party, if not the governing party then at least the official opposition. If not federally, then at least provincially. If not in BC or Ontario, then at least in Saskatchewan or Prince Edward Island. Half a dozen large nonprofit clients would retain him and his associates for on-the-spot advice on government relations, media, and communications strategies. One or two large corporate clients, alternative energy companies like Ballard Power or large communications or internet companies, would subsidize his pro-bono work. The ridiculous amounts of money that he earned for his advice and insight would allow him to do free work for groups like Peggy McSorlie's ragged band of crusaders.

Instead here he was, three years into his solo fling, and the Eastern Slopes Conservation Group (ESCoG as they clumsily called themselves) was currently his second biggest client. His second client, period. And the only client that threatened to pay him.

Cole became aware of the silence and realized that Peggy McSorlie's introduction was complete. He focused and looked around the room, smiling faintly. He tried to appear as though the silence was planned.

Then he stood and cleared his throat. "Thank you, Peggy," he said. "We have a tough job ahead of us." He looked around the room, making eye contact with each person. "This will not be easy. It isn't a game. The stakes are high. A place we love is being threatened. Our opponents have huge resources: smart people, lots of money, the media, and the government in their pockets. This is going to be a long, tough fight. But that isn't going to be the hardest part," he said. "The hardest part won't be facing down angry miners at a public hearing. It won't be the cold stares you get when you walk into the local diner or the Tim Hortons. It won't even be the crank calls you get at midnight. Or the threats from people you thought were your friends. No, the toughest part will be working together, staying together, bleeding together. Finding a strategy that you all believe in and then seeing it through. Not turning on each other. Not parting ways. Not stabbing each other in the back. Not running. Not leaving. Not giving up."

He let his words sink in and looked around the room. "That will be the hardest part. If someone here is not a team player—" he let his dark eyes fall on Dale van Stempvort a second longer than the others, "this is your chance to leave. This is your chance to walk. Nobody will think less of you. In fact, we'll thank you for your honesty. You'll have our blessing to do what you feel you must. But from this point on, we are a team. There is no room for heroes, for all-stars, for lone wolves." Again his eyes met van Stempvort's. "If we develop a plan together, and execute it together, then we can win *together*. That's why I am here. To win. My grandfather said that close only counts in horseshoes and hand grenades. I believe that. Aiming to come close will not stop this mine, and it will not save the Cardinal Divide. It won't save grizzly bears, wolves, or cougars. It won't save harlequin ducks. I'm here to help you stop this thing once and for all. Stop it so it stays stopped. But we're going to have to work together. That's the only way we will win."

Cole thought his sermon sounded pretty good. But that was the easy part. The consultant had it easy. The real work, the work that mattered, was up to these volunteers. Still, he would do his best, over the next two weeks, to give them what they needed to win.

The morning went as expected, with the group excitedly outlining all the myriad opportunities that they had to put the kibosh on the mine, and ranking them against a scale they devised to decide on which tactic they would use to start. Cole finished early for lunch. The group had made excellent progress, he thought, and he didn't want to enter into the next phase, which he knew would be harder, until they had been fed and had a little stretch outside in the sunshine.

Peggy retreated to the kitchen to work with two local volunteers who had brought soup, sandwiches, and a veggie platter for lunch. The rest of the group stood and talked, reluctant to stop when they were flying high. Cole shuffled them toward the kitchen where they fixed sandwiches and bowls of soup, then headed outside to eat, standing in the midday sunlight.

Cole stood alone to collect his thoughts and looked out across the fields and the turned soil of the vegetable garden, eating an egg salad sandwich. The noon sun was strong and he stretched his arms forward and back.

"I know you were talking to me," said a thickly accented voice. Cole knew it was Dale van Stempvort.

He finished his stretch, turned, and smiled at the big man.

"I know you were talking to me when you said we got to be team players," said van Stempvort again, taking a bite of his sandwich.

"I was talking to the whole group," replied Blackwater.

"But mostly to me," said Dale, holding up his hand to cut off further objection from Blackwater. "It's OK, really. It's OK. I know what my reputation is."

Cole said nothing. He noticed how Dale's eyes couldn't hold Cole's gaze, and how he shuffled his feet.

"I got it coming to me," he said with a smile, pushing dirt back and forth with the toe of his boot. "In the past, I have not been the best at playing as a team."

"Do you think this time will be different, Dale?" asked Cole, and watched him closely.

"I don't know. It's hard to teach new tricks to an old dog. But I want to stop this thing, and if you think sticking together is the way to do it, then it's worth a try. I just hate sitting on my hands while those bastards get away with raping places like Cardinal Divide."

"Well, I don't aim to have anybody sitting on their hands," said Cole quietly.

"I suppose you don't. But you don't know these people," said Dale, looking around him. Then he leaned closer. "They don't like conflict too much. They are afraid of it."

"Can you blame them? I mean, they are going up against their neighbours, their customers, their friends."

"Well damn it all," said Dale; his voice rose and his head bobbed. "They have got to put all that aside if they want to win. They can't be afraid to do what it takes. If that means making a few enemies, then that's what they will have to do." He spoke quickly, his accent thick.

Dale went on. "Sooner or later somebody is going to have to draw a line in the sand and say: this far and no farther. Sooner or later somebody is going to have to say: we're going to stop these bastards at all cost."

The two men stared at each other in the noonhour sunlight. Cole Blackwater's face was impassive. Dale van Stempvort's was agitated.

"Have you seen Cardinal Divide?" Cole asked.

Stephen Legault

"Of course I have," said Dale, slightly perturbed by the infer-ence. "It's beautiful."

"Do you think that the people who plan to mine there, build roads over it, and bring the outside world to it are motivated by hate, greed, power, fear?"

"I don't know what motivates them. It's not the same thing as you and me. I don't even think they are people."

Cole raised his eyebrows. In fifteen years of activism Cole had heard this line of thinking many times, and he rejected it. When we stop thinking the people we disagree with are worth the same dignity we insist on for ourselves, and for wild creatures, we head down a slippery slope. The way Dale spat out those words, so full of anger, worried Cole.

"And what motivates you?" Cole queried.

Dale was silent. He looked back down at his feet and rearranged a ridge of sand he had built there. "I don't know ..." he said after a minute. Then he looked around at the woods bordering the Mc-Sorlie spread, as if seeking inspiration. Would Dale explain that love of nature inspired him? He doubted it. When polled, ninety percent of Canadians said they loved nature. Few of them ever lifted a finger in its defence.

Finally Dale looked up and said, "I hate to see those bastards get away with destroying another beautiful place."

The two men regarded each other. Cole nodded his head. "I hate it too," he said, in genuine agreement. "But what worries me, quite frankly, is that I think you hate the people more than you hate what they are planning to do, and that's trouble. That blinds you to the fact that they *are* people, like you and me, with chil-dren they love, and passions of their own. To win, we have to treat them as people, capable of love and worthy of our respect. If we don't, we're not better off than they are."

The look of disdain on Dale's face showed that he didn't agree. He shook his head and repeated, "They aren't people. Not like you and me. Not like Peggy."

Their stalemate was interrupted by Peggy McSorlie's voice from the stoop of the house. "Time to get started again, folks."

The two men regarded each other. Then Dale said, "Peggy hired you to help us, and I'm willing to give her the benefit of the doubt. I know you've won some battles. You got the scars to prove it," Dale grinned. "But at the end of the day, this is our fight. It's my fight. Win or lose, you get paid, and go back to Vancouver, and move on to the next client. But we're stuck here. We've got to stay. It's our backyard. I aim to do what I have to do to win."

Cole smiled at the man. "I'll do everything I can to help you," he said, putting his hand on the big man's shoulder and guiding him toward the door. "Let's get back at it," he said congenially. It was truly dangerous to have a man like Dale van Stempvort involved on this campaign. Dale van Stempvort seemed to Cole to be a man whose hatred made him capable of almost anything.

5 A telephone rang. Where was he? In the unfamiliar darkness he probed for clues. No streetlights, no sirens, no car horns. Not Vancouver. He peered around the room. Rim Rock Motel. Oracle, Alberta. The phone—he fumbled for it, knocked it off the bedside stand onto the floor. It rang yet. He bent over, sheets twisted around his legs, reached for the receiver, and pressed it to his face.

"Hello," he said finally, groggily, into the mouthpiece.

"Cole?"

"This is Cole Blackwater."

"Oh hi, Cole, it's Peggy McSorlie. Did I wake you? I'm sorry, it's just that—"

"It's OK, Peggy," interrupted Cole, "I'm sure that the day is already well underway," he mumbled. He looked at the clock on the bedstand, where the phone had once stood. It was 8:30 AM. He closed his eyes.

"Anyway, I'm sorry to call so early, but we've got a problem."

Second day on the job, he thought, and we already have a problem. "What is it?"

"Well, it's Dale."

"What has he done?" said Cole, rising up on an elbow.

"I think you had better read the Red Deer newspaper and then call me back, Cole."

"You can't tell me over the phone what it is?"

"I can, but I think you'll want to read it anyway."

"How bad?"

"Pretty bad."

Cole grumbled something under his breath. Then, "OK, I'll pick up the paper and call you back."

He hung up the phone.

He walked stiffly to the shower and, without turning the light on in the bathroom, stepped in and turned the water on as hot as he could stand. He put one hand against the tiled wall under the shower head and let the other hand hang at his side. The hot water blasted over his head, neck, and shoulders and ran down his back and chest. He stood that way for five minutes, letting the water revive him.

He had left Peggy McSorlie's around 7 PM the previous night, picked up a sandwich and sixpack in town, and came straight back to the Rim Rock Motel. While his laptop slowly downloaded his email (dialup, no wireless for the Rim Rock) he washed and changed into clean clothes and quickly read the day's headlines on *The Globe and Mail*'s web site. He drank a beer, sorted his email, responded to a few messages, and then took a look at his notes from the day. He ate his sandwich, drank two more beers, and by 10 PM had typed his notes and ordered his thoughts, mentally and on paper.

He watched *The National* on television, drank his last two beers, and then, finding no solace in Peter Mansbridge's dulcet tones, ventured downstairs to The Quarry for a nightcap. The bar was as crowded and noisy as the night before, as comforting as a home away from home. After his perfunctory scan of the joint, he bellied up to the bar and drank two Jamesons, neat, while chatting with George Cody about the Canucks' chances, and whether or not Calgary and Edmonton were playoff contenders.

It was an educational conversation. He learned that George *had* played football, but only in university, and at his own admission, he wasn't very good. He had been a running back. "Big," he had said, "but not very fast." Not fast enough to go pro.

Cole learned that George had met Deborah while working in Fort McMurray, before the tar sands boom, and the two had migrated further west, bound for BC, when they had stopped in Oracle and learned that the Rim Rock and its adjacent bar were for sale, the owner in some kind of financial trouble. They scrapped together money they had saved, bought it, and stayed.

Then Cole had a chance to try out his own story, telling George that he was a freelance business writer interested in the Buffalo Anthracite Mine, and the new project they're working on at the McLeod River. Cole had studied George's reaction: the big man had nodded, rubbed his moustache and said that "project might work, if that new hot shot they've got running the show out there gets his head out of his ass and looks out for the mine and the community, not just the company, or his own self. If that new project doesn't pan out, we'll have to change the name of this place."

Cole had raised an eyebrow in inquiry.

"Call it the Watering Hole or the Trout Pond, not The Quarry. For the tourists. If that mine closes, we're going to have to hope that the tourists heading to Jasper find this joint appealing, or Deb and I will be on the road again."

By the time Cole returned to his room it was 2 AM and he was comfortably drunk. He slept deeply but not for long enough. The hot shower was slowly easing the previous night's poison from his body and brain. A coffee would help.

He stepped from the shower, towelled off, and dressed in the bedroom. He opened the curtains and winced at the daylight. Alberta is bright, he remembered. He had been on the coast long enough to grow accustomed to weeks without seeing the sun.

He swallowed two Advils with a slug of water (breakfast of champions) and stepped into the day. He walked to the front office to find a newspaper. Deborah greeted him warmly.

"Good morning," she said, beaming.

"You always behind that desk?" Cole asked, mustering a smile.

"Almost," she said, and she winked at him. He hoped it was a sharing-the-joke kind of wink. Or just a charming but innocent habit. Not a come-up-and-see-me-sometime kind of wink.

He cleared his throat. "Have you got today's paper?"

"Well, the local rag doesn't come out 'til Thursday," she said. "But the Red Deer paper's daily. There are a few on the table there." She pointed to the coffee table by the fireplace.

"Can I take one?" he asked.

"Be my guest," she smiled.

He grabbed a paper and beat a hasty retreat. He walked the four blocks to the highway and made his way to the Tim Hortons to read the news and coffee up. The place was quiet. By nine most of Oracle's working class was already at the mill, at the mine, or in the woods. He sat at a table by the window, drank his coffee, and flipped through the paper.

There it was. "Greens gear up to fight new mine," read the headline.

Cole sipped his coffee and scanned the story.

A coalition of local activists, small business owners, and scientists is preparing to go head to head with Athabasca Coal, the proponent of the McLeod River Mine, located south and west of the town of Oracle.

The group hopes to stop in its tracks plans for a new open-pit mine that will extract 30 million tonnes of coking coal in the region, saying that the mine will destroy wildlife habitat and put Jasper National Park at risk.

That's good, thought Cole. They got the small business owners and scientists angle in, so it's not just a bunch of berry-suckers doing the whining.

But local Mine Manager Mike Barnes says that the company has every intention of protecting fish and wildlife in the region, and says that the new mine will actually enhance local populations of wildlife in the long run.

Barnes says that the open pits will be reclaimed so that after the mine closes in thirty years, there will be a series of lakes that will be stocked with trout, and the slopes levelled and seeded for sheep habitat.

Barnes adds that the local economy, in a slump since a previous mine project was scuttled nearly a decade ago, needs this project to stay afloat. "We're talking about our kids' future," says Barnes, who has been the Manager at Athabasca Coal's existing Buffalo Anthracite Mine for six months.

Not so good, thought Cole. This guy Barnes knows his stuff. He got a line in the paper about economy and kids practically in the same sentence. The story went on:

But local activist Dale van Stempvort ...

Rats, thought Cole.

...says that the mine is a "disgrace and an abomination," and that activists are developing a plan to stop it. When asked what they had planned, van Stempvort said that no plan had been finalized yet, but that he was "willing to do anything necessary to keep the mine out of Cardinal Divide."

69   Stephen Legault

Cole stopped reading. He put down the paper and looked out the window. His job just got a lot harder.

He dialled Peggy McSorlie's number on his cellphone and listened to it ring. She answered the phone.

"I've read it," he said without saying hello. "I told you," he said angrily.

"I know you did. What can we do?"

"Nothing, I guess," he sighed. "I think we're just going to have to carry on with our plan of yesterday."

"OK," agreed McSorlie.

"But it's like he wasn't even there. Wasn't even listening when we talked about keeping a lid on this for a while. What did he do, call the reporter from his truck as he was leaving? He would have had to make the print deadline."

Peggy was silent a moment. "I'm sorry, Cole."

"No, I'm the one who should be sorry. I should have come down a little harder on him."

"It wouldn't have helped."

"Likely not," he said, less angrily. "OK, well, on with the show."

"You're still going to call Mike Barnes and ask to see him?"

"More reason now than ever. In fact, in some ways, this fits well with my cover story."

"And what about Dale? Should I call him?"

Cole thought a moment. "No, let me. I can lean on him a little without risking a long-term relationship."

They said goodbye and hung up.

Cole sipped his coffee. Then he checked his Palm Pilot for the mine office number and dialled it, taking a deep breath as he did.

"Buffalo Anthracite Mine. Sophie speaking."

"Mike Barnes, please."

"Just a moment." Cole waited while the call was transferred.

"Mike Barnes' office. Tracey speaking," said a woman with a cool voice.

"This is Cole Blackwater calling," he said. "I'd like to make an appointment with Mr. Barnes."

"Will he know what it's about, sir?"

"I don't think so. I'm a business writer and I'm interested in doing a story on Mr. Barnes and the McLeod River project."

"OK, let me see." After a minute she returned. "Mr. Barnes is in meetings all morning, sir. Would you like to talk with Mr. Henderson, our Assistant Mine Manager instead?"

"No thanks," said Cole, "and I'm not in that much of a rush. I was hoping for an hour or so of Mr. Barnes' time, face to face."

Cole made a mental note to see if Henderson's position on things was just the same.

"Well, he could see you at the end of the day today," she said.

"That would be fine," replied Cole. "What time?"

"Five?"

"That would be great." .

"OK, I'll leave your name at security. They'll give you directions to the administration building. You know how to get to the mine site?"

He said he didn't, and she told him.

He hung up. That was easier than he'd expected. No questions about which magazine, no questions about his credentials. But then, why should there be? There was no reason for the mine to suspect that the local activists had brought him in as a hired gun to help them stop the new mine. Not yet, he reasoned.

He sipped his coffee, now nearly cold. He looked up Dale van Stempvort's number in his Palm. How would he handle this call? Clearly van Stempvort had violated the group's wish for confidentiality, and only a few hours after assuring Blackwater that he would do no such thing. Cole looked at the number. This call required more caffeine. He went to the counter and ordered another coffee and another doughnut. He sat back down and wondered what might motivate van Stempvort.

In his years as an activist, Cole Blackwater had rarely worked on a file where someone like Dale van Stempvort didn't show up as a fly in the ointment. People's motives for working to protect the environment were complex. While nearly everyone who volunteered to protect places like the Cardinal Divide did it for noble reasons — protect nature, leave a legacy, care for wildlife — some people's motives had nothing to do with the environment at all. The environmental movement was by nature an outsider's game. And outsiders came in all shapes and sizes.

Along with the everyday people who simply cared about nature, Cole Blackwater believed that the movement did attract its share of people who were disenfranchised by society, who were mentally ill, or who simply felt that the way to get attention was to stand out by speaking out. More often than not these people took drastic positions, looking for media attention, or created conflicts within environmental groups, choosing infighting over working to solve the real problems. Had these people lived in the nineteenth century, they would have circled the wagons and shot *in*.

Dale van Stempvort certainly seemed to crave attention, even to revel in the conflict he created among his fellow activists. Blackwater thought him unbalanced. He seemed dangerous. He had a propensity for rash statements, like the one staring at Blackwater from the pages of the newspaper spread open in front of him.

So the question Blackwater posed to himself over his second cup of coffee was this: just how far *would* van Stempvort go to stop this mine?

He looked at Dale van Stempvort's number again on his Palm. He had taken everybody's name, email, phone number, and address down after the first meeting at Peggy McSorlie's farm and entered them there for safekeeping. He picked up his cell and was about to dial the number when a familiar-looking pickup truck pulled into the doughnut shop parking lot. Cole watched, amazed, as Dale van Stempvort parked his truck and stepped out, adjusting his ball cap. Cole hid behind his newspaper. He didn't want to be seen talking with Dale. He needed another couple of incognito days in town to interview the President of the Chamber of Commerce and others under the guise of a magazine story. Talking with Dale could cast suspicion on his cover, and at the very least make people think that the story was for *Canadian Geographic* rather than *Report on Business*.

From behind the paper Cole watched Dale order a coffee and a muffin and then, without a word to anybody, walk back out. Cole swept his phone, paper, and Palm Pilot into his arms and followed Dale into the parking lot.

Dale stepped into the truck. Cole checked over his shoulder and, certain he wasn't being observed, deftly moved to the passenger side of the truck, opened the door, and slipped in.

If Cole Blackwater's sudden appearance in the cab of his truck startled Dale van Stempvort, he didn't let it show. Instead he simply said, "Good Morning, Cole."

"Morning, Dale."

"Saw you behind the newspaper in the shop there."

"Well, I didn't want to blow my cover quite yet," Cole said, somewhat embarrassed.

"Oh yes."

"Shall we go for a little drive, Dale? Have a chat?"

"All right. Where to?"

"How about just to the outskirts of town and back?"

Dale backed the truck from its stall and turned right on the highway, heading west toward the mountains.

"Listen, Dale, I wanted to talk with you about this story in the paper this morning. Have you seen it?"

"Yes, I saw it."

"It's quite the story."

"It sure is."

"Dale," said Cole. "I'm a little disappointed that you went to the media after all we discussed yesterday."

"Now just wait a minute, Cole," said Dale, turning his head sharply. Cole thought for a minute that Dale was going to explode, and prepared himself for the possibility of physical violence. He suddenly questioned the wisdom of jumping, unwitnessed, into the cab of a pickup with a man whose sanity he had only moments ago questioned. "Wait a minute," Dale said again, more calmly, turning his eyes back to the road. "That reporter called me. I didn't call him."

"How do you mean?"

"The reporter called me. The telephone was ringing when I walked in the door. I've never even heard of him before. Somebody from Red Deer that doesn't normally work this beat."

"Did he say how he knew to call just then?"

"I didn't even ask. I just assumed that it was blind luck that we had wrapped up our strategy meeting. You know, a coincidence."

"Some coincidence."

"Well, the story has been pretty hot, and I have been in the paper a lot."

Cole looked at the paper in his hands. The byline was given to Richard T. Drewfeld. He made a mental note to call Mr. Drewfeld later that morning.

"So you didn't call the reporter."

Dale stiffened. "Cole, I know you don't like me. Maybe I'm too rough around the edges for a big city environmentalist like you.

But an agreement is an agreement, and we agreed to hold off the media for a week while we developed our plan."

"But you were quoted."

Dale hunched forward a little. "Yeah, well, what was I supposed to do? Tell the guy to fuck off, that there wasn't any story?"

"But Dale, you told the guy that you would be willing to do anything to stop the mine. That's hardly a mush-ball quote. And the reporter knew that we'd been in a strategy session! Did you tell him that too?"

"I did no such thing!" barked Dale in his thick Dutch accent. "Look, the guy seemed to have already known that we were planning to oppose the mine. It wouldn't take a rocket scientist to surmise that we were going to go head to head over this one. And as for the comment about doing anything necessary, well, he took that out of context."

Cole was silent. They had left town now and were still driving west on Highway 16. "Let's turn around," he said, as calmly as he could.

Cole knew from years of experience that Dale van Stempvort, if he was telling the truth, had fallen for two of the oldest tricks in the journalist's book. First, the reporter had conned Dale into believing that he already knew certain things. A statement as open ended as "I understand local enviros are gearing up to fight this mine" could have tricked van Stempvort into believing the writer knew about that day's meeting.

The second trick was to get van Stempvort talking and then just sit back and listen. People are uncomfortable with long silences, and often avoid them by continuing to talk. In this case Drewfeld may have simply asked what was being planned to stop the mine, and van Stempvort could have rattled on for 15 minutes. Then the reporter could have taken a sentence, even half a sentence, that met his needs and used it to make van Stempvort sound like the frothing-at-the-mouth radical he was.

They drove in silence for a few minutes. Then Dale said, "I screwed up, didn't I?"

Cole breathed out heavily. "It could be worse. It could be that nobody was interested in this as a story at all. But yes, you did screw up. You should have told the reporter that you didn't have anything to say or told them to call Peggy."

"Look, Cole, I'm sorry. Sometimes I just get a bit hot under the collar. I hate it so damn much what those bastards are doing, and are going to do, that I don't think."

"We need to think, Dale, if we're going to win."

Dale stared toward the approaching town of Oracle. "I know it," he finally said.

"Stay out of the media. Deal?"

"Deal," Dale said, smiling. Then, "Where can I drop you?"

"Pull off 16 up ahead. I'll hop out."

Dale pulled over on the shoulder of a side street about four blocks from Cole's motel. Cole began to open the door. Dale grabbed his arm and Cole stiffened. Dale relaxed his grip, "Wait a minute, Cole."

Cole sat back, but left the door ajar. "What is it?" he said.

"I know you think I'm some kind of raving lunatic. An eco-terrorist. A mad bomber," Dale grinned at the labels. "I know that's what everybody thinks. That I'm some kind of psychopath. That I'm dangerous."

Cole was silent. He watched the big man. Dale gripped the wheel with both hands intently, not making eye contact. "I'm none of those things, really, Cole. It's just an act. It's for show," sighed Dale, looking over at Cole. "I didn't have anything to do with blowing up gas wells."

"But you didn't deny it when the stories came out."

"I didn't and I know that seems pretty stupid. But it was a good opportunity to tell *my* story, and as long as nobody was laying charges against me, I didn't see any reason to assert my innocence. I know that may seem dumb to you, but it gave my issue a lot of attention, Cole."

It gave *you* a lot of attention, Cole thought, but remained silent.

"Anyway, I just really want to stop this mine. And if you say that means *not* talking to the media, well, then I'm willing to listen. For now."

Cole regarded him for a long, silent moment. He saw in Dale van Stempvort's face no malice. He saw no guile. He saw simply a big, rough man fighting for something that he believed in. Did Dale van Stempvort conceal something dark and sinister behind his mask of innocence? Cole had no way of knowing. I'm a liar myself, after all, mused Cole.

Cole sighed deeply. He swung the door open, and said, over his shoulder, "You gave me the benefit of the doubt yesterday. I'm giving it back to you now. Let's hope neither of us comes out of this too disappointed." He stepped out of the truck.

He puzzled over the question of Dale van Stempvort as he walked the four blocks to his motel. He needed to trust Dale in order to continue with his work. He needed to know that there wouldn't be a story in the paper the day after every strategy session. Some of the tactics they were considering required the element of surprise to be effective.

The morning was bright and the temperature climbed steadily. It must be fifteen degrees, a respectable spring day in the Eastern Slopes. May could be bright and sunny, but as often as not it could shepherd in weeks of rain, even snow. Ian Tyson's lament came to mind: *Just like springtime in Alberta, warm sunny days, endless skies of blue. Then without a warning, another winter storm comes raging through.*

As he walked he found himself humming the tune. That melody catapulted him into Saturday morning breakfast with his brother Walter and their dad at the Coral Café in Clairsholm. After their morning's tasks at the feed store, they would stop for breakfast before driving back to the ranch. Cole and Walter would fight to see who got to sit in the middle of the pickup. Whoever lost had to jump in and out of the truck a dozen times on the drive, opening and closing gates on the way home. He stopped humming. No sense in letting in any more of *those* memories. Cole pushed thoughts of his father back under the dark and heavy anchor that kept them in place.

He reached the Rim Rock Motel and crossed the now nearly empty parking lot. It was 11 AM, and Blackwater guessed that nearly every person staying there was out on a job site. It was his intention to join them just as soon as he could. He climbed the outside stairs and followed the walkway to his room. His computer was waiting. He had some digging to do. When he reached his room he rummaged through his pockets, fishing for the key, digging through the usual collection of receipts, wrappers, coins, money, lint, and other rubbish. He heard a loud shout from a room a few doors down to his right. He looked up quickly, and noticed for the first time the open door, and the maid's cart protruding slightly onto the catwalk.

Cole held his breath, listened, and then heard another shout, a loud male voice. The voice was familiar. Curiosity overtook him, and he quietly walked the twenty metres down the catwalk toward the open door.

"You're a filthy whore!" a man's voice yelled through the open door.

Cole stopped.

"Fuck you, George."

"Fuck me? Seems like you're fucking everybody *but* me!" George roared.

He took a step back from the open door and tried to peer into the room through the window, through the tiny gap between the drawn curtains. He was aware that he might easily be seen through the drapes because he had daylight behind him. He took another step back and glimpsed Deborah Cody making a bed, while George Cody stood behind her, his meaty hands on his hips.

"That's a lie," Deborah Cody said, tucking the sheets into the foot of the bed.

"Have you been fucking *him*?"

"I don't know what you're talking about."

"Have you been fucking Mike Barnes?"

Good God, thought Cole Blackwater, and took another step back.

"Have you?"

Deborah Cody turned to face her husband.

"I found *this*," said George, his voice quieter. Cole could see George waving a slip of paper at Deborah.

"That doesn't mean anything," he heard Deborah say.

"It says plenty."

"He was a guest here, George. He must have left that in his room."

"It wasn't in *his* room," George spat.

Deborah turned her back on her husband and finished making the bed.

"You're fucking hopeless," George said. "You disgust me."

Cole realized that George was about to storm out of the room, and he turned as quickly as he could, careful not to make a sound, and padded to his own door. He didn't relish the idea of an enraged George storming from the room, finding him lurking there, and soundly thrashing him, taking out his rage for his wife on Cole. Nor did he want to endure the mother of all awkward moments.

He breathed heavily and fumbled with his key. His heart pounded as his vulnerable back faced the open doorway, where George and Deborah quarrelled. Several wrappers and a crumpled five-dollar bill fell to the ground in his haste to locate his key. Finally he opened the door.

He kicked the detritus into the room as he entered and gently pushed the door shut behind him. He stood and panted in the darkness. Why was it so important that he not be caught listening? Surely George and Deborah wouldn't involve a blameless guest in their dispute. But there was something in George's voice, and in Deborah's cold ambivalence, that made Cole Blackwater panic. George had sounded on the edge of rage. And the way Deborah had simply brushed the issue aside, as if she were brushing the sheets smooth as she made the bed, struck Cole as calculating.

He stood with his back to the door. In the darkness he peered around the room. His bed was a mass of twisted blankets and the towel from his morning's shower hung over the straight-backed chair by the small desk where the phone and his computer sat. His room hadn't been made up yet.

He quickly switched on the lights and peered through the curtains before parting them. He flipped open his computer and turned it on. In a moment Deborah would enter his room to clean it, and he would be deeply engaged in his work when she did.

He was checking his email when he heard a tap on the door and the sound of a key scraping in the lock. The door opened and he looked up and smiled.

"I'm sorry, Cole," smiled Deborah, as if she were having a pleasant, run-of-the-mill day. "I didn't know you were in here."

"No problem. I'm just getting some work done between interviews." He continued with his cover story, though he realized it had one glaring hole in it: Peggy McSorlie had made his reservation for him. He hoped that Deborah wouldn't make the connection.

"Do you want me to come back later?"

Cole weighed the options in his mind. Shooing Deborah away would ensure he wouldn't become entangled in this domestic dispute. On the other hand, he was curious about Deborah Cody, and wanted to learn the truth behind George's accusations.

"No, you can tidy up now, if you like," he said. "As long as I won't be in your way, you won't be in mine," he smiled again.

"Fine with me," she said and started to pull the sheets from the bed. He sat with his back to her and typed while she put new sheets on the bed and straightened the covers. He watched her surreptitiously in the full-length mirror screwed to the wall next to the desk. She moved purposefully about the bed, making quick work of the job. She was a beautiful woman, he noted, confirming his first impressions. Faded blue jeans hugged her shapely butt and a cotton T-shirt rode up to expose her smooth midriff when she bent to flatten the blankets. Her sandy hair was tied up above an elegant neck. Cole Blackwater felt the attraction. Any man could succumb.

Deborah Cody said nothing as she moved to the bathroom to clean it and change the towels. If he didn't act now, he would lose the opportunity.

"I'm working on a story about the Buffalo Anthracite Mine," he said, typing with emphasis. "I do mostly freelance work, and I hope to run this piece in *Canadian Business* magazine."

She continued to clean in the bathroom, behind the door. Had she heard him? He continued typing.

"I'm focusing on, you know, how the economy of this region is tied to mining. Uh, since the prospects for the new mine look good, how's the economy of this place going to buck the current trend by, um, remaining vibrant while other towns, like Cache Creek, have crumbled as opportunities have disappeared?"

There was silence, and then, "That sounds interesting," Deborah said as she stepped from the bathroom, a heap of towels in her arms.

"I think so," he lied. "I'm heading out to the mine this afternoon to interview Mike Barnes." He looked at his computer and tried to gauge her reaction from the corner of his eye.

If she had any, he could not discern it. She walked behind him to the open door and dumped the towels and used sheets into the waiting hamper.

Cole decided to go for broke. "Do you know Mr. Barnes?" he asked.

"Oh yes," she said, and Cole took a breath. "He was a guest here for a few months when he first came to town, before he found

a place to rent. We have a few suites with kitchenettes in them."
Cole could detect no strong emotion one way or the other in her
words. Her voice was flat. Uncharacteristically so.

"What's he like?"

"He's all business," she said, arranging some cleaning products on the trolley. "People say he's going to turn that mine
around, save the community. He certainly spends enough time at
it. While he was staying here, I hardly saw him. He was always
out at the site."

Cole smiled and attempted to employ the journalist's trick of
silence. Deborah Cody either didn't fall for it, or didn't have anything else to say. "Anything else I can do for you, Cole?" she said,
her voice taking on the slightly sultry tone that Cole had grown
accustomed to.

"I don't think so," he lied again. He could think of half a dozen
things she could do for him, but thought better of it. "Thanks so
much," he said and turned back to his computer.

When she left, Cole pondered the information. All business,
she said. Turn the mine around. Save the community. A lot was
riding on Mike Barnes. Maybe Cole's speculation about the man
was right. Maybe Cole's cover wasn't so far fetched after all. If
what he suspected was true, the little group of environmentalists were in for the fight of their lives. It wasn't only the Buffalo
Anthracite Mine and Athabasca Coal they were fighting. It was
the whole town. Cole had visions of lynch mobs and torches.
Bricks with death threats taped to them heaved through windows. It wasn't unlikely. In the United States clashes over the use
and exploitation of natural resources – timber, oil, ore – sparked
violence, and even murder. People's homes had been burnt to
the ground. Forest Service offices had been bombed. And the
violence wasn't always perpetuated by the right-wing proponents of development. In one high-profile case the Earth Lib-
eration Front, or ELF, had burned a resort development in Vail,
Colorado, to the ground. Nobody was injured, but the cost was
in the millions.

Both sides of the ideological spectrum spawned their share of
raving lunatics. People with strongly held views on either side of
the issue sometimes came unhinged as they struggled for what
they believed was right.

For ESCOG to stop the new mine, they would need to make more than an environmental argument; they would need a well-constructed and community-supported economic argument. How was this mine going to be bad for the people over the long haul? Cole considered this as he scanned his emails.

Then he thought back to the loose ends created by his morning's conversation with Dale van Stempvort. He Googled the story and read it again in the online version of the *Red Deer Advocate*. He found the paper's phone number, broke the connection with the internet, then picked up his room phone and dialled the number.

A receptionist answered the phone and he asked for Richard T. Drewfeld. What a name, Cole thought. What does the "T" stand for? Timid? Tepid? Tenacious?

"Drewfeld here," came a gruff voice on the other end of the line. OK, not timid, thought Blackwater.

"Cole Blackwater here," said Cole in his roughest, whiskey-soured voice. It was pretty rough.

"What can I do you for?"

"Mr. Drewfeld, I'm a writer doing a piece on the Buffalo Anthracite Mine for *Canadian Business*. Read your piece in the *Advocate* this morning. Good bit of writing," said Blackwater.

"Thanks. Who did you say you write for?"

"Doing the piece on spec. Hope to place it with *Canadian Business*," said Cole, slinging the lingo.

"Right, well, what can I help you with?"

"Little bit of journalistic indulgence. Some tit-for-tat, say. I was wondering how you got the tree-huggers to talk? They seemed kind of tight lipped to me? You must've really worked your address book."

There was silence, and Cole let it linger. Even journalists got anxious with the silence eventually. "Well," said Drewfeld, "not really. That van Stempvort likes to spout off any chance he gets. He's a real talker."

"So you just phoned him up out of the blue? Just like that?"

"Well, you don't need to write for the big boys to figure that those fish kissers would be planning on putting up a fight, do you?"

"Guess not," confessed Cole. "But still, seems like you really got the timing right. How did you know to call van Stempvort when you did?"

"Let's just say a little birdie whispered in my ear."

Cole didn't say a word. He held the phone against his face, listening to the other man breathe. Finally he said, in as calm a voice as he could, "Got a source, do you?"

"Maybe, maybe not. What's the tat part of this equation? What did you say your name was, Blackwater?

He could hear the other man typing, likely doing a web search on his name. Cole's mind raced. He had shut down his web page last night when ESCoG had decided that he would go undercover. He hoped he had covered this tracks well enough. "I'll call you when I've got something," Cole said quickly and hung up. But there would be no need to call the reporter back. He already knew enough. There was a mole in the Eastern Slopes Conservation Group, and it wasn't Dale van Stempvort.

6 Cole muttered expletively under this breath. He slammed his fist onto the shaky table. His laptop jumped dangerously. Papers spilled onto the floor. He did it again.

He pressed his head into his palm and slumped over. This was entirely unexpected. Cole closed his eyes, the better to picture each member of the group. Faces came and went in his mind, blurring and melding, but he didn't have the foggiest idea who the snitch was.

He pulled himself upright and dialled Peggy's number. He broke the news to her.

"Oh, Cole, what now?" she asked, her voice shaking.

Cole exhaled slowly and said, "We've got to work fast, Peggy. It may be that whoever has burrowed into ESCOG is working alone, but it's unlikely. I'm betting that our mole is connected to the mine. From what I hear of Mike Barnes – smart, strategic, more than a little devious – he could be capable of placing someone inside to monitor our work and report on our actions to keep one step ahead of the berry-suckers. But they've played their hand too early."

"What does it mean for your cover, Cole?"

"It's probably blown," said Cole. "But I'll string it along for a few more hours and see what I can milk from the community. My meeting with Mike Barnes is this evening ... either his secretary doesn't know about it, or Barnes doesn't care."

"Maybe he's using you, Cole."

Cole laughed. "Maybe. We'll see who gets the upper hand."

"Be careful, Cole. Whoever gets the upper hand gets the Cardinal Divide," reminded Peggy.

Cole sobered: "You don't need to remind me, Peggy."

Peggy heard the defensiveness in Cole's voice. "You're right; I don't need to remind you. What should I do, Cole?"

Cole thought a second. "We'll cut the planning team to no more than a few trusted people, Peggy. We'll keep folks informed, but I only want you and a few others that you can absolutely trust, people you've known all your life, that you can vouch for one hundred percent."

"That's no problem, Cole. I can do that."

"Good. I'm going to run. I need to make hay while the proverbial sun shines on my cover story, Peggy." He hung up.

Stephen Legault

Cole gathered his things, picked the papers off the floor and stacked them on the desk, then left and locked the door behind him. He headed downtown in the Toyota and stopped for fuel and a coffee at a gas station before turning off the highway. Main Street, the original heart of the city, ran perpendicular to Highway 16. On it was a block of charming heritage buildings, bordered on both sides by newer offices including the mandatory, and startlingly ugly, post office at one end, and the squat, institutional Royal Canadian Mounted Police detachment and a bright, but Spartan-looking Chamber of Commerce building at the other.

That was Cole's destination.

The single-storey building was bordered tightly by a sidewalk and buffered by planters displaying a few small wild rose bushes not yet in bloom. Cole walked up the steps and entered the broad front doors. A bell chimed as he entered.

"May I help you?" A young woman seated behind the front desk looked up as he approached.

"Hi," he said, "I'm a freelance writer doing a story on Oracle and the Buffalo Anthracite Mine. Can I speak with anybody about that?"

The young woman picked up her phone and looked at Cole. "Let me see if David Smith is available. What's your name?"

"Cole Blackwater," he said. This was no time to further complicate things with a pseudonym.

The woman spoke into the phone and then placed it back on the receiver. "He can spend a few minutes with you if you like." Cole followed her to a back office.

David Smith was a large man with broad shoulders and a thick neck who carried thirty extra pounds on his chest and belly. He rose from behind a wood-panelled desk and reached out his hand when Cole entered his office. When the two men shook, Cole sensed the power in his massive hands and arms. Like most in this part of the world, thought Cole, he must have spent a fair portion of his life hewing wood and drawing water.

"Have a seat," ordered Smith, and pointed to one of two chairs arranged on the opposite side of a broad, wooden desk. Cole sat. "So you're a reporter?"

"Thanks for seeing me. I know I should have called, but just happened to be walking by and thought I'd come in and introduce myself," Cole began. "I'm a freelance writer, actually. I don't write for any particular magazine or paper. I come up with story ideas and pitch them to publications —"

"I know what you do," said Smith, smiling broadly, and Cole felt a lump in his throat. "I wasn't thrown off a turnip truck yesterday." The man smiled again. Cole relaxed. "What are you writing about?"

"The new McLeod River Mine is seen as Oracle's saviour. How does the Chamber view that?"

"You got a tape recorder?" asked Smith.

"No, I hate the things. Always messing up. I'm an old fashioned guy," said Cole. He found a pen in his pocket and began to scribble in his notebook.

"Well, I know that mine like the back of my hand. I worked there for almost twenty years. I started out on the shop floor and made my way up to mill foreman. I did well for a guy without a college diploma. It was good work, but after a while I moved on. Started a business selling parts to the Buffalo, and to other mines in the region. Now here I am," he said. He opened his arms wide, gestured to the room, and leaned back in his chair. "It's been a long journey from the shop floor to this office, and I'm proud of every step I've taken.

"I tell you that so you know I'm not just blowing smoke when I say that without the Buffalo Anthracite Mine, and that new one, the McLeod River project, there wouldn't be much left of this town. Mining is this town's past, it's certainly our present, and you better believe that mining is this town's future. We built Oracle on rocks and trees. We've got our share of oil and gas, but we're not swimming in the stuff like out around Drayton Valley, where they can get at it just under the surface. Here the oil is way down underground. And you've got to break a sweat to get at it. So there's not much incentive for the big companies to come this far into the foothills. But the coal, now that's another story."

"What about the flagging markets for coal?"

"Ahh," Smith said, waving a hand dismissively. "It comes and goes. I don't see the world using any less steel, do you? They need our coal to power the blast furnaces to make that stuff. There's always going to be a market. If not in Japan, then elsewhere. China and India are coming online as our biggest markets. We just have to bide our time, be ready for the increased demand. And when it comes, I'll tell you, Oracle is going to be on the map. With that new mine, we'll be the coal capital of Canada!"

"But you've tried to dig at Cardinal Divide before, haven't you? It didn't turn out so well, as I recall."

"That was on the other side, the side closest to Cadomin. This is a new project. I'm confident that it will happen. Things are different this time around."

"Like what?"

"Well, we got that new manager for one. He's a real go-getter. The company brought him in from head office to make things happen. He is full steam ahead, let me tell you. Mike Barnes is not going to disappoint me. He's a fellow who gets things done."

"You've been disappointed before?" asked Cole.

"Sure. When that last project got stalled, I was furious. We had it all planned. The timing was perfect. We were going to put this town on the map. That was six years ago. I had just taken over here at the Chamber and things were really starting to happen for me, for the town. But the goddamn feds got their hands in it and really messed things up. I got to tell you, when it comes to messing things up, just ask the federal government to get involved.

"This time things will be different. We're going full steam ahead, but we're taking a different tack. Smarter. Much, much smarter."

Cole felt a wave of heat move through him. What did the man mean by that? He asked.

"Well, for one thing, we've put the enviros in their place this time around." Smith winked, not smiling, and Cole wondered what the wink meant. "They haven't got a leg to stand on."

"How do you mean?" asked an intently interested Cole Blackwater.

"Well, first off, the greens are hopelessly disorganized. All the rich national groups are off chasing polar bears and butterflies, and our little bunch of local tree huggers are just that. They don't know what they're up against. They don't know how serious this is. This is our town's future. A little band of housewives and hippies isn't going to stop this mine." Cole wrote furiously.

"I understand they have some business people working with them."

"Ahh," said Smith dismissively, waving his hand and looking off to the side. "A couple of fellows who think that Oracle is going to be the next Canmore or something. They look south at a place like Canmore and think, hey, we can do that here. These folks think that because Canmore was a coal-mining town, and that it's there next to Banff, that there are somehow parallels."

"You mean the world might come flocking to your door and send real estate prices sky high?" Cole asked.

"Oracle is no Canmore. In Canmore they have Banff just fifteen minutes down the road. And they had the Olympics to publicize how lovely their little town was for the whole world. We're too far from the mountains and there's no Olympic cross-country skiing to provide free global marketing for us. No, this town is a mining town, always has been, and that's the way it's going to stay. That's my plan."

"What about this Dale van Stempvort character?" asked Cole. "He says he'll do anything to stop the mine."

"That guy should be locked up," said Smith, seriously, sitting forward and clasping his meaty hands together. "He's a menace to this community. He shouldn't be allowed to walk free."

"You think he's dangerous?"

"Dangerous to the future of this town. Dangerous enough to blow up a gas well. He's going to kill someone with his antics one of these days."

Cole pretended to review his notes. "You mentioned a plan for the town. What is it?"

"I've got lots of plans, and the ones for the town and the ones for David Smith are one and the same. First, we've got to get the McLeod River project approved. That's going to happen quickly. We've got that all worked out. Then the road and the rail line will be constructed. We're already in negotiations with the railway to develop a spur line, so that won't hold us up. After that it's only a matter of time before we start digging." Smith was gleeful, his face wide with his toothy smile. "That will give this town a needed burst of economic activity. Lots of money, you understand, for housing, for infrastructure, for new business. We'll put this town on the map. And that's when the second part of my plan will come into effect."

Cole raised his eyebrows.

"That's when I run for office."

Cole smiled and nodded.

"Its no secret," said Smith. "I ran for the Reform nomination eight years ago; lost by a few hundred votes. I was just a businessman back then. Now I'm the President of the Chamber of Commerce. I've been making the rounds of every town in this riding. I've got a great team in place: three local mayors, two reeves, and a pocketful of business people all backing me. The Conservative MP says he won't run again, and when he steps down, I'll step up. I'll be the Member of Parliament for this riding inside a couple of years, you mark my words," said David Smith, pointing at Cole's notepad. "Hell, they might even make me Minister of Natural Resources. Now wouldn't that be a story?" He beamed. "Shop floor to Minister in charge of mines for all of Canada. And when I'm in Ottawa, I sure as shooting won't let red tape get in the way of projects like McLeod River. I'll have that process streamlined before you know it.

"Well, I'm getting ahead of myself," he said, sitting back in his leather chair, the material creaking under his girth. "My point is that this town's future is the McLeod River Mine. I aim to do whatever I can to make sure it's a success. Nobody is going to get in the way this time around."

Cole rose. "Well, you've been very helpful. I really appreciate your time." He turned and looked around the room for the first time. Until now he had focused exclusively on Smith. The windows on one wall faced Main Street. Floor to ceiling shelves filled with books and trophies covered another wall. Cole walked over to examine them.

"Trap and target shooting's my thing. Relaxes me," Smith said. His presence behind Cole was palpable. "I've won the Alberta Federation of Shooting Sports championship the last two years in a row. When I was young I won a national juniors title in trap. I almost went to the Olympics, you know. I busted my shoulder in the mill a long time ago, and can't move side to side as quick anymore," Smith demonstrated. "But I'm steady as a rock, and can see for a mile."

Cole looked at the impressive display of trophies.

"So you'll put me in this story of yours?" Smith asked, and reached out his hand.

"Sure will. I appreciate your time," said Cole, shaking hands again. "OK if I keep in touch?"

Smith held on for a second. "Absolutely!" Then his voice dropped, "I'm going to do what it takes to make that mine a success, you hear?"

Was Smith merely driving home his point? Or was he making a new point altogether? A point aimed not at Cole Blackwater, freelance writer, but at Cole Blackwater, hired gun.

Cole Blackwater had plenty to think about on his drive to the Buffalo Anthracite Mine. Who double-crossed ESCOG? The *why* was simple; that was no mystery: to undermine the efforts of the grassroots conservation community. He was furious with himself for not seeing this sooner.

The mole damaged the group's element of surprise when he or she leaked the story to the press that activists were strategizing to fight the McLeod River Mine. To finger van Stempvort, and not the more reasonable Peggy McSorlie, as the ringleader and spokesperson was cunning. Whoever was behind the ploy knew that van Stempvort could be counted on for off-the-cuff remarks that would inflame the local community. It made Cole Blackwater's job a lot more difficult.

Cole drove his Toyota pickup over the gravel road marked Route 40 toward the existing Buffalo Anthracite Mine. He rode up and down rolling hills clad in fir and pine and spruce, the dark mantle of conifers decorated with highlights of brilliant green larch. Above the hills the sky was the kind of blue that Vancouverites quit their jobs for, and his truck kicked up a plume of dust that hung in the air like pollen on a summer's day. It was early afternoon. Though his meeting with Barnes, the mine manager, wasn't until five, he wanted to arrive early to have a look at the operation and clear his head.

Blackwater believed that his ill-conceived cover must have been blown, despite Richard T. Drewfeld's innocence of the matter. The more he thought about his meeting with David Smith, the more he was convinced that Smith knew who he was. He had done a good job at stringing Cole along, but there was something in his handshake that Cole could not put out of his mind. A warning.

Stephen Legault

Could that mean that Smith and Barnes were in collusion? Had they worked together to orchestrate the placement of the mole inside ESCOG? Perhaps the mole hadn't told the reporter that Cole was in town to stop the mine. Maybe that part of the story was being saved for the next leak.

Cole's mind raced, and as his thoughts consumed him, his foot got heavier and heavier, and his pickup fishtailed on loose gravel around a corner. He took his foot off the accelerator to control the skid. The truck straightened and in a moment Cole was back in the spring-green foothills, driving along this gravel road, more aware than before of the dangerous curves ahead.

There wouldn't be another leak. He had instructed Peggy to cut the planning team down to three or four trusted people. They would accelerate their time line. Instead of giving the mining company a month or more before their strategy was fully hatched, Blackwater would see to it that the little team executed their plans in the next two weeks. His blood flowed faster as he scanned his memory of the faces and names in the room during the planning session at the McSorlie farm.

Two pickup trucks roared past in the opposite direction. Gravel peppered his Toyota like machine gun fire. Dust obscured his vision and Cole drove blind on the unfamiliar road. Good thing he wasn't driving a rental. The drivers of the racing trucks were likely oil and gas field workers heading home after a day of surveying. The foothills south of Oracle were criss-crossed with seismic lines, the long, arrow-straight lines that divided the landscape into explorable segments of oil and natural gas. Shallow holes drilled at regular intervals along the seismic lines were packed with small explosive charges that sent shock waves into the earth when detonated. Ultra-sensitive geophones recorded the sound as it bounced off layers of rock, water, and pockets of oil or natural gas. The finished product was a map of the subsurface geology and hydrology interpreted by a geologist to determine where a company had a good chance of finding oil or gas.

Some people said that more forest was clearcut for oil and gas exploration and development than for timber in Alberta, though the oil and gas industry disputed that claim. And Alberta's timber industry itself had a voracious appetite. Tens of thousands of kilometres of seismic lines were cut annually, and twenty thousand wells drilled each year. Cole slowed until the sky above reappeared. At night, or in bad weather, this section of highway would be downright dangerous, Cole contemplated.

He drove through the tiny hamlet of Cadomin, big enough for one store where Cole stopped for a Coke and a bag of Doritos. From there the road headed up into the foothills, where the snow-covered ramparts of the Rocky Mountains' Front Ranges rose beyond the forested domes of spruce and fir. The intense glare of midday relaxed now, and the hills reflected a softer glow. The bountiful spring light seeped like golden molasses over the folds of the earth. This afternoon's moment conjured memories of his childhood in Alberta's southern foothills. There the earth wore short, rough fescue, green in the spring and brown in the dry summer months. The foothills in the province's south were cloaked in aspen, stunted pines, and spruce on their leeward aspects; their windward slopes, which faced incessant western gales, were swept bare of anything taller than a yearling heifer. Toward the Cardinal Divide, they wore a thicker coat of pine and spruce forests that darkened their leeward aspects, while their domes were often peppered with wildflower gardens.

Cole marvelled at the spring light, how it set each tree into distinct relief. He was distracted enough that when the earth fell away in front of him, he gripped the steering wheel and veered reflexively, crossing the imaginary centre line on the gravel road. "Whoa, horse, take it easy," he said, laughing shakily, and brought the Toyota back onto the right side of the road, where he slowed, then stopped on the shoulder. He sat, dust rising like smoke.

When his heart rate resumed a normal pace he stepped from the cab of his truck and walked around its nose to peer into the open pit of the Buffalo Anthracite Mine. The open-pit mine came within a hundred feet of the road and stretched back a kilometre toward the mountains. Entire hills disappeared into its maw. At its deepest, the mine burrowed several hundred feet into the earth, and at its most distant point rose several hundred feet up the side of another foothill. A haul road entered it at the far side, and massive Caterpillar dump trucks inched along the road, dwarfed to the size of real caterpillars by the expanse of the operation. The trucks' rumble and the loaders' growl were carried from the bottom of the operation to his ears by a strong and consistent wind that rose off the Front Range peaks well beyond the mine.

"Holy huge hole in the ground, Batman," Cole said and whistled through his teeth.

Strangely, Cole's first thought was awe at humanity's might, its way with technology, its ability to manipulate nature to gain affluence and comfort. Open-pit mining was one of the most destructive things people did to the earth: it left nothing of the original landscape. No tree, no hill, no creek, no habitat for anything wild. Nothing. Though the mining companies argued that the pits could be reclaimed, Cole knew, standing next to this hole in the earth, that the mine had eaten these foothills forever.

Cole's second thought was even less hopeful: a corporate machine capable of undertaking such a massive project was deeply invested in continuing to dig and rip and consume. Cole Blackwater was up against a more formidable foe than he had bargained for. He definitely wasn't being paid enough. Briefly he wished he had stayed in Vancouver, where he could hit the Coach and Horses or the Cambie for a few brews, and count on his weekend with Sarah to cheer him up.

Cole was depressed. He felt very old and very tired, not to mention very small. And not in a comfortable, humble sort of way, but in an unimportant, trivial way. Anger welled up in him as his gaze drowned in the hole before him. His anger didn't diminish when he thought of his meeting with the hot-shot, Mike Barnes. Cole had to do something to calm himself before meeting with the mine manager. He straightened up and stretched his back.

He stepped back into the cab of the Toyota and turned the ignition over. Putting the truck in gear, he started down the gravel road. He fumbled through his CDs and found what he was looking for. Midnight Oil blared from the speakers: *And some have sailed from a distant shore. And the company takes what the company wants. And nothing's as precious, as a hole in the ground. Who's gonna save me? I pray that sense and reason brings us in. Who's gonna save me?* Cole howled along with the song, which made him feel a little better.

He passed the entrance to the mine and continued down the highway, the beat of the music absorbing the pulse of his anger. He had a couple of hours and he knew exactly what he had to do.

After fifteen minutes the truck began to labour up the Cardinal Divide, a north-south watershed divide whose waters flowed south into the South Saskatchewan River drainage, to the Atlantic via Hudson's Bay, north to the Athabasca River watershed, and finally to the Arctic. The wide road narrowed after it passed the mine itself, and soon trees pressed in on the narrow gravel track. The road snaked up the steep north slope of the Divide. In places Cole wondered if there was room for two of the monster pickup trucks to pass one another.

As it neared the top, the road levelled out, the trees thinned. Cole pulled over and shut down the engine of his truck. He stepped out into the cool, quiet spring air and took a calming breath. He grabbed a pair of binoculars from the glove box and headed east on a narrow trail up the crest of the divide. Legs burning, he emerged from the trees and was rewarded with an inspiring view of the landscape. Now he wished he had taken the stairs more often.

The flowing mats of grasses and early wildflowers calmed him further. Though it was too early in the spring for the full bouquet of wildflowers that would carpet the Divide in June and July, even now there were enough white pasque flowers, yellow glacier lilies, and purple forget-me-nots to cleanse his mind's palette of the anger.

He climbed upward and the trail petered out, but Cole no longer needed it. Intuitively his body knew the way: up, toward the precipice that fell away to the north, toward where he had come, toward the existing Buffalo Anthracite Mine. He gained that crest after another five minutes. His breath was ragged and he felt a disquieting ache in his calves. Sweet mother of pearl, he moaned to himself, you are one sorry, out of shape so-and-so. He thought of his brother Walter, a few years older than he, who still climbed the peaks and ridges of Waterton Lakes National Park as a back-country warden. That was one more reason not to head south after his stay in Oracle. He'd be too embarrassed to be seen in such pathetic condition.

Now the earth fell away in a different sort of panorama. Cole stepped to the edge of the ridge. To the south, alpine meadows sloped gently into Mountain Park below. To the west, the Divide rose up into the Front Range peaks a mile away. Directly below his vantage point, to the southwest, the McLeod River emerged through the jagged mountains from Jasper National Park. All of this beauty was destined to be devoured if Cole and ESCoG were not successful. He took a deep breath and turned north. Here the earth dropped off sharply in a band of rocky cliffs more than one hundred feet tall. Below that sharp drop, the jumbled terrain sloped gradually in folds to the Mountain Park area a thousand feet below, and a kilometre distant.

On the gracefully arching promenade of Cardinal Divide, Cole heard the pure music of nature. The existing mine was far enough away to be inaudible. No cars or trucks passed on the road far below or up over the Divide. Birds called and sang; their names he couldn't recall. Insects buzzed and droned, and a colony of marmots far below went about their daily business with many piercing whistles. He heard the scream of a hawk high above. Cole took his binoculars in hand and trained them on the bird circling overhead. Cooper's Hawk? He could not be sure. He was a pathetic naturalist.

But he was a superb aesthete. He sat on sun-warmed rocks on the lip of the Divide and let his eyes sweep across this world that he loved while his feet dangled over the precipice. Something far below, to the north and west of the existing road, caught his eye and he trained his binoculars on a small meadow: grizzly. You could not mistake the gait, the muscular amble, the broad hump on the shoulder. Head down, the bear made its way through the meadow, plucking glacier lilies as it went. Midway across the clearing it stopped and looked back. Had it heard something? Smelled something? Then two small bundles of fur emerged from the forest's edge and bounded toward the big bear. Cubs of the year! Cole caught his breath. He had lived in grizzly country for nearly half his life and this was the first time he had seen cubs of the year. He watched through the glasses as the mother made a motion with her head, which Cole assumed was accompanied by a grunt or woof, and the cubs beat a path to her side. Then, together, they grazed across the clearing, and were gone again, swallowed by the forest.

He sat for another five minutes, binoculars trained, hoping the trio would emerge to graze again. But they didn't. He lowered the binoculars. What an opportunity for the city slicker he'd become. He thought of Dusty and Martin in their downtown Vancouver office towers, hoping to convince him to come and work for the corporate world. He shook his head and laughed audibly.

His anger was both assuaged and inflamed by the sighting of the sow and cubs. What would happen if the McLeod River Mine was built? The skinny road below would be blasted wide and deep for the huge trucks that hauled ore from the mine to the mill. Cole knew that such a road, though a permeable barrier, would claim more than its share of wildlife over the course of a year. Grizzly bears would have to contend with the wheels of commerce as they roamed their wide territory. And the improved road would bring both legal hunters and poachers too. The bears, attracted to the wide shoulders of the road and their banquet of wildflowers, would become easy targets for those men, too lazy to step from their vehicles to hunt.

He looked up and down the long, curving spine of stone called the Cardinal Divide. Such an evocative name for so distinct a landscape. But it occurred to Cole, the memory of the grizzly bears still rich in his mind, that this wasn't the only divide to be found in Oracle, and it certainly wasn't the cardinal, or principal one. After only a few days of kicking around town, to Cole it seemed that the principle divide in Oracle was between those who looked ahead for the town's future, and those who looked back. People like Peggy looked forward, trying to imagine Oracle building a twenty-first century economy without really knowing what that might look like. David Smith looked back, pining for the boomtown economy of the nineteen fifties. That divide seemed as sharp to Cole Blackwater as the rugged edge of the landform he was sitting on.

Now it seemed that there was one man whose presence in the community might seal its fate. Mike Barnes had stirred the pot since arriving in Oracle, evoking powerful emotions, hope and fear, in the tiny town. One man determining on which side of this cardinal divide the town would land.

Cole rose to his feet. It was time to face the enemy.

Cole got back to his truck, threw the binoculars on the passenger side floor, and drove back to the mine compound. The anger was still there. He felt it in his belly. He felt it as a quickening of his pulse and his breath. For the first time since taking the job last Friday, Cole felt a sense of purpose.

He arrived about an hour early. At the security booth by the chain-link gates, a middle-aged man in a black uniform asked to see his driver's licence to prove his identity, a precaution that Cole Blackwater thought a little overzealous. This was, after all, a mine site, not 24 Sussex Drive or the House of Commons. Were they on to him? Was the guard actually calling the RCMP at this very moment to report him for impersonating a writer? Would it have been better to be straight up with Barnes and the others?

"There you go, Mr. Blackwater," said the security guard, handing him his ID. "What time do you expect to be through?"

Cole looked at the man's name tag. It read "JP."

"Not sure, JP," answered Cole.

"It doesn't matter, really. I'll be here or on my rounds when you come by, so if it wouldn't be an inconvenience, would you mind signing out on your way past? The clipboard will be on the ledge here." He pointed.

"I don't mind at all," Cole said, relieved.

"You know where you're going?"

"No, I've never been here before."

"Well, it's easy to get lost. Lots of buildings. Most empty these days, but easy to lose your way. Follow the signs for the main Transfer Station, and when you get there, turn left — that will be west — and follow that road past the old power plant to the biggest building on the site. That's the mill. There's a yard between the mill and the admin building. You can't miss it. It's about as far away from where we are now on the site without ending up the trees." The guard smiled.

"Thanks," said Blackwater.

"No trouble. Have a good evening."

"You too."

Cole rolled up his window and drove up the road. He wove his way between a number of buildings: maintenance sheds, garages, a fuelling station for the massive dump trucks he had seen hauling rock from the open-pit mine. Beyond an enclosed conveyor that was used to move ore from the transfer station to the mill, he found himself beside an enormous building with doors large enough to accommodate dump trucks loaded with ore. Here trucks unloaded their burden of rock laced with coal to be separated into waste and rough mineral coal, which would then be loaded onto train cars to be shipped to market.

Cole turned west and followed the guard's instructions. The main administration building was small compared to the grand scale of the other structures around it, and constructed of red brick with neat, rectangular windows that faced east, and simple double doors that opened onto a gravel parking lot. Half a dozen cars and trucks were parked there. The cars seemed out of place, since he'd seen nothing but trucks since leaving town. Maybe the cars were driven by female clerical staff or receptionists. After the thought he scolded himself for the sexist nature of his thinking. His ex would have lambasted him. Then he grinned. Pointy-headed accountants might drive the sedans, too.

Cole parked in the visitors' section, turned the engine off, and collected himself. He knew very little about Barnes. He had done a hasty Google search before leaving his hotel room. He had planned to do more research on the man before this meeting, but the events of the day had pre-empted that, and he was feeling unprepared.

Barnes was married. This much he knew. His wife and two school-aged children would be arriving in Oracle in the next few weeks, or so he had been told. Barnes had been in town for nearly six months without them. Why? Was the posting to Oracle so sudden? Was housing so hard to come by? Hell, in six months they could have built a home. Blackwater made a mental note to learn more about this man, if only to follow Sun Tzu's advice to "know thy enemy."

Maybe Barnes had other reasons for not wanting his family to come to Oracle: marital reasons. Cole recalled George Cody's angry accusation and Deborah Cody's cool rebuttal.

Blackwater had learned that Barnes had married into the company business and was likely being groomed for senior management. He had worked at two different mines in Northern Ontario, Cole recalled, neither one a coal mine. Cole made a mental note to check on Barnes' track record. Maybe he would learn something that would reveal how the mine manager handled conflict. If Barnes was noted for being aggressive in his approach with those who opposed him, it might help Cole Blackwater to know in advance, so he could better prepare his clients' strategy.

Cole Blackwater had more questions than answers about Barnes as he stepped from the truck. He pulled a spiral-bound notebook from his bag and walked up the steps to the office. He was nervous about the whole cover story. He knew he was on thin ice.

But then, he'd been on thin ice before. Thinner ice than this, he recalled.

Cole was distracted by this thought when the double doors in front of him burst open. He snapped his head up and saw a small, wiry man march toward him. He looked to be in his late fifties or early sixties, with close-cropped hair and a weather-beaten face. In a second they would collide if Cole didn't move or say something.

"Hey there," he said.

The man stopped and looked up. "Who the hell are you?"

Funny way of greeting a stranger, thought Cole. "Cole Blackwater," he said, uncertain if a handshake was called for.

"What do you want?"

"I've got a meeting with Mike Barnes," Cole said.

The man sneered. "College boy," he spat.

Cole paused.

"Well, don't just stand there," the man spat again. "Go on up and see his eminence."

Cole forced a smile and walked past him to the doors.

"You that reporter?" he heard the man ask, over his shoulder.

Cole stopped, hand on the door. "Yep, that's me."

"Right," said the man, and headed down the stairs to his pickup.

Friendly fellow, thought Cole, feeling the panic around his meeting grow in his stomach.

Cole stepped into the administration building. There was a wood-panelled desk that held a computer and a telephone, but no receptionist. The walls were bare, the space inhospitable. A woman walked out of an office adjacent the entrance and strode toward him. She was attractive, dressed in black pants and a grey, form-fitting turtleneck over which she was donning a coat. She looked at Cole and said, "You must be his 5 PM."

"I'm Cole Blackwater, and I'm here to see Mr. Barnes, if that's what you mean," he said with a weak smile.

"It's what I mean," she said, smiling back. "I'm Tracey, Mr. Barnes' assistant. We talked on the phone. He's on the fourth floor. No elevator. Stairs are at either end of the hall."

"Who was that angry little man who just left?" Cole asked as she passed him.

"Oh, that was Hank Henderson," Tracey said, smiling. "Our assistant mine manager. He's all charm, isn't he?" she said. She smiled again as she exited. A whiff of her perfume was all that remained. She walked down the stairs to the black Toyota Celica in the lot.

Cole looked for the stairs and found them at the end of a hall past a row of empty offices. The staircase was wide, with polished wooden railings with brass fittings on either side. He climbed to the fourth floor, aware that his heart rate was higher than he'd like, and headed down the hall toward the centre of the building, looking for the mine manager's office. The fourth floor offices were mostly empty; their vacancy seemed stark and unsettling. In the centre of the building was a reception area. A man sat behind the desk and typed at a computer. He was mid-thirties, clean-shaven, with short, blonde hair styled in a modern cut that struck Cole as being distinctly out of place in Oracle, Alberta. His dark green shirt was open at the neck and he wore no coat. Small wire-rimmed glasses made him look both a little nerdy and intelligent.

Cole presented himself. "I'm here to see Mr. Barnes. I'm Cole Blackwater."

The man swivelled his chair to face Cole. "So you are," he said, and stood. "And you're looking at him. Glad to meet you."

Cole shook the hand. It was dry and firm. "Nice to meet you, sir."

"I was just checking some email. Note from my family. They're on their way here next week."

"I'm sorry to interrupt."

"No no, not at all. I was expecting you. Come, let's sit down in my office. Tracey just left for the day, so I was just using her computer. Mine is on the fritz. You wouldn't believe how hard it is to get a computer fixed in Oracle. No big deal, really. I keep my appointments in my old fashioned Day-Timer, and can always bum Tracey's machine. He closed the email window but not before Cole spied a photo of Barnes with a beautiful woman and two picture-perfect children.

"Nice looking group," Cole said.

"Sure are."

"You must miss them."

"I do," said Barnes. "Come, let's sit down." Barnes held the door to his office open. This room was very large, with windows that looked over the back of the compound and to the foothills beyond. There was a desk in one corner, a board table in the other, and in the centre of the room several leather chairs and couches were clustered around a low wooden table which held a pitcher and several glasses. The room was much more elegant than others he'd seen, its dark wood-panelled walls lit by the sunlight that even at this hour poured through a bank of windows.

Cole stepped into the room. Into the lion's den, he thought.

7   "I know you're not a reporter." Mike Barnes spoke calmly as they sat down and faced one another.

Cole nodded, and slowly inhaled a long, slow breath to calm himself.

"It was a pretty stupid idea, actually," said Barnes, watching carefully for Cole's reaction. "I had Tracey do a web search on your name when you called. I try to keep informed. It took a little digging. It seems you don't have your own home page. But she found a reference to your name on a First Nations website out on the coast. She called them and asked about you. She told them she was checking references. They were very effusive. You must be good at what you do. Aside from masquerading as a reporter, I mean."

Cole smiled ruefully in appreciation of Barnes' thoroughness.

"My guess is that you're in town to work for the environmentalists, and that you'd like to get inside the mine to scope us, use something to stop us. Know thy enemy stuff. Am I right?"

Cole cleared his throat, and made to rise from his chair. "So, I guess I'll be going now." He grinned.

"What for? Sit down. Let's talk."

"Really?" said Cole cautiously, dropping back into his seat.

"Sure. The best way for us to solve our differences is to talk them through. No?"

Cole sat back down. He gestured to the pitcher on the table. "Do you mind?"

"Not at all, here, let me," said Barnes and he poured Cole a tall glass of water. Cole sipped.

"It might come as a surprise to you to know that I don't think this community should be so dependent on mining. I guess we're likely in agreement on that."

Cole choked on the sip of water in his mouth and nearly spat it across the table. What was Barnes going to say next, that he planned to take out a membership in ESCOG?

"I mean it. Oracle has been a one-horse town since it started. Sure, it's got the lumber mill, but how many people work out there? Fifty? Seventy-five tops. The Buffalo employs five hundred and in its heyday more like a thousand people worked in the mine. That was all fine and dandy in the nineteen fifties, but this is the twenty-first century, and Oracle can't rely on coal forever. Don't get me wrong.

Stephen Legault

I don't think the market for coal is going to dry up. On the contrary, I think it's going to continue to grow. China, India, Brazil ... these countries are the next wave of the industrial revolution. China alone will keep the market for metallurgical coal hot for the next fifty years. The problem isn't demand, though newer technology means we don't need as much coal to make steel as we did before. No, it's not demand that's going to kill us. It isn't even supply. There's lots of coal left, thought it's a little bit trickier to get at now. We've got to dig deeper, which costs more. No, the problem is competition." Mike Barnes poured himself a glass of water and took a sip.

Cole sized up Barnes. He was a sturdy enough man, possibly cruiserweight, though Cole doubted he'd ever thrown a punch in his life. He was fit, tanned. He probably liked to mountain bike on his days off. His hands were strong but smooth and well taken care of. His strength was born from his morning workout, not from slaving in the mill as the rest of the men in Oracle had.

"Competition will be our downfall. The Buffalo Anthracite Mine simply can't complete against less expensive, more productive mines elsewhere in the world," continued Barnes. "We simply can't compete with low production costs off shore."

"Do you mean Indonesia and other developing economies?" asked Cole.

"Sure. There are plenty of countries where coal is mined and milled for a lower cost than in North America. We pay ourselves too well. We have high standards for workplace safety. And though you may not agree with this, we have tough environmental regulations. All of those factors put a huge onus on the company to spend money on up-front measures to minimize our impact, and on remediation and mitigation. It all adds up."

"Back up a little," Cole interrupted. "You *bet* I don't agree with you about high environmental standards. High maybe if you compare us to Peru or Burma."

"It's all relative," said Mike Barnes, smiling. "My point is, this mine will have a declining presence in the local economy. *Has* had a declining impact on the local economy for more than a decade. People just refuse to see it. Acknowledge it. Oracle needs to accept this and learn how other similar economies have diversified, and take measures now to ensure its future, or it can dry up and blow away."

Every word out of Barnes' mouth sounded familiar. He could have been listening to Cole's conversation with Peggy McSorlie after the strategy session. He smiled.

"What is it?" asked Barnes.

"You're singing from the same song sheet as my employer. How strange is that?"

"Peggy McSorlie? Smart lady. People should listen to her."

"Some do, some don't."

"Problem with ESCOG is that they're fighting below their weight class. They think like kitchen-table locals. And the disreputable elements in the group don't exactly win them any friends in town. And if you think I don't have to listen to those disreputable sorts even in here," he looked around the room, "you're mistaken. Anybody who asks for a meeting here gets one. Even Dale van Stempvort."

Cole nodded, sipped his water, cleared his throat, and replied: "We both agree that Oracle needs to diversify its economy. Don't clearcut and send your trees overseas for someone else to make them into Ikea furniture. Set up secondary manufacturing right here. Every man who works at this mine or at the mill has a basement full of tools. Imagine the stuff they could build. Someone else can do the marketing. This creates new businesses in town, generates money for the local economy. Guys are afraid that if they give up mining and logging they'll be flipping burgers or telecommuting to Calgary or leaving home to slave in the oil sands. But a town like Oracle has options. A small-scale manufacturing economy values skills and rewards them with good-paying work. But big companies like Athabasca Coal get in the way."

"I agree," said Barnes.

"You agree?"

"I do. We create a dependence on our employment for the people of this town. Everybody in Oracle, in some way, needs us to make a living. Am I right?"

"You're right, but there's more. You frighten people so they fight change."

Barnes shrugged. "We don't do that on purpose. There's no sinister plot. We don't pass out leaflets that tell our employees to fear change."

Cole leaned forward, "Actually, Mr. Barnes ..."

"It's Mike."

"ok, Mike, I've seen that happen. Maybe not here, but in other company towns."

Barnes shrugged again. "I won't argue with you. But people are afraid of change by nature. If you're making seventy or eighty thousand a year punching the clock at the mine, driving a nice truck to work, with a big house for your wife and kids, it's pretty hard to imagine yourself going into business for yourself and making four-poster beds to sell over the internet."

Cole stood up and walked to the windows. He looked out over the mine site to the forested hills beyond. "Here's another thing," said Cole, noticing how the evening light slanted across the spruce and fir forest. "Oracle wants to bill itself as the gateway to Jasper National Park instead of the gateway to a humongous hole in the ground."

Mike Barnes allowed himself a smile. "Think, Cole. To get to their second homes in Canmore, Calgarians don't mind driving right past Exshaw where Lafarge and others have been levelling an entire mountain and grinding it up into cement. And the millions of tourists who visit Banff National Park drive right past that hole in the rock too. Canmore's growth isn't slowing one iota, despite the plume of cement factory exhaust and the massive scar on Grotto Mountain. Mining certainly hasn't hurt Canmore's prospects. Maybe it's even helped."

Cole heard the words, but right now his attention was riveted to the hills, their shapes and shadows. "Yes, Mike, you're absolutely right. But there's bears in them there hills." He pointed and Mike's gaze followed his fingers. "I happen to believe strongly that to have a diverse economy Oracle's got to keep some of the ecological pieces intact. It's got to be a place where grizzly bears are protected, not persecuted. That's part of the whole picture."

"But it's not up to Athabasca Coal alone to protect them, Cole. This town has to want a future other than mining if this is going to work."

"So why are you pushing so hard for the McLeod River project? There's a disconnect between what you're telling me and what you're doing."

"At the end of the day, Cole, I've got a job to do. That job is to ensure that through this operation, the best interests of Athabasca Cole are served."

"So there is no middle ground?"

Mike Barnes stood, put his hands in his pockets, and walked to the windows. Cole wondered if Mike Barnes saw the same thing that he did. Was their view of the world so different?

"Cole, I'm not going to lie to you. We plan to push ahead with the McLeod River project. That's in the best interest of Athabasca Coal. We aim to have the road built this fall, and the rail line soon after. We intend to minimize our impacts on wildlife. Maybe your friends at ESCOG can give us some help with that. I'd promise to deal with any recommendations they make myself. But we're not going to pull the plug on this operation. I'm sorry, Cole."

"I'm sorry, too." Cole appreciated the frank exchange of views with Barnes. The man was not from the stone age. What on God's green earth was he doing in a place like Oracle? "Because we're going to stop you," Cole concluded. "That's in the best interest of humans and grizzly bears and the future of this planet."

"I would expect nothing less," said Barnes, smiling. "But do me a favour. Two favours, really."

Cole looked at the man. "What's that?"

"First, keep the lines of communication open. No more games."

"Deal."

"And let's keep it civil. I can't control some of the rougher elements around this place, and there are some people in your camp with bad reputations, but let's do our best to keep this a clean fight."

"I'll do what I can, Mike."

They shook hands. "Now," said Mike Barnes, "If you'll excuse me, I have another meeting, if you can believe it. I need a few minutes to collect my thoughts for this one." He consulted the full-sized Day-Timer on his desk, scrolled a finger down the day's appointments, and said, "Seems everybody wants to talk right now. I doubt this conversation will be as civil as the one you and I just enjoyed."

"I appreciate your time, Mike. I'm glad we can be straight with each other. That's refreshing."

They shook hands again and Cole left the office. He found the stairs and walked down to the main floor. He passed no one. His head was spinning. It was after six when he exited through the double glass doors and found his truck in the parking lot. He pressed his back on the driver's door and leaned his head against the truck.

Maybe Mike Barnes should be in charge of this campaign, he thought. He's got all the answers. I should just head back to Vancouver and get a job as a Greenpeace door-to-door canvasser. Barnes had made quite an impression on Cole.

Cole shook his head, got into his truck, and headed back to the gatehouse. JP was nowhere in sight, so Cole stopped and signed the ledger, as instructed. He scanned the sheet to see if anyone else had signed in, but there were no names on the list after his own. He turned his truck onto the gravel road and began the journey back to Oracle. He stopped in Cadomin for a snack and continued on his way. Traffic was light; he passed only a few pickup trucks headed in the opposite direction. His thoughts returned to Barnes. Who was he seeing so late in the day? Why was he so accommodating with his time, and so forthcoming with his opinions? Was that in the best interest of the company? More importantly, the question of the hour became how was Cole Blackwater, hired gun, going to stop a mine that by its manager's own admission was not what the town needed, but everybody seemed to believe was a done deal?

By the time the lights of Oracle hove into view, Cole was certain of one thing at least. Mike Barnes, good natured as he appeared, was not to be taken lightly. The man was intelligent, and a clever, perhaps even brilliant, strategist. Had he planted the mole in ESCoG? With the company's best interest in mind, of course.

Deep in thought when his cellphone rang, Cole jumped, startled. He rummaged beneath the newspapers on the passenger seat, spilling them onto the floor, and knocked the binoculars down too before he found the phone.

"Blackwater," he said.

"Cole, Jim Jones here."

"Hey Jim, good of you to call."

"Sounds like I caught you driving."

"I'm on my way back into town after a very interesting visit with Mike Barnes."

"What, did he surrender?"

"Not exactly. That wouldn't be in the best interest of the company. But we found a lot to agree on."

"Oh?"

"Well, we agreed that the last thing Oracle needs right now is to become more dependent on mining for its future."

"But Cole, haven't you heard. Mining is *everybody's* future."

"Yeah, that was some good PR a few years back. But it's not the way Mike Barnes sees it. He actually came out and said that Oracle should be diversifying its economy, not consolidating around the mine."

"We've been saying that for years, Cole. But the mayor, and this David Smith character who runs the Chamber of Commerce, are both hot to trot on the McLeod River project. I heard Smith on the radio staking his political reputation on the project."

"Yeah, I met with him today too."

"You've been busy."

"So's the other team, Jim. Barnes is determined that the haul road will be pushed into the McLeod River headwaters by the fall, and the rail line shortly after."

"Well, that makes sense," said Jones. "It's consistent with what I read in the draft environmental report just this afternoon."

"You got a copy of it?" Cole asked excitedly.

"I sure did. Wasn't really that hard, actually. I just called up our mutual friend Jeremy Moon at Wild Rose and asked for one. Courier brought it this morning. It wasn't much of a read, really, a hundred pages long if that."

"That's it? The last time the thing was as thick as the Calgary phone book, wasn't it?"

"Yeah, like five times as thick."

"What gives?" asked Cole.

"You want the long version, or the Reader's Digest one?"

"I want the long one, but I'll probably get into town before you can tell it all, so give me the condensed version for now and I'll call you later this evening, if that's OK."

"Sure thing. So here's the short answer: I don't think they intend to go ahead with this mine."

Cole paused, then: "Sorry, say again?"

"I don't think they intend to dig the pit."

"OK, Jim, I'll need the full page in the Reader's Digest, not just the headline."

Jim Jones laughed. "Well, here's what I see in the EA. Lots of upfront work to evaluate the impact of a four-season haul road over the Cardinal Divide connecting with the existing mill at the Buffalo Anthracite Mine. Lots of charts and graphs about mitigation for bull trout where the road crosses the McLeod River, and a lot of effort to address grizzly bear mortality on the highway, including posting a 30 km speed limit through Mountain Park."

Cole thought of the sow and cubs. "Wow, that's unheard of."

"Sure, and you'll see why it's unheard of in a minute. So they have some top-of-the-line mitigations in place for the haul road and for the rail line. They don't actually propose infrastructure moderations, understand? It's not like they will fence the road and build wildlife underpasses. They propose speed limits, no hauling early in the day or early in the evening. Pilot cars for the trains to clear the tracks."

"That all sounds pretty good to me," said Cole.

"Like I said, wait for the catch," said Jones. "And here it is: there is no back-end clean up plan for the mine. They don't even talk all that much about how they plan on doing the mine work itself. And there are no details on how they would restore the pit. They talk about a lake and bull trout, et cetera. But there are no details. No time lines. Nothing."

"Weird," said Cole.

"Yeah, and all of that only comes in the section on Cumulative Effects, which is required by law. You know, the part where the company has to explain how the impacts of this project, when taken into account with everything else that is happening or could happen in the future, will impact wildlife. So what we have here, Cole, is a very detailed plan for a road and a rail line, and very little at all for the rest of the mine."

"So it's the old trick of breaking the project into little pieces so that it seems less menacing." One hand around the phone, Cole steered his truck with his knee and geared down as he came into Oracle.

"Maybe," said Jones. "But I've seen enough of these to know when the intent is to slip something past a sympathetic regulator, and when the plan is to simply get away with murder. I don't think either is the case here. I'd bet you a case of Kokanee that Athabasca Coal is really only trying to get approval for this road and rail line and if they get it, we'll lose Cardinal Divide, and Oracle will lose its main employer."

"You think they'll build the road and the rail line and then cut bait?" Cole pulled into the Rim Rock Motel and managed to park with one hand between a behemoth Dodge Ram 1500 and a Ford F250, and not stall his little Toyota.

"It's not unheard of."

"But why?" He switched the ignition off.

"Could be any number of things. But my guess is simple: economics. Coal is too expensive to produce right now. Labour costs and shipping costs make it too expensive to produce here and ship to market in Japan, so the company wants to sit on this for five or ten years until the market is more favourable. They could wait even longer. Maybe never develop it. But in the mean time, they have a lot invested in this region, and their shareholders are eyeing all of the existing infrastructure nervously. So the company makes a lot of noise about the McLeod River project to keep its shareholders happy right up until the moment they pull the plug. My guess is that Athabasca Coal has got something big happening overseas that they'll be announcing in the next few months, and when they do, they will quietly slip out of Oracle's back door."

"Won't be so quiet around here," said Cole, and walked up the steps to his room.

"Maybe not in Oracle. But in Toronto and New York, where it matters, nobody will hear a peep. The news will be focused overseas on something big, something new, and not on a backward town on the eastern slope of the Rockies that had its chance and blew it."

Cole dug into his pockets for his key. It was attached to two rubber bands and a gum wrapper. He untangled it and unlocked his door.

"Ok, Jim, this has been enlightening. Thanks for all the digging."

"No problem. Little bit more than the Reader's Digest version, I know."

"It's fine. It's a complex theory."

"It is that. And listen Cole, the thing about all of this is, they can do this and come out smelling like roses, you know."

"I was just thinking that. They can blame the market, they can blame labour, they can even blame the berry-sucking, fish-kissing, sandal-wearing environmentalists if they want. They've got lots of options, my friend."

Jim was chuckling. "We don't wear sandals in Alberta, Cole. Hiking boots here. Sandals are for you crystal gazers on the wet coast."

Cole cracked a smile. "I'll be in touch, Jim." And he hung up.

Cole Blackwater sat down on his bed. He put the phone down and let his body fall backward onto the covers. Was it only this morning that he watched Deborah Cody make up this very bed after a thunderous encounter with her husband? "What a day," he moaned.

Flat on his back, he dialled Peggy McSorlie on his cell. She answered on the first ring.

"Sitting by the phone?" Cole asked.

"Hi Cole. Well, yes, I guess I was wondering how things went."

Cole filled her in. He told her about all of his meetings: with David Smith, his brief encounter with Hank Henderson, his long meeting with Mike Barnes, and then his recent conversation with Jim Jones.

When he was finished there was silence on the line. "You there?" he asked.

"I'm here," she said. "Just digesting."

"Don't blame you," he said wearily.

"Do you really think that's their plan? To push in the road and the rail line and then leave? Seems like a lot of money just to string their shareholders along."

"Seems that way to me too, Peggy, but I don't know enough about this sort of thing to measure the trade-off. They spend, what, four or five million dollars, maybe ten, on the road and rail line? What would their stock have to do to make that worthwhile?"

"I don't know, Cole. I don't own a single stock. I'm totally out of my league."

They discussed their intent to trim the planning team down to just a few trusted colleagues. Cole urged Peggy to cut Dale van

Stempvort out of the mix, and she reluctantly agreed. "I don't trust him, Peggy; he's not stable. I don't know what he might be capable of, but he's not an asset. He's a liability," he repeated.

After they hung up Cole went to the washroom to wash his face and brush his teeth. He realized that he was hungry. He went back to the bedroom and found the phone number for a pizza place and ordered. While he was waiting he flipped the television on, opened up his laptop, and dialled into the internet.

So Mike Barnes had checked him out online. Fair enough, thought Cole, waiting for his web browser to open. When it did, he searched Mike Barnes again. He came up with the smattering of references he had seen that morning, mostly on the company website, and a few in *The Globe and Mail* and the *Toronto Star*. Then he decided to expand the search, and keyed in Barnes' name and the names of the towns that he had worked in before Oracle. He found several stories in small community newspapers whose content was online.

"Let's see what you've been up to, Mike Barnes," said Cole, clicking on a link.

The first story was about a mine in New Liskeard, Ontario, where Mike Barnes had been the manager for about eighteen months. The story was about the impact that the mine's closure had on the tiny town.

He clicked another link. This was a story from a paper in The Pas, Manitoba, where Barnes had been managing the operation for nearly a year before it had unexpectedly closed. The editorial praised Barnes for his dedication to the community.

Cole sat back. His pizza arrived while he was deep in thought, and he paid for it and began to eat without stopping his stream of consciousness.

Two stories. Two mines. Two closures.

Was Mike Barnes a hatchet man?

Had Athabasca Coal hired him not to make a mine like the McLeod River project a roaring success, but to quietly shut down its existing operation at the Buffalo Anthracite Mine without raising suspicion, or upsetting shareholders?

Cole went over his conversation with Barnes. Dangerous, Barnes had told him, for the town to put all of its eggs in one basket. Darn tootin', thought Cole.

Cole ate another piece of pizza. Athabasca Coal had definitely picked the right man for the job, he mused. Mike Barnes was smooth as Ex-Lax.

But was he clever enough to plant a mole inside ESCOG to ferret out information, or maybe even plant information, to help the environmentalists mount an effective opposition to the project? Even aid and abet the environmentalists through the placement of the mole so that the company could then blame the extreme greens when the proposal for the McLeod River project failed? Cole had no doubt that Mike Barnes was that clever and then some. Now he wished he had asked Mike Barnes that question directly. He was angry with himself for not thinking of it sooner.

He stood and stretched. It was ten o'clock. He flipped to CBC and watched the evening news. Nothing new. The pizza had satisfied his hunger, but now his thirst needed quenching. He'd check his email, and retreat to The Quarry for a night cap, just one or two beers, and then turn in early. Big day tomorrow.

He downloaded his messages and scanned through them. His heart leaped when he saw the message from Sarah. "Hi Daddy," it said. "I miss you. I hope that you are saving the world. I love you! Sarah."

He pounded his fist on the little desk and the pile of papers he'd picked up that morning cascaded back down to the floor. He let his head fall forward into his hand. He hadn't called Sarah since arriving in Oracle, despite telling her that he would.

He grabbed the phone from the desk and dialled Jennifer Polson's number. It rang. And it rang. On the fourth ring he heard her voicemail click in. She'd probably checked her call display and chosen not to answer. He thought uncharitable thoughts about his ex-wife.

Then Cole closed his computer, grabbed his keys, and beat a hasty retreat to the bar.

How could he be so stupid, he thought as he walked into the now familiar, crowded place, and made a bee line for the service counter. How could he forget to call his little girl? The number of stupid things Cole had done since arriving in Oracle was piling up, it seemed. This was supposed to be his chance to prove himself.

He arrived at the bar expecting to be served by George Cody, but was instead served by a man in his early twenties.

"Where's George?" Cole asked, and ordered a pint of Alexander Keith's.

"He got called away this evening," said the young man, serving him his beer. "I usually just work on the weekends, but he called me in. Said he'd be back late."

"Cheers," said Cole hoisting the pint and drinking deeply, distracted by his self-loathing.

He resolved then and there to call Sarah every second or third night from now on. Resolute, he turned his mind to the new challenge of stopping a mine that might very well stop itself. How do you get any leverage against a project that for all intents and purposes doesn't want to proceed? Cole would have to devise a tricky little bit of strategy to stop the road and the rail line from destroying Cardinal Divide. He guessed that there wasn't a single piece of paper that said that the company didn't really plan to go ahead. And if pressed, Athabasca Coal would simply say that the road and rail were necessary to set in place the operation to take advantage of evolving market conditions. What were five or ten years to them? But to this town? And to Cardinal Divide itself? It meant life and death.

Cole swallowed the last of his beer when he was jostled heavily from his left. "Watch it, faggot," came a gravely voice.

Every nerve in Cole's body exploded. "My fault, sorry," he managed as his heart rate soared and a surge of adrenaline rushed through him. All his distractions vanished and the world around him slowed. He could see everything in front of him with sudden clarity.

"Fuck you," said the man who had jostled him. He was facing Cole now. Cole sized him up quickly: baseball cap, short dark hair, scruffy beard, dark eyes. He wasn't a large man. Cole guessed welterweight, around a hundred and fifty pounds and maybe five nine. Wearing a jean jacket, so he'd be a little slow. He wasn't holding anything in his hands. Cole pushed his glass away so it wouldn't get caught in the scrum.

"Here, let me buy you a beer," said Cole, cursing himself for failing to see this coming. For not seeing this waiting for him when he stepped into the bar. My cover is really, really blown, he thought, and then the man took a swing at him. It was a big roundhouse swing and Cole had been right, the jacket restricted

Stephen Legault

his movement and made the punch a little slow. Cole easily stepped back and the blow went wide, the man sprawling on the bar from his own momentum. Glasses and beer bottles crashed to the floor and the room was suddenly silent. As Cole feinted back he bumped into another patron, blocking his escape. Instead Cole stepped forward with a quick left jab as his attacker straightened himself, and another to set up the knock-down blow. As his assailant stepped back from the second left jab, Cole delivered the right hook. The force of the blow sent the ball cap flying from the man's head, snapping his face back. A spray of blood erupted from the man's mouth and painted the bar. The attacker stumbled and dropped onto his butt on the floor in a daze.

Landed it that time, Cole was thinking.

But it wasn't over. Cole reeled as he was hit from behind with considerable force, the blow connecting with the back of his neck and the base of his skull. He fell forward and tripped on the man he had just knocked down, stumbling along the tavern's hardwood floor. He guessed the brute that had slugged him used a sap, a plastic club about six inches long that could be easily concealed in a pair of jeans. Stumbling, feeling suddenly sick to his stomach, he turned to face the new threat. The man bore down on him. The room was silent, the eyes of every person on him. The big man stepped into him. Cole knew that a giant like this could kill him if allowed to get a hold of him so he quickly stepped to his right, away from the bar, and brought his left knee up into the man's solar plexus. This wasn't the ring. This was the real world. As the big man doubled over, Cole stepped up to him and stood at a right angle to his attacker, and used all his might to hit him with a right jab in the ear. The head is softest there, and he saw the giant wince in pain, close his eyes, and collide with the bar with a dull thud. Cole also felt a hot rush of pain in his hand that extended all the way to his shoulder. Good Christ, he thought. I just broke my hand.

That's when the chair hit him and Cole's lights went out.

8 The phone rang. The sound felt hollow and distant at first, like a mosquito buzzing in his ear in the darkness. That's a rotten way to wake up for the second morning in a row, Cole Blackwater thought. It was as if he had his very own personal wake-up service jangling in the hollows of his brain. But this morning he couldn't make his hand reach for the phone even when the ringing seemed to grow louder, as if insisting the urgency of the caller.

Cole lay still, his eyes closed, his memory swimming back to break the surface of the day. He wasn't at home. This wasn't east Vancouver. But where? He lay still, eyes pressed shut, waiting for memory to return. Oracle, Alberta. A motel room. The ringing phone felt like daggers in his ears.

Yesterday he had been awoken with bad news. What had it been again? Dale. Dale had mouthed off to a reporter and now Cole's strategy to stop the McLeod River Coal Mine had been blown. Ringing. He'd only been on the job for two days now and already his plan was DOA. His head ached, but not just from the constant ringing.

Cole pressed his eyes closed to will the jangling to stop and was rewarded with a brilliant burst of painful fireworks right where the ringing had been. That stopped it. He cautiously opened his eyes and the fireworks were replaced with a sensation like shards of glass piercing his eyeballs. At least the ringing has stopped.

He lay prone on the bed and fought through the layers of unconsciousness, something dark and thick, much deeper than sleep, trying to wake up. His face hurt. His head ached. He realized his hair was wet and his right hand seemed to be caught in a vice grip.

He was in Oracle, Alberta. He closed his eyes and groaned. Now he had been awakened by the phone again, though he had never managed to answer it. Cole Blackwater was accustomed to laboured starts to his days. But this didn't feel like a hangover. He reached up and touched the back of his head with his throbbing right hand. "What happened?" he asked himself out loud.

"You were jumped by three goons," said a voice from the bathroom. Then Cole heard the toilet flush.

Despite his various maladies, Cole Blackwater sprang up from the damp bedsheets, hands held up in front of him in a typical

Stephen Legault

boxer's stance as the bathroom door opened. He stumbled and tried to focus, but his eyes would not cooperate. His feet caught in the tangle of sheets and he lurched sideways, knocking the phone from the nightstand, sending it crashing to the floor. Cole made out a hulking shape emerging toward him as his hands shaped themselves into painful fists.

"Easy slugger, easy," said the shape. "It's George Cody."

Cole Blackwater let his hands fall down to his sides. "George?" he asked, and swayed unsteadily. "What the fuck were you doing in my can?"

"Nature called. Are you OK?"

"What?"

"Are you OK?"

"Your john busted?"

"I've been here all night, Cole. Sorry I couldn't get to the phone. Shitty way to wake up."

"I'm going to be sick," said Cole, shaking his feet free of the sheets, and stumbling toward the bathroom. He collapsed in front of the toilet and managed to get the lid open before retching.

He slumped beside the bowl and pressed his face against it. The cool porcelain eased the ache in his face and head. Thank you toilet bowel for being so cool, he thought.

"You OK?" said George Cody again. He sounded very far away.

Cole didn't move, and moaned in response.

George righted the phone and stepped into the bathroom and helped him get up. "Come on fella', time to get back into the game."

"What time is it?" asked Cole.

"About eight o'clock."

"In the morning?"

"Yup."

"What happened?"

"You got beaten up pretty good." George guided him out of the bathroom toward the club chair, but Cole stopped him. George was broad across the chest and shoulders, and had the powerful arms of the football lineman he had been in college. Though Cole was taller than the man, he felt small next to his girth.

"Wait, George, let me get a look at myself."

George grinned and said, "You might want to hold off on that, Cole."

"I can take it. I used to do this for fun."

"Suit yourself."

Cole felt his way back through the bathroom doorway and flicked on the light. Eyes closed, he steadied himself with both hands on the sink, hunched forward toward the mirror. Slowly he opened his eyes.

"Good God," he said, and heard George chuckle behind him.

His right eye was black and blue and swollen half shut. A nasty gash under the eye extended from his nose across his cheek more than an inch. It was red and raw, but was neatly taped and had long stopped bleeding. By the look of it, a stitch or two were required to ensure he didn't go home looking like Frankenstein. His nose was all in one piece—still crooked and bent—but no moreso than before.

When he lifted his right hand to touch the battered eye he noticed that the hand too was blue and swollen. He flexed it and extended the fingers and decided that nothing was broken, but it was badly bruised. Then he felt his head and near the crown he discovered a goose egg as big around as his fist.

Sarah would be plenty disappointed in him.

"Somehow the chair didn't break the skin," said George. "Just dumb luck, I guess."

The chair. Last evening's festivities started to come back to him.

"I've been icing it on and off all night. I don't think you suffered a concussion. But to be on the safe side I woke you every hour or two."

Cole touched the top of his head with his bruised right hand. He grimaced at his face in the mirror. Just like old times. "How many of them were there?" he asked, watching George in the mirror.

"Three."

"I only saw two of them."

"Third one got you from behind with the chair."

"Right. I remember seeing it break around me, but never saw who hit me."

"You hit the ground after he hit you."

"What happened after that?"

"That's where I came in."

Cole recalled now that George Cody had not been in the bar of the Rim Rock Hotel when he had entered. Cole thought back on the events, touching the puffy red bruising around the gash on his face. He had been distracted by his own long list of shortcomings, and by something else, and had failed to notice the thugs that jumped him moments later. He had let his guard down again. He shook his head, which felt as though it rattled his brains. A wave of nausea washed over him.

"I walked in the door to see one of my chairs being broken across your back. Good thing I'm a cheap bastard and that chair wasn't much more than toothpicks and carpenter's glue." George laughed. Cole grinned too, which hurt.

Cole turned on the faucet and cupped water in his left hand and rinsed his mouth out. There was no blood in the water: a good sign. What had been so distracting that he had failed to make his customary and precautionary scan of the bar? The meeting. The meeting with Mike Barnes.

"I guess you handled yourself pretty good up until that point," said George. He turned and walked to the bed where he picked up the ice pack, dumped the ice into the sink, and threw the bag into the trash.

"I used to do a little boxing," said Cole. He poured water into the sink, gently rinsed his hands first, then splashed his face. The cool water revived him. "But I've never fought anybody who used a chair before. That's a pro-wrestling trick," he quipped.

"Did you know those guys?" asked George as he tidied the room.

"Never seen them before in my life. You?"

"Nope. But I got their names before I tossed them out, so if you want to press charges, you can. I'll back you up."

"We'll see," said Cole. The gravity of the situation began to set in. "Did you call the cops?" asked Cole.

"I did, but they said it would be a few hours before they could get a car over because they were tied up with something. Said if you weren't dead you didn't rate. Whatever that meant."

Cole walked to the bedroom and sat on the foot of the bed. Even that much movement hurt.

"I've got to go," said George, and grabbed his jacket from the chair by the desk.

"George," Cole said weakly.

"Yeah, Cole."

"Thanks." Cole looked at him. A big lad, George was a good man to have at your back when things got hairy.

"No problem. I'm sorry things got so out of hand in my joint."

"Things are pretty out of hand period," said Cole, and looked down at his swollen fist.

George smiled thinly, "Yeah, I know what you mean." He closed the door behind him.

Cole leaned back onto the bed and considered just how out of hand things were. Two days on the job and what was supposed to be a simple strategy to stop a mine had turned into a mess. In the two days since he had arrived in Oracle the whole campaign had unravelled. He was supposed to be helping the locals protect grizzly bears, harlequin ducks, and wolves. But his hasty and ill-conceived cover as a reporter, developed to ferret information from less willing sources, had been blown. The Eastern Slopes Conservation Group had a mole who was leaking information to the media and likely to the mine proponents. And Dale van Stempvort, a first-class malcontent, who most of the town of Oracle believed was responsible for blowing up natural gas wells, had spilled the beans about the group's plans to a reporter who had been tipped off by the infiltrator. When Cole confronted Mike Barnes, the manager of both the existing Buffalo Anthracite and the proposed McLeod River Mine, he had been bested by a man who was clearly no small-town hick. Now someone—maybe the spy, maybe someone else altogether—had set three thugs onto him last night in the bar. If George hadn't shown up when he did, who knows how far the goons might have gone? Whoever did that knew where he was staying and was aware of his habits of the last couple of days. Somebody had been watching him very carefully.

Cole picked himself off the bed. He needed to shower, to change out of his blood-stained clothing, and to swallow some Advil. Then he had to find a cup of coffee. He stepped into the bathroom and pulled his T-shirt off. His back ached from the blow it had sustained.

He was about to drop his pants when the phone rang. He stepped to the side of the bed and snatched up the receiver.

"Blackwater," he growled.

"Cole, it's Peggy."

"Hi Peggy," he said, his tone lightening. "Did you try to call earlier?"

"Yes, that was me. Your phone just rang and rang. Were you out?"

"In a manner of speaking."

"Listen, Cole." Her voice was rushed and breathless. "We have a problem."

She's not kidding, thought Cole. "Has Dale shot his mouth off again to the media?"

"That's not it, Cole." Her voice trailed off.

"What is it, Peggy?"

Peggy McSorlie drew her breath in sharply and said: "Mike Barnes is dead."

"Holy fuck," spat Cole Blackwater, beyond caring about his choice of words. He sat down heavily, too close to the edge of the bed, and nearly slipped to the floor. He grabbed at the tangled sheets to steady himself and pulled the phone off the stand. It crashed to the floor for the second time that morning, and he dropped heavily to his knees to find the pieces.

"Are you still there?" asked Peggy.

"Still here." His mind raced. Had Barnes driven his SUV off the road late last night and crashed into a tree?

"How?" he finally asked.

"Cole, he was murdered."

Cole let the phone slide down the side of his face. It came to rest on his lap. Peggy still spoke, but he couldn't make out what she said. Instead he heard Mike Barnes' voice in his head. He could see him, sitting comfortably across the coffee table in his office, his shirt tailored, his shoes polished. He saw himself shake Barnes' hand and watched as the young man turned back to his office to prepare for his next meeting.

And now Barnes was dead.

"Cole, are you there?" he heard the tinny voice in the phone ask.

He lifted the receiver again. "I'm here, Peggy."

"Did you hear what I said?"

"No, sorry, I was lost for a minute."

"I said that we should get caught up on this as soon as possible. I think this is going to have an impact on our work."

"You think?" Cole said sarcastically.

Now it was Peggy's turn to be quiet.

"I'm sorry," said Cole. "I'm just a little overwhelmed. This news about Barnes comes as quite a shock. I was just with the man twelve hours ago. And I had a bit of a run in myself last night." Cole described the fight and how George Cody came to his rescue and sat with him through the night.

"Jeepers, Cole, you should go to the hospital to make sure you're OK."

"I'm OK, but I will swing by for some stitches this morning so I don't have to play Scarface this Halloween," he grinned.

"We should expect calls from the RCMP, don't you think?" asked Peggy.

"I know *I* should. In fact, I'll probably save them the trouble and give them a call before I get breakfast."

There was a long silence.

"Cole, you don't think Dale had anything to do with this, do you?"

"I don't know, Peggy. I want to believe that he didn't, but I don't know."

"I've known him for ten years, Cole. He's crazy but he's not a killer."

"I want to believe you, Peggy. But I'm not the one who will be making that judgement. He really stepped in a pile of it this time, if you ask me."

"It was a harmless comment, Cole."

"It wasn't harmless, Peggy, and you know it. Lets not play naive. He said he'd be willing to do anything to stop the mine. That's far from harmless for a man with Dale's history."

"Come on now Cole, you know that quote was out of context. He would do anything *legal* to stop the mine. And you know as well as I do that Dale has never been convicted of anything, he's never even been in jail. It's all just rumours and hearsay, likely the product of the same people who tried to crack your skull last night. There's a lot riding on the development of the McLeod River Mine."

Cole was silent. How far down this rabbit hole did he want to go? He was in unknown territory. Finally he said, "I'm not the one who will be making that judgement."

"Well." She sighed deeply, "Let's keep in touch today, ok?"

"ok. Thanks for the call, Peggy."

"No problem, I guess," she said softly.

Cole sat on the bed and held the receiver. A sliver of light poked through the heavy curtains. A Leonard Cohen song came to mind: *There is a crack, a crack in everything. That's how the light gets in.* For Mike Barnes there was no longer any light and that made Cole sad, unexpectedly and overwhelmingly so. Though Barnes was the man responsible for the imminent destruction of the Cardinal Divide, Cole Blackwater had not considered him the enemy once they had met face to face. They had become human beings to one another.

Mike Barnes was reasonable and straightforward, likeable: a fellow human. Flesh. Blood. Bone. Memory. Gone.

Cole stared at the crack of light. In all the years he'd worked to stop ventures like logging of old growth forests, drilling of oil and gas wells in the wilderness, and mining in places like the Cardinal Divide, he had never wished his opponent dead. Sure, he'd made jokes that his life would be a lot easier if so-and-so got run over by a cement mixer, but he didn't really mean anything by that. Now a man he had worked to oppose was dead, and Cole Blackwater was one of the last people to see him alive.

Murdered, no less. Cole watched the sliver of light grow sharper as the sun moved higher. Murder: how many people could even consider such a barbaric act? Cole wondered. He closed his eyes against the thought. It would be a lie to say that he had never considered it as a solution to some of his own problems. But it had never been about work. And Cole knew all too well that acting on such an impulse was another matter all together.

Cole sat on the floor, his back to the bedraggled bed, his fist, face, back, and head aching, and looked at the seam of light in the heavy drapes over the motel room windows. He couldn't get much closer to the floor unless he fell over, he thought. A pretty fair metaphor for his life. Now what? he wondered. Pick himself up, dust himself off, as the Peter Tosh song implored? Start all over again? He steadied himself with his left hand and was preparing to do just that when the phone rang.

He looked at it a moment. Seemed as though everything bad that had happened in his life had started with the jangling of a telephone. That's how this folly had begun, less than a week before. He reached for it and picked up the receiver.

"Blackwater."

"Mr. Blackwater, this is Staff Sergeant Reimer from the Oracle RCMP. I wonder if you might have a moment to come into the detachment this morning. We have some questions we'd like to ask you concerning the death or Mr. Mike Barnes."

Beaten to the punch again.

Stephen Legault

9 Cole closed his eyes as he listened to the Staff Sergeant request his presence at the RCMP detachment. "I can. It will be about an hour or so. There are a few things I need to deal with first."

"Come as soon as you are able, please," she said politely, but firmly enough to leave no doubt in his mind that his presence was not optional.

"Do I need a lawyer?" he asked.

"You're welcome to have counsel present, but you're not under suspicion in the death of Mike Barnes, if that's what you're asking. You were likely the last person to see him alive, and that makes you an important witness in his murder."

"I'll be there shortly," Cole said, and hung up. He stood hesitantly and made his way back to the bathroom. Not more than ten minutes had elapsed since he had started to undress, but in that time his world had altered perceptibly. Ten minutes ago his biggest problem was that he had been beaten unconscious by thugs, likely hired by someone who didn't want him to do his job. Now he was, at the very least, a witness to the last hours of a man's life. Even worse, the suggestion of murder had unlocked a memory he had buried so deeply it had remained hidden for three years.

He reached into the shower and turned the water to hot. While he waited for the cold water to exit the pipes he stripped off his pants, then stepped into the shower. The hot water relieved his aching back. He stood and absorbed the heat. The water massaged his neck and shoulders and cascaded down his bulky frame. The cuts on his face stung, but the pain helped push that unpleasant, unwanted memory from his mind. Standing with his left hand pressed against the tiled shower wall, the water coursed over him and he let it wash away the past, if only for a moment. Finally he lifted his head to wash his face beneath the shower. Fresh blood ran down his body and turned the water in the shower stall to the colour of faded roses.

As he drove from the Rim Rock Hotel toward Main Street, he contemplated: stitches or coffee? His need for caffeine was definitely greater, but the stitches would have to come first. The cut beneath this eye had opened in the shower and bled into a hunk of toilet paper that Cole pressed to his face. It probably wasn't the first time someone in this town asked for an extra large double

double while bleeding on the counter at Tim Hortons. Just the same, he made his way to the hospital and found the emergency room blessedly empty. He was given a gauze pad for the cut, ushered into a small room that smelled of disinfectant, and told to sit on the tissue paper-covered bench to wait for the doctor. He wished he'd picked up the *Red Deer Advocate* to read local coverage of the murder. Instead he stood and perused the charts and posters on the wall.

A knock at the door was followed by the doctor in black pants and a black turtleneck. He introduced himself with an extended hand. Without thinking Cole shook it and winced in pain.

"Oops, sorry about that," the doctor said. "Have a seat." He pulled on a pair of gloves and poked at the cut beneath Cole's eye.

"What happened here?"

"Bar fight."

"How's the bar look?"

"Funny," said Cole, grimacing.

"I try."

The doctor looked at his head. "You're lucky. This could have been much worse. Let's have a look at the hand."

Cole held it out, and the doctor gently turned it over. "We'll need to have this x-rayed." He scribbled something on a form. "Why didn't you come in last night?"

"I was unconscious, I think."

The doctor frowned. "That's not good, Mr. Blackwater."

"You don't have to tell me."

"Someone should have brought you in. No friends in the bar with you?"

"Just the bartender. He says he woke me every hour throughout the night."

The doctor nodded, opened a cabinet, and removed a suture set. "Not too squeamish, are you?"

"I've had my share of stitches, Doc," said Cole. He felt macho until the first suture was inserted into the cut, driving a hot nail of pain into his eye. "Christ almighty," he grumbled. "I think one of those will be enough."

The doctor smiled. "We're going to need about a dozen of these to make sure you don't end up scaring small children and pets."

125   Stephen Legault

"Can you at least give me a caffeine drip?" Cole begged. "This is a little much to take without so much as a coffee."

The doctor smiled and completed the job. Then he directed Cole to Imaging. "The results will only take a minute or two. If it's broken, you'll be sent back here to have it immobilized."

Cole did as he was told and half an hour later was in the Toyota headed downtown. His hand, badly bruised but not broken, was wrapped with a tensor bandage to prevent further injury, and the black stitches beneath his eye looked like a caterpillar had lodged on his face. Now it was almost noon and he still hadn't had a cup of coffee. He was hungover, bruised, aching, beaten, and grumpy as a buckshot bear.

He drove to the highway and made a beeline for Tim Hortons. It was lunch hour as he walked stiffly across the lot to the double doors and into the line up with construction workers, bank tellers, and a couple of yummy mummies with small children. People waited for soup and sandwiches, cups of coffee, and doughnuts, and Cole overheard the name Mike Barnes more than once. He kept his ears open to pick up on the gossip. By the time he reached the front of the line and ordered his coffee and sandwich, he'd also heard Dale van Stempvort's name mentioned no less than half a dozen times.

The townsfolk of Oracle had connected the dots between van Stempvort's reputation, his comments in the newspaper the day before, and the murder of Mike Barnes as easily as Cole had. Cole Blackwater predicted a lynching. Keeping his eye open for anyone who might look as though they could swing a chair, he ordered coffee and sustenance, eliciting a slightly fearful look from the girl behind the counter. He caught sight of himself in the doors as he left and understood why.

He retreated to his Toyota and burned his tongue on the first few sips of his day's first coffee. Dale van Stempvort could have arranged a meeting with Mike Barnes last night. He could have been on the mine property when Cole left, or Cole could have passed him on the road without recognizing his faded red Chevy S10 in the fading light. Maybe Dale van Stempvort hadn't scheduled himself in; maybe he waited for the Barnes to finish work and killed him when he left the office.

Cole rubbed the back of his aching head. He took a deeper draught of his coffee now that it was cooler.

Was van Stempvort capable of killing a man? That was a tough question to answer. Killers came in all shapes and sizes. He'd fought a number of boxers who'd seemed inclined to kill Cole had he given them the chance, but those young men had been punched in the head too many times, and some of them used boxing to vent their rage. The coffee ran through his veins and sped up his thoughts. What about Dale? He was a pretty angry dude, thought Cole. But despite his super-heated rhetoric, Dale didn't come across as a killer. Not for a mine. And not for the Cardinal Divide, as lovely as it was.

Cole was long overdue for his visit to the RCMP. He started the Toyota and turned stiffly to shoulder check as he backed out of the busy parking lot. He drove to Main Street where the RCMP detachment office was located. Like others of its kind in small towns all across Canada, it was a square brick building, landscaped with anonymous shrubs, and decorated with the maple leaf up a flagpole. Cole parked next to the only cruiser in the five-car lot and stepped out of his truck, carrying the dregs of his coffee. The sunlight made him squint and the swelling around his eye was tender where the sutures were threaded.

Steps led up to the main doors of the detachment. Cole entered into a cool reception area with a white linoleum floor. A bulletin board displayed posters of Canada's most wanted next to a small sitting area. Cole presented himself at the reception desk, as unpresentable as he was. The woman behind the glass was on the phone and motioned that she would be a moment. He stood, looking around the sparse sitting area at plastic plants, a small coffee table with last year's magazines on it, and three grey, threadbare boardroom chairs. Beyond that a door led to what Cole guessed were the inner offices of the detachment.

"Can I help you?"

Cole looked back to the woman. Her phone rang again.

"Busy morning," he smiled.

She said nothing, and raised her eyebrows to hurry him along.

"Cole Blackwater to see Sergeant Reimer."

The woman picked up her phone and gestured to Cole to take a seat beside the plastic fern.

He shuffled over, sipped his coffee, and chose to stand, reading the "Most Wanted" posters rather than back issues of *Time*

127   Stephen Legault

magazine and *Maclean's*. A minute later the door by the reception desk opened and a constable walked briskly through.

She was maybe five-and-a-half feet tall with dark hair pulled back and twisted into a knot. The grey-blue long-sleeved shirt and black tie hugged Reimer's compact body, suggesting a rower or weightlifter. Cole's fleeting fantasy was interrupted by her businesslike voice: "Mr. Blackwater?"

"That's me." Cole reminded himself that this woman led a murder investigation into the death of a man, and he was among the last to see Barnes alive. Even so, he liked the way her gun belt, loaded with service weapon, extra magazines, handcuffs, pepper spray, collapsible baton, and radio, hugged her hips. A number of female police walked Vancouver's downtown eastside beat, and Cole couldn't help but appreciate them as they performed their service to their community.

"I'm Sergeant Reimer," she said. "Would you join me in the back?" It wasn't really a question.

Cole followed her through the door and down a hall into a sparse interview room. A second officer joined them as they arranged their chairs. "This is Constable Paulson. He'll be sitting in on our conversation. Have a seat," said the Sergeant. "Can I get you anything? Coffee?"

Cole motioned to his Tim Hortons cup and sat down. "Kind of formal," he said, taking a sip from his coffee to steady his nerves.

"Standard procedure," said the Sergeant. "We don't do informal when investigating a murder." She sat opposite him. "Looks like you had a rough night."

Cole managed a smile. "Could say that."

"What happened?"

"I got jumped at The Quarry, the bar at the Rim Rock."

"Pressing charges?"

Cole considered it. "I don't think so. Just a little disagreement over a game of pool."

"OK," said Reimer, ending that conversation. "Tell me about your meeting with Mike Barnes yesterday."

Cole took another swallow of his coffee, now almost cold. He wondered if he could interrupt to take Reimer up on her offer. He decided against it. "Well, I went to the mine under the pretence of interviewing Mike Barnes for a story for *Business Week* magazine."

"What do you mean pretence?"

"Well, I wasn't really writing a story."

Reimer jotted something in her notepad. "Go on."

"I work for the Eastern Slopes Conservation Group. They've hired me to stop the mine from being built. So I invented this cover to interview Mike Barnes so I could learn how the company plans to push through their application for the new mine at Cardinal Divide. But Barnes had me figured out. And the strange thing is we had a really good chat anyway."

Reimer made notes and didn't look at Cole. "So you impersonated a journalist?"

"I guess so," he said. "Is that illegal?"

She allowed herself a slight smile. "I think we have a more serious crime to discuss."

The seriousness of the conversation sobered Cole. He was in an interview room with an RCMP officer to discuss the murder of a man he had seen only the night before. He swallowed hard.

"What did you and Mr. Barnes talk about last night?"

Cole cleared his throat. "We talked about a lot of things. About the existing mill, its operations, its productivity. We talked about the market for coal, and the various problems with getting the product to market. We talked about labour, and about the union at the mine. Mike Barnes was very forthcoming with me."

"Did he have any reason not to be?"

"Well, he could have just thrown me out when he learned who I was. That's what I would have done. Mike Barnes struck me as a very bright man. I frankly couldn't figure out what he was doing running a mine in a backwater place like Oracle."

Reimer looked up from her notebook.

"Sorry, didn't mean to offend you," he said honestly.

"I'm not from Oracle, Mr. Blackwater."

Cole put his coffee down and folded his hands before him.

"OK, let's move on. What time did you arrive at the mine?"

"About quarter to five."

"Did you talk with anybody when you arrived?"

"I signed in with security. The fellow there told me that he might be on rounds when I left, so I should sign myself out."

"Anybody else?"

"I talked with Hank Henderson, the Assistant Mine Manager.

He was just leaving. He didn't seem too impressed with Mike Barnes," Cole added.

Reimer made more notes. "How do you mean?"

"Just seemed not to like Barnes is all. Called him 'college boy.' Not really how you'd expect the Assistant Mine Manager to refer to his boss. Called him 'his eminence' too. Struck me as petty."

Reimer made another note in her pad. "And what time did you leave?"

"I think it was about 6:20 when I left the grounds. I signed out at the gate and jotted the time down there. Barnes told me he had another meeting."

"Was anybody waiting to see him when you left?"

"I didn't see anybody."

"Not in his office, not down in the main reception?"

"Like I said, the building was empty as far as I could see, but it's not like I was looking into other offices."

"Did you see the security guard when you left the mine site?"

"No. I signed myself out."

"And then where did you go?"

"I drove back to town. To my hotel."

"Did you see anybody on the road as you drove back?"

Cole counted the trucks in his mind. "I must have passed a dozen or more trucks."

"Anybody you might recognize?"

Cole shook his head and winced. It felt like his brain was sloshing around.

"Are you OK, Mr. Blackwater?"

"I'm sure I'll live."

"After leaving the mine you drove back to your hotel. Is that when the alleged assault on you occurred?"

"No, that was later in the evening. Closer to midnight. I did some work in my room first, called my daughter in Vancouver, had a shower. Then I went to the bar. And as you can see, the assault isn't alleged." He held up his bruised hand and pointed to the stitches under his eye.

Reimer ignored the remark. "Can you remember the make and models of any of the vehicles you passed on your way back from the mine last night, Mr. Blackwater?"

Cole rubbed his eyes, which stung, and thought. "Some big SUV types. I think a Ford Expedition. A couple of Ford F150s. A Dodge Ram. A few smaller trucks."

"Can you remember any of the smaller trucks?"

"No, it was getting dark by then."

"Do you remember if one of the trucks was a Chevy?"

"I got a telephone call as I was getting closer to town, so my mind was on that call, not on the types of trucks that passed. I really can't recall."

"A Chevy s10?"

Cole was silent for a moment, then said, "Why do you ask?"

"Tell me about the injury on your hand. It looks like you gave as good as you got," said Reimer.

"I used to do some boxing," said Cole, still thinking about the types of trucks on the road.

"I assume there were witnesses to the fight?"

"About forty or fifty."

Reimer made some notes.

Cole shifted uncomfortably in his seat. "How was Mike Barnes killed?" His voice sounded suddenly very small in the empty interview room.

Reimer looked up from her notes. "I'm not at liberty to say just yet."

"Well, you're asking me about my hand. Do you think that I beat him to death after my meeting with him?"

The Sergeant levelled her gaze at Blackwater. "As I said, I'm not at liberty to say right now. But I told you, you're not a suspect."

"If I am a suspect, I think I should know. I'd want to talk to a lawyer."

"You're not a suspect," she repeated. "Someone saw Mike Barnes alive after you left the mine."

"Who?"

"I can't say."

"How was he killed?"

"Mr. Blackwater, I am the one conducting the interview. Or are you playing reporter again?"

Cole smiled.

"Tell me about your client, the Eastern Slopes Conservation Group."

Cole sat back in his chair. He thought about Peggy McSorlie and her band of community activists. He thought of Dale van Stempvort and shook his head. "There's not much to tell, really. Peggy McSorlie called me last Friday and asked me to come out to help put together a strategy to stop the mine. I normally don't take on such small projects, but this one is really important. The Cardinal Divide is very special."

"Besides Peggy McSorlie, who else are you working with?"

"There were about twenty people in a meeting I facilitated a couple of days ago," said Cole. "I can't remember everybody's name, but Peggy could probably give you a list."

"We might ask her for that list," said Reimer, returning to her notes. She stopped writing and looked up at Cole. "Now I want you to tell me everything you know about Dale van Stempvort."

10

It was late afternoon when Cole left the RCMP detachment. A squall had rumbled past like a giant bulldozer while he was inside, and now he had to squint against the glaring wet blacktop. He fished in his jacket pockets for sunglasses but found none. Eyes closed, he walked blind down the sidewalk to his truck, feeling about two hundred years old. He leaned his forehead against the hot blue metal of the truck door, and took one, two, three big breaths, slid his hand down the panel and into his pocket, and pulled out a handful of debris. Pine needles, the tab off the top of his Tim Hortons coffee cup, a strangely short pencil like the ones you find at IKEA, and finally keys. He slung himself into the driver's seat and let his head fall back against the back of his seat. His sunglasses sat on the dash, casting golden brown prisms of light onto the windshield. He eased his eyes open again.

The Toyota's engine roared to life with one turn of the key. At four hundred and fifty thousand kilometres, this truck was just getting warmed up. Cole's body clock was tuned to listen to the CBC every hour: what time was it? Four o'clock in the afternoon. He turned the radio on and caught a static-laced signal; likely the storm was messing with the reception. He turned off the engine and, through hiss and crackle, Cole heard the top story.

"The RCMP is preparing to make an arrest in a sensational murder in Oracle, Alberta, where the manager of the Buffalo Anthracite Mine, the town's largest employer, was found dead late Wednesday night. Mike Barnes had been in the community for just six months when he was killed. Police say they have interviewed a number of people who might be connected to the murder, and that an arrest will be made soon. Chamber of Commerce president David Smith says that the mine is a vital component of Oracle's economy and that Barnes' death must not be allowed to derail plans for its expansion."

Cole clicked the radio off and closed his eyes. A real compassionate fellow, that Smith.

Preparing to make an arrest was how the CBC had put it. That seemed like pretty brazen language for the RCMP to be using. They must be getting a lot of pressure from the town's fathers, thought Cole, David Smith among them.

Cole opened his eyes and a wave of dizziness washed over him; the truck's dashboard spun. Was he fit to drive? The lump at the back of his head was painful to touch and his head ached. There should be a bottle of aspirin in the glove box, he thought. Without water, he swallowed hard to get two of the white tablets down. When had he eaten last? No breakfast this morning. Then the RCMP station. The day-old bagels hadn't appealed. What about the night before? The meeting at the mine, his hotel room, the bar, blackout. Pizza at dinner the day before was the last time he had eaten. No wonder he was weak.

A good square meal was what the body needed. And a couple of drinks to kill his hangover.

He found, or rather his truck found, the Big Sky Restaurant. He guided the Toyota into a parking stall, and as he turned the engine off his cellphone rang.

"Hold on a minute," he said, picking it up, and then clutching the steering wheel to avoid a minivan packed with kids, before pointing the truck into a parking stall.

"Blackwater here," he said.

"Cole, it's Peggy. Where have you been?"

"RCMP," he said, and stepped out of the truck.

"All afternoon?"

"Well, the hospital before that."

"How is your head?"

"Awful, thanks for asking. I feel like someone hit me with a chair."

Peggy laughed. "That's funny. I feel like I haven't laughed in ages. Cole, what did the RCMP ask you?"

Cole leaned against the front bumper, and faced Big Sky Restaurant's large front windows.

"They asked me a lot about the Eastern Slopes Conservation Group."

Peggy stopped laughing. "Me too."

"You?"

"Someone came to the farm this afternoon. They were here for over an hour."

"I spent nearly three hours at the detachment this afternoon. I'm starving. Haven't eaten since yesterday."

"You better get something to eat."

"I will, but I want to tell you about my interview with Sergeant Reimer first. And I want to hear about your meeting with the cops too."

"You first."

"Well," said Cole. He shifted his weight and tucked one foot up under him against the truck so his weight was balanced on his right leg. "First they wanted to know about my meeting with Barnes. I was the second last person to see him alive."

"Who else saw him?"

"The night watchman at the mine saw Barnes sometime around ten. The Mounties wouldn't say at first, but I finally got that much out of them."

"That's a lucky break for you."

"I'll say. I didn't catch many more details, though; the sergeant was tight lipped. Sometime after I left, Barnes was killed."

"I might be able to fill in some of the blanks there, Cole, but tell me more."

"There are a lot of blanks to fill in Peggy. Tell me what you know."

"I will, but I want you to finish first. I need to keep all of this straight."

"Alright. Well, next they launched an inquisition into ESCOG. Sounds like you're on their terrorism watch list." Peggy sighed at the other end. "They wanted to know everything about your operations, your members, your activities, your plans. But that was only a warm-up to the main event."

"Which was?"

"Dale van Stempvort."

"Figured."

"I swear, Peggy, I knew Dale was trouble from the moment I met him."

"He hasn't done anything, Cole."

"Peggy, please, are you defending Dale? The RCMP have been keeping very close track of him."

"Well, there are only *suspicions* that Dale is involved in eco-sabotage. In Canada people are innocent until proven guilty."

"Dale has never publicly denied or denounced violence, and that leaves a lot of people to draw their own conclusions."

"Including the RCMP."

"Their line of questioning suggests that they're treating this as a case of escalating violence. They see Dale as an eco-vigilante who started with tree spiking, graduated to blowing up gas derricks, and has now moved on to murder."

"Still, to blow up a well when there are no people for ten miles, and to kill a man are very different things."

"Tell that to the cops."

"I did."

Cole rubbed his aching head. "They questioned me on the connection between Dale and ESCOG. I told them that Dale is a lone wolf who causes more trouble than he's worth. They can't think Dale acted on behalf of ESCOG or they'll pin a conspiracy charge on you."

"Cole, you make it sound like Dale is already behind bars."

"I wouldn't be surprised if he is before the end of the day."

"He's innocent."

"That may be, but the RCMP are getting pressure from the mayor and the Chamber of Commerce, and Barnes' family are insisting an arrest be made."

This sobered Peggy: "What else did you learn?"

"That's about it."

They were silent for a few seconds, then Cole said, "What's your news?"

"The constable that came to the house is an old friend. He was quite chatty – they don't investigate a murder in Oracle every day. He told me that Barnes was found dead on the ground in the mill. Looks like he was hit on the head with a heavy drill bit. They found evidence: blood on a big steel bit and on the ground."

"Who found him?"

"That security guard, around midnight."

The trusty Toyota caught him as Cole's legs buckled under him. "That's it, Peggy, I have to eat or I'll fall over. Our next task is to create some spin. If Dale's arrested, the town, hell, the whole country, is going to think ESCOG is somehow responsible for the murder. We have to nip that in the bud."

"OK, Cole. We'll do whatever you suggest. Get something to eat and call me later."

"Right," he said and hung up.

Cole walked to the front door of the Big Sky Restaurant on rubber legs. The place was Smitty's Pancake House with a face lift.

Cole didn't care anymore. In his previous life he wouldn't have been caught dead in a place like this. Sure, he liked a greasy spoon, but it had to be *genuine* grease. He liked the Windmill on Elgin in Ottawa where he always ordered sausage and eggs with toast. And The Stem on Queen near Spadina in Toronto was an open kitchen diner straight out of the nineteen thirties. At The Stem they used actual duct tape to patch the cracks in the red vinyl benches, and even the coffee was greasy.

Of course, his tastes also aspired to the upscale restaurants in Ottawa's Market where you were likely to sit next to a Cabinet Minister or senior political staffer, or sometimes a national correspondent for a major newspaper.

He shook his head side to side to get rid of the memory. He wondered what made him think of that.

The hostess approached: "Just yourself?"

Cole looked up to see an attractive and very young woman in uniform before him. He hated it when they put it like that. It made him feel like such a loser. "Only me, unless you're not doing anything."

"Sorry?" She was too young to have a sense of humour. He was too ugly at that moment not to.

"Just me," he said and followed her to a table near the back. He scanned the room, determined not to let his guard down.

"Can I sit in that booth?" said Cole, motioning with his chin to a booth along the back wall, where he could see the door. With only the slightest roll of her eyes, she seated him and asked, "Can I bring you coffee or something to drink?"

"A Kokanee would go down well," he said.

She turned without a smile.

He had to admit that he was in a foul mood; even a pretty face couldn't fix that. His list of woes was long. He hadn't eaten, his face was bruised and scarred, his body was battered, his hand ached, his head throbbed, and his only paying client was closely associated with a murderer. Not a good day for Cole Blackwater and Blackwater Strategies.

He picked up the menu and scanned it quickly.

His beer was delivered by another woman, not as pretty as

the hostess, but she had a down-to-earth feel, and her authentic smile eased some of his pain. "I'm Pat," she said, "Have you decided or do you need more time?"

"Pat," he said, "I'm Cole. I haven't eaten in a day, and someone beat the heck out of me last night. I'm hungry and worn out, and if I say anything mean while I'm here, I'm sorry in advance."

She grinned. "OK, Cole. I'll try not to say anything mean either. If I do, I'm sorry too."

Cole smiled, and felt the sutures in his face stretch. "Good. Now that that's settled, I'll have your twelve-ounce steak dinner. I don't want to see the thing still chewing its cud, but I don't want it to have been dead for long either." He handed her the menu. "And you can bring another one of these with dinner." He motioned to the beer, and then added, "Please."

"You bet," she said and smiled again.

Cole drained half the frosted mug of beer with one long, slow swallow. That helps too, he thought.

Better empty the bladder, he mused and walked, still a little wobbly, to the bathroom. The men's room smelled strongly of industrial cleaning products. The lighting was stark and in the smudged mirror he saw his miserable face. His left cheek was black and blue and red, the angry gash held together with neat black stitches. He probed it gently. It would heal well enough, but for the next week he was sure to scare the children. He leaned closer to the mirror and saw that his eyes were dark, whether from being beaten or from weariness, he didn't know. Maybe both. Quite the handsome devil, he thought. At least he had his charm.

He used the urinal and then washed his hands and waved them under the automatic dryer for a few seconds before wiping them on his jeans. The instructions on these hot air dryers should read: 1) wash hands 2) wave under dryer until impatient 3) wipe on pants.

Hands still damp, he opened the door. On the way back to his booth he scanned the room, not entirely certain who he was looking for, the identity of at least one of last night's assailants still unknown to him. The other two he would remember. They would be the ones with the bruises. He smiled. His eyes moved from table to table, from booth to booth, and then, as he was about to sit down, he glanced at the front entrance. "Sweet mother of pearl," he breathed, it couldn't be. He seated himself quickly, ducking so he could not be seen from the doors.

He steadied himself with another deep pull from his beer, hid his face with the dessert menu, and watched. He held his breath as the hostess turned down his aisle. Maybe it wasn't her. "Jesus Christ," he muttered, and drained his beer. It was. Nancy Webber had just walked into the Big Sky Restaurant and back into the ruin of his life.

_____

Nancy Webber had walked into Cole Blackwater's life for the first time seven years before. She had walked into a press conference Cole was giving, along with Jennifer Polson and two other national level activists for the federal Species at Risk Act, sat down in the front row, and proceeded to rake Blackwater and the others over coals, peppering them with question after question. The others, Polson included, had grumbled about the new *Globe and Mail* reporter after the news conference, but Cole sat silently, sipping his beer at a corner table at Darcy McGee's. He was still buzzing with adrenaline from the news conference, the glare of publicity washing through him like an aphrodisiac, and he sat silently watching the others debating questions and answers, and plotting parliamentary strategy to pass the law protecting Canada's endangered plants and animals.

"You're awfully quiet," said Polson, turning to him.

"What?"

"You out to lunch or something, Blackwater?" Mike Bonnet asked. He was a big man and smoked constantly. He was drinking a rum and coke.

Cole rubbed his eyes. "You're damn quiet, I said," Polson repeated. "What's the matter with you?"

Cole sipped his pint and looked at his friends, and at Polson. "Nothing's the matter," he smiled. "I just met my match."

Neither he nor Polson could know it at the time, but his words bore a double meaning. In the meantime, they carried on as they always had.

Jennifer Polson and Cole Blackwater had met when he took the job of National Conservation Director for the Canadian Conservation Association. She was Communications Director for The

International Fund for Animal Welfare. Jennifer was on the eleventh floor, he the tenth floor of the "Green Building" in Ottawa, a ten-minute walk from Parliament Hill. They started collaborating on a legislative agenda shortly after he took the job, and soon found themselves collaborating on much more. A steamy romance ensued that produced grist for the Ottawa rumour mill and, within a year, a baby girl. They got married. A shotgun marriage, Cole joked. They had mock wedding invitations made up with a picture of Jennifer's father pointing a 12 gauge at a startled-looking Cole Photoshopped into the background. That's how it started. It was all a good laugh. They moved into the home Jennifer owned, just a twenty-minute walk from Parliament in the Glebe, a trendy downtown neighbourhood. Sarah was born, and for the first few months the young family enjoyed a blissful honeymoon at home together.

But something changed for Cole soon after he returned to work. Sure, he slipped back into career mode. Now he had his share of a mortgage to pay, and it seemed that baby Sarah churned through an extraordinary number of diapers. And organic baby food cost an arm and a leg. He felt the dual pressures of saving the world and having to save his money at the same time.

But career pressure was only the most obvious of the troubles vexing Cole Blackwater in the months after Sarah was born. He felt unnerved by the responsibility of being a father. It was an awesome task. His friends who were also fathers said it changed them. Turned them into better people: more reasonable. This was not his fortune; what fatherhood brought him was fear. Fear that he was not up to the task of raising and caring for a baby. Fear that he would, in some inexplicable way, let Sarah down.

Fear of himself.

So he worked late and spent weekends at the office. While his relationship with his family didn't advance, his career did. He became a media darling because of his impassioned work on National Parks, endangered species, and a host of other environmental issues. He spent more and more time at the National Press Club across the street from Parliament Hill.

His became a household name in Canada, or at least in the households who cared about nature. He had access. The Prime Minister's office called *him*. He had the ear of the Minister of the

Environment. He was drunk with the sense of accomplishment that it provided.

And he was often simply drunk. Darcy McGee's, behind the Blackburn Building and the PMO, was just a small detour on his way home, and it was rare that he didn't stop in for a pint or two on his way. The place was often packed with political staffers, members of the Prime Minister's office or Privy Council office, and the air was charged with political gossip. Cole Blackwater lived for that. He consumed it. He would sit at the bar, or a corner table, and hold court.

And he fell prey to other distractions.

Nancy. His match. They were sitting in a basement lounge, the room thick with the sound of jazz, the table crowded with tumblers and beer bottles.

"You really get off raking me over the coals, don't you?" said Cole, looking across at Nancy Webber, her hair so black that it seemed to be absent of colour. In the darkness of the room she blended into the shadowy walls.

"I'm just making you earn your living, Blackwater. Everybody around here treats you like you're some kind of superstar."

He smiled. "But not you?"

She stirred her drink. "No. I'm not a member of the fan club."

"But here we are," he said, looking around. They had started the night with half dozen other reporters and advocates after a meet-and-greet at the Press Club. They were the last two standing.

"Maybe I'm just waiting for you to say something off the record. Something I can use as deep background."

Cole shrugged. "I'm willing to take my chances."

"Like to live on the edge, eh Blackwater?"

"If you're not living on the edge you're taking up too much space," he recited.

She threw her head back and laughed, the light catching in her raven-black hair, a shining, iridescent blue. "You really are something."

They made love that night on her living room floor, and he stumbled home at three to a silent house. Baby Sarah was asleep with Jennifer in her bed so he lay down on the couch and slept in his clothes.

Stephen Legault

Ottawa wasn't a city for clandestine activities, and his affair with a national correspondent for *The Globe and Mail* was soon the worst-kept secret in town.

What drove Cole drove him and Jennifer apart. By the time Sarah was three years old, Cole Blackwater was sleeping on the couch nearly every night he slept at home. By her fourth birthday he had moved out of their place in the Glebe and taken an apartment across the river in Beachwood.

When he moved out of Jennifer Polson's life, he was almost relieved. His affair with Nancy had been on again, off again for so long that he couldn't keep track of where he was supposed to be sleeping anymore.

The relief, he reflected, was a temporary emotion. He had been more than a little distracted from his relationship with his wife for some time. What had drawn them together—the hot spark of passion for their work—repelled them after a time. Sarah had been unplanned, and Cole believed Jennifer blamed him for what he imagined was an inconvenient interruption in her non-profit ladder climbing. But they never spoke of it. And the unspoken anger silently corroded them.

Despite the split, it came as a shock to him when she phoned one afternoon a year after he moved out to tell him she had taken a position with a west coast environmental group and that she and Sarah would be moving to Vancouver. In a month.

He was sitting at his desk on the tenth floor, and his first instinct was to say, "Jesus Christ, why now woman? I'm up to my armpits in Bill C-65." He wisely suppressed that. His second instinct was to run up the flight of stairs and confront her. But his call display showed him that Jennifer was calling from home. So he just sat there, the phone against his ear.

"Are you there?" Polson asked.

"I'm here."

"Of course, you can see Sarah whenever you want, Cole."

He couldn't entirely suppress a harsh laugh. He said, "It's a long way from Ottawa to Vancouver. Who's going to pay for the flights?"

A long silence followed. "Cole, we both know what you've been up to. I've known about Nancy Webber from the start. Don't insult me by trying to deny it. We both know where your priorities lie. If you had cared about me or about Sarah you would have kept your pecker in your pants, and made your daughter a priority." It was a matter-of-fact statement. She was moving across the country, with his daughter, and there was nothing he could do about it.

It was, he reflected later, the beginning of the end for him in the nation's capital.

"Here's your dinner, Cole," said Pat, suddenly at his side. Cole flinched to hear his name broadcast. He watched through shielded eyes to see if Nancy Webber turned to look, but the kitchen noise and the sound of fifty dinner conversations saved him. He nodded his thanks to Pat and reached for his beer.

How long had it been?

Three years since he'd left Ottawa, almost to the day. A year before that while he looked, unsuccessfully, for work in the nation's capital. A week before that between the time he was fired and when he had last slept with her. Four years, give or take a week or two. Four years since things began to come undone. Four years since the gradual downward spiral of his life accelerated to the lie that ended his career and the affair that ended his marriage.

He put his beer down and picked up his fork, but his hunger was suddenly gone. He stared at his food. How could he get out of the restaurant? The room tilted again and he knew he should eat something. He took a bite of mashed potatoes and cut into the steak.

He chewed but all he could think of was her. One glimpse of her brought long-buried memories to the surface. The smell of her hair as it lay across his face. Her smooth skin against his weather-beaten hide. Her taste. How she tasted when he kissed her sweaty body after a wrestling match on her living room floor.

He ate his steak.

His phone rang. He ignored it and swigged his beer. Like everything else in his life, their affair had ended with a phone call.

Cole ate the steak and started in on the potatoes. His hunger returned as he began to eat. He had to get the heck out of dodge before she discovered him. Otherwise there would be a scene that the Big Sky patrons wouldn't soon forget. He scoped out the emergency exit at the end of the corridor by the bathrooms.

Stephen Legault

She must be here because of the murder. Just his luck that she was a reporter and his client was about to be featured in a national story.

He reached into his pocket, fished out a crumpled wad of bills, and spilled a few coins and gum wrappers onto the floor. He reached down to retrieve them and banged his head. "Son of a—" He caught himself, remembering his oft-overlooked promise to Sarah.

Sarah, sweet Judas; he hadn't phoned her. He dropped a twenty and a five on the table and stood to leave.

"How was dinner, Cole?" Pat's voice, still pleasant, rang shrill as it called attention to him.

Cole flushed, glanced over at Nancy's table, and replied with his head down: "Just fine, thanks, Pat."

"You were very well-behaved." She winked.

"I try." You don't know how hard.

"Follow me to the till," she said. "I'll make change."

Only if you can change me into someone Nancy won't recognize. He checked again. From where he stood he saw the back of her head, her raven-black hair tucked behind her ears.

"I don't need any change, Pat, thanks. And I've got to, you know...." he nodded toward the washrooms. He thought maybe he could escape out the fire exit that he'd seen at the end of the hall that lead to the washrooms.

He turned and slunk down the hallway. The corridor was empty, all that stood between him and a clean break. Five feet from the exit he heard a voice behind him: "Can't get out that way." Cole stopped in his tracks. At least it was a man's voice.

"Door's alarmed. Stops people from dining and dashing."

Indeed, he could see the white sign with bold red letters: "Use in case of emergency only." "Thanks," he said, but his good Samaritan was already in the john.

The jig was up. He was not going to get out of here alive. Did he think he could hide from Nancy Webber in this one-horse town? She would turn up his name the minute she began to dig. That was, after all, her speciality. She was one of the best, even reporting on hog prices in Saskatoon. Which is where she had been banished when yours truly had pretty much ruined her career.

He turned to exit the restaurant as any other free man would do. He hoped beyond hope that she wouldn't notice him. He longed to disappear into the night, lie low for a few days until the RCMP said he could go, then slip back across the Continental Divide, down the Fraser River, and back to his life, such as it was, in Vancouver.

She was twirling a forkful of noodles against her spoon — she always did that with long pasta — when he walked past her, head averted. It looked like he was about to get away with it when she raised the spaghetti to her mouth and looked up to meet his last backward glance.

Her eyes widened. "Cole Blackwater?" Her voice, deep and distinctive, that he'd heard in all manner of passionate moments, was incredulous now and fierce and very, very loud. "What the hell are you doing here?"

He froze, a deer in the headlights of her big green eyes.

"Nancy!" He attempted surprise. But he was a lousy actor and he came across as a jack lighter, caught red-handed hunting at night.

"What the hell are you doing here?" She was as lovely as ever. Her black hair hung to her shoulders; her skin was sun-browned and smooth. And by the sounds of it, she was no less angry than she had been four years earlier.

Heads turned. He stepped toward her table, hands jammed awkwardly into the pockets of his jeans. "You're looking well."

"You're not. What happened to you? Like I care."

"Family restaurant, Nancy," said Cole, nearly tearing his sutures with his forced smile.

"What are you doing here?" she asked, loudly enough that patrons at the surrounding tables stopped eating to look at them.

"I'll tell you if you just shut up," he growled.

"Don't you dare sit down," she hissed.

His reply was to sit. And before his back was against the booth she slapped him. The pain blinded him and his first impulse was to hit back. His jaw clamped and he restrained himself.

"What are you doing here, you bastard?"

"You used to have such a great vocabulary." He looked at her and looked around. Eyes were trained on him. She swore at him and hit him but everybody assumed he had it coming.

And they were right.

It looked like she was about to swing again and he said, between gritted teeth, "Don't."

Nancy Webber must have seen the intent in his eyes because she lowered her hand.

"Or what, Cole?" She looked around. "You'd be in the alley with the rest of the trash if you lifted one finger at me, tough guy."

"Maybe," he said.

They stared at each other.

"You haven't answered my question," she finally said.

"Why don't you try asking me nicely?"

She exhaled a long, slow breath. "Cole," she said with exaggerated sweetness, "what brings you to Oracle?"

How could he hate her so much after loving her too? "I'm working here."

"Really?" she continued in the patronizing voice. "In the mine, or running a skidder?"

"Neither." His voice was low. "I'm working for some folks who are trying to stop the mine at Cardinal Divide."

Nancy couldn't hide her interest. "Really, Cole? And just how is that campaign going?"

"Not very well," he said, looking sideways.

"You don't say? Sounds like one of your clients has popped the mine manager. Was that part of your strategy? Or was it, as you used to say, collateral damage?"

"I thought reporters were supposed to cover the story, not invent it, Nancy. Or don't the Saskatoon hog report readers expect unbiased journalism?"

"Sources close to the police say otherwise."

"Oh yeah? Someone with a vested interest, perhaps?"

Nancy was silent; her green eyes betrayed nothing.

"You really have fallen far. Covering small town murders," he said.

"You ought to know, you pushed me."

"You were the one who printed it."

"And you were the lying bastard who fed me the story."

"You were the willing reporter who gobbled it up."

"I won't be making that mistake again."

"Sounds like you already have."

"I'm just following leads, Cole."

"Right, Nancy, you're following whatever leads the owners of this town and your two-bit newspaper feed you."

"You're one to talk, Cole. Look at you. Talk about how the mighty have fallen."

Cole was running two for two with scorned ex-lovers.

"We're done here," he said and prepared to rise.

"Don't get in my way on this story, Cole."

"Or what?"

But she didn't answer because her Blackberry buzzed as her mouth opened and, like all reporters, she was wired to her technology. She scooped it up off the table and read the message. Cole saw her grin, the smile wide and triumphant. Her green eyes met his and as they locked gazes, he knew what was in the message she had received.

His phone rang. Without taking his eyes from Nancy Webber, he answered: "Blackwater."

"It's Peggy."

"Go ahead, Peggy."

"Dale van Stempvort was just arrested. He's been charged with murder."

11 "I'm going to the RCMP detachment now." Peggy's voice shook. "To make sure Dale gets a lawyer." Her voice trailed off.

Nancy tucked her Blackberry into her purse and zipped the bag. "Do you want me to meet you there?" asked Cole.

"Would you? I don't know anything about this," said Peggy.

"It's not exactly in my job description either, Peggy."

"Well, two heads are better than one."

Cole sighed. "OK, I'll see you in twenty minutes," he said and hung up.

"This has been a blast, Cole," said Nancy. "But I have to go. Story to file, you know."

"And what exactly do you think the story is, Nancy?"

"Pretty clear, isn't it, Cole?"

"Illuminate me."

"Angry environmentalist bludgeons mine manager," she said.

"Can't argue with you about that."

Nancy turned to leave.

"You could always tell the back story. Dig a little deeper. You were good at that once upon a time."

"If it bleeds it leads, Cole. Don't talk to me about the good old days."

"Fine, whatever." Cole waved her away and watched her go. But he knew he hadn't seen the last of Nancy Webber.

The evening air was refreshingly cool when he left the Big Sky Restaurant. In the indigo sky Cole saw Arcturus and followed its arc to Spica, barely visible on the horizon. The air revived him, but nothing could fix the ache in his bones. And miles to go before I sleep, he thought. The driver's door of his truck protested when he opened it. Don't you start acting up on me, he thought. I need something in my life to be dependable. And then he thought of Sarah.

He pulled his cellphone from his pocket and dialled Jennifer's number. On the fourth ring, Polson answered, saying, "It's about bloody time, Cole."

"Hi Jennifer." He had no energy to argue.

"Sarah is worried sick about you."

"How are you, Jennifer? I'm fine."

"Cole, you are an asshole."

"Well, Jennifer, things are a little nutty in Oracle."

"Cole, do you even care about Sarah?"

Cole closed his eyes and felt the familiar heat of adrenaline flood his neural pathways. In a moment, if he wasn't careful, his vision would narrow and obliterate the peripheral until all that remained was a narrow band right in front of him. And when that happened, as it had so many times in his life, trouble usually followed.

"Has something happened to Sarah?" he finally asked.

"No, nothing, Cole."

"What about you, have you been in an accident?"

"No, Cole."

"Have either of you contracted a mysterious disease that impairs your ability to dial a telephone?"

"Jesus Christ, Cole, you are a prick."

"Can I talk with Sarah, please?"

Finally there was silence on the other end. He heard a muffled conversation in the background. Finally his daughter's voice.

"Hi Daddy!"

"Hi sweetheart. How's my girl?"

"I'm good. How are you?"

"Just fine."

"You don't sound fine."

"Don't I?"

"What's wrong? Are you OK?"

"I'm OK," he said, and felt the unwelcome constriction in his throat that could lead to tears. The adrenaline drained from his system at the sound of Sarah's sympathy, and despair was beneath it.

"Don't be sad, Daddy. I love you."

She made the heart glad. "I love you too, sweetheart."

"So, are you saving the world from evil corporations?"

"I'm just getting started. Listen carefully," he said, "something has happened here that you might see on the news tomorrow."

"Are you OK?" she asked anxiously. He loved her so much.

"I'm fine. But a man has been killed. He was the manager of the mine that we are trying to stop, and someone I know is accused of killing him."

The line was quiet as Sarah absorbed the information. "Did he do it, Daddy?"

It occurred to Cole that he hadn't actually asked that question. "I don't know."

"What do you think?"

"I don't know what to think, Sarah."

"Are you going to stay in Alberta for much longer?"

"I don't want to. This is a lost cause and I want to head home."

"Are you going to see Grandma?"

He was silent.

"You should."

"Now don't you go should-ing all over me," he said with a smile, which he hoped she felt through the phone.

"You should," she said again.

"I know."

"When will you be home?"

"I'm not sure."

"Will you call me and let me know?"

"Of course, or you can call me."

She was silent. Cole could feel something there, something that he should ask about but dared not, so far away.

"I'm going now, honey. I have to go to the police station."

"Be careful."

"I will. There's nothing to worry about." He had said that a few days ago before he left Vancouver. He had meant it then, but now he wasn't so sure.

"I love you, Daddy."

"I love you too, Sarah. Be good for your mom."

"I will. Bye."

He hung up and his hand fell to his side. He needed to sleep for a week. Was it only four days since he had seen Sarah?

The Toyota started with a reassuring roar and he drove to the RCMP detachment. The previously empty parking lot was overflowing with rental cars and TV vans whose satellite dishes pointed skyward, ready to beam the news to the nation.

Cole parked a block away, and walked along the sidewalk. People, likely reporters waiting for the RCMP to make a statement, stood outside the police station. He approached slowly, as if headed toward a cage of dangerous animals. He feared being recognized almost as much as he feared *not* being recognized.

In the shadow of a cedar shrub he watched for Peggy. He counted a dozen reporters, including TV crews from two of the four national networks. Their lights flooded the front door of the RCMP detachment. Huddled together, reporters chatted in conspiratorial tones. How juicy, thought Cole. A wet dream for the *Calgary Herald*, the *Alberta Standard*, and all the other right-wing mouthpieces. For so long the story had been Developer Kills Grizzly, Conservationist Loses Battle. Now the table was turned.

Cole scanned the crowd of journalists and saw Nancy Webber talking to a reporter he didn't recognize. He inhaled deeply and slowly released his breath. Things had gone about as badly as he expected they would at the Big Sky Restaurant. He expected that they would get worse before they got any better. But he really didn't see how he could avoid her.

"Someone's coming out," a reporter called and all eyes turned to the front door. Cole realized he was holding his breath and he made himself exhale.

Peggy McSorlie walked through the door. She stopped and blinked as her eyes adjusted to the glare.

Keep walking, thought Cole, his body tense and sore.

"Did Dale van Stempvort kill Mike Barnes?" shouted a reporter.

Peggy stood, uncertain if she should stay and answer or push through the throng. "No," she said. "He's innocent."

You're in the animal soup now, Cole thought to himself.

"Have you been charged too?"

"No! I'm here to arrange for a lawyer for Dale."

"Does your group advocate violence to stop the mine?"

Cole pushed his way from the back of the group to rescue Peggy.

"The murder of Mike Barnes is a tragedy," said Peggy, regaining her composure. "Our prayers are with his family tonight."

Cole caught Peggy by the arm and pulled her through the crowd. More questions were hurled at them. Someone asked, "Who the hell is he?"

Nancy's face appeared in the crowd. "More lies, Cole?" she asked, and he grimaced.

He spoke into Peggy's ear. "Where's your car?"

"Up the street."

"We'll take mine," he growled.

A few reporters followed them to his truck, where Cole tried to brush them off. "No story here, ladies and gents," he said as amicably as he could. They were saved by shouts that the RCMP was about to make a statement.

"Shouldn't we wait to hear what they have to say?" Peggy turned toward the station.

"Not unless you want to answer more questions on Dale van Stempvort's behalf."

Peggy was ready to cry.

Cole put the truck in gear and drove past the RCMP station, where Sergeant Reimer was now in the spotlight.

"Where can we talk?" asked Cole.

"My farm?"

"Too far," he said. "I'd never make it back."

"There's a guest room."

"No thanks. Any place here in town that's quiet?"

"Andy's."

"A friend?"

"No, it's a bar."

There is a God, thought Cole. "Sounds good. Where?"

Peggy directed him to a small storefront off Main Street.

"I didn't know this place existed," said Cole as he parked.

"You've only been here for four days," said Peggy.

"Feels like four years," Cole said without a smile.

Andy's was empty except for a couple at the bar. Half a dozen tables sat in the centre of the small room, which might once have been a diner but was now a jazz bar. Another half dozen booths lined the walls. John Coltrane infused the room with a blue sound.

"This is the cultural centre of Oracle," said Peggy.

"As long as they serve whiskey, it can be anything it likes," said Cole.

Peggy and Cole slid into a booth. Cole was tired. He didn't know how he would stay awake. He slumped and Peggy sat upright across from him.

A man approached their table. "Evening, Peggy."

"Hi Andy."

"What'll you have?"

"Big Rock."

"And you?"

"Jameson, rocks."

"Coming up," said Andy.

Cole was silent.

"I know what you're thinking," Peggy said.

"I don't think so, Peggy."

"You're thinking this was a really big mistake. You're thinking, I told you so."

"OK, so you *do* know what I'm thinking." Cole almost smiled.

"You're also thinking you'd better quit while you're ahead."

Their drinks arrived. The whiskey warmed him immediately and he relaxed. "Had occurred to me," he said.

"Dale said he didn't do it."

"Well, then, we're off the hook. When do they release him?"

"Come on, Cole."

He took another drink. "He didn't do it? That's great. Can he prove it?"

"Dale says that he was at home all last night."

"Got a witness?"

"He lives alone."

"He doesn't have a leg to stand on."

"The police say they've identified his truck at the mine. But there are dozens of beat-up old Chevy s10s and Ford Rangers in Oracle. That's not evidence."

"Peggy, he has said publicly that he would do anything to stop the mine. The cops have a clear motive. And they have his truck at the scene."

"They don't have anything, Cole."

"Then why is Dale behind bars?"

"Guess."

Cole sipped his Irish whiskey. "My money is still on guilty. But he's behind bars right now because of pressure from the mine, the town, the Chamber of Commerce, and from the family."

"Small town politics, Cole. And there's something else. People have been calling Dale's place with death threats. Someone drove by his farm and threw a brick at the house."

Cole finished his drink.

"You can't leave now, Cole."

He raised his eyebrow. "Can't?"

"Cole, we need you now more than ever."

"It's nice to be needed, Peggy, but a man is dead. One of your group members is in jail. I spent the morning in the hospital getting stitched back together and the afternoon in the cop shop getting interrogated by a surly sergeant. In twenty years of activism, I have never, ever had a bad day like this one. And I've had my share of bad days."

"If you quit now, Cole, we'll lose."

"You've already lost!" Cole shouted. "You can't save Cardinal Divide now. You'll be lucky to avoid a charge of collusion or conspiracy, or whatever they call it. Dale van Stempvort kills the mine manager, and your whole group is fingered as a bunch of murderous thugs bent on any level of violence to protect bears and butterflies. I don't see a way out of this for you, ESCoG, or Cardinal Divide."

Peggy looked at her hands.

"We're not going to quit," she said finally.

"Well I am," said Cole.

"Don't run away from us, Cole. Don't run from yourself."

Cole signalled Andy for another drink. "Don't get all psychological on me, Peggy. You don't know anything about me."

"I know enough, Cole. Stay and help us save Cardinal Divide."

"This is mission impossible," scowled Cole. "And I am not Tom Cruise."

"That's for sure," grinned Peggy.

"Nice," he said. "Look, to save Cardinal Divide, you will first have to save Dale van Stempvort. I hope you've got a good lawyer."

Andy brought Cole another whiskey. Cole took a sip.

"Someone from Legal Aid will come from Red Deer in the morning," Peggy said when Andy left.

"Legal Aid? Good Lord, Peggy."

"Dale has no money. I have no money for a lawyer. If this goes to court, he'll likely have to sell the farm, literally."

Cole shook his head and finished his whiskey.

"Help us clear Dale's name."

"He looks guilty to me. Why in the he—" He caught himself. "Why should I help clear his name?" he said more quietly.

"Dale is a loudmouth and a bit of a firebrand, but he's not violent."

Cole remembered his conversation with Dale the day before when Dale had professed his innocence. Still, he wasn't sure. "What about the wells?"

"What about them? Destroying technology is different than murder."

This was the familiar argument that supported eco-sabotage. He shook his head.

"We don't know how to play the game at this level, Cole. You do. Please don't leave now."

"Peggy, I'm a strategist, not a private investigator. I don't know the first thing about clearing a man's name of murder."

"The lawyer will know."

"Then let him do it!"

"He can use your help. He can use your expertise on the issues."

They sat across from each other. She finished her beer. His drink was done.

"Sleep on it," she said finally. "Things won't look so bad in the morning."

"I seriously doubt that, Peggy."

He drove Peggy to her car and took himself back to his hotel, aware that he'd consumed two beers and two whiskeys in the last few hours. He really didn't need a DUI on top of everything else. Every part of him, including his ego, ached.

The hotel parking lot was nearly full. The reporters were staying here, he guessed. Cole sat in his truck for a moment.

In the morning he would put Oracle in the rearview mirror en route to Vancouver. He could cobble together a stopgap strategy for Peggy long distance to help her save her reputation, maybe her organization. But Cardinal Divide was lost. Dale van Stempvort was lost. And he, Cole Blackwater, had now lost his only paying client. He put his head between his hands on the steering wheel and dozed off.

He woke with a start to hear a familiar voice. On the second floor catwalk Nancy Webber, her black hair illuminated by the glow of the light above her room's door, called goodnight to someone he could not see. So, things *could* get worse: she was staying in the same hotel as he was.

Now he knew he had to leave.

Stephen Legault

12 Cole's eyes opened. He waited for the phone to ring or the other shoe to drop, expecting further news of murder or mayhem. When none came he looked out the window through the half-open curtains. The morning was lovely, a blue bird day as they called it in Alberta, and over the parking lot and the tops of the houses that lined the road he could see the sculpted forms of foothills beyond. Each hill was carpeted in a thick pattern of dark and light green, the morning sun igniting the tip of each tree with a golden fire. It was so beautiful, thought Cole, that it would be hard to leave. Hard, but not impossible.

Sleep slowly trickled from his soggy mind. But one thing was for certain: he was outta here. He rolled onto his side and pushed himself up with his good hand. He stretched gingerly, felt his whole body tighten.

When he fought, he could wake in the morning too stiff to move. It often took twenty minutes for the kinks to work out of his body. The combination of ranch work, riding, and getting his ears boxed somehow disagreed with his body. His doctor said he had loose ligaments, that his tendons were subject to higher than average buildup of lactic acid. His trainer encouraged more stretching, even yoga. But Cole Blackwater would have nothing to do with that. If his friends at school found out he was doing a downward-facing dog, he would never hear the end of it.

So he stiffened up. The stiffness slowed him down and likely ended his career as an amateur boxer. Lack of flexibility was only one of the things that contributed to his final defeat inside the ring, and out. Lao Tzu said that "that which does not bend breaks." Pretty clever for a guy who had been dead for a couple of millennia.

He sat on the edge of the bed, dropped his head, and bowed forward to loosen his spine. From that vantage point he got a bird's eye view of his spare tire. At least he could still see his own dong when he looked down. This morning's stiffness was come by pretty honestly, he had to admit, but his overall lack of fitness was his own fault. If his brother saw him today he'd shake his head, speechless.

He held his forehead in his hands and let his neck release slowly. Walter was as fit and trim at forty as he was at twenty. That's what clean living did for you. Thoughts of Walter brought up the memory of the last time they'd been together. Three years ago. He saw himself and Walter standing together in the barn, looking at the boxing ring with its sagging hemp ropes, and the now red-stained canvas floor. The four overhead lights still hung over the ring.

Neither brother spoke a word or shed a tear.

Cole asked himself why he did not keep in touch with Walter. None of it was his brother's fault. There was nothing Walter could have done. He was a boy then too, only a few years older than Cole. Quieter, steadier, more level-headed for certain, but just a boy.

And at forty he was a park warden. He rode the trails in the summer, helped lost tourists find the washrooms, and brought little children down off the rocky mountainsides. In June he herded cattle into the high country, and brought them out in October, keeping alive his family's grazing permit. Walter was not married but he lived with a woman. Beth? Betty? Cole was sad that he didn't remember her name.

He groaned as he stood up, padded naked to the bathroom, and turned on the shower. While the water found its way through the pipes to his room, he turned on Newsworld, a morning show from Toronto. At least there was no news about the murder of Mike Barnes. He entered the shower, let the water warm him and loosen him and wash the stiffness and pain from his body. It took a full ten minutes.

Peggy gave him no argument.

He expected to have to defend his decision. While meditating in the shower, he had worked out all of his rebuttals. He'd even practiced the lines under his breath: "I signed on to stop a mine, not stop a man from being sent to jail." And, "Solving a murder mystery isn't in my contract." And, his favourite, "I'm a strategist, not a PI." To Cole Blackwater it sounded like Bones protesting to Captain Kirk, "I'm a doctor, Jim, not an iguana."

But when he told her that morning that he had to leave, Peggy simply said, "I'm so sorry for how this has turned out, Cole."

He listened to her cry on the other end of the line. Not because he was leaving but because everything she had believed in was in peril, and his departure hammered that home.

Stephen Legault

"I'm sorry for the inconvenience to you, Cole," she said. "We pulled you away from important work, and from your family, and this is the last thing that you need right now."

He was dumbstruck. What kind of goodness was required to allow *her* to apologize to *him*? The Cardinal Divide was almost certainly lost and one of her colleagues likely to spend the rest of his life behind bars for killing a man responsible for the destruction of the wilderness she loved so dearly – to apologize to him?

"I'll do what I can from Vancouver to salvage something." Cole wanted to encourage Peggy, at least. "Try to use this turn of events to our advantage. Maybe we can get a few feature stories on the Cardinal Divide out, the back story to the murder. I'll see what I can do."

"Thank you, Cole," said Peggy McSorlie.

He hung up.

Considerably lighter now that he had decided to head back across the Continental Divide, he dressed in jeans and a colourful shirt reserved for festive occasions. He stuffed the rest of his clothes into his backpack and jammed his computer and accessories into his briefcase.

He scanned the room to make sure he hadn't left anything behind and checked in the bathroom and under the bed. Satisfied, he shouldered the pack, with some discomfort, and opened the motel door. He checked that Nancy Webber wouldn't see him slinking off, then walked to the Toyota, tossed his bag in the back, and headed to the Rim Rock office to settle up his bill.

Deborah Cody appeared at the sound of bells ringing. "Need anything Cole?"

"I'm checking out, Deborah."

"I have you down for two weeks, Cole." She smiled at him.

"Yeah," he sighed, "things have changed."

"I guess so." She smiled again, offering him a check-out slip to sign. "But we hardly got to know each other."

He looked up from his signature. Her eyes searched his, then held his gaze. "Don't you think that's a shame?" She touched his pen hand lightly.

A terrible shame, thought Cole.

"How is your face?" she asked, suddenly very concerned. "George told me what happened."

Cole thought of George Cody and his baseball bat. What might the man do to Cole if he caught his wife flirting with him?

"It looks painful." Deborah Cody reached out to touch his face and Cole pulled back involuntarily.

"It's pretty sore to the touch," he said, and managed a half smile.

Deborah smiled too. Her dark blonde hair was loose and fell to her shoulders. Her eyes were bright and very sympathetic. She wore a T-shirt and her arms were well-muscled and brown. She was firm in all the right places and soft in the others. No wonder Mike Barnes had decided to seek some solace there.

He dropped his gaze from his paperwork and let his eyes trail down the long, shapely arms to the hand that rested near his on the counter. What was that on her right hand? Her knuckles were bruised, swollen, a little red.

"What happened to your hand?" he asked.

She looked at it as if she had only now noticed the bruise. "Oh, that? A window I was cleaning fell right on my knuckles."

"Looks painful," he echoed.

"Oh, it is," she said, inviting sympathy.

I'm outta here, Cole thought to himself, and said, "I must be off."

"See you again," Deborah said with a wink.

Not likely, he thought, but smiled and, yes, he winked back.

Outside the motel office the morning air was cool, but Cole felt flushed, warm from his encounter with Deborah Cody. Good gravy, but that woman was brazen. Not only was she an incontestable flirt, but she was the wife of baseball-bat-wielding George Cody. What was Mike Barnes thinking? Messing with a woman like that could get a man killed.

He unlocked the door of his Toyota and climbed in. When the engine growled Cole inserted a CD, turned the volume up to ear-drum-piercing levels, put the truck in gear, and drove out of the parking lot, singing along to the Eagles: *Well I'm running down the road trying to loosen my load, got a world of trouble on my mind.*

But just before he drove away he saw Nancy Webber emerge from her motel room. And here he thought he'd made a clean get away. No such luck. Surely she had seen him leave, could hear the rattle of his slowly disintegrating Toyota as it lurched from the parking lot. He didn't care. He just kept singing to beat the band.

But even music couldn't push Nancy from his mind. All of our ghosts come back to haunt us, thought Cole Blackwater. Every mistake we've ever made, no matter how great or small, lurks somewhere in the darkness waiting to return and claim its due. Well, his ghosts had certainly caught up with him this week. Whatever. It was all in the rearview mirror now.

He bought a coffee at Tim Hortons for the road and managed to get in and out without incident. That was a good sign, he thought. Cole pointed his truck west, toward the mountains, and headed for the highway. He and Thoreau agreed that "Eastward I go only by force, but westward I go free." Cole Blackwater always loved the feeling of driving toward the mountains.

A memory surfaced. When he was a kid his family drove into High River for groceries in the red Dodge pickup truck that his father had owned since the end of the war. When they needed more than the tiny foothill town offered they rose early, finished the morning chores before sunrise, and drove for three hours to Calgary. There they loaded the truck with supplies: socks and underwear for the boys, groceries, a few pieces of equipment and spare parts that the old man couldn't find in High River. Their chores done, the old man made the obligatory trip to Prize Fight, his alma mater, a boxing club in the rundown section of the city, south of downtown.

The old man talked with his cronies, threw a few jabs at a heavy bag, and picked up whatever was needed to continue Walter and Cole's training. The boys sat ringside and watched the fighters train. The low ceiling, the heat, the pervasive odour of sweating bodies, and the iron smell of blood got under a person's skin; this is where Cole had returned when he was seventeen to further his amateur boxing career.

Late that afternoon they left the city and drove home in the last light of evening. Cole loved sitting on the wide bench seat between Walter and their mother. He leaned his head on her shoulder and fought sleep to watch the mountains rise steadily on the horizon.

They drove down Highway 2 as far as High River and then turned west. Orange evening light as thick as honey spilled across the fields. The blue mountains of the Fisher, Opal, and Highwood Ranges rose up on the horizon jagged as bent saws, their tops white with snow late into June. When the blacktop disappeared after High River and they rumbled across the gravel, Cole, and sometimes even Walter, fell asleep.

Then Cole heard through the dew of slumber the voices of his parents talking quietly about how Calgary was getting too big for its britches, drunk on oil wealth, and how the price of a pair of shoes was murder. The cab of the truck always smelled of whiskey on the way home, after the old man stopped by a social club near Prize Fight to hoist a few and pick up a bottle for the return trip. But the close quarters of the Dodge's big seat and the proximity of their mother quieted his father's rage, or at least kept it at bay. The old man was always happy, at least for a few days, after a visit to his old club. But that never lasted long, Cole remembered.

Cole hit the highway. As he left town he felt the anticipated guilt well up within him. He knew this would happen, so he was prepared for it, as prepared as he had been to counter Peggy Mc-Sorlie's arguments that morning.

He slipped the town limits just after nine, and saluted the "Entering Oracle" sign from his rearview mirror. A clear blue sky sat atop the forested foothills, and to the west the dark, craggy line of mountains leaned up against Jasper National Park. His stereo was on full blast: *It's just another Tequila Sunrise, starin' slowly 'cross the sky. He said goodbye.* Cole tossed back his coffee and dropped the cup on the floor with the rest of the detritus of his life.

He'd be home by midnight, wake up tomorrow in his own bed, see Sarah on the weekend. His heart lightened. My Lord, how he loved his little girl. They'd go out for a big breakfast on Saturday and then go to Stanley Park, or maybe to the north shore mountains for the day and walk the trails up into the canyons and over the craggy hills, draped with cedar and spruce and ferns.

He would put this mess behind him. Yes, it was time for a clean start. Let the ghosts of the past haunt him no more. He pounded the steering wheel in time with the music. He crooned, *She wasn't just another woman, and I couldn't keep from coming on, it had been so long.*

Come Monday morning, Blackwater Strategy would be reborn with a clean slate. On Monday morning he'd develop a new business plan. He was good at planning. It was time to apply those skills to his own interests for a change. By Friday he'd have another client lined up and ready to go. The past would be in the past, where it belonged.

It occurred to him to let the RCMP detachment know he was skipping town before he got out of cell range, so he rolled the window up, muted the stereo, and found the phone on the passenger seat. He dialled the number, keeping one eye on the road, and got through to Sergeant Reimer.

"It's Cole Blackwater, Sergeant."

"What can I do for you, Mr. Blackwater?"

"I'm heading back to Vancouver today. I just called to let you know."

There was a long silence on the phone that made Cole uneasy.

"We would have preferred that you remain in Oracle, Mr. Blackwater."

"I've got to head home to my family, Sergeant," he lied.

Another long silence.

"We may need you for a further statement."

Now Cole was silent. "I thought you'd found your man."

"We have, but we're still compiling our case against him. Some of the forensics have yet to come back from Edmonton."

Cole thought about that for a moment. "I'm sorry? What do you mean?"

"Just what I said. Some of the items that we've sent off to Edmonton for analysis haven't been returned to us, so we are still in the process of building our case. We may need you to make another statement."

"But you arrested Dale van Stempvort."

"Yes, we did. He's in custody, awaiting arraignment this afternoon."

"On what grounds did you arrest him if you haven't got your evidence back?"

"We have established motive and opportunity, and we need only finalize our work on method to have an open and shut case."

Cole switched the phone from his right hand to his left hand and geared down.

"How can you arrest a man for murder if you don't know how he did it?"

"Mr. Blackwater, the RCMP have considerably more experience in criminal investigation than you. You're going to have to accept that we know what we are doing. We have the killer of Mike Barnes in custody."

"Tell that to David Milgard."

Reimer ignored him. "I suggest that you phone the Vancouver police when you arrive in the city to let them know your whereabouts. You are an important witness to this criminal investigation. Is that clear?"

"Clear enough," he said, repressing the growing urge to tell the sergeant to go take a flying leap. "But what's not clear is that you have a case against Dale van Stempvort."

"I think we've talked long enough, Mr. Blackwater," said Sergeant Reimer. "Good-bye."

Cole dropped the cell on the seat next to him, slowed, and pulled the Toyota into a rest stop next to the highway at the top of a hill. The rugged peaks of Jasper National Park thrust upward toward the morning sun.

Cole turned the ignition off.

He sat, observing the mountains. Banks of clouds ripped their bellies on the front range peaks and spilled rain, snow, or hail into one valley, while the next was bathed in sun.

Cars whizzed past on the highway. A tractor trailer shook the Toyota with its afterdraft.

The RCMP sought an open and shut case, but it didn't seem like they had it yet.

Cole Blackwater was prepared to accept that Dale van Stempvort was a killer, but not without proof. What had Reimer said? They had motive and opportunity, but not means? Sounded like dime-store detective talk. Motive had been established, Cole assumed, when Dale, via the *Red Deer Advocate*, had publicly declared that he would do anything to stop the mine. Opportunity, Cole reasoned, was established by the Mounties when Dale couldn't produce a sufficient alibi for his whereabouts. Cows made poor witnesses. His truck had been seen in the vicinity, Reimer said. Or at least a truck matching Dale's truck's description, an aging Chevy s10. How many of those were in the Oracle region? Peggy McSorlie had asked the same question.

Means. Reimer said she was waiting on forensic evidence to establish means. Hadn't Cole heard that Mike Barnes was bludgeoned? His skull cracked open. Cole shuddered at the thought of that handsome head split down the middle, blood and brains spilling out. That would make one hell of a mess. There were lots of big, heavy things lying around a mine mill that could do such damage, reasoned Cole. A length of drill steel. A drill bit. A pipe wrench. What *else* could do such damage?

A baseball bat?

Cole watched a dark cloud pass over the mountains, scudding toward the dark green foothills. Behind it trailed the opaque shadow of rain, dousing the woods in a brief but much-needed shower.

Cole shook his head. By this afternoon the lab would send confirmation of the murder weapon with while Dale van Stempvort's fingerprints all over it, and that would be the end of the story.

He went to start the truck, but dropped his hand. What if, in their haste to satisfy the Chamber of Commerce, the dead man's family, and the mining company, the RCMP arrested the wrong man? It happened all the time, didn't it?

Cole didn't want to believe that an innocent man would be put behind bars simply because of his politics.

And now that he let himself think about it, Cole knew it didn't make sense for Dale van Stempvort, after that piece in the paper fingered him as a loose cannon, to make an appointment with Mike Barnes, drive out to the mine, and club the man over the head. Dale came across as a passionate man, but not violent. Cole flexed his fist and observed the bruised knuckles on his right hand. Now Cole Blackwater, he mused, there's a man with a streak of violence in him. He looked at his hand, watched the knuckles turn white as he clenched, and turn blue and red as he opened the fingers.

No doubt where that violent streak came from; he smiled thinly. He made a fist again and threw a soft jab toward the windshield. He cut the air so crisp and quick that his coat made a snapping sound. No doubt where he had picked up the habit of sorting out his troubles with his fists.

But if Dale didn't kill Mike Barnes, who did?

Leave that to the RCMP. He shook his head again and threw

another jab, this time a little harder.

He could still throw a decent punch, he mused. That night in the bar he had done well. He'd cleaned that first dude's clock, and the second one too, with the knee to the solar plexus. He wished now, looking at his hand, that he'd held back a little with the punch to the ear. But he had let his guard down, had forgotten his father's cardinal rule.

His father had learned about letting *his* guard down, too.

In the end it was George Cody's baseball bat, and not Cole's skill as a fighter, that had saved him.

It didn't surprise Cole that George Cody stashed some Spalding muscle behind a bar that catered to roughnecks and miners. Especially in a town where the only police backup was a 120-pound woman. No, the baseball bat didn't seem out of place.

Where had George been? It sure had been handy of him to show up in the nick of time.

Life's events hung on a delicate hinge of timing, mused Cole. Timing was everything, wasn't it? In his old man's life, for sure. And thus in his own.

On June 6, 1944, Henry Blackwater was determined to be the first man up Juno beach. He wanted to be the first man in his company to kill Jerry. But, as luck would have it, his life was spared, and an anger that spanned generations was born.

For three years Henry Blackwater was stationed in England, and during that time he won himself a reputation as the meanest son-of-a-bitch in his whole division. Maybe in the whole Canadian army. He didn't start out that way. He was of average build, weighed maybe 170 pounds, and stood just shy of six feet; he wasn't a physical menace. One night in a pub some boys from a Limey machine gun squad poked fun at the Canadians, called them a bunch of country hicks and poor cousins. The fun turned sour when one of the Brits got in Henry Blackwater's face and wouldn't let up. Henry knocked four of his teeth out with one punch. The whole pub got into it and the constabulatory was called out. By the end of it, Henry was in the klink along with half a dozen other Canadian lads, while the Limeys got sent home with a stern warning.

The next morning Henry and the others were sent back to barracks, where they faced further disciplinary action for missing curfew. The bobby that accompanied them warned the base commander that such behaviour wouldn't be tolerated. Henry protested, but it fell on deaf ears.

Henry was assigned to mess duty for thirty days. By the end of it, he had discovered the base's gym and started boxing as a way to relieve his frustration, his anger, and his restlessness. For nearly three years, while the Canadian expeditionary force sat in England as part of the home guard, Henry Blackwater boxed. He gained fifteen pounds of muscle. Cruiserweight class. Along with the fifteen pounds of muscle, he gained a reputation as the meanest man to step into the ring. He boxed the nose, face, and chin of nearly every man that stepped into the ring with him.

Nearly every man. There was one man Henry couldn't beat. They fought to a draw twice. He was a hulking black man from Central Africa who was in the British forces as an artillery man. Bombshell Bismarck, the men called him. He weighed twenty pounds more than Henry, topping the heavyweight scale, and towered over him by four inches. His reach was at least three inches longer than Henry's. But what Bombshell had in brawn, Henry Blackwater made up for in pure rage.

Cole wondered now: rage at what?

Bombshell and Henry Blackwater clashed for the last time in early May of 1944. They fought for fifteen rounds 'til both men were beaten to a pulp. By the end of it neither man could stand, but neither man would fall. They simply clung to each other, their glistening, muscled bodies entwined, trading jabs, head butts, and low blows when the referee could not untangle them.

And then the order came that there was to be no more boxing. Henry Blackwater knew it meant that soon they would invade Europe and that their commanders wanted all the men to be fit and ready to fight Jerry, not one another.

And so the morning that Henry Blackwater loaded into his landing craft, he didn't have the distinction of being an uncontested boxing champion, but merely a boxing legend. He planned to become a legend in combat too.

Somewhere while crossing the English Channel, his plan went awry. Master Sergeant Henry Blackwater was not a good sailor. He took the tablets they provided that morning as he ate a solemn breakfast, but they did no good, or if they helped, it was impossible to tell. By the time the shores of France were in sight, Henry Blackwater was curled up on the bottom of the landing craft in a pool of his own vomit. The medic tried to revive him with smelling salts, but Blackwater was as seasick as a man could be. He was heard to curse himself as shells exploded in the water and the boat revved its engine for the final push up onto the sand. When the craft finally beached and the gangplank was dropped, a hail of machine gun fire ripped into the boat and killed half a dozen of the men in the front. The others pushed through them and were cut down as they did. Their blood sprayed the deck of the boat and coated Blackwater, who lay in the bilge.

Henry Blackwater held onto his Enfield rifle for dear life, determined not to die under a heap of bodies, in a swamp of vomit, blood, and salt water. With all of his considerable strength he pulled, but to no avail. And then a shell exploded a few feet away, tossed the boat onto its side, and with it Henry Blackwater's hope of becoming a hero.

His injuries weren't life-threatening, but they warranted a return trip across the channel, this time on a medical frigate. He suffered multiple shrapnel wounds, all of which were superficial. He broke his ankle and his left arm when he landed on the side of the boat in the explosion. He suffered a minor concussion. He fared better than most in that craft. Of the sixty men on board, only thirty-five made the beach, and fewer than ten were alive at the end of the day.

None of those who survived ever spoke of Henry Blackwater's seasickness. None blamed him. It could happen to anyone, they all reasoned. It's not like he had run away. It's not like he had turned tail. Nobody accused him of that. Nobody blamed him. But Blackwater blamed himself, blamed his body for letting him down. His anger boiled during this stay in an English hospital. He was reassigned four months later to a unit doing mop-up work in the Netherlands. He saw a little action there, exchanging small arms fire with a band of Germans who refused to surrender a strategic point on a farm road. Try as he might, he didn't kill any of them. Didn't even wound a man. As the allies advanced across Europe, Henry Blackwater found himself in the rear, and it ate at him for the rest of his life. He never forgave himself for the involuntary cowardice that saved his life on that

Stephen Legault

frightful crossing.

And Cole could not forgive him for what he did with that rage.

Cole looked at the horizon. The storm had passed. He looked at his hands. At the damage done by years in the ring. His fingers were bent, and he could feel the stiffness there that would soon turn to arthritis. My God, his father had been an angry man.

He closed his eyes. The world was murky since the killing of Mike Barnes. He needed to see through the pain and sorrow of this man's untimely demise back to the clarity of white and black and the time when he knew what he had to do.

The long sweep of Cardinal Divide came into focus. He saw himself, as if from the vantage of a hawk wheeling high overhead, climbing the slope up the divide's south side. He watched himself crest the ridge and discover the expansive valley below. He watched himself pick his way over the barren slope and step from rock to rock, from one grassy hillock to the next toward the apogee of the curving ridge. And then, across the valley, he spied the family of grizzly bears, the mother with her cubs of the year eating glacier lilies as they went.

Cole saw the mother stop now and again to sniff, to test the air for threats. They disappeared into the woods, but Cole Blackwater knew they were not gone, not yet.

He opened his eyes and breathed deeply.

He turned the ignition over and the Toyota roared back to life, and with it the Eagles at full blast. Cole hit pause, extracted the CD, and inserted Ian Tyson. *Cowboyography.* Singing along, Cole checked his mirror, looked over his shoulder, swung into the eastbound lane, and drove back toward Oracle.

13

If Dale van Stempvort didn't kill Mike Barnes, who did? Two names struck him as obvious. George or Deborah Cody.

As he drove back to Oracle he considered, as Sergeant Reimer had, means, motive, and opportunity. George Cody had a clear motive. Mike Barnes had been boning his wife. That flagrant act must have stuck in George's considerable craw.

Cole thought of his own infidelity and wondered, had murder ever been on Jennifer's mind? Likely. And he guessed that it still was.

George also had the means to kill Mike Barnes; he could certainly swing a bat.

Finally, George Cody had the opportunity. Had he not been absent from his usual duties behind the bar on the night that Mike Barnes was killed?

Deborah Cody? She had motive: she was a woman scorned, though from Cole's perspective she didn't seem all that broken up about it. Maybe she was just the kind of woman who, even in the throes of murderous rage, took time out to hit on her customers.

Opportunity? Who knew Deborah's whereabouts that night? Not Cole. And means? Hard to tell. What about that bruise on her hand? Maybe she injured herself in a struggle with Barnes. Her arms looked strong. She could likely swing a crowbar or pipe wrench well enough.

Which of the two had more reason to want Barnes dead? Or did they do it together as a weird way of making amends to one another? Cole shook his head and frowned. That was too strange to contemplate.

The highway sign read "Oracle, next exit." Now what? Go back to the Rim Rock? Not with his amateur assessment of Deborah and George Cody weighing on his mind.

No, he needed someplace quiet where he could think and stay out of trouble while he tied up these loose ends. He stopped at a gas station to fill up and called Peggy McSorlie to tell her he was coming back.

"You can stay with us, Cole."

"After all the trouble I've caused, you want me at your place?" Cole was genuinely touched.

"You haven't caused us any trouble, Cole."

"OK, but aggravation. Now I'm leaving, now I'm staying."

"I'm just glad you're back, Cole. Come and stay with us. It's quiet. You and I can talk things over more easily out here."

A few nights of peace and quiet would help him think through this whole mess. "OK," he agreed, "I'll come out later this afternoon. I want to follow up a few leads around town first."

"OK, stay safe."

"I will," he said, despite not having the foggiest idea how to accomplish that.

He hung up the phone, filled the truck, and drove downtown to have some lunch and think. He sat down in a café on Main Street to mull things over.

He realized that he didn't have the slightest notion where to start with his so-called private investigation. Nothing in his life had prepared him for this. Sure, he had done his share of research, using the Freedom of Information Act, into environmental crimes committed by big corporate players. He requested correspondence and documentation of environmental misdeeds, sorted through the blacked-out sections of thousands of pages of information, and pieced together what was often, at best, a sketchy story.

No, he needed to find someone who knew what they were doing. Someone really good at digging, at getting at the story behind the story.

Anybody but her.

But he couldn't think of anybody else. She really was the best. At that.

"Sweet mother of pearl," he muttered aloud, picked up his cell, and called directory assistance.

"*Edmonton Journal*," he said. Two calls later he had Nancy's cell number. He stared at his phone for a full minute, weighing the pros and cons.

"You are such a pussy," he said, loudly enough that other customers in the bagel shop turned to look at him. He ignored them.

He dialled.

"Nancy Webber," came the familiar voice.

"It's Cole."

The line went dead.

"You are such a b—" But he bit his tongue, grimacing, evoking further glances of sympathy and condemnation from fellow customers.

He dialled again.

"What?"

"Don't hang up."

"Why the fuck shouldn't I?"

The woman could make a sailor blush. "We need to talk. Dale is innocent."

The line went dead.

He took a deep breath in and exhaled loudly through pursed lips.

He dialled again.

"Flunked out as an activist and a consultant, and trying on the PI hat now, Cole?"

"Try just for a second to act like an adult, Nancy, and listen."

Now it was Webber's turn to breathe. "Speak," she finally said.

"I talked with Sergeant Reimer this morning."

"So did I."

"Could you try just shutting up for a minute, Nancy, and listen?"

"I'm listening."

"I spoke with Reimer. She told me that they still don't have confirmation of a murder weapon. So why do they have Dale locked up? I think they're jumping the gun." He stopped and waited for her reaction.

"Go on," was all he got.

"Don't you think it's strange that they would lock someone up for murder without having a murder weapon?"

"Cole, this isn't a game of Clue. It's not like you have to say 'the butler did it in the dining room with the candlestick.' The Mounties know what they are doing."

Cole shook his head. "Since when did you become such a fan of authority? Didn't you once tell me that a good reporter never trusts anyone?"

"I was talking about you, dick-head."

"Maybe so," he said. "But I think a healthy dose of cynicism right now might get you a front page story, and might help keep an innocent man out of jail."

"My activist reporter days are long gone, Cole."

"Don't blame me."

"I do blame you, Cole, and don't try to pretend I shouldn't."

"Listen Nancy, I didn't ask for this mess. I didn't go looking for it. And I sure as shooting didn't expect to find you here in the middle of it. But here I am. And here you are. And however you might feel about me, this is what we've both got to work with. Maybe we should start working together."

"You must be out of your mind. Have you been smoking weed out there in lotus land? There is no way in hell I'm going to be caught dead working with you. If you were the last source for a story left on earth, I wouldn't print a word that you said."

Cole smiled thinly. "I get the picture, Webber. That's fine, have it your way."

"I will, thank you."

"I just thought that you might be interested in some insider info on the Eastern Slopes Conservation Group."

Nancy was silent. He could hear her brain at work. "Now I'm suddenly going to trust you?"

"I'm not saying I want to go on record, Nancy. Just deep background."

Silence again. "What have you got?"

"Let's meet and talk."

"Not in a blue moon. Not if you were the last source for a story on earth." She hung up.

Anger heated his veins. Hard to believe that at one time he would have given up so much to be with her. Did, in fact. He put his elbows on the table and held his head in his hands.

"Do you want some more coffee, sir?" asked the waitress.

"What time do you serve alcohol here?" he asked.

"Eleven AM."

"And what time is it now?"

His phone rang. The call display showed the number was blocked.

He ignored the waitress, who retreated to another table. "Blackwater."

It was Nancy. "Four o'clock at the Legion Hall."

"OK." And the line went dead.

Of course she had every reason to hate his guts. But she had a particular way of expressing it that left nothing to chance.

He paid his bill and walked out into the spring sunshine. The town looked as it had just a few days earlier. A neatly laid out Main Street: false fronts, red brick buildings. Trees in planters. In the summer there would be flowers hanging from the lampposts in baskets. Except now, the Cardinal Divide that ran between the part of the community that resisted the dominant industrial paradigm and the part that embraced it had split open, as visibly, he imagined, as the fracture in Mike Barnes' head.

He had a couple of hours to kill before meeting Nancy. He could drive out to the McSorlie ranch and stow his gear, but that meant an hour of driving back and forth, and he had had enough of back and forth for one day. Instead he strolled down Main Street toward the cop shop. Sergeant Reimer might be happy to know he was back in town.

There was no media presence as he approached the RCMP detachment. Inside he asked to see Sergeant Reimer.

A few minutes passed before the doors to the back office opened and Sergeant Reimer appeared, along with a man dressed in Docker pants and a cheap polo shirt. Cole heard the word "defence" used a couple of times before the young man left by the front door.

"Didn't expect to see you again so soon, Mr. Blackwater."

"I just can't enough of this place."

Reimer smiled.

"I'm not heading back to Vancouver."

"Changed your mind, did you?"

"Something like that. I decided to stay and try and help my client stop the mine, despite this unfortunate event."

"I assume when you say client, you're not referring to Dale van Stempvort."

"As I told you, Dale was never my client."

"Well, you're free to stay in Oracle as long as you like, and as long as your presence here doesn't interfere with our continued investigation."

Cole smiled. "Thanks. Nice to be made welcome."

The sergeant turned to go. "Sergeant," said Cole. She stopped and looked at him. "Any word on the results of the tests on the murder weapon?"

Reimer's smile faded. She turned and closed the door behind her.

Cole left through the front door. The young man wearing a polo shirt paced the parking lot while he spoke on his telephone. Cole waited for the man to hang up. It took some time. When he finally hung up, he shook his head and exhaled with vigour.

"Tough day?" called Cole.

The young man looked up, suspicious. "It's just fine, thanks."

"Doesn't look like it. Fight with the wife?"

"Boss."

"Tough. Who do you work for?"

"I'm with Legal Aid. I've got one hell of a case on my hands."

Cole smiled and walked toward the man. "I'm Cole Blackwater," he said, and extended his hand.

The young man shook it. His grip was firm and Cole winced. "Sorry," he said.

"It's OK, force of habit. I got in a fight last night and bashed up my hand pretty good."

Like Cole, the lawyer wore a few extra pounds around the middle. He was five ten with a youthful, almost boyish, face with a conservative haircut, and soft, white skin.

"What's your name?" asked Cole.

"Perry Gilbert. I'm out of the Legal Aid office in Red Deer."

"And you're on Dale van Stempvort's case?"

"That's right. Who are you again?"

"I'm Cole Blackwater. I was hired by Peggy McSorlie and the ES-COG to help develop a plan to stop the mine at Cardinal Divide."

"Lots of luck. Especially now," he said, and looked genuinely sad.

"It's not over 'til it's over."

"I'd say this one is over."

"Not very optimistic for a defence attorney. How long have you been at this?"

"Three years," said Gilbert.

"How many cases have you handled?"

"Fifty, maybe sixty."

"How many murders?"

"This is my first," he said. "But I've got lots of help."

Cole looked around.

"In Red Deer," added Gilbert.

"Right. The phone call."

Gilbert shrugged.

"Did Dale van Stempvort tell you he killed Mike Barnes?"

"Look, I don't think I should be talking with you about this."

Now it was Cole's turn to shrug. "Suit yourself. But your client's already been convicted by this town, and I just thought you'd like to compare notes."

Gilbert looked down at his shoes. He kicked a stone across the parking lot and it hit the tire of an RCMP cruiser. "Guess that couldn't hurt."

"Let's take a walk," suggested Cole.

They strolled off Main Street and into the older residential neighbourhood adjacent to downtown, turning up Fifth Street toward Andy's bar. Cole asked, "What do you think of this Sergeant Reimer? The one who's leading the investigation?"

Gilbert shrugged. "Seems competent enough. She's just the local Horseman. They sent a team in from Edmonton yesterday. You know, a detective and a scene-of-crime team. They only stayed the day. Figured it was cut and dried. They headed back to Edmonton with the forensics."

"And now it's in Reimer's hands?"

"Looks like."

Cole shook his head.

"What?"

"Just feels wrong to me. To leave the whole thing up to a bunch of backwoods cops."

"They all get trained in the same place."

"Yeah, but when was the last time anybody in this detachment had to handle this sort of case?"

"Maybe never. But they move around a lot."

Cole looked at Gilbert. "You have faith in them?"

"I didn't say that."

They walked along the quiet streets of town. Gilbert changed the direction of the conversation. "So the first time you met my client was on Tuesday?"

"That's right, at Peggy McSorlie's ranch."

"And the following morning you and he argued about the newspaper quote that appeared in the *Red Deer Advocate*, the one the RCMP suggest establishes motive?"

"That's right, he drove me around and we argued about the wisdom of saying such a stupid thing to a newspaper reporter." Cole snarled the word "stupid." "At the time I never imagined the RCMP would use it as grounds to put the man in jail."

"So what you're telling me," said Gilbert, "is that Mr. van Stempvort didn't call the reporter but the reporter called him?"

"That's what I'm telling you," said Cole.

"And that means that someone else who was in that meeting on Tuesday called the reporter to tip him off?"

Cole was getting frustrated. "That's what I said."

"I'm just getting up to speed on this case, Mr. Blackwater," said Gilbert. "I'm trying to understand all the angles."

Cole nodded.

"You think that the environmental organization you represent has a mole?"

"Look, I don't represent them. I'm a strategy consultant, and the answer to your question is yes, I think someone inside the organization leaked information."

Perry Gilbert walked at a brisk pace. Cole figured Gilbert was an athlete in high school, whose law degree and career as a PD kept him off the track or court.

"Whoever tipped off the reporter," said Cole, "probably tipped off Mike Barnes. Barnes had a lot to say. He knew I was working for ESCOG and he still wanted to talk. Maybe Barnes planted the mole himself."

Gilbert thought about this. "Maybe he learned about you some other way?"

"Maybe so. Why?"

"Well, I'm only guessing, and really, but was Dale van Stempvort set up?"

Cole stopped walking, waited until Gilbert stopped too. "How do you figure?"

He shrugged with one shoulder: "I don't know. I'm just guessing."

"Well, guess out loud."

"Somebody infiltrates ESCOG. They'd have to do it a while ago, right, because the environmentalists won't let just anybody come to their top secret strategy meeting, right?"

"Right," said Cole, thinking hard.

"So the infiltrator calls the reporter from the *Red Deer Advocate* after the meeting and suggests that Dale van Stempvort is the leader of the group. The reporter, knowing that Mr. van Stempvort is a hothead, calls him up for a quote, and gets a doozy."

Cole listened and nodded.

"The next day the quote appears in the newspaper. Months of tension boil to the surface as environmentalists are pitted against the mining company in a battle for Cardinal Divide." Gilbert ran his hand across the space in front of him as if outlining a newspaper headline.

"You've been watching too many movies," said Cole.

Gilbert was on a roll. "Maybe. So the newspaper story runs and everybody now looks at Dale van Stempvort. He becomes a known commodity. Wing nut, eco-terrorist. And that's when our man ..."

"Or woman," Cole said.

"Or woman," added Gilbert, "decides to make his or her move."

"So she calls up Barnes and asks for a meeting that night and drives out to the mine and clubs him on the head with a piece of drill steel," said Cole.

"Knowing full well that with the temperatures running hot, the heat will come down on Dale van Stempvort. Maybe he calls up Mr. van Stempvort and invites him to a meeting at the mine that night so that his vehicle is seen at the scene of the crime."

"Now you're sounding a little thin," said Cole.

Gilbert shrugged again. He turned and began to walk. "Look," he said "it's not really my job to find out who killed Mike Barnes ..."

"Me neither!" said Cole.

"My job *is* to defend Mr. van Stempvort, and I've got to consider what else might have happened that night."

"Fair enough," said Cole. "And my job is to save the Cardinal Divide."

"That's right, which you can't do if Dale van Stempvort is convicted. So we had better come up with some other possibilities for who caused the untimely demise of Mike Barnes."

"Can't argue there," said Cole. "And on that note, I should tell you about another little piece of information I came across."

Cole told him about Deborah Cody's affair with Mike Barnes, what Cole believed was a scrap of paper with damning evidence on it, the confrontation between the couple, George's absence from the bar on Tuesday night, and Deborah's bruised hand.

"This is starting to sound like a Dick Tracy comic," said Perry Gilbert with a grin.

Cole smiled weakly. "I don't do hats," he said.

It was after four when Cole and Perry Gilbert walked back to Main Street. Cole's head hurt and the stitches in his cheek itched and if Nancy Webber slapped him again, he'd have to slap her back. The lawyer said he would keep Cole in the loop. Perry Gilbert's cooperation provided Cole with access to helpful information. Gilbert had some plausible theories about how Mike Barnes had really been killed. What was more, he actually believed Dale van Stempvort was innocent, which was more than could be said for Cole Blackwater, at least at first blush.

And now? Was Dale innocent? Cole mulled this question over as he walked to the Legion. He was certainly leaning that way, otherwise he wouldn't be here. But why had van Stempvort fallen into the trap so easily? He didn't strike Cole as a scared rabbit. Who had set the trap?

Cole walked up the front steps of the Legion Hall.

Oracle's Legion was like a hundred Canadian Legion Halls. Administrative offices and meeting rooms were upstairs as well as a large assembly room where, once or twice a year, the community's vets assembled to remember fallen comrades. Cole had been in the High River Legion Hall almost as often as he'd been in Prize Fight, at least until he was a teenager and able to choose where he spent his time.

The social club downstairs served beer and light snacks to vets and the public alike. That's where Cole found Nancy. Seated at a table in a dark corner of the room, past the pool table and toward the emergency exit (which Cole noted) Nancy sipped coffee from a porcelain cup. As Cole scanned the room, alarm bells went off left, right, and centre. A table of three men drank beer and smoked cigarettes and eyed him suspiciously as he walked past, as did two vets playing pool. Now Cole knew why Nancy chose the venue.

He sat down at the table across from her. She wore a black leather jacket and blue jeans which fit her very well. A classic white button-down shirt completed her ensemble. Her black hair hung loose and fell over the shoulders of the leather coat. He smelled a familiar fragrance. He damned himself for being so weak and pushed the arousal from his mind.

"Thanks for agreeing to meet," he said cordially.

She stared at him. "I haven't agreed to anything."

"Let me tell you what I know," he said, trying to start off on the right foot.

Cole ordered draft beer and he began. First he told her about his meeting with Barnes, and about the fight in the bar. She sat expressionless.

He told her about George and Deborah Cody, and Deborah's affair with Mike Barnes. He told her about the mole within ESCoG and the suspicion that whoever leaked information to the media might have set up Dale van Stempvort, or worked with someone who set Dale up to take the fall for the murder. He didn't mention Perry Gilbert. No need for Cole to divulge all his sources. That was all he had right now. It was thin. But it was his.

Throughout his explanation, Nancy sat and stared at him, drank the last of her coffee, and looked sour. Her beauty had become overshadowed as bitterness had seeped into her every pore. Cole looked at this woman who had once been so lovely, and was sad.

"I don't know what I ever saw in you, Cole," she finally said. Cole was startled to hear her express his own thoughts. He was silent. "I can't imagine why I ever trusted you. I was young and stupid and ambitious and thought that you, somehow, were part of the ladder I could climb to success. That's the way it is in Ottawa. I know that now. Snakes and Ladders. With greased rungs. In real life, you can fall off the board," she said, and fingered the rim of the cup. "You were the greased rung for me, Cole. You were the one wrong move. You were the snake."

"Then I guess we're even," he finally said.

He saw it coming. She had to let go of the coffee cup to swing and he was ready for her. He blocked her hand with his arm and shoulder. None too gently. The sound of her smack against his own leather jacket was loud. The few heads in the Legion turned to look and conversations hushed.

"You're a bastard, Cole. You know that." Despite his earlier notion that he might strike back, he had no desire to do so. He could see tears in Nancy's eyes. If she knew that her eyes betrayed her, she didn't let on. She rubbed her hand on her leg, trying to dull the sting.

"Yes," said Cole. "I know it. I've heard it enough to make me believe it." Neither Cole nor Nancy returned the stares that the patrons directed their way, and conversations finally started again.

"You ruined my career, and you have the audacity to tell me that we're even."

"I ruined my own career too. I guess that's what I meant."

"Don't play cute with me, Blackwater."

"ok, Nancy." He looked her in the eyes. "I'm really just trying to say that I'm sorry."

She was silent. The tears that had welled in the corner of her eyes now spilled down her cheeks and she wiped them away with the back of her sore hand.

"I really am sorry."

"It's too late for that. You lied to me. You took advantage of our relationship and lied and I printed it, and the truth came out, and I got fired for it."

"It was my fault," he said. "No ifs, ands, or buts about it."

"I got fired from the best job in the business, Cole. I will never get to report from Ottawa again. Do you understand that? I can't go back. It doesn't work that way in my business. In your business, people can come and go. In mine, once you're gone, you're gone. For good. I had to move to fucking Saskatchewan to find a job as a reporter. Do you know what goes on in Saskatchewan? Not a fucking thing. Nothing happens. I was the senior parliamentary reporter for *The Globe and Mail* one day, and the next day I'm covering agricultural fair visits by the deputy agricultural minister in one of the least populated places on the planet." She shook her head, the tracks of her tears obvious across her face. She wore no make-up to smudge.

"What do you want me to say, Nancy?"

"There is nothing you can say."

"I know it was my fault. I know I was the one who made the mistake. It was my lie."

"But I printed it, is that what you're going to say?"

He was thinking it. She printed it, and her editor didn't check it. But he simply shook his head.

"I've paid for this mistake, Nancy. Big time paid. I lost my wife."

"Don't give me that shit. You lost your wife long before we started fucking."

"I lost my little girl. I lost my job. My dream job. I had to leave Ottawa too. It's not been easy for me in Vancouver."

"Am I supposed to shed tears for you, Cole?"

"I don't want your sympathy," he said, his temper on the rise.

"Good."

"What I want," he said, breathing out through clenched teeth, "is your cooperation. And for you to stop hitting me."

Nancy smiled. It was the first time he'd seen her smile since before his moment of indiscretion more than four years ago. It changed her face. The bitterness drained, if only for a moment, and once again she was impossibly beautiful. It lasted only a moment.

They sat in silence.

"Truce?" he said.

"For what purpose?"

"To get to the bottom of who really killed Mike Barnes."

She shook her head. "Dale van Stempvort killed Mike Barnes."

"Maybe so. But I'd like to know for sure before he's condemned to prison for the rest of his life, and before the Cardinal Divide is handed over to the coal miners because of it."

"Is that what this is about? You trying to save some wilderness for the grizzly bears?"

"What did you think it was about, Nancy. It's what I do. It's what I've always done."

"I thought that maybe it was about people this time, not just about some God-forsaken valley with a few grizzly bears in it."

"It's about both. It's about Dale and about the ESCOG and about this stupid town, and about the Cardinal Divide. It's about Mike Barnes, and his family. It's about lies and deception," he said.

"And redemption?"

"I don't believe in redemption," he said. "There's no such thing."

She watched him.

"Deep background only," she said, finally.

"Yes, deep background only."

"If my editors knew I was talking to you, I'd be writing for the *Red Deer Advocate* before the week was out."

"Funny you should say that," said Cole Blackwater.

The drive back to Peggy McSorlie's ranch was longer than he remembered. The road wove in and out of the woods, across meadows and a few clearcuts, and past natural gas wells. He had a lot of time to think.

Nancy agreed to talk with the *Red Deer Advocate* reporter who started the whole mess to discover his source within ESCoG. Cole reasoned that if they knew who tipped him off, they might be able to determine if Dale was being framed. Nancy thought it was a longshot, but saw no harm in a simple conversation between peers.

She also agreed to talk with Deborah and George Cody. Cole warned her that one, or maybe both of them, might have split Mike Barnes' skull open with a baseball bat. Nancy thought that talking with them as part of a background story on the man's life in Oracle was a good place to start.

Cole's job was to attempt to find out the mole's identity from inside ESCoG. They agreed to talk the next day.

"I'm not doing this for your cause, Blackwater," Nancy said as they rose from the table at the Legion. "And I'm not doing this for you. I'm doing this for a story. That's all this is to me," she said.

What she meant was, that's all *you* are to me. A path to a story. Cole figured that's all he had ever been. But he didn't really want to believe it, given the years they had spent together sneaking around a city that didn't tolerate sneaking.

He was weary from the day, and drove carefully along the gravel road toward the McSorlie place. There were so many loose ends and dead ends and fatal ends that Cole could hardly keep them straight. He wasn't even certain what he was trying do to. He had better figure that out first before he set off on some wild goose chase.

His conversation with the lawyer from Legal Aid nagged at him. Perry Gilbert said that they ought to try and figure out who might have tipped the *Red Deer Advocate* reporter. Was the mole working individually, or with someone else in the community? And if so, was that person, or those people, trying to frame Dale van Stempvort for murder, or merely drive a wedge into the community for some other purpose? To make sure the mine was dug.

Then he thought about Jim Jones. Was it only two days ago that he and Jones had talked? When Jones speculated that the mine was merely a paper tiger? Cole thought about that, and how Mike Barnes had said it was dangerous for Oracle to depend on the mine so heavily for its economic future. Dangerous was not a word to be used lightly by an educated man like Barnes. He had written his dissertation on the social and economic implications for communities like Oracle when a company decides to pull up stakes. Mike Barnes knew what it was like to work for projects that shut down.

College boy, thought Cole Blackwater. Mike Barnes certainly was that.

Cole rubbed his head. Where had he heard that before?

14

Cole Blackwater opened his eyes, awakened by the invigorating smells and sounds of bacon frying, bread toasting, eggs sizzling, and coffee perking. He looked at his cell-phone for the time, and groaned. It was 6:10 AM. That's life on a ranch. He shook his head to clear the cobwebs, pulled his jeans on, and buttoned his shirt.

Gord McSorlie sat at the kitchen table reading the newspaper and drinking coffee. Peggy McSorlie stood at the stove. She of-fered Cole coffee, for which he was deeply grateful.

"How'd you sleep?" Peggy asked.

"Like a baby."

She smiled. "I'm sorry to hear that. You were up every two hours?"

"I didn't hear any crying," said Gord between sips of coffee. His eyes didn't move from the paper in front of him.

"It is a stupid saying, isn't it?" said Cole, adding cream to his cup. "But I sure did need that good sleep."

"It's the country air," said Peggy, and handed her husband a plate of food.

"This looks great," Gord said, and kissed her on the cheek as she served him.

"Are you hungry, Cole?"

"I'll start with coffee and work my way up," he said, and raised his cup in a toast to Peggy.

A few minutes later the McSorlie boys appeared and in a whirl-wind downed their breakfast, kissed their mother and headed out the door with backpacks across their shoulders, walked to the end of the drive to await a ride that would take them to a basketball tournament in Red Deer. Cole watched them go, and thought about Sarah.

Breakfast finished and the dishes cleared, Gord headed to the barn to begin his day's work. Peggy and Cole sat across the long, wooden table in the large, open kitchen and lingered over another cup of coffee.

Fully caffeinated, Cole said, "So, now what?"

"I guess we get back to work," said Peggy. "Where do we start?"

"Let's review what we know."

"About the mine, or about the murder?" she asked, and took a sharp breath when she said "murder."

"Both," said Cole. "One is so mixed up with the other that I don't think we can untangle them."

"You first, Cole."

Cole started. He told her everything he knew. Peggy alternately looked down at her coffee or straight at Cole as he dumped the information out in a tangled mess for them to sort through. George and Deborah Cody, her affair with Barnes, his absence, and her bruises. He recounted his conversation with Perry Gilbert and his theory that the mole inside ESCOG might have set Dale up, or worked with someone who did. He told her what Jim Jones uncovered in his review of the yet unseen draft of the Environmental Assessment.

He told her everything, except, of course, about Nancy. Peggy didn't need to know about her. Not yet.

"I still can't believe that someone is spying on us," she said when he was done.

"What else could account for the call Dale got from a reporter that night after our meeting?"

Peggy shook her head, more in disappointment than in disbelief. "Who could it be?"

"Is there a new person in the group? Or someone who is overly enthusiastic or just plain suspicious?"

Peggy thought for a moment. "I don't know, Cole. I'll have to give that some consideration. It would be too easy to blurt out names. That's what got Dale into this trouble."

Cole nodded in agreement.

"Is there someone in the community who could be behind this?" Cole asked.

"Are you asking me to say who I think wanted Mike Barnes dead, or who I think wanted to make our group look like crazies?"

"I don't know. Both."

"Mike Barnes seemed like a nice enough man. None of us had a lot of affection for him, but nobody I know, including Dale, wanted the man dead. Maybe on the first plane back to Toronto, but not in a coffin," Peggy grimaced at the thought. "Who would want to make us look foolish? Well, that list is pretty long, Cole."

"Can we come up with a short list?"

"Any number of business owners, including George and Deborah Cody. Their business caters mostly to people in town who work for the mine as contractors or short-term workers, though I bet they'd do as well if tourism took off and Oracle became a gateway to Jasper, as we propose. Most of the businesses on Main Street are for the mine and against our efforts. The Chamber of Commerce. The local union. The Downtown Improvement Association. You name it, Cole. We're up against serious odds."

Cole jotted notes in a pocket notebook, hoping to keep it all straight.

"What about people at the mine itself?"

"Well, Mike Barnes didn't wish us any luck, but he was always cordial. Which is more than I can say for others there."

"What do you mean?"

"Mike Barnes sat beside me at a public meeting once. We disagreed on most things, but we did so with respect. Other people in the room jeered and cat-called during our presentation. As I recall the assistant mine manager was there too. Hank Henderson. Not the friendliest apple in the barrel. He scowled at us through the whole meeting. Scowled at Mike Barnes, too."

"College boy!" That's where he'd heard it.

Peggy raised her eyebrows. "Not our man, Hank. He's strictly a learn-on-the-job type."

Cole frowned. "I met Henderson the other day. Wednesday, I guess. He was upset about Mike Barnes, called him 'college boy' like it was the worst name he could think of. Not the sort of thing you'd expect from a man in a position of authority, talking about his own boss to a complete stranger. He really spit those words out, made it sound as if going to college was a detriment to the job of managing a mine."

"In this town that might be the case," sighed Peggy.

"Well, whatever the case may be, I'd say that Mike Barnes was not Hank Henderson's favourite person. What do you know about him?"

"He's lived in Oracle all of his life, started working in the mill down in the valley, made his way up from the floor to the offices where he became a production manager. About fifteen years ago he was hired by the mine to be the mill foreman. I can't remember when he became assistant mine manager. Before Barnes was hired he acted as mine manager for a year or so. The rumour is that he was pretty busted up when the top job didn't go to him."

"Is he the acting manager now?"

"I don't know."

"Stands to reason."

"They'd want someone with experience in that post while this whole mess gets sorted out."

Cole was silent for a moment.

"What are you thinking, Cole?"

"Was Hank Henderson angry enough to kill Mike Barnes?"

Peggy shook her head and rubbed her eyes. "I can't believe we're drawing up a list of murder suspects."

"Still, Hank Henderson could have planted our snitch. And he could have engineered it to frame Dale, don't you think?"

"Hank *could* have done it. He knows just about everybody in town."

"Henderson asked if I was 'that reporter' when I met him at the mine the other day," said Cole, recollecting. I felt stupid enough about that cover, and when he said it, I got the distinct feeling that he knew it was a hoax. I wonder...."

"What?"

"Did Henderson know who I was?" Cole smiled and shook his head. "I'm beginning to think my cover was blown pretty early."

"What if he did?"

"Well, he might have sent those goons to The Quarry to teach me a lesson."

Peggy's face fell. "My goodness, this is a rough piece of business," she said.

"It certainly is," said Cole, and felt the gash on his cheek. The swelling was down and it had started to heal.

Cole changed tracks. "What do you think about Perry Gilbert's idea that van Stempvort was called out to the mine for a meeting in order to place him at the scene of the crime?"

"Can we ask Dale?"

"We should probably get Gilbert to do it."

Peggy rose and refilled their coffee cups. "Thanks," Cole said, and added cream. "I don't know about you, but my head hurts."

"Mine too."

Cole looked at his notes. "The first thing we do is identify the mole."

Peggy sighed.

Stephen Legault

"We've got to do it, Peggy. That person might lead us to Mike Barnes' killer."

"I know we have to do it. It just makes me so sad."

"It pisses me off," said Cole. "Which is why I want to find this person." He took a sharp breath. "Can you draw up a list of people we should talk to?"

"You mean interrogate?"

"I'll be gentle."

"I have a hard time believing that," Peggy said with a wink.

Cole let that slide off. Sure he looked rough, but he could go easy when he had to, couldn't he?

"What are we looking for?" asked Peggy.

"Someone who joined the group in the last six months. Someone fairly knowledgeable about the mine and its operations. Someone who's enthusiastic."

"Why enthusiastic?"

"To cover their deception with an excess of exuberance."

"I'll think about it."

"There's one more thing that bugs me," said Cole, and stared out the window into the woods.

"What's that?"

"Before I left, Mike Barnes told me he had another appointment after me, something that came up late in the day. He pointed to his Day-Timer, which tells me that he wrote that appointment in his book. But the Mounties didn't mention anything about that, did they?"

Peggy shrugged. "Not that I've heard."

"No, me neither. I wonder if Dale's name is in that book."

"How are we going to find out?"

"Ask him, I guess."

Cole got a sense of progress from totting up a to-do list, and for a few hours that morning he felt positive about the whole mess. Peggy agreed to pay him to continue to work on a strategy to stop the mine, and later that morning he spent a couple of hours writing out revised goals and objectives. He downloaded his email on a sluggish dial-up connection, checked the news sites to learn what was being said about the Barnes murder, and even called Sarah, it being Saturday morning.

While he was on the phone with his daughter, Perry Gilbert left a message and invited Cole to call him back. Cole did.

"Can you come to a meeting today, Cole?" Perry Gilbert sounded even younger on the phone than he did in person.

"Sure, who with?"

"Dale van Stempvort."

"How are you going to swing that?"

"I'm his lawyer. I'm inviting you to join me to assist with my research on this case."

"Is that kosher?"

"Depends on who you ask. I've cleared it with the RCMP. They will have an officer in the room with us."

"I'll be there. What time?"

"One. Let's meet at twelve-thirty for a coffee and chat before we go in."

The arrangements made, Cole let Peggy know of this next step and they agreed to share information later that night. Then Cole packed his things and headed back along the winding dusty road to Oracle.

Perry Gilbert was waiting for him when Cole arrived at the bagel shop on Main Street. "Did you know that the family is in town?" Gilbert asked Cole when they sat down with coffees.

"I had no idea."

"They arrived yesterday to take the body back to Toronto."

"Sweet Mother of Theresa."

"You said it," Gilbert sighed. "Wife and two young kids."

Cole shook his head. "The guy was cheating on them, you know."

"You told me."

"Not just a one night thing, but an affair."

"It tears families apart."

"Don't I know it," mumbled Cole.

"I want to ask Dale if he had an appointment with Barnes that night," Cole said.

"I don't know if that's such a hot idea. If he says that he had an appointment, then it establishes him at the scene."

"The RCMP already have him on the scene. They say they have his truck there that night."

"Yeah, but that likely won't stand up in court."

"No?"

"Too many S10s in this area. I looked it up. There are almost a dozen in and around Oracle. Without a licence plate that won't stick."

Cole was impressed. "But Barnes had an appointment after me. He wrote it down in his book."

"Yeah, I wanted to ask you about that. The RCMP told me that the calendar for the day was empty. Even you weren't on it."

"I was on it. I saw my name written down."

"Well, it wasn't on his secretary's computer. The calendar was blank."

"That's because he used an old fashioned Day-Timer. An appointment book, with pages made of paper, you know? Didn't Tracey tell them?"

Gilbert scratched his head. "You're kidding. Paper? Wow. I wonder if they even asked."

"I kid you not. They guy said it was cause his father used to give him his old Day-Timers."

Gilbert looked at him. "You guys became quite good buds, didn't you?" He smiled and said, "The Mounties haven't said anything about it. I don't think they've found a handwritten Day-Timer."

Now it was Cole's turn to say, "You're kidding me."

Perry smiled. "I kid you not."

They walked to the RCMP station and arrived just before 1 PM. Sergeant Reimer met them in the waiting area.

"I want to establish the ground rules for this meeting, Mr. Blackwater. You are here as an invited guest of the defence council. You are also an important witness in this investigation. I caution you not to interfere with the proceedings here. Do I make myself clear?"

Cole nodded. "Clear."

"Let's go. Mr. van Stempvort is waiting for us."

They followed her into a room with a long metal table at its centre and straight-backed chairs arranged around it. Dale van Stempvort sat with his back to the door. He didn't turn his head when they entered. Constable Paulson stood against the wall opposite Dale, and left after Sergeant Reimer entered the room.

Reimer sat at one end of the table. Cole and Perry Gilbert sat across from van Stempvort. Dale was pale and wore a couple of days' growth of beard. His eyes lacked the fire that had troubled Cole. He appeared to be puzzled to see Cole. His brow wrinkled, and then he looked angry.

"You know Mr. Blackwater," said Perry Gilbert.

"What's he doing here?" asked van Stempvort, cutting to the chase.

"I've asked him to join us, Dale, because I think he might be able to help us clear your name."

Dale regarded Cole coldly. Finally Dale said, "Have you changed your mind about me, Blackwater?"

"I don't think you killed Mike Barnes, if that's what you mean."

"And what about everything else? The gas wells, and the tree spiking?"

"Right now that doesn't seem so important."

"It matters to me."

"Well you're just going to have to live with it, aren't you?" said Cole, raising his voice.

Perry interrupted them: "Gentlemen, let's play nice, if only for the sake of the good sergeant. Cole here was likely the last person to meet with Mike Barnes before the murder. He wants to get to the bottom of this to help stop the mine," said Gilbert. "Surely that is in both of your interests?"

"His only interest is protecting his reputation," said Dale sourly.

Cole laughed. "If I had one to protect."

Sergeant Reimer spoke. "It doesn't appear as if Mr. van Stempvort wants your help, Mr. Blackwater. I think it's time for you to leave."

Cole shook his head. "You are such a stubborn prick," he said. "Begging your pardon, ma'am."

"Wait!" Dale called. "Wait," he said more quietly. "Let him stay for this meeting. I guess it can't hurt."

"Nice to be wanted," said Cole, sitting back down.

"Let's review some things, shall we?" said Gilbert, opening his notebook.

Dale answered Gilbert's questions in a calm, flat voice.

"Nobody but the cows saw me on Tuesday night, I'm afraid," he repeated.

"You didn't leave your ranch that evening?" questioned Perry.

"No."

"Didn't travel to the mine for a meeting?"

"No. I was home all evening."

"Did you make any telephone calls?"

Dale glanced at Cole. "No. No calls. Not even to a reporter."

"OK, Mr. van Stempvort. Let's talk about what the Crown calls your motive. You're on record as saying that you would do anything to stop the mine. The Crown seems to think that this includes killing Mr. Barnes. Can you tell me what you meant by that statement?"

"Only that I would do anything legal to stop the mine."

"But you understand how that sort of statement must sound coming on the eve of a man's murder. The murder of a man who was controlling the development of this new mine."

"It's a turn of phrase and nothing more. Just a saying. Like 'happy as a clam' or 'easy as pie.'"

Cole shook his head, "Come on, Dale. You knew that sort of phrase was incendiary in a place like Oracle and that's why you said it."

"Sure, but that doesn't make me guilty of murder."

"The Crown seems to think it does," said Perry, and cast a sideways glance at Sergeant Reimer.

"I may not want that mine to be built, but I didn't kill Mike Barnes. That would be stupid. He was a company hack. There's an endless supply of MBAs to replace him. The company will just send in another guy to see this project to completion." Dale's face went red and he spoke through clenched teeth.

"What if Mike Barnes' job wasn't to build the mine, but to kill it?" Cole's question hung in the room.

No one spoke. Through the single window set high on the wall, the sun caught dust motes as they drifted through the room. Traffic on Main Street could be heard. Through the closed, barred window Cole could make out the song of a red-winged blackbird.

"What are you talking about?" Dale van Stempvort asked finally. Even Sergeant Reimer became more attentive.

"Mike Barnes was not sent to Oracle to complete the mine. I believe he was sent here to kill it. The man's previous two jobs in the mining sector were to close mines in northern Ontario and northern Manitoba. He wrote his MBA thesis on the very topic. He was a hatchet man."

"So why would they go to all the trouble of making it appear as though they were proceeding with the mine?" asked van Stempvort.

"I don't know. I don't even know if that was what Mike Barnes was really doing. Maybe he was turning over a new leaf. But I do know that he had a history, and it suggests that his presence in town wasn't to ensure that the dominant employer here remained viable."

Dale shook his head. "It fits with one of our suspicions. The coal here isn't as high in value as it is elsewhere, even in the Rockies. And the market is increasingly competitive. I bet the company is planning to create some sort of income fund and sell a stack of trust units in the future mine, and once they've covered all their bases, they'll skip town. They find a more workable project to turn their attention to, use the money they raise on the McLeod River project to finance something in Indonesia or South America, somewhere that they didn't have to follow all the rules we have in Canada." Dale looked at Cole with at least some respect.

"Build the road and even the rail line to make it look like the mine is proceeding and then cut bait and head out of town, leaving five hundred men out of work, and the town reeling from the loss of its biggest employer," added Cole.

"And blame us for it," said Dale.

"That's right," said Cole quickly. "Pin the blame on the local environmentalists so the company could say they tried to build the mine but the tree-huggers and fish kissers got in the way."

"That would make you part of their plan, wouldn't it?" said Dale, with the first smile of the day.

Cole pursed his lips into a smile and nodded, resigned. "I guess it does."

The room was silent as Cole and Dale regarded each other across the table.

"Nice theory, gentlemen. But I want to remind you that Mr. van Stempvort is under arrest for murder," said Reimer. "We're not here to investigate some kind of income trust fraud."

Cole inhaled and was about to retort, but Perry Gilbert silenced him with a hand on his arm and a quick glance. "Dale, you've been in Oracle for a long time," he said.

"Fifteen years now."

"Given this new piece of information, who do you think would want Mr. Barnes dead?"

"What's the current population of Oracle?" he asked, deadpan.

The Sergeant escorted Perry and Cole into her office after the interview with van Stempvort.

"Because you're new to murder investigations, Mr. Gilbert, I am going to remind you that your job is to defend your client against the charges laid, not open your own investigation into murder."

Cole interrupted, "Don't you think someone should actually investigate who killed Mike Barnes?"

"That, Mr. Blackwater, is exactly what the RCMP is doing. We have our suspect behind bars."

"You have a scapegoat behind bars."

"Mr. Blackwater, you are treading on very thin ice right now. I'm warning you for the last time not to interfere with a murder investigation."

Perry Gilbert interrupted. "Can I ask a couple of questions without everybody getting all upset?"

Reimer sat back in her chair. "Ask."

"I'm told that Mr. Barnes kept a handwritten appointment book. Mr. Blackwater says that he saw Mr. Barnes referring to it the afternoon they met. He says he saw his own name in it, and that Mr. Barnes noted that he had another meeting that night, and that it too was written in the journal. Have the RCMP determined the whereabouts of this journal?"

"Mr. Blackwater didn't mention this journal in his first visit to us, but Mr. Barnes' secretary told us about it. She says Mr. Barnes kept it on his desk, and that when she made appointments for him she had to go into his office to check availability and to write the appointments in. She says he often took it with him in the evenings when he left for town."

"Have you found it?"

"No."

"So it's missing?"

"Yes."

Perry sat back in his chair. "Don't you think that's an important piece of evidence?"

"We do, Mr. Gilbert. We're looking for it."

"The murderer's name is likely written in it for all the world to see," said Cole.

"Maybe."

Cole exhaled loudly and sat back too.

"Another question, if I may" said Gilbert, leaning forward. "Have you got the results back from the tests on the possible murder weapons?"

"Not yet," said Reimer.

"What's the hold up? Doesn't this usually only take a day?"

"We have a drill bit with hair, blood, and a trace of bone. That we know for certain. What we don't know is if it's the murder weapon," said Reimer.

"How big a bit?"

"It's a twenty-pound bit used in open-face drilling."

"Fingerprints?"

"None. But it seems likely that the suspect would have used gloves."

"Have you recovered these gloves?"

"We have found a number of pairs of gloves in Mr. van Stempvort's possession that are being tested."

"When will you get the results?"

"Later this week."

"I want to be notified when the results are back, please."

"Yes. Anything else?"

"Where was the drill bit found?" asked Cole.

"It was on the shop floor, just inside the main loading bay for the mill."

"Was there a lot of blood?"

"There was enough."

"I'd like to have a look at the scene, Sergeant. Can you arrange that?" asked Perry Gilbert.

"Sure. There's an officer on the scene. I'll radio him and let him know that you'll be coming. When?"

"This afternoon. I understand that Dale is to be remanded to the provincial facility at Red Deer on Wednesday, and I'd like to clear up any further questions by then."

Wednesday, thought Cole. To the big house on Wednesday.

"Site rules will be in effect, Mr. Perry. You're not to touch anything. Am I understood?" Reimer looked specifically at Cole.

"Understood," said Gilbert. He rose and led Cole to the door.

They agreed to drive to the mine separately and meet at the mill. Cole had to collect a few things from his truck and Gilbert needed to check in with his office. Cole headed down Main Street on foot. It was midafternoon, springtime in Alberta. The sky above was clear and blue, but Cole noticed a faint halo around the sun. Sun dogs were the harbingers of stormy weather. Sometime in the next few days it would rain. Or worse.

Cole saw his truck ten paces ahead when he heard his name spoken. He tensed as he turned, and expected another attack.

"Cole Blackwater," the man repeated.

Who was he? His voice sounded familiar.

"You don't know who I am, do you?"

Cole shrugged, removed his hands from his pockets. The man was of average height and build – Cole guessed welterweight at best – with a face like a basset hound. It was broad daylight on Main Street, but after the week Cole Blackwater had endured in Oracle, he would rather be safe than sorry.

"I know who *you* are, Cole," the man said. He wore a plain brown jacket, clean blue jeans, and a red checked shirt. A notebook was tucked into the breast pocket of his shirt.

"You got me, mister," said Cole, "but if it's all the same to you, I'll be getting along."

"Still playing reporter, Cole?"

"Drewfeld?"

"That's right. Richard Drewfeld, *Red Deer Advocate*."

Cole turned to leave. "I don't have time for games, Mr. Drewfeld."

"You had plenty of time for games four days ago."

"Well, things are more serious now." It was the second time he'd issued that refrain.

"You sure seemed to enjoy games three years ago."

Cole stopped as if he'd hit a wall.

"Not having fun anymore, Mr. Blackwater?"

Cole stood still. His vision narrowed. Things in his peripheral vision dimmed. It was always like this. The adrenaline forced its way through his system, alerting all of his muscles that they would shortly be called into service. His heart beat faster, his lungs expanded, his senses became more acute. It was always like this right before the fight.

Cole took a deep breath and forced his throat open so that when he spoke he wouldn't sound panicked or anxious. "That was a long time ago."

"Not long enough for you to have learned your lesson, obviously." Drewfeld seemed to enjoy this. Baiting him. And Cole was falling for it.

"I've learned to leave the past in the past."

"Apparently not. Lying seems to be the one thing that you're good at Mr. Blackwater, of Blackwater Strategies, West Cordova Street, Vancouver. I checked you out. Do you think I'm stupid? Do you think that because I'm a rural newspaper man that I don't have access to sources? After I tracked you down online — it was very clever of you to take your web site offline last week when you put on your disguise — I tracked down much of your information through provincial registries. After that it took me five minutes to find out that Blackwater Strategies has all of two paying clients. Two. What kind of strategist are you?"

Cole smiled. "I'm focused," he said. If Drewfeld didn't know that his second client, a small First Nations group on the central coast of BC, hadn't actually paid him in a year, he wasn't going to point that out to him.

"You're a flop, Blackwater. Three, four years ago you were a rock star. Big ego. Big name. Always on TV. Fighting the good fight. Then you fucked up, didn't you? Lied to *The Globe and Mail*. Got caught. Got fired."

"I've paid for that," said Cole.

"Not dearly enough. You swagger into town here, all bluff and bravado, and you think because you're a big time, big city consultant that you know how to run the table, so you pass yourself off as a reporter. Did you not think that people wouldn't see through that?"

Cole took a deep breath. His mind was racing. How much did Drewfeld know about Ottawa? He'd seen this before. He was being lured into saying more than he should to fill in the gaps in the reporter's story, and he wouldn't do it. He wouldn't reveal anything.

"Didn't you think that the people you planned to interview would do some background research? Hell, I even got a call from one of them to ask if I knew you. When you called me to ask about my source I already had my suspicions. But now I see that your habit of lying has landed you in hot water before. You can't hide in the age of the internet."

"This has been fun, but I really should be getting along." If Drewfeld knew about Nancy Webber, he was either not saying, or waiting for the right moment. One way or another, Cole would do nothing to compromise her. Not anymore.

"Funny how things just go around in life," said Drewfeld, pleased with himself.

Here it came.

"The reporter you lied to, and got fired from a plum job in Ottawa, lands in Edmonton, and finds herself in Oracle, Alberta, writing about a murder that one of your clients committed."

"Is alleged to have committed," Cole corrected him. "Dale is innocent. You'll be eating crow in a week's time. This whole town will be."

Drewfeld grinned. "We'll see. First you were a reporter, now you're a PI. That will make good copy. Care to go on the record, Mr. Blackwater?" The reporter mockingly pulled his notepad from his pocket.

If Richard T. Drewfeld knew the depth of his relationship with Nancy, he didn't let on. Maybe he didn't know. It was never published in the press but it was common knowledge on the street.

"Like I said, I've got to be going." Cole turned away from the man and began to walk. The adrenaline petered out; his limbs were weak. Was he even walking straight?

"I'm not done with you Cole," called Drewfeld. "I'm just getting started!"

Things were unravelling, and fast. It was only a matter of time. Drewfeld would learn that Cole and Nancy Webber had an affair, and that pillow talk that led to the now infamous story, printed in *The Globe and Mail*. That story had resulted in the loss of their jobs, and contributed to his year-long estrangement from his daughter Sarah. The mistakes of our past are always there, he thought. They lurk in the darkest corners, wait to reappear, and slide up to us like an unwelcome suitor. Of course, it doesn't help if you don't learn from the mistakes, thought Cole. It doesn't help if you just keep making those mistakes over and over again.

And now that the spotlight was on him, thought Cole, were his other secrets safe?

He opened the door to his truck and got in, rolled down the window, and took a deep breath before turning over the ignition.

How much time before Drewfeld learned the truth about him and Nancy? It was only a few days before Dale van Stempvort was transferred to Red Deer, where he would be held in protective custody awaiting his preliminary hearing. Time was running out.

15

Cole Blackwater needed a drink. He needed a half dozen, but would start with one. He steadied himself with hands on the steering wheel, closed his eyes, and let the adrenaline drain away.

His drink would have to wait. He wanted to see the place where Mike Barnes was killed, and he was late for his rendezvous with Perry Gilbert. But he would reward that wait richly when he had done his work.

He mounted up and drove out of Oracle, turning south along Route 40, the rough, winding gravel road that snaked between foothills, following the valley of a tiny creek over a saddle and down into the next valley. The road was wide, but harrowing in places where blind corners and steep hills hid what was around the bend. Several times Cole gripped the wheel as a much larger pickup truck barrelled around the turn and slipped over the middle of the road into his lane. The encounter with Drewfeld had eviscerated him. How could he get through the rest of the day? Now he met the deluge of traffic as miners were coming off shift, making their way back to Oracle. Giant Ford F-150s and F-250s. Chevy Tahoes. Dodge Ram 2500s. Explorers and Renegades and the occasional brutish Expedition. None of them cost less than $40,000 and they were all, with a few exceptions, brand new. No dinky Chevy S10s among them. And few imports. Cole's pint-sized, aging Japanese truck was seriously inadequate in this company.

Cole considered slaking his thirst with a soda in Cadomin, but Perry Gilbert was likely already waiting for him.

As Cole approached the mine gate, he recalled his first visit to the site. Mike Barnes had still been a healthy, clean cut, neatly dressed young mine manager, whose body must now be on its way back to Toronto to be buried. That thought led him to consider the man's family. Cole Blackwater felt more sympathy for Barnes' family than he did for the man himself. Barnes had likely never missed a trick; probably found a lover wherever he went. He'd cut a swath, Cole guessed, everywhere he ventured. Nancy would dig up rumours of infidelity in the other communities Barnes had lived in. One thing was for certain: Mike Barnes had cut a swath through Oracle wide and deep enough that somebody, for some reason, had killed him.

Cole drove up to the gate. He checked in with JP, the night watchman who was on duty the night Barnes was killed. Cole knew the way. He drove slowly through the compound. The mine site had twenty-five or thirty buildings. It struck Cole that the giant compound was a mammoth-sized machine designed to digest, process, and ship coal. The machine needed fuel. If it wasn't fed, it died.

Cole parked next to an old blue Dodge Caravan and stepped out of his truck. His body ached and he stretched, felt his stomach press into his shirt in a way that made him stand up straighter and suck it in. He really should deal with that.

"Cole?" It was Perry Gilbert. "What took you so long? We've already started."

Cole hurried over at a half run. He stepped through the door that Gilbert held open for him and waited to let his eyes adjust to the dimness of the room.

"The RCMP think Mike Barnes entered the mill through this door the night he was killed," said Gilbert. "They figure he was attracted to the mill by some kind of disturbance. Something was broken, or the door was left open, or maybe he saw an unfamiliar vehicle."

Gilbert handed Cole an orange hard hat with built-in ear protection. He put one on himself.

As Cole's eyes slowly adjusted to the light, he studied the cracks and markings on the floor for some sign of Barnes' passing, but saw nothing. A cement pad outside the door had been recently poured, but like the floor inside, revealed no clue.

The two men stood in a large room with a high ceiling that held fluorescent lights, several of which were burned out. It was devoid of furniture, but cluttered with mining equipment. A five-foot wide corridor exited at an awkward angle from the door and led to a set of double doors that Cole guessed opened to the main mill. Skids loaded with drill bits and drill steel, hoses and fasteners, and even a few drills stood against the walls of the room. It smelled of oil and metal. Industrial noise from the mill rumbled through the walls and Cole felt a slight vibration in the floor.

"This room used to be kept clear of equipment, but in the last year the mine has been closing down buildings and these spaces have been pressed into service as storage," said Perry Gilbert. He led Cole through the maze toward the double doors. Cole stumbled over something and almost fell face forward.

"Watch yourself," said Perry helpfully.

Cole looked down. A coil of hose had fallen off a skid of similar hoses. He pushed it aside with his foot.

"The RCMP think Mike Barnes got as far as these doors. They think that Dale waited for him on the other side and conked him on the head with a drill bit when he walked through. A big, heavy drill bit."

Perry opened the doors. The noise grew oppressive. Cole flipped his ear protection down. This dampened the roar of the mill, but blocked out Perry's voice.

The room was vast. Large loading bay doors at one end allowed massive trucks to enter and exit with equipment and machinery. An overhead conveyor belt came into the room twenty feet off the ground and ended in a huge machine that Cole guessed separated ore from the overburden of limestone. From there the coal was fed into the coking ovens, and waste rock was crushed for tailings, or to be used for other purposes. The coking ovens occupied more than half the space, and from fifty metres away Cole could tell that they where white hot.

Light spilled through the giant bay doors and through widows high above the floor, letting long, slanting rays into the otherwise dim room. The white light caught on the backs of a million dust motes, giving the air and the light the appearance of water, shifting and moving through the room. The space was utterly devoid of colour in the muted light.

Inside the door were randomly arranged skids of bits and drill steel. A uniformed RCMP officer in a hard hat with ear protection wore a scowl. A taped-off area twenty feet long and fifteen feet wide encompassed some of the skids of drill bits stacked three or four high on the pallets. Cole didn't notice them at first, given the scale of the room. It was only after he stubbed his toe on one that he looked down and noticed them. A wide path lead between the pallets. On the floor inside the tape lay a few drill bits the size of a man's head, and a pallet that had been knocked to the ground.

Cole bent down to examine the area inside the tape.

The concrete floor wore oil stains and dust. Where the dust

had been recently disturbed, he could see the ghostly outline of what he knew to be Mike Barnes body. It wasn't as obvious as a chalk outline, but it was clear enough. Mike Barnes had met his untimely demise here. The place was a few feet inside the doors from the outer room, in a straight walking line into the mill. Cole examined the floor. He felt a tap on his shoulder. He looked up to see the RCMP officer standing there. He stood.

The officer leaned close and Cole removed the ear protection from his left ear.

"Don't touch the floor inside the tape, please," the constable yelled over the din of the room.

Cole gave the thumbs up and squatted back down to look at the floor. It told a jumbled story at best. Perry Gilbert squatted beside Cole. He pulled a small flashlight from his pocket and shone the beam onto the floor. It was light enough to see, but the flashlight allowed Gilbert to direct Cole's gaze.

Seven oversized drill bits lay on the floor. It looked like they had been knocked off the pallet that leaned at a forty-five degree angle against a neighbouring stack of bits. From where Cole and Perry squatted, they could not see any sign of blood on them, but Cole assumed that those that had blood had been sent to Edmonton for forensics testing.

The bits were randomly scattered in a wide half circle. Inside that circle was an area that had recently been disturbed. This area was off to the side of the clear area that provided passage between the outer room and the mill itself. Perry moved the light into that disturbed area, that place where Mike Barnes body had been found, to examine it more closely. There was blood, but not much. Droplets, really, and in one place a small dark stain, maybe where Barnes' head hit the floor after he had been clubbed.

There were no obvious footprints in this area. There was too much traffic. Cole examined the floor around the taped off area. There he saw many footprints and tire tracks too. Cole saw a forklift at work in the mill and assumed it was used to move these pallets of bits and steel out into the yard for use in the mine. How were the pallets removed from the smaller room, Cole wondered? Was there some kind of power-assist lifter around? He looked but could not see anything.

Perry shone the light across the other pallets of drill bits, getting as close as he could to them, and examined them carefully. He pointed to a few bits where tiny red dots of blood were visible.

Perry stood stiffly. He turned his back on the mill and put the taped off area between him and the double doors that led to the outer room. Cole stood, body creaking, and moved beside him. Wordlessly, using the flashlight as a pointer, Perry retraced the last seconds of Mike Barnes. He waved the light at the double doors, then swept it down along the floor, bouncing the light to indicate footfalls. And then the attack: Perry jigged the beam to indicate the violent act, and then shone it on the floor to show where Mike Barnes had died.

Cole watched. His eyes swept across the scene. He had never investigated anything more felonious than falsified pollution reports by an oil and gas company. But something wasn't right. Did Gilbert see it too?

Cole tugged on his sleeve, and motioned with his head toward the doors. Perry nodded and the two men made their way between the pallets of drill bits toward the outer room. The doors closed behind them, the sound dulled, and both men gratefully took off their ear protection.

"Let's go outside to talk," shouted Perry and Cole gave him the thumbs up.

They stepped into the late afternoon sunshine like breathless men breaking the surface of a lake.

Cole took off his hard hat and leaned back against the wall, grabbing his ear lobes, first the right and then the left, and tugging at them to stop the ringing in his ears. "Can you imagine that, every single day?"

Perry rubbed his eyes and leaned against the front of his van. "No way. I'd go crazy."

"How could a man hear himself think in there?" asked Cole.

"I don't think thinking is high up on the job description," said Perry. "It's pretty mindless work, loading coal onto conveyor belts all day."

"So tell me how the RCMP figure it again."

Perry shifted his weight from his right leg to his left and rubbed his hand over his face. "They think that Dale must have made an appointment with Mike Barnes sometime early in the day, right after the *Red Deer Advocate* story ran. They figure he drove out to the mine after five, possibly aware that he could get through the gatehouse unseen after hours. They think he might have cased the joint to see if the security guard came and went at regular hours."

"Does he?"

"Don't know. Don't know. We'll have to find out. Anyway, they figure that he got onto the property unseen and went up to Barnes' office around eight or so. What happened then is a mystery. But sometime after ten and before midnight, Mike Barnes left his office and for some reason went across the yard to the mill."

Cole looked across the dusty yard to the three-story brick building that was the mine's office. It was a hundred yards or so, the length of a football field. "Why?"

"Don't know. Maybe Barnes saw someone who didn't belong. Remember, the mill only operates on a day shift right now. Anybody wandering around here after six or so would seem suspicious. I'm told the mill shift ends around then."

Cole stared across the yard.

"So let's just say that he met with someone that evening," said Cole, "and he came out after the meeting and saw this person prowling around the mill. He walks across the yard thinking he'll deal with it faster than trying to find the security guard. Maybe he followed the murderer into the room full of drill steel and what have you. Maybe he thought the prowler was there to do damage to the mill. He wanted to catch him red-handed. So he followed him through the big double doors into the mill."

"And *whappo*."

"Right, *whappo*. Someone clubs him on the head with a twenty-pound drill bit, and it's lights out."

"Lights out."

"That's what I said."

Cole still stared across the yard. "Let's walk."

Perry shrugged. "OK."

They set off across the dusty yard toward the mine offices.

"You said lights out," said Cole.

"So?"

"Made me wonder if they turn the lights out in the mill at night is all."

Stephen Legault

"What difference does it make?"

"Maybe none, but maybe a lot."

"What's eating you?"

"It just doesn't make sense to me," said Cole. They walked up the steps of the mine office and turned around. The mill loomed across the yard. It was five stories tall at least, with windows halfway up, and several sets of massive doors to allow for the transfer of ore or machinery. The door beside which their vehicles were parked seemed very small and very far away.

"Where did Mike Barnes park, I wonder?" asked Cole.

"Right here, I imagine," said Gilbert, pointing to the stall labelled "Mine Manager" in front of the building. "Whose truck is that parked there now?"

"That's Hank Henderson's." Cole remembered seeing Henderson climb into it after their meeting on these very steps the night he had visited Barnes. The night Barnes had been killed.

"Hasn't wasted any time taking over, has he?"

"I'm told he feels he's been passed over for the job on a couple of occasions."

"Wonder how strongly he felt about it?" asked Gilbert, looking around.

"You should ask him," said Cole. "He's very friendly."

"So do you think that Mike Barnes could have seen someone at that door at ten o'clock?"

"I don't think I could see anybody there now," said Cole, squinting. "At ten it's nearly full dark. I can't see how."

Both men were silent.

"I don't think Mike Barnes was killed in the mill," Cole said finally. "It just doesn't make sense."

"If not in the mill, then where?"

"I don't know. But even if someone did lure Barnes to the mill with lights or something, I can't see how he could have been surprised by that person when he came through those double doors."

"What do you mean?"

"There's nothing to hide behind. The bits only come up to my thigh. Unless the place was pitch black, it would be hard for someone to get the drop on him, don't you think?"

"What if the assailant was standing on top of the pallet?"

"You'd have to be a gymnast to balance like that. Those bits roll all over the place."

They walked down the steps and started back across the yard.

"So how did the body end up in the mill then?" asked Perry.

Cole was silent. He looked at the building, and turned around as he walked, scanning the yard, the office, and the other buildings. "I have no idea. But whoever killed Mike Barnes likely dragged his body to the mill from somewhere else, intending to dispose of it here. I think he probably went in through this door," said Cole, and pointed to the door in front of them. "And when he dragged the body into the mill itself, knocked over some of the drill bits."

"But why leave the body? If you were hoping to get rid of him and go through all the trouble of dragging it from wherever you clubbed him, why dump it at the last minute?"

Cole shook his head. "I don't know. Got spooked by something or someone?"

Perry shrugged again. "Maybe." Then he said, "Do you want to have another look?"

Cole grimaced. "Not really, but I guess we should."

They donned the hard hats, flipped down the ear protection, and went through the door into the outer room. They retraced the last steps of Mike Barnes according to the RCMP, through the maze of drill steel to the big double doors. They paid careful attention to how it might feel to step through them and be surprised by an assailant. Cole looked left and right as he walked through the doors, wondering if a man might conceal himself there. He doubted it. The path was too wide, and the pallets of bits too low, and the bits themselves gave no place for a man to crouch and strike with any stability. Cole was shaking his head. It was all wrong.

They finally finished after six o'clock. Cole was exhausted. When he and Perry Gilbert parted ways outside the mill, Cole was determined to drive directly back to Oracle, find a quick dinner, and retreat to Peggy McSorlie's farm for the night. Then he would reward himself with a drink.

But the long rays of spring sun slanted through the mine property and reminded him that the day was far from over.

He sat in the cab of the Toyota a long time before putting the key in the ignition.

So what if Mike Barnes was killed somewhere else on the property and not in the mill? What did that change? Was it was plausible that Dale van Stempvort had been waiting for Barnes by his car, or even in his car? Surely the RCMP would have scoured it for signs of a struggle. Maybe the killing had taken place in Barnes' office? Cole decided that he needed to have another look around there.

There was also the need to find Mike Barnes' appointment book. Without that, it would be hard to follow through on the numerous leads that this inquiry was generating. It was possible that the killer's name was written there in black and white!

And what about Cole's other suspects? Could George Cody have driven out to the mine that night and clubbed Mike Barnes out of revenge? It seemed like a risky move for Barnes to make, thought Cole. Why would he meet a man whose wife he'd been screwing in a quiet office on a nearly deserted mine site so late in the evening? Unless Mike Barnes had wanted no one to witness the meeting, that is. So George arrived at the mine and the men met, and in a rage George clubbed Barnes right there in the office. What did he use? Surely Mike Barnes' secretary would have noticed if anything was missing. And the RCMP would have scoured the office for blood and signs of a struggle. George would have killed Mike Barnes somewhere else. But where? Cole shook his head, which pulsed a little, and he touched the bump on the back of his skull, still tender.

What about Deborah? Many of the same questions applied: where? With what?

Was Deborah strong enough to kill Mike Barnes? He figured she was, especially if she took him by surprise. What would have convinced Mike Barnes to see her again after writing her a note that Cole could only assume terminated their affair?

Maybe Deborah made him an offer he couldn't refuse. Maybe she had threatened to go public with the story herself, an act of self-destructive vengeance that would surely ruin his career and marriage and cause more harm to him than to her. Maybe she felt she had nothing left to lose? Maybe she was bribing him?

Or maybe she had come to the mine hoping to seduce him one last time. Maybe when he rejected her she flew into a rage and killed him.

But Mike Barnes was a big man, weighing what, 180, 190 pounds? Light heavyweight to cruiserweight class, Cole guessed. As if Mike Barnes would ever tape up his hands. Cole pegged her at welterweight, around 140 pounds. But he doubted that Deborah could carry him from his office to the mill. It was just too far. She would have had to load him in her car and drive him, or drag him. Or find some other way to move the body. He made a note to look for blood in her car.

He stepped out of the Toyota and walked around the yard, looking in the sand and gravel for drag marks. He walked in little circles and then big circles, but found nothing.

He got back in the truck, turned the ignition over, and decided to drive back to Oracle before he grew too weary. He started the truck, turned it around, and drove toward the gatehouse. He signed out, and drove up Route 40 toward Cadomin.

Who else? Who else? Faces and names flowed through his head. If in fact George and/or Deborah Cody killed Barnes, what was their connection to the mole inside the Eastern Slopes Conservation Group? And was there any link with Jim Jones' information that the company never really intended to dig the mine, but merely push the rail line and road into the wilderness in order to keep investors and shareholders happy? He could see no possible connection there. It was possible that these were all unrelated threads, but Cole Blackwater somehow doubted it. It seemed too neat and tidy to be coincidence.

He drove the winding gravel road, snaked through the hills, and followed the path of tiny creeks and streams as they wove their way through the sculpted foothills.

Who else might want Mike Barnes dead? Nearly everybody in town, had they known what he was up to, thought Cole. Who else knew?

He nearly swerved off the road when it occurred to him. College boy. Hank Henderson knew. He was the assistant mine manager; he *had* to know.

The disdain Hank Henderson felt for the mine manager was palpable. Cole could remember very little of the conversation they'd had, but he knew that Henderson had been twice passed over for promotion to the mine manager's job after working at the mine for most of his adult life. And had he learned that Barnes meant to shut down the mine, it would have been easy for Henderson to snap under those circumstances. It would have been easy for him to confront Mike Barnes, and in a fit of rage take his life. It would have been easy for him to dispose of the body, too, thought Cole. He knew the mine inside and out, and wouldn't have had a problem coming up with the best solution for an unwanted corpse. Dump it into one of the giant conveyor belts that carried the coal. Gone. To become part of a Toyota or Hyundai or Mitsubishi. Cole allowed himself a slight grin at the morbid thought. Might impact the structural stability of a vehicle to be made from the pulp of an MBA, he mused.

Now what? Here was a new path to follow among many. He was nearing Oracle when his cellphone rang. He snatched it from the detritus on the passenger seat.

"Blackwater."

"Webber."

"Hi, Nancy."

"Where are you right now?"

"Driving into Oracle."

"I've got some news."

"Me too."

"Hold your horses, I go first." The cellphone crackled.

"You're breaking up, Nancy. Can we do this in person?"

More static, then silence.

"You still there, Nancy?"

"Come by the hotel. Room 245." The line went dead.

"That woman can be such a ..." he said aloud, and bit his tongue.

It was nearly eight o'clock when he arrived at the hotel.

He found his way to her room. Nancy answered the door and let him in. The room smelled like her. It was neat and clean, everything in its place. On the small desk she had set up an orderly work station with laptop and keyboard arranged just as they would be on her desk at the *Edmonton Journal*. Clothes were hung neatly in the open closet. Cole assumed that the drawers of the dresser were likewise tidy. The bed was made. On the small round table Cole saw that Nancy had eaten pizza for dinner. The smell of the pizza mixed with her perfume made him a little dizzy with various hungers.

"What have you got to tell me, Cole? This isn't a social visit."

"I thought we were working on this together, Nancy."

"We are not working on anything together Cole. You're a source. I'm a reporter. What have you got?"

"I'm hungry," he said. "I'm going to eat some of your dinner." He walked over to the table and flipped open the box. Half a vegetarian pizza was left. He picked up a slice. A couple of mushrooms dropped to the floor. He began to eat.

He could tell that this infuriated Nancy. The mushrooms and the delay.

He sat down in one of the chairs, stretched out his legs, and chewed. "What have *you* got?"

"Christ, you can be difficult, Cole."

"You're no walk in the park yourself, Nancy."

She sat down at the little desk across the room from him. She ran her fingers through her long dark hair and sighed. It was so familiar. The long hair cascading down across her shoulders. The way she tilted her head slightly to the left when she spoke. The way her eyes looked in the half-light of a darkened room. He was beginning to remember her the way she was before the disaster. Before the disaster called Cole Blackwater.

"So Mike Barnes has a history. It's not a long one, but it's colourful," she said. "Before he worked in mining, he spent some time in the forestry sector. This was before doing his MBA, and before marrying into the mining industry. He worked for a medium-sized logging company in northern Ontario and Manitoba called East Woods. They specialized in salvage operations and in taking over timber licences that had been abandoned by smaller operators. They would buy up the licences of operators that were going out of business one way or another, assume the operation, sometimes even with the outgoing company's crew and equipment, and after cutting everything that they could, wind down operations quickly and efficiently. I guess that's where Barnes got his skill as a hatchet man."

Cole listened. He ate a second piece of pizza.

"Interesting enough on its own, but I did some digging with a few contacts in one of the communities he worked in. A few years ago, after you ruined my journalism career, I was covering a flood in Manitoba and got to know a few local reporters in the area. Anyway, I called in a favour, and I'm told that Mike Barnes has a history of fooling around. No big deal, I guess, but it's led to trouble. About ten years ago, in one of his very first jobs, he slept with one of the forestry mill workers' wives, and the worker found out and tried to kill him."

"You're kidding me," said Cole. He held a third piece of pizza in his hand.

"I guess Barnes scheduled the man on night shift so he could come over and bone the wife. The worker got suspicious – you know, little things that the wife would say or do. He came home one night during his meal break and found Barnes in the sack with the chick. He flew into a rage and tried to strangle Barnes with a belt."

Cole shook his head. "How did that end?"

"The wife conked her husband on the head with a lamp and knocked him out. Barnes got the hell out of town. No charges were ever laid."

"Guy hasn't learned his lesson."

"Looks like it might finally have killed him," said Nancy.

"Not so fast, Sherlock," said Cole, getting up to go to the bathroom. He spotted a half-full bottle of wine (when it came to booze, the bottle was *always* half full in Cole's view) on Nancy's night stand, and he retrieved one of the plastic-wrapped cups from the bathroom and poured himself a full glass.

"Like some wine?" Nancy rolled her eyes.

"Don't mind if I do. So you think that George Cody is our man?"

"Makes sense, given what we know."

"Because someone else tried to kill him for boffing his wife, you figure this time George Cody was successful?"

"Why not?"

"I'm not saying it's not possible, but I don't see how an incident ten years ago could catch up with Barnes in Oracle. I doubt George Cody found out about Barnes' past and decided, on behalf of men everywhere, to put an end to his philandering ways."

"It was easy enough to find out," said Nancy. "A couple of phone calls."

"Yeah, but you're a sophisticated reporter with a major newspaper. George is a bartender with a baseball bat."

"*Was* a sophisticated reporter with a major newspaper. Then I met you, shithead."

"Whatever. My point is, it doesn't seem possible that George would have known about Barnes' past."

"Nevertheless, it could be that Barnes' past finally caught up with him."

"Or that at least his bad habits did," added Cole. He took a slug of wine and drained his glass. He was feeling more relaxed, thanks to the food and the wine. "I was thinking along these same lines this afternoon. I was out at the mine looking at the crime scene with the lawyer from Legal Aid."

Nancy raised her left eyebrow. "Really? What did you learn?"

"I don't think that Mike Barnes was killed where the RCMP think he was killed." He told her about the crime scene and his belief that whoever killed Mike Barnes likely hadn't been hiding among the drill bits and steel.

"Then where?"

"I don't know yet. We need to check a few things out."

"We?"

"Yes, we, as in you and me. I need you to check and see if there is any blood in either George or Deborah Cody's car. If either of them—"

"Or both of them," interjected Nancy.

"Yes, if either or both of them killed Barnes somewhere else on the mine site, they might have used a vehicle to get the body from the site of the murder to the mill. It's a big place, and Barnes was a big enough man that Deborah, and maybe even George, would have needed some assistance in getting Barnes to the mill for disposal."

"Why would they choose the mill as a place for disposal?"

Cole cocked his head to one side to indicate he wasn't following.

"Why choose the mill? Why would George or Deborah gather that the mill was the best place for disposal?"

"Beats me," said Cole.

"Me too."

"But I'm not so certain that the Codys are our best suspects."

"Really? Then who?"

"Hank Henderson."

"You're kidding me. The assistant mine manager?"

"Now *acting* mine manager," said Cole.

"You think ambition led him to club his boss and take his job?"

"Why not? The man has been at the mine for half his working life. He's been the assistant mine manager for a long time. Passed over twice for the top job. And then in walks Mike Barnes with a plan to kill the mine. I think that might be enough to rattle a couple of screws loose from Hank Henderson's head and lead him to commit murder."

"I don't know. Seems a little weak."

Cole grinned. "When you lost your job at *The Globe and Mail*, what did you want to do?"

Nancy looked down and then up into Cole's eyes. Hers were burning. "I wanted to kill you, you bastard."

"Case in point."

16

"You got in late." Peggy McSorlie dropped pancake batter into a hot pan. "I hope you don't mind," Cole said and made a beeline for the coffee pot. In a moment he had a cup full, with cream, just the way he liked it. It was half-past eight. Gord McSorlie was already at work in the yard. Cole sipped his coffee. "This detective work involves a lot of late-night snooping around." Cole winked.

"Just be careful about what you're snooping around. Remember the old cliché, curiosity killed the cat?"

"I'm very careful," said Cole with a grin. This PI work wasn't too bad after all. He was almost looking forward to his day, something that hadn't happened since he'd arrived in Oracle. Something that hadn't happened for a long time, period. He rubbed his cheek. He needed a shave. Had to take better care of himself. Not let himself go to pot. He needed to stay sharp. A man's future was at stake, after all, and so was an amazing landscape.

Cole ate a stack of pancakes, and when he was done he cleared the table and washed the breakfast dishes. That settled, he and Peggy sat down with a second cup of coffee to discuss what came next.

"I need to go back to the mine today," he said. "There are just too many loose ends out there. There's the mysterious disappearance of the appointment book. And I can't believe that the night watchman didn't see anything out of the ordinary that night."

"Do you think he might be in on it too?"

Cole sipped his coffee. "As far as I'm concerned, everybody in this town might be in on it. One thing I'm reasonably sure of is that Barnes was here to shut the mine down, with special orders to make it look like things were actually going full steam ahead."

Peggy nodded. "Maybe that's why he was so forthcoming when you talked with him."

Cole grinned and sipped his coffee. "Don't forget, Peggy, my cover was already blown then. In fact, it never was a cover at all, knowing what we know now about the mole. Maybe Mike Barnes himself placed that mole inside our group to ensure we stayed on track with our plan to shut down the mine for him."

Stephen Legault

"Wow. That's one serious conspiracy theory."

"Maybe, but I'm not willing to rule anything out right now."

Peggy grinned. "Speaking of moles."

"What have you found?"

"I'm at work on that list. I'll have it by the end of the day."

"How many names on it?"

"Five right now, but I should have it down to three by this afternoon."

"Can you set up meetings with these people for me tomorrow?"

"What do I tell them?"

"Say we're on the move with a strategy and that I want to check in with each of them personally about their part."

"And what are you really going to do?"

Cole was silent. Then a smile spread across his face.

"What is it?"

"I just got a really good idea."

"Tell me!"

"What if I feed each of them a separate story, something juicy, that the mole would certainly want to leak to the press? And then we see what happens."

Peggy leaned forward. "We watch to see which of the stories turns up somewhere that it shouldn't, and then we know who our mole is. Do you think they might be wise to that trick?"

Cole finished his coffee. "Maybe. But we can try to diffuse suspicion by telling them that I plan to meet with everyone. It's worth a try."

They agreed to brainstorm a few different stories for Cole to feed the suspected moles. Peggy's job was to find out when Dale would be transferred from Oracle to Red Deer.

"While we're on the subject of the press, Peggy, there's something I need to tell you," said Cole, a little bashful.

"What is it?"

"Well, I've been working with Nancy Webber on this."

"The *Edmonton Journal* reporter?"

"Yes. We knew each other in Ottawa, and I trust her. She loathes me, but I still trust her. She's helping me dig up some material that I couldn't get on my own."

"I don't know, Cole. What if she's just using you to get a story?"

"I'm pretty sure she is, Peggy," said Cole with a doleful smile. "But I trust her to keep quiet until I give her the OK. I won't do that without talking with you first."

"All right," said Peggy, but she wasn't entirely convinced.

They finished their coffee. Cole said before leaving, "Peggy, I get the feeling that we're running out of time on this."

"Why?"

"It's been a week since Mike Barnes was killed. In a couple of days all our help will to disappear. Dale will be transferred to Red Deer. Perry Gilbert will be back there as well. Nancy Webber will have to head back to Edmonton, and she's been the most helpful of the three, despite the fact that she hates my guts. We need to wrap this up and soon."

"Let's get cracking then," said Peggy.

Cole called Perry Gilbert on his way into town. "Anything on the murder weapon?" he asked.

"You're not going to believe this."

"Try me."

"The results got lost."

"You're right. I don't believe it."

"They have to redo them."

"How long?"

"Another two days. Friday."

"And when does Dale go to Red Deer."

"Friday. Saturday at the latest."

Friday then. Two days. Cole could feel time working against him. But he had to admit that he liked this part of the fight: the clock running down. It made time for one last play. For one last flurry of punches. And then what? Then either you hit the mat, your opponent did, or you both sat back down.

As he drove through Oracle he dialled Nancy Webber.

"Webber."

"Blackwater."

"Ha ha. What do you want?"

"They're moving Dale on Friday. Saturday at the latest."

"I heard this morning. I'm a reporter you know."

"I know. We have to pick up the pace."

"What do you suggest?"

Cole hit the gravel road and pressed the pedal down. "Can you follow up on George and Deborah today? I'm headed out to the mine right now."

"Cole, do you really think that the killing could be linked to Mike Barnes' job? You know, to shut the mine down?"

"Could be. That might be Hank Henderson's motivation."

"How do we find out who knew that the mine was actually slated for a shutdown?"

Cole thought about it.

"Hello?"

"I'm deep in thought. What if I call someone and see what I can learn?"

"Who?"

"Can't say. I need to keep him out of this."

"Fine, be that way, but call me back."

He hung up without saying goodbye. He dialled Jim Jones. "Jim, it's Cole."

"Cole. How's the body count?"

"Funny."

"Not exactly how I expected you to stop the mine, but I'll take what I can get."

"Jim, this call is probably being monitored."

"Fat doughnut-eaters can listen all they want," laughed Jones. "They won't take you alive. Good work, kid."

"Seriously Jim, I have a favour to ask."

"Go ahead."

"Who got copies of the environmental assessment? And when?"

"I can try to find out. The thing is still not in the public domain. I worked with a review draft."

"Can you look into this ASAP?"

"I'll try, Cole. What has this got to do with anything?"

"I better not say, Jim."

"It's going to cost you."

"I'll stock up on my way back through Jasper. Spend the night. We'll have a real hoot."

"Deal."

"Call me."

"It might take a few days of sweet-talking."

"We're running out of time, Jim."

"I'll do what I can, Cole."

What next? He drove and pondered.

At 11:30 he reached the mine. He learned at the gate that JP Juror, the night watchman, started his shift at 2 PM.

"Can I wait for him at the office?"

"He doesn't report there," said the guard.

"Can I wait there anyway? Beats sitting around in my truck."

"Hold on," the guard said and picked up the phone. "OK," he said after quick conversation. "You can wait in the front entrance hall."

Perfect, thought Cole. Then all I have to do is figure out how not to be seen by Hank Henderson, and find my way up to Mike Barnes' office.

He parked in visitor parking and walked up the steps. He glanced at the mill and shook his head. No way was Barnes lured across a hundred plus yards of darkened yard to the mill building. Unless, of course, he suspected a trespasser. Cole ruled that out. The only person likely to throw a monkey wrench in the mill was van Stempvort, and Cole was pretty much convinced of Dale's innocence.

The office building was quiet. Mike Barnes had let a dozen people go when he came on board, in the name of reducing redundancies, and until a week ago anyone not involved with the running of this particular mine site was weeded out. How many of them had foreknowledge of the plan to close the mine? Did any of them have the necessary motivation to kill Mike Barnes? Come on, Jim, Cole thought, I need something to point us toward a suspect.

Cole walked right past the empty reception desk and mounted the stairs at the south end of the building. At the top of the third flight of stairs Cole had to take a rest. By the fourth floor he was breathing so hard his stomach felt tight and his heart protested. He was repulsed by himself, by what he'd become, and promised himself to get back into shape if he ever got out of Oracle.

He walked down the hall to the former manager's office. Tracey sat at her desk.

"Hi there," he said. "It's Cole Blackwater."

"I remember we met that night.... I'm Tracey Blake, remember? I'm Mr. Barnes' secretary. *Was*, I guess," and she looked down at her hands.

"In the front hall, right," said Cole, then added, "I'm sorry for your loss."

"Me too. He was a good man."

Did she know anything about Mike Barnes' private life?

"The front gate called and told me that you'd be waiting at reception and asked if I'd look in on you. You're supposed to be downstairs, aren't you?" she raised an eyebrow at Cole. "Do you have a meeting with someone?"

"Well, there was nowhere to sit downstairs," Cole shuffled his feet. "I'm here to talk with the night watchman, but I don't have an appointment and I'm early. Tell me, how are you holding up?"

Tracey sat back in her chair and pressed her knuckles into her eyes. "I'm OK." She sighed. "I guess I'm in denial. I keep expecting him to walk in through the door like he was just back from a trip to Toronto and say 'Hi'ya Trace.'"

"Did he travel a lot?"

"He went to Toronto once a month to visit his family and work out of head office for a week."

"Did he seem happy to be heading there, or happy to be coming back?"

Tracey thought about it. "He seemed pretty happy either way. He was a pretty happy man."

Tracey's eyes were red. The talk of Mike Barnes brought on fresh tears.

"You miss him?"

"Of course," she said, almost defensively. "We worked together for almost a year. He was a great boss. If I needed an extra day off, or if I had to leave early to take my kids somewhere, it was never a problem. He was easygoing and never grumpy."

"Now what?"

"I don't know. I'm holding down the fort until they find a new manager."

"What about Hank Henderson?"

"Oh, him. What about him?"

"He's parked his big Chevy in the mine manager's stall."

"He'll never be manager."

"Why do you say that?"

Tracey grew quiet. Her gaze roamed over the desk and down the hall. "He's just too old school. He doesn't see the role this mine plays in the bigger picture of the company. To him, it's all about *this* mine. But it's a global market today, and this mine is part of a company that leverages other investments for its shareholders."

So Tracey knew.

"But shouldn't the manager be looking out for the best interests of the mine?"

"Not at the expense of the company."

Cole put his best face forward. "Tracey, I need a favour."

His best face wasn't much. She looked at him. He didn't have much left to charm with. His nose was out of whack. The bruise on his eye had faded, leaving the eye puffy and pink. The jagged cut across his cheek was still bright red and bristling with black sutures like hair growing out of an ear. "Like what?" she asked.

"I need to have a look around Mike's office."

"Oh, I don't think that's possible, Mr. Blackwater."

"Tracey," he said calmly, "I think the person who killed your boss is still loose."

She looked at him askance. "The Mounties got their man. Dale van Stempvort is in jail."

"I don't think he did it. I think someone else killed Mike Barnes."

"You would, wouldn't you, Mr. Blackwater?"

"I'm an environmentalist, yes, but Dale van Stempvort is not a killer. He's a big mouth and a bit of an idiot, but I don't think he killed Mike. I'm trying to figure out who did."

Cole held her gaze. "I don't think so," she finally said. "I think you want to get at some company files to get inside information to help out your friends. To help them stop the mine."

"Tracey, you and I both know that this mine is stopping with or without the Eastern Slopes Conservation Group."

She looked surprised. "How do you know that?"

"A little detective work. I put two and two together. It may be that the real killer did too."

She looked down at the desktop.

"There's more, Tracey. Did you know that Mike was having an affair?"

She looked up, her eyes swimming in tears. "It was nothing," she said, the tears spilling over. "We just had some innocent fun."

Good God, Cole thought, Mike Barnes should have been giving lessons. How many women was he sleeping with?

Cole knew he had to get out a big gun. "Look, Tracey, I'm sorry to be the bearer of bad news, but Mike Barnes was having an affair with Deborah Cody."

"From the hotel?"

"Yes."

She put her face in her hands and cried quietly, her shoulders shaking with waves of despair and disappointment. After a minute she straightened up, wiped her face, and handed Cole a key from her pocket.

In silence he took the key and walked past her to the mine manager's office. He inserted the key into the lock.

Inside, the office was as he remembered.

Except Mike Barnes' appointment book was missing.

"Tracey?" he called.

She walked into the room, Kleenex in hand.

"Mr. Barnes' Day-Timer?"

"I don't know."

"Did the police ask you about it?"

"They did and I told them he must have taken it home with him that night. He often did that."

"The police haven't found it."

"Really?"

"Really."

Tracey stood by the door while Cole searched the shelves, the drawers, and under the chairs. He excused himself and closed the door slightly to look behind it.

"Do you recognize this coat?" It was a charcoal suit jacket, hand-tailored, very expensive.

"It's Mike's, it was Mike's I mean."

"When did you see it on him last?"

"I can't say for sure. But I think," and she took a little breath, "I think he was wearing it on Wednesday."

"When I met with him he wore suit pants and a green shirt."

"He often took the jacket off as soon as he walked in the door. I told him he could show up in jeans and nobody would care. At least he stopped wearing ties after the first few weeks."

"Did he ever leave his coat at the office, you know, just

forgetting that he had worn a coat?"

"No. He was a really classy guy. Always finished things right. Tidied up the loose ends. Plus, you don't just forget your coat at minus twenty."

So Mike Barnes hadn't left the building. He had been killed here. But where?

Cole got down on his hands and knees and peered under the desk. He checked under the tables and chairs and looked closely at the carpet.

"What are you doing?"

"Looking for blood."

Tracey covered her mouth. She joined him on the floor. "You think he was killed here?"

"Well, I don't think he left the office building that night. The RCMP think he was killed in the mill, but I don't see it."

On hands and knees they examined the furniture when a voice at the door startled them. "What the hell are you doing?"

Both Cole and Tracey looked up guiltily.

"Mr. Henderson!" said Tracey. She stood up and straightened her pants and shirt.

"Miss Blake. And Mr. Blackwater."

Cole stood but didn't say a word.

"What are you doing, Miss Blake?"

"Looking for something we think Mr. Barnes misplaced," she said weakly.

"And what would that be?"

She shot a look at Cole. Help, it said.

"I came here to try and find a piece of paper I think Mr. Barnes had in his possession the night he was killed." Cole stared directly at Henderson, aware that if his eyes drifted, the man would know he was lying through his teeth. "It had a name on it of someone who had called him. I think he was going to see that man that evening. If I can find it, it would lead me to the killer."

"Miss Blake, why did you let Mr. Blackwater into this office?"

"I'm sorry, Mr. Henderson," she said, and returned to her desk.

Hank Henderson turned his angry gaze back to Cole. "How about I call the RCMP and have them arrest you for trespassing?"

Cole shrugged. "I came here to talk to you too, Mr. Henderson. I think you know more than you're letting on."

Hank Henderson laughed. "So you're not done jerking my chain, are you Blackwater?" he spat.

"I'm not jerking anybody's chain. An innocent man is behind bars and I think you know more than you're telling me."

Henderson laughed again, a loud, aggressive snort, the kind that preceded the first punch in a bar fight. He sounded like a bull right before all hell broke loose.

Henderson turned to Tracey. "Call security and have them escort Mr. Blackwater off the property." She looked briefly at Cole and then picked up the phone.

"Now, if you don't mind, Mr. Blackwater, some of us have a job to do. Mine, as it turns out, is to dig a hole so deep into the Cardinal Divide that you and your pathetic band of duck-loving friends won't be able to see daylight should you fall into it. Now get the hell out of my sight!" This last sentence was delivered as a yell. He turned and walked back toward the stairs.

Cole followed him. "They were going to shut you down, weren't they?" he called as Henderson disappeared down the stairs. Cole trotted down the hall. "They were going to shut this mine down and you were going to be out of a job, weren't you?" Cole caught up with Henderson at the bottom of the stairs.

Henderson stopped and Cole almost ran into him.

"Are you trying to get yourself in more trouble, Blackwater?" said Henderson, hissing through his teeth. He was not a big man. Cole guessed him to be a featherweight, super featherweight at best. Cole had fifty pounds on him, but Cole's bulk wasn't muscle. Hank Henderson was long and lean, and when he moved his arms, Cole could see the compact bulge of his biceps through his shirt. He might be older than Cole, but Cole didn't doubt that Hank Henderson could still throw a punch.

"They were going to take your job from you before you could become manager," he went on, betraying his excitement and fear with the quickness of his breath.

"I don't know what you're talking about," said Henderson. He walked down the hall to his office, which was located directly below Barnes' office, and closed the door.

Cole followed after him, opened the door, and walked into the room. It was smaller than the office above it, and it lacked the reception area. It was so unlike the mine manager's office that Cole was momentarily disoriented. Where Mike Barnes' office looked like it belonged on Bay Street, Hank Henderson's office looked as if it belonged in the shop room of the mill. The walls were dark and covered in maps and side-cut illustrations of open-pit mines. The large windows that looked west from the building were covered with cheap Venetian blinds that were dusty and drawn tight. An overhead light fixture gave the room a yellow glow. Two tables in the room were both covered in maps, a hard hat, goggles, drill steel, a few large drill bits, core samples, gloves, and other tools of the trade.

"Get the fuck out of my office," said Henderson, and sat down behind his desk.

"Who else knew that this mine was closing?"

"Blackwater, I don't know what you're trying to prove, but you're heading down a dangerous road for damn certain. Haven't you had enough misery for one week? Isn't one trip to the hospital enough?"

"When did you find out that the mine was going to close?"

"It's not."

"It was when Mike Barnes was manager."

"Things have changed."

"The environmental assessment seems to suggest it will."

"Well, plans can be redrawn. With the right leadership."

"Looks like that's you now."

"Looks like."

"Convenient."

"What do you mean by that?"

"Mike Barnes was killed just before the plan went public that suggested this mine had no future."

"And you think I did it?"

"Did you?"

"You're crazy to come in here and accuse an upstanding citizen of killing his boss to keep a mine from closing. You must be grade A, one hundred percent, certifiably crazy." Henderson stood.

"Did you?"

"I'll tell you what I'm going to do, Blackwater. I'm going to count to three, and if you're not out of my office, I'm going to throw you out." Henderson moved toward Cole now, his hands clenched in fists.

Stephen Legault

"Did you kill Mike Barnes to keep this mine from closing?"

"One."

"You were passed over twice, Henderson. That must have really stuck in your craw."

"Two."

"You knew they would never promote you. Were you going to kill the next manager they sent too?"

"Three."

Hank reached for Cole and Cole stepped sideways. But Henderson was surprisingly fast for a man his age. He managed to get his hands on Cole and manhandle him through the open door. Cole skidded on his feet into the hall.

"You are one crazy son of a bitch," growled Henderson. "Keep a good look out over your shoulder. Next time it'll be more than just a couple of goons gunning for you."

"So it was you I have to thank for the welcoming party," said Cole.

"Watch your back, Blackwater."

"I'd be watching more than that if I were you."

Cole didn't have time to think, the punch came so fast. He only had time to react, to let his body do what it had done so many times: respond. He leaned back and arched his spine, but not fast enough to dodge the blow. Henderson's fist connected with his chin and Cole stepped back, reeling from the punch.

"Hold it, hold it, hold it!" came a shout from down the hall. Cole leaned into the wall as Henderson came forward and readied himself to step forward and land a right jab at the advancing man when JP, the night watchman, came between them. "What the hell is going on here?"

"Get this jackass away from my mine," spat Henderson, his anger made it hard for him to speak. "Get him off the property, and make sure he never comes back. Call the RCMP."

Cole stood silently, breathing hard but otherwise unscathed. He'd been in enough scrapes; this one didn't phase him. JP turned to him and said, "Let's go."

"Lead the way."

"If I see you on this property again, Blackwater, you're a dead man!" shouted Henderson.

Cole smiled to himself. Some guys just didn't know when to keep their mouths shut.

They reached the stairwell when Cole touched his chin. It was cut and he was dripping blood. "Mind if I clean this up before we go?" he asked.

The security guard pursed his lips and looked over his shoulder at Henderson's office. "Sure," he said, "but let's use the can on four. Don't want you and the old man there to get into it in the bathroom. One of you is likely to drown."

They took the stairs to the fourth floor.

"You got the old man pretty riled up," said JP as they walked down the hall.

"Is he always like that?"

"He's got a hair-trigger temper," said the guard. "People tend to give him a pretty wide berth."

"No wonder he's never made manager."

"There are many reasons," said the guard, "and that's just one of them."

"How long have you worked here?" Cole asked.

"Almost twenty years. I started working in the pit itself, but I messed up my arm so I took a job as watchman eight years ago."

They stepped into the bathroom. Cole said, "I've got to take a leak."

"You're not going to pull a Houdini in there, are you?"

"Not likely," smiled Cole. He tried the first stall, but it was locked. A little piece of paper on the door said that it was out of order. He tried the second and it was open. He stepped in, wadded up some tissue and held it against his chin as he relieved himself.

"I haven't seen Henderson hit anyone in a while, mind you," JP was saying. "I think the last time was three or four years ago. He got into it with one of the mill workers over something. Can't even remember what."

Cole finished and stepped to the mirror. He threw the tissue in the garbage and looked at himself in the mirror while he washed his hands. There was a half inch cut on his chin that bled. He splashed water on his face and dried it with paper towels, which he also threw in the garbage.

"You're going to need more stitches," smiled JP.

Cole looked at him. "Funny."

"I'll call Doc Frankenstein, see if he's in." JP was chuckling.

Cole grinned back. "You don't happen to have a bandage, do you?"

"No."

"Would you mind going to see if Tracey has one?"

"I don't know, you seem like a good candidate for flight from custody," smiled JP.

"Isn't that what you want? Me to get my butt off the mine property?"

"Boss said something about the RCMP."

"Look," said Cole, and dabbed at his chin. "If you want, I'll march right over to the constable at the mill and turn myself in. Make it easier for me to press assault charges. I even have you as a witness."

JP shrugged. "I'll go get you something for your chin." He stepped out of the bathroom.

"Thanks," said Cole. He bent toward the mirror and pressed his fore and index fingers around the cut. He dabbed at it with another paper towel and reached for more, but the dispenser was empty. "Great," he said, and flipped open the lid of the paper towel holder. Nothing. He used the blood-soaked towel in his hand to clean up his chin. The bleeding slowed. Cole figured a couple of Band-Aids might help, and reached into his pocket to see if there was anything there that might fit the bill. He tugged at something that felt like a Band-Aid and pulled it out, spilling a wad of papers, money, and six deck screws onto the bathroom floor.

"Mother of Pearl," he muttered, and discovered that all he had for his efforts was a crinkled gum wrapper. He stuffed it back into his pocket and bent over stiffly to scoop up some of what had fallen to the floor. On his knees he chased down a dime from beneath the sink, looked up, and stopped cold.

Under the counter, dry and dark red and unmistakable, was blood, sprayed in tiny droplets against the bathroom wall.

17

Cole was still on his knees when JP opened the bathroom door. The door hit Cole's feet.

"What the hell are you doing down there?"

"Dropped something," he said, and picked up the last of the rubbish that had spilled from his pockets. He let the image of the blood burn into his mind. It was sprayed in a pattern more than three feet wide. A terrible image formed in Cole's mind as he hunched on the floor: the last brutal seconds of a man's life.

He stood up and steadied himself on the counter, sick to his stomach. He'd seen plenty of blood in his life, mostly his own, but this was different. Where he stood now Mike Barnes had last stood alive.

"You OK?" asked JP.

Cole said nothing. He saw the door to the bathroom open and well-dressed Mike Barnes walked in. He saw him step into one of the bathroom stalls and flush the toilet. He heard the throaty sound of the flush. Barnes stepped to the mirror to examine himself while he washed up. Then the bathroom door opened. Or did the assailant hide in the other stall? Cole could not know. Wherever it came from, the attack was swift. A piece of drill steel or a baseball bat, swung hard and wide. The bathroom was large enough that a man could swing a bludgeon at full arm's length. Had Barnes turned at the last moment to ward off the attack? Had he seen the attack coming and tried to defend himself? Or did it happen so quickly that he was clubbed in the side of the head and dead before he hit the floor? His head connected with the ground with such force that blood from his wound, and from the new one made where he hit the ground, sprayed around the wall under the counter. Cole opened his eyes.

"You OK?" JP asked again.

"I'm OK," he said. "Just a little light-headed."

"I got you a Band-Aid," said JP and handed Cole a couple of butterfly bandages. Cole ripped one open and applied it to his chin.

Mike Barnes had been killed in this bathroom. Cole could see that plainly. What he could not see was the face of the man, or woman, who had done the deed.

"You ready to go?" asked JP.

"Sure," said Cole, and turned to leave.

Stephen Legault

They walked back to the stairwell and passed Barnes' office.

"Hold on a minute," Cole said.

"You fixing to get me fired?"

"Just a second," Cole said, and poked his head into the office.

"Nice face," said Tracey.

"Thanks for the Band-Aid." Cole tried to muster a grin, but couldn't. "Listen, how long has the one stall been out of order in the men's room?"

Tracey looked at him, thinking. "I don't know. About a week."

Cole said, "Seems like a long time to go unattended."

Tracey shrugged. "No men left on this floor," she said, her eyes reddening.

"Right," said Cole. "See you."

"Bye," she said, and returned to the papers on her desk.

They stepped out of the building into full sunlight. To the west Cole saw clouds piled high over the mountains, above them a bright blue sky. The kind of day when Cole missed living in Vancouver.

"Where's your car?" asked JP, squinting in the sunlight.

"Right over there." Cole pointed at the Toyota.

"Seen better years," said JP.

"Haven't we all?" said Cole.

"This place sure has," said JP and looked around.

Cole nodded. "Let's go for a drive." He said it on impulse.

"What, you and me?"

"Why not?"

"You really are trying to get me fired. Look, if Henderson saw us driving around I'd be out on my ass. I've got three years to go until retirement, and I need this job to put enough away to get by in my golden years."

Cole looked at the ground and kicked a stone. "JP," he said. "Can I call you JP?"

"It's my name."

"JP, I've got a little problem with the official version of events from the night Mr. Barnes was killed."

The watchman was silent. He squinted at Cole.

"First, I don't believe that Dale van Stempvort killed Mike Barnes. You probably think, of course I'm going to defend him." Cole waited for JP to say something, but he was quiet. Blackwater continued, "I don't know who did it, but I'm convinced of Dale's innocence. I also don't think that Barnes was killed in the mill."

"Where do you think he was killed?"

"I'm not sure," he lied, "but it wasn't the mill. No doubt you found him there, but he wasn't killed there."

"What's that got to do with us taking a drive?" JP asked warily.

"The cops say you saw him alive after my meeting with him."

"Yeah, he was in his office. I walked by and said 'Evening Mr. Barnes' and he said, 'Evening JP.' Same as most nights."

Cole nodded. "Then you found him on your rounds. I want to know what might have been going on around here before you came across Barnes."

The watchman looked up at the red brick office building. "If Henderson sees us, my ass is grass."

"I hate to tell you this, JP, but this mine isn't long for the world, and it ain't us environmentalists you need to be worried about."

"You're bullshitting me."

"I wish I was. Look, the company isn't going to dig another mine. Not right now. Maybe in five or ten years, when the price of coal makes it worth their while. What they are going to do is string this town along until they get their permits, sell lots of stock or trust units or what have you, and then take their money and run. Run straight to Indonesia or Brazil or wherever they can dig without having to pay you union wages."

"Or worry about your ducks."

"That too."

JP sighed. "OK," he said. "Get in."

They drove the route that JP made once every two hours throughout the night, a wide circle around the outside of the mine, slow but steady, so that the guard could shine his flashlight into windows and look between buildings. At this time of the day he stopped from time to time to chat with someone. After making the sweep of the perimeter, JP drove between the buildings.

"Why are you doing this?" the watchman asked Cole.

"Doing what?"

"Well, sort of sticking your nose where it doesn't belong."

"You mean, trying to find out who killed Mike Barnes?"

"Yeah. I mean, it's not going to bring the man back to life."

"No, but another man's life is at stake."

"We don't hang 'em in Canada anymore."

"Twenty-five years in prison and you might as well."

"Fair enough."

"There's also the fact that Barnes' death is going to make it pretty hard for my colleagues to save Cardinal Divide. Public opinion runs against convicted killers, and Dale, like it or not, is part of the gang trying to stop the mine."

"You said it's not long for the world anyway."

"Yeah, but it's going to destroy Cardinal Divide before it's done."

Cole regarded the security guard. He figured him to be in his mid-fifties. He was trim and neat and close-shaven. His left arm, injured years ago, was thinner than the right, but he looked strong and capable, steady. There were a thousand men like him in the community: regular, everyday guys who watched hockey on Saturday night, took their kids to practice at six in the morning, spent evenings in the basement woodshop, worked for thirty-five or forty years and retired. Went fishing.

"There's another reason," said Cole.

JP looked at him.

"It's people like you," he said.

"Oh," said JP, slowing the truck and looking between two buildings. "And what do people like me got to do with it?"

"You deserve a future. You deserve a future that is dignified. When this mine closes, then what? Are you going to work at McDonalds?"

"We got a Wendy's too," said JP, smiling. "I got options."

"You deserve real options. All your life you've been told that mining is what this community is built on. And there's no doubt about that. Mining is what built this community, and what sustained it for the last fifty years. But mining is not its future. The world is changing, and this town has to change too. You've been backed into a corner by the Hank Hendersons and Mike Barnes of the world."

"What's that got to do with solving this murder?"

"Everything, and nothing I guess."

"Speak plainly, man."

"Well, it's got everything to do with this town's future. I believe

Mike Barnes was killed because he was here to engineer the closure of the mine. If I figure out who killed him, this town might have some options. If Dale goes to prison, and the company continues to pull the wool over Oracle's eyes, then the mine will close and your options will be few. Cardinal Divide will have a hole in its side, and yahoos on ATVs will be using the haul road and rail line to get into the wilderness up against Jasper Park. But if we can prove that Dale didn't kill Barnes, and in fact someone else did because of Barnes' plans for the mine, then maybe folks around here will wake up in time to remake their future. One way or another, things are going to change. The question is, will the people working in the mine today be a part of that change, or will they be observers, left on the sidelines?"

"Nice speech," said JP, and waved to some men coming off shift. "You said there was another theory about why Barnes was killed."

"A skirt."

"That will do it to you every time," said JP. "Look, we're coming up to the mill. What do you want me to do?"

"Just what you did before finding the body."

"It's a little different during the day."

"Well, can you do what you do at night?"

He looked at this watch. "Shift is just ending, so I think I can."

He drove the truck up to one of the sets of doors, left the engine running, and stepped out. Cole looked at his watch. JP fished a set of keys from his pocket and unlocked a box on the wall, opened it, and flipped a switch. He then stepped to the doors, unlocked them, and pulled them open. As the doors swung open, the darkness inside the mill was illuminated by the headlights of the truck. JP pegged the big doors down with long bolts that anchored into the cement pad that led to the doors. He stepped back into the truck. Cole looked at this watch again. "About a minute," he said to himself.

"It's not a race," said JP.

"I know, but timing is important."

They drove into the mill, toward the coking ovens, in a wide sweep through the building. Cole looked at the speedometer. Dead slow: 5 km/hour.

"You always drive about this speed?"

233   Stephen Legault

"Yeah, inside I do. Can't hear anything if you're going faster." Cole noticed the big building was very quiet without the mill operating.

The back wall of the mill came into view and there were the double doors leading to the storage area. Cole saw the pallets of bits and steel.

"Where were you when you saw Barnes?"

"I didn't see him at first. I saw the pallets knocked over." JP stopped the truck. "I was right about here."

Cole's heart quickened. The lights of the truck shone squarely on the double doors. "Were the doors opened or closed?"

"Closed."

"What did you do then?"

JP left the ignition running and opened the truck door. Cole did the same. He followed JP as he crossed the twenty yards from the truck to the pallets. The RCMP officer was gone, but the tape was still up. "I was about here when I saw the body. It was lying on the ground in a heap, with bits all around him. I couldn't see who it was at first, but it wasn't no mill worker."

"How did you know?"

"No coveralls, no hat." JP stepped to the tape. "I got to here and knew it was Barnes. The nice shirt. Man always dressed like he was going to a wedding."

"Or a funeral."

"Right. Anyway, I saw him crumpled on the ground and ran over. There was a small pool of blood, but not too much really. His eyes were wide open so I knew he had to be dead. I radioed the RCMP from the truck. Cells don't work out here."

"You obviously didn't see anybody else around?"

JP shook his head. "No other vehicles. I told the RCMP that there were no other vehicles parked in the main lot or around the mill."

"Where did they get the idea that there was an S10 on the property that night?"

"Not from me."

Cole made a note to follow up on that. "And you didn't hear anything?"

"Nothing."

"JP, my friend, I think you are a lucky man."

"Oh, and how's that?"

"Well, I'd bet my left arm that when you found Mike Barnes' body right there, the person who killed him was on the other side of those doors."

━━━━━━━━━━━━━━━━━━━━━━━━━━━

"After you called the police, what did you do?" Cole leaned against his Toyota. He and JP were parked side by side outside the gate at the entrance to the mine.

"Once I was certain he was dead, I drove here to wait for the RCMP. It took them about forty minutes to get here."

"You didn't see anybody come or go?"

"Not a soul."

Cole was silent. Then he said, "Is there any other way in or out of the property?"

"Sure, plenty. But they're all locked."

"Who has keys?"

"Well, lots of folks do. Too many to count, really."

Cole sighed deeply. "I better get going." He looked at his watch. It was after seven. "I appreciate your willingness to show me around."

"Mike Barnes was hurting the working people around here," said JP. "There used to be three of us on night duty just a year ago. We covered the property once every half hour, instead of once every two hours. But he cut two of the posts right away. Those fellas are on pogey now. I don't have any love lost for Mike Barnes, but the man didn't deserve to die like he did."

Cole considered that. "If anything else comes to mind, give me a call, OK?" He handed JP his card with his cell number scribbled on the back.

"Will do. Take care. Watch out for Henderson."

Cole nodded. He'd be watching Hank Henderson for sure.

It dawned on him as he drove back to town that Mike Barnes' decision to cut the night watchmen from three down to one may have cost him his life, or at least let the killer get off scot-free.

As he drove to Oracle he mulled over what he head learned and what to do next.

Mike Barnes was killed in the washroom on the fourth floor of the office building. That meant that someone transported the body from the office to the mill. That someone almost certainly had to have keys to the building unless, of course, they had lifted Barnes' keys and used them to open the mill building. Were Barnes' keys accounted for? Another thing he would have to look into.

How did the assailant get off the mine property? That was less mysterious. Though he didn't know for certain, Cole guessed that whoever had the keys to the mill had keys to every other gate on the property. How they drove their car off the property without being noticed was another question all together.

Hank Henderson loomed large in his contemplation. He touched his tender chin. Quite the temper on the man. Hair trigger. Certainly capable of the sort of violence that ended Mike Barnes' life. Hank Henderson clearly wore his motivation on his sleeve. He had enough heavy mining paraphernalia lying around his office to beat a marching band to death. The only thing not clear to Cole was whether he had opportunity. Where had Hank Henderson been one week ago tonight?

Cole Blackwater had played his own hand. He told Henderson to his face that he suspected him of murder. If Henderson were the killer, then Cole Blackwater had *better* watch his back. Hadn't Henderson said as much?

He drove on as the day waned. He was weary. At this point in the campaign, energy started to drain and it took all his strength to persevere. But persevere he must, he thought, looking around him at the hills and rolling stands of forest. Behind their veil were wild things like the mother grizzly and her cubs he had seen from the crest of Cardinal Divide. As he always had, he would persevere not for his own salvation but for theirs.

He was lost in that thought when his cellphone rang.

"Blackwater."

"It's Nancy."

"What happened to 'Webber'?" he chided.

"That was yesterday."

"I have a hard time letting go," he joked.

"I know. Listen, can we meet? I've got some news for you."

"Me too."

"Well, get in line."

"Where?"

"My place. It's safest. Just make sure George Cody doesn't see you."

"I'll be there in half an hour."

"Good." She hung up.

He went first to the liquor store and bought a decent bottle of red wine. Then he drove to the Rim Rock and sat in his truck on the street, checking the parking lot and hotel for any sign of George Cody. It didn't look like George was around the hotel. He grabbed the bottle of wine and made for Nancy's room.

"What took you?" she asked, and let him in.

"Had to return the favour," he said, and handed her the wine.

"Don't think that because I drink this that I'm drinking it with you," she said, with a half smile.

"I wouldn't dare."

She opened the bottle, poured herself a full glass, and put the bottle down on the table between them.

"Don't think that because I'm helping myself that I'm drinking with *you*," he said, pouring a glass for himself.

"I'm not even paying attention," she said.

"What have you got?" Cole asked, and sat back in the chair.

"It's been quite a day," she said.

"Tell me about it."

"You just sit there and shut up and drink the wine you're not drinking with me."

"Right-ee-o," he said, finishing the glass and pouring more.

"So it's been a big day," Nancy started again. "I wrote a profile of the town for tomorrow's paper. Had a very interesting conversation with the president of the Chamber of Commerce. He struck me as an ambitious man. Seems to think that mining, as they say, is in everybody's future."

"Yeah, we met. Quite the booster. Old school. He said the same thing to me."

She smiled. "I know you met. He asked to see my press credentials. I haven't had that happen since, well, *ever* I guess. Smith stuck me as one of the people most likely to run for office."

"I got the same impression. He told me that he was setting himself up for a run for the Conservative nomination when it comes open."

"Should be soon. Old Chester Thomas is due for his next heart attack right about now," said Nancy, looking at her watch. "Doubt that he'll be able to run after number five. Four *should* be the limit. Anyway, David Smith is a driven man. He had a lot to say about the future of Oracle."

"No storm clouds on his horizon, are there?"

"I get the sense that he's the kind of guy who would change the weather. After that I did some follow up with the RCMP on logistics. Dale is being moved on Saturday morning, first thing. Seems like there was a mix-up with the forensics and they aren't getting the results from the suspected murder weapon back until Friday at noon, so they're holding him here a bit longer. I also talked to Reimer about a few odds and ends. I think she's getting suspicious. Most of the other press has left, and she wanted to know why I'm still hanging around. So did my editor for that matter, but I was able to tell him I was onto something juicy."

"He believed you?"

"Sure, I just haven't told him that you're involved is all. Everybody believes what I say so long as I don't mention you."

"Nice," he said, and tilted his head back to finish the second tumbler of wine. His chin had stopped aching. "Well, that's all great."

"I'm not done."

"Carry on," he said. He filled his glass and topped up hers.

"So I snooped around both Deborah and George's vehicles today."

"Ohhh, do tell."

"Well, Deborah's is as clean as a whistle. It was unlocked so I was even able to get a look inside. George's is another story."

Cole felt his pulse quicken. He sat forward.

"He actually has two vehicles. A 2002 Ford F150 king cab, which is registered to the hotel."

"How do you get that information?"

"Trick of the trade. He has the F150 and he has a 1983 Pontiac Pinto."

"You're kidding me."

"I am not kidding. I couldn't believe it either. The truck's clean. Looks like he uses it for hauling booze from the liquor store and bottles to the recycling depot."

"How very environmentally conscious of him," said Cole, his words slightly slurred.

"He must hose the thing down every other day, 'cause you could eat off the bed of the truck. It has a cap on the back and it was unlocked. I got a good look around. The front of the truck is pretty clean too, but it was locked up tight and I couldn't look in. The Pinto is another story. It was locked too. But the back seat was down and from what I could see through the window, there was some kind of tarp over the hatchback."

"Really?"

"Really. I couldn't tell if it was there to cover something up, or protect the seat from something. "

"Or both."

Nancy nodded. "There wasn't anything on the tarp itself, mind you, but the way it was tucked into the corners of the seat and the hatch, I'd guess that it was done pretty deliberately. Anyway, George Cody has had something in the back of that Pinto that leaks or spills or makes a real mess."

"Like Mike Barnes' head?"

Nancy made a face. "Maybe."

Cole was silent. He watched Nancy intently, holding the now empty glass loosely in one hand. He sat that way for almost a minute, regarding her, until she said, "Well, what have *you* got?"

"A lot."

"Do tell."

"You don't have any more wine around here, do you?"

"No," she lied. "And if I did, you don't need it."

"Need and want are two different things."

"Tell me what you've got, you bastard!" she said loudly, but she smiled when she said it.

"OK, OK." He told her about his calls that morning, and about the confrontation with Hank Henderson, and the tipping of that hand. He told her about his conversation and ride with JP, and about his revelation that when JP had found the body the murderer was likely still in the mill. And then he told her about the bathroom and the blood.

"Have you called the RCMP?"

"What for?"

"It's important. It might force them to reopen the case!"

"It's not enough yet. They'll just say that Dale clubbed Mike in the john and dragged him to the mill."

"They might take it more seriously than that."

"Come on, Nancy. You know they won't. They don't care about Dale, or even about Mike Barnes. They're just doing what they're told. They're protecting pricks like the corporate brass who run the mine, and wankers like David Smith. People who don't care about other people, only their own selfish interests. People whose only motive is to make sure that their own butts are covered."

Nancy sighed. She finished her own wine. "That was good wine," she said.

Cole stood up. He felt flushed and a little dizzy. "As I see it, we're down to two."

"George Cody and Hank Henderson."

"That's right. I haven't ruled out Deborah entirely, but somehow this seems more, I don't know, *manly*. I mean, you should have seen the blood in the bathroom."

"Pretty awful?"

Cole nodded and steadied himself on the desk.

"Now what?" she asked.

"Now what?" he repeated. "Now what? Now I have to catch a mole. I have to flush a mole from a hole." Cole slurred and told her about Peggy McSorlie's effort to narrow down the possible moles in the ESCOG from a score to just three or four names, and their plan to trick the mole into revealing himself.

"Can I get in on it?" she asked, eyes twinkling.

"No way," he said. "For all I know it has nothing to do whatsoever with the death of Mike Barnes. It's just a hunch. Plus I've got to protect my client. There might still be something left to save when this is all over with."

Nancy shrugged.

"And we've got to follow up on a couple of things. First, were Mike Barnes' keys found on him when he was killed? And what about that blasted Day-Timer?"

"Reimer says nothing has turned up about the appointment book. I asked about it today. She says they have searched the mill, the admin building, Dale's truck, Dale's ranch, and even Mike Barnes' place, but nothing."

Cole steadied himself against the wall. "It's got to be around somewhere."

"Cole, it could have been thrown out of a car window into the woods and eaten by a bear."

"Bears have better taste than that," he quipped.

"You know what I mean."

"I know what you mean."

"I'll look into the keys," she said. "And I'm going to try and find out more about George Cody's past. See if he has any history of violence."

Cole stood against the dresser. "This is just like old times," he said.

Nancy's face soured. "No it isn't, Cole. It had better not be. Because if this is just like old times, you're about to fuck me over, and if you do, you and Mike Barnes are going to have a lot in common, got it?"

"Calm down. I just meant, you know, you and me working together."

"There was never a you and me working together. There was you working to jerk off your own ego, and there was me, getting bent over and fucked because of it."

"You liked it."

She grabbed the empty wine bottle and threw it at him. Maybe because he had drunk most of its contents, he was able to step aside quickly enough that it grazed his shoulder and bounced off the wall and hit the dresser behind him. "You take that back, you shithead."

"I'm sorry. I was only joking."

"It's not funny. I lost my job. My career. I'll never be able to work the Hill again."

"Sorry." He let his head hang down, but didn't take his eyes off of her lest she throw something else.

"And I loved you, you asshole."

He was silent.

"You broke my Goddamn heart. You shattered me. Losing my job was bad enough. But I lost you, you fucker. It nearly killed me."

For the first time Cole Blackwater became aware that he wasn't alone in the world. It had never really occurred to him that she had loved him. He always felt that to her he was just entertainment, the sort of thing you do when you're bored and you want to live a little closer to the edge of things.

"I'm sorry," he said again.

"Yeah, well so am I. Now get the fuck out," she said, and turned her back on him.

18 He knew he should head straight back to Peggy McSorlie's ranch, but he went to the bar instead. He inspected every face in the joint deliberately as he entered. So intent was he on watching his back that he didn't see George Cody behind the bar until George greeted him.

"Howdy stranger!" he said cheerfully when Cole leaned against the counter.

Cole turned quickly, startled. "Hi George."

George peered at him "Your face is healing up. You're no uglier now than you were when you first got here. Though it looks like you cut yourself pretty good shaving this morning."

"Close shave of another kind."

"You like to mix it up, don't you?"

"Keeps me from being too big of a horse's patoot."

George laughed. "Around here that's called a horse's ass."

"Where I come from too, but I promised my daughter I'd clean up my language. Its hard, but I'm trying."

"Very noble."

"Thanks. Can I get a Jameson? Rocks."

George poured. "Didn't make any promises about the booze though, huh?"

"You my counsellor now?" said Cole testily.

"None of my business," said George, holding his hands up. "Just giving you a hard time."

Cole took a hearty pull on the Jameson. It burned a little after the wine, but it felt warm in his belly. "Forget it. I'm just in a foul mood."

"I thought you had headed home. Deborah told me you checked out."

"I did. I was. But I changed my mind. Unfinished business."

"Oh?" George drew beer for the waitress.

"Don't like the way things turned out with the mine and with Mike Barnes and with Dale van Stempvort." Cole finished his whiskey, put the glass on the bar, and tapped it lightly. George looked at him and poured another measure.

"Don't like it at all," said Cole, and pulled on his fifth drink of the night.

"And what don't you like?"

"None of it. First, Dale van Stempvort is an idiot, but he's no killer. Second, Mike Barnes was a prick, but he didn't deserve to get his brains splattered all over the b—" Cole checked himself. "All over the place. Third, the Buffalo Anthracite Mine has had its day, and something new is needed around here, but that isn't going to happen if Dale gets framed for Mike Barnes' murder." Cole spoke quietly and quickly, and looked at his hands wrapped around the tumbler of Irish whiskey.

George leaned on the bar, resting his elbows there. His head was low, but his eyes were on Cole. "You've got some strong opinions."

"Sure do. Always have."

"Seems to get you in trouble."

"Nothing I can't handle."

"Seem to remember you not being able to handle the chair the other night."

"OK, so the chair was a surprise. I was out of practice. I'm back now."

"So you stuck around Oracle to solve the mystery of Mike Barnes' murder."

"That's right."

"Got any suspects?"

"I got a few."

"Care to share?"

Cole sipped his drink. He felt both foggy and razor-sharp at the same time. His peripheral vision had vanished and all that remained was straight ahead. Dead straight ahead. "Two types of people," he said. "People who didn't like what Mike Barnes was up to at the mine, and people who didn't like what Mike Barnes got up to when he wasn't at the mine."

"That sounds like a lot of people."

"Yep. Whole town pretty much."

"You narrowing it down?"

"Yep." He sipped his drink.

George poured a couple of beers and mixed a rum and coke. He came back and resumed his place across from Cole. "So you've narrowed it down."

"Yep," Cole said again. "Two people."

"That's pretty narrow."

"Pretty narrow," Cole agreed.

"You going to tell me who those two people are?" George spoke evenly.

Cole sipped his drink. He set it down and looked at his hands. He used to have fast hands as a boxer. How fast were they tonight? "Nope," he finally said. After five drinks, slow as molasses at Christmas.

"Suit yourself. But I've read a lot of mystery books, and I got a pretty good eye for this sort of thing."

Cole shrugged. The adrenaline born from being so close to one of his murder suspects was now wearing off. He finished his drink. When George served him this sixth, he said, "I even got a magnifying glass somewhere around here, and one of them silly hats, if you want it, Sherlock." Cole smiled as George laughed. Funny, he thought. Very funny.

He drove himself back to Peggy's place. George wanted to call him a cab, but it was a half-hour drive, and would cost him half a day's wage, so he drove slowly with the window down and the music turned way up. When he pulled into the yard he felt a bump and thought maybe he'd run over a piece of wood, or if he were lucky, a cat, but didn't bother to check. He stepped heavily out of the truck, almost fell, and staggered across the yard.

He walked to the barn, figured he was drunk enough to find a saddle blanket or two and fall asleep in the hay. Better than crash through the unfamiliar house, wake everybody up, and explain how he drove home snot-hanging, toilet-hugging drunk. That wouldn't go over big.

But when he opened the barn door, sleep was the last thing on his mind. The swarm of hay-scented air hit him like a leather glove in the face and he reeled in the thick aroma. He took two steps and tripped on a loose floorboard and fell heavily to the ground. He lay on the floor, feeling a trickle of fresh blood seeping from his face. He felt so tired. So tired.

A golden cloak of evening light draped itself over the gentle folds of Alberta's Porcupine Hills. Summer insects buzzed and droned. The delicate light slanted across the rolling hills and caught the myriad insects in their evening dance, like so many dust motes.

The hills rose and fell, rose and fell, sparse clumps of aspen trees tucked in among them. On their flanks, grasses grew thickly, making the Porcupine Hills some of Canada's finest ranch country. In the distance, the Front Ranges of the Rocky Mountains towered like the fortified ramparts of an ancient castle. Free of snow in early June, they formed a blue-grey wall of limestone rising three thousand feet above the gently rolling plains that broke like shattered waves at their feet.

The slopes of the Porcupine Hills were pocked with the black and brown forms of free-range cattle grazing their way downslope toward evening pasture. Where once buffalo roamed, now domestic breeds took sustenance on the rich nutrients of rough fescue.

At the base of one hill, a ranch was laid out among a few spreading cottonwood trees that lined a tiny creek. The trees gave meagre shelter from the harsh summer sun, the biting winter winds, and the nearly constant howl of the Chinook that blew year round.

The ranch house was a rambling, single-story affair with a wide porch and shuttered windows and a small kitchen garden on the creek side of the building. First built in 1895, it was added to when the market for cattle would permit and when war did not pull the homestead's men overseas. A chicken coop, pig pen, tack shed, and drive shed were scattered around the ranch house. Half a dozen derelict automobiles and a ramshackle assortment of barrels littered the near pasture and interrupted the picturesque ranch image.

Light shone from the kitchen of the ranch house, but no shadows passed across its windows.

The barn, set back against hills that rose toward the west, leaked light though its weathered boards. The broad doors stood open and the incandescence spilt across the ranch yard.

The sound of a man's voice rose above the hum of the evening. A dog barked. Feet shuffled on canvas. The heavy sound of bodies colliding went out like a dull call into the night.

Inside the barn the walls were piled high with hay, the bales stacked ten or twelve high around the outside of the barn. But at its centre there were no bales. Where in other barns there might be cattle feed or farm machinery a boxing ring stood. No crude arrangement of hemp ropes strung between crates or chairs, this ring was complete with a raised canvas floor and cloth-covered ropes strung tightly between corner poles fixed firmly in place in the barn floor. Four overhead lights hanging from the barn ceiling filled the ring with a harsh white light and cast tall shadows of three bodies onto the straw-lined walls.

Two boys circled each other in the ring. One of the boys is nearly a man, fifteen or sixteen years old. The other is younger, not more than thirteen. They each wear heavy gloves and trunks, and sweat streaks their bodies. Farm boys both, they wear the broad shoulders and lean, muscled arms of those accustomed to pitching bales of hay onto the bed of a tractor. They circle each other while a man, also in gloves, call to them.

"That's it, boys, that's it. Keep light on those feet," he says.

The border collie circles the ring, herding the boys, barking.

"Watch for the opening, Walt, watch for the opening. That's it. Now step in," shouts the man.

The older boy feints and then steps in with a quick right hand jab, and the younger boy is knocked back. The older boy steps out and the two continue to circle each other.

Stockier than the younger boy, Walter is 5'11", heavy across the chest, with short-cropped dark hair and a heavy, brooding brow. But he smiles as he circles the ring, and winks at his brother as they trade jabs.

Walter dances sideways as the younger boy throws a left and then a right that glances off the older boy's shoulder.

"He saw that coming, Cole. He saw that coming! You can't tell him you're going to hit him!" The man's voice is hoarse. The smell of liquor is thick on him. He steps sideways, heavily, watching the boys. "You've got to set him up." Henry Blackwater wears his faded boot-cut Wrangler jeans and a white undershirt, sweat stains spreading from under his arms across his chest. His hair is grey and cut short, and his face hard and cut deeply with lines. A broad man who has not lost any of his youthful muscle, he lurches around the ring, yelling.

The boys continue to circle. "Watch him now, Walter. Watch him. Wait for him."

Leaner than his brother, Cole is not skinny. His arms, long and corded with muscles, give him an immense reach. His arms dangle to his mid thighs when at his sides. His chest and back, though not

Stephen Legault

broad like his older brother's, are nevertheless strong from evenings and weekends spent working on the western ranch.

"Watch him now, Walter," shouts Henry Blackwater. The older
boy feints as Cole throws a left jab. Before Cole can throw the right,
Walter hits him with a wide left and Cole stumbles backward.

"Jesus Christ," grumbles the man. "Jee-sus Christ." He paces
around the ring, holding onto the ropes for stability. "Cole, what
the hell are you doing? Don't you pay attention, boy? Don't you
listen? You've got to move quick if you want to hit him. You can't
wind up like you're in one of those Goddamn cowboy movies. You
can't tell him you're going to hit him!"

The two boys circle each other. Cole throws another left-right
combination that grazes his brother's gloves and shoulder. Neither
boy is smiling now.

"You never listen do you, Cole?" His father shouts. "Always
want to do it your way. Well, your way is going to get you knocked
on your ass. It's going to get you punched in the nose, is what's
going to happen!"

The boys trade jabs but neither seem to be into the boxing
match anymore. Their father wheels around the ring, his hands
waving above him.

"If it's not one thing it's another with you, boy. You bitch about
how I try to teach you to box. If it's not that, you're bitching about
how I run the ranch. Bitch about how I take care of them wolves
that are killin' our cattle. Bitch at me about using pesticides on
the place, like you want to grow a crop of Goddamn weeds rather
than putting aside some hay!"

The old man gripes the upper rope with both hands, sways a
little, spitting as he yells. He shakes his head and seems to realize
that he is in the barn beside the boxing ring. He stops shouting.
The air is still. The dog had stopped barking. The two boys do not
look at Henry Blackwater, but at each other, at their feet, at the
mat. Anything to avoid his furious eyes.

"Well, what the hell are you standing there for?"

"Take it easy, Pop," says Walter quietly.

"Don't tell me what do to, Walter. You shut up and box now."

The two boys raise their hands again and begin to dance side
to side, throwing a few exploratory punches. Walter lands an
easy right jab that Cole stumbles back from. Cole then steps in

to throw the left-right combination they have been working on all night, but Walter steps aside and Cole trips over his brother's feet and hits the mat. Walter stoops to help Cole to his feet. Both boys are dog-tired after a long day of work and a long workout at night.

"Goddamn it, Cole!" shouts Blackwater. Both boys stop. "How many times I got to tell you? You can't just poke at him with that left if you're goin' to set him up for a knockout punch. You got to hit him hard and get him leanin' into that right!" The man is sweating and his face is flushed. He steps back from the ropes and demonstrates, his hands up in front of his face, his back bent and his body bobbing in the typical boxer's stance.

"You got to watch for your man to step a little off balance and then pop, pop!" He throws two quick left jabs. His flesh and the leather in the gloves pop in the air. "And then pow!" He swings out with his right. "That's how you do it." Henry straightens. The boys puff hard, beads of sweat dripping from their noses. They stand close to each other, their bodies slick and coated with the dust from the hay.

"Now you put those Goddamn gloves up, Cole, and show me how you can do it." Henry swings under the rope and pushes Walter none-too-gently aside and takes up a stance in front of Cole.

Cole looks at Walter. Walter looks down at his younger brother. Cole steps forward.

"Come on now, put em' up!" The father shouts. He starts to scuffle sideways, his feet heavy.

Cole looks again at Walter. He steps forward and begins to circle before his hulking father. They trade a few punches.

"Now watch for it," the father says, circling, his feet dragging. The boy's eyes are fixed on his father's.

"Watch for it."

They circle. They trade a few exploratory punches. Henry Blackwater stumbles a little. "Watch—" As the father lilts sideways, Cole strikes quickly with two left jabs, landing them on his father's chin, cutting the man's sentence off, and knocking him back a little. Henry Blackwater's eyes open with surprise.

Then Cole steps forward with his right foot and lands a right hook squarely on the father's cheek, knocking him backward against the ropes.

Cole brightens and lowers his hands a little. Walter grins behind him. Cole begins to speak, relaxing. "I got it!" he says as his father's right glove lands squarely in the middle of his face, knocking him off his feet, sending him crumpling to the mat. A trail of blood follows him down, streaming from his nose. The sound of his body colliding with the canvas is quickly absorbed by the hay-lined walls.

The dog explodes in a frenzy of barking and runs out of the barn into the night.

Walter quickly drops to his knees beside his prone brother.

Henry Blackwater remains standing, swaying, hands up and at the ready.

"Cole, are you OK?" The boy's nose is crooked and bleeding, but his eyes are open, conscious of the swirling world around him. He says nothing.

Walter looked up at his father. "His nose is broken."

"He's got to learn," says his father distantly. "Got to learn. You can't let your guard down. Not once. Not ever."

Walter cradles his brother's head in his arm. Cole focuses on his brother's reassuring presence.

"Can't let your guard down just cause you land a punch. Got to learn! I never let them get in. Not once. Just cause you land a punch, you got to watch for what's coming at you next. Never let your guard down!"

Cole Blackwater lay on the canvas mat, bleeding, his head spinning, his brother holding a towel to his face while soothing Cole with his voice: "We'll get some ice. I'll get Mom. It will be OK, Cole. Just lie here and don't say a word. Don't say a word."

That had been nearly twenty-five years ago. Cole blinked the hay dust from his eyes and managed to roll over onto his back. He rose to his feet and found his way, swaying, to the tack room where he retrieved a couple of saddle blankets that smelled sweetly of horses.

It was three years since he had been in his parents' barn.

Fleeing disgrace and shame in Ottawa, on his way to much of the same in Vancouver, Cole took a detour. He stopped in Calgary on the long drive across Canada and turned left to make the two-hour drive south along Highway 22, a lovely little road that wound through the foothills. Then he turned east and travelled over the crest of the Porcupine Hills and down into their lee to the family homestead.

He was there for a week before the old man showed his face at a meal. Cole didn't care. Being on the ranch was a nasty piece of time travel. All of a sudden he was fourteen years old, boxing every day and getting the living hell beaten out of him. He would have left after the first two days but he saw his mother only once every two or three years.

So he stayed, helped around the house, seeded a field, and repaired a manure spreader his father had let fall into disuse. Cole was aware of his father's presence in the yard. He could hear his father in the barn where the cows slept in the winter. Late at night the old man listened to a tinny radio in the basement workshop. Cole could see his father's shadow moving between the weathered boards. Could hear his cursing, and then the long silences.

Cole avoided the old man and steered clear of the barn except when he wanted to ride. Then he would stand outside the barn doors for five minutes to work up the courage to step into that hated place to look for saddle, blankets, halter, and bridle, and choose a horse that needed running.

At the end of the second week, Cole was out riding an old mare named Blue when his father suddenly rode up beside him. Henry Blackwater looked every bit the cowboy. He wore a tight, checkered, pearl-button shirt with a felt-lined tan vest over it, the zipper done up nearly to the top. He had a pair of dark blue Wranglers on and wore a sweat-stained Stetson on his head at a peculiar angle. Cole suspected that he had already been drinking some of his home brew, sour mash, by the way he held the reins so lightly. If he fell off his horse and hit his head on the rocks below, that was fine with Cole. The world would not miss Henry Blackwater.

"Your mother's pretty glad you're here," said the old man.

"It's good to see her," said Cole, eyes staring straight ahead at the horizon of blue peaks above the bristled Porcupine Hills.

"Got yourself in a bit of trouble back in Ottawa, did you?"

Cole was silent. Had his father been waiting for Cole to let his guard down before striking?

His father spat. "Got yourself in a little too deep, didn't you, boy?"

Cole shifted his weight and the saddle creaked.

"You don't have to answer me, Cole. We both know that you fucked up good this time, if you take my meaning." The old man laughed harshly. "I should have made sure that you knew right from wrong better. Should have taught you your lessons better. Should have made sure you knew how to take care of your family right."

Cole realized he was holding his breath and let it out with a low whistle.

"Ain't you going to say anything?"

"Not to you," said Cole, and he turned his horse around.

The old man trotted to catch up. "What the fuck were you thinking, Cole? Fucking around on your wife. Making a mess of your job? Bringing shame on your daughter? What the fuck were you thinking?"

Cole pressed his heels into Blue and she stepped up her gait.

"You can't outride me, city boy. I live in the saddle. You're just a fucking tourist here."

Cole looked over at the old man. He grinned at Cole.

"What made you such a hateful bastard, I wonder?" Cole finally asked.

"Having to put up with good-for-nothing pricks like you all my life," his father growled.

"If we're lucky," said Cole ruefully, "we won't have to put up with *you* for too much longer."

"I'm going to outlive you all," his father said, spat again, and turned his horse away from Cole.

That was the last time Cole spoke with his father. By the end of the day the old man was dead.

Cole stayed on to help with the funeral, got drunk with his brother Walter, and then drove to Vancouver to start the next chapter of his life. He hoped he would be able to get on with things with the old man finally gone, make a clean break with the violence of his past. Indeed, Cole became good at forgetting. He routinely went days without a thought about that final night in the barn under the glare of the lights, and the sudden end there on the mat. On those days Cole was just like everybody else walking down the streets of Vancouver.

But the final act of violence in Henry and Cole Blackwater's explosive relationship flooded back as he lay wrapped in blankets on the floor of the barn. The barn was where it always happened. Under the swinging lights, on the mat, or if he refused to step in as he sometimes did, against the bales of hay, or on the blood-soaked floor. The barn was where it always happened, and the barn was where it came to a bloody end.

Cole rolled in his blankets, pushing the evil memory back into the darkness where it had secreted itself for the last three years. His thrashing upending a table full of tools that crashed to the floor around him. He shouldn't have come back to Alberta. Should have left the past behind him. Shouldn't have dug so deeply. But like the miners he was trying to stop from destroying Cardinal Divide, Cole Blackwater pushed on, regardless of the consequences. He had stopped asking why or why not. He was digging steadily toward where he had buried the awful truth in his own past.

She had loved him and he destroyed her. That was what Cole Blackwater did to the things that dared love him. That was what had been done to him, and in turn he passed that rare gift of destruction on to those who loved him.

His brain swam. He pulled himself to sitting and leaned against one of the barn's pillars.

The rich smell of horses churned his memories. His father was a broken and angry man who, if there had been any justice in the world, would have been killed on the shores of France. But then Cole and Walter, and Cole's progeny, Sarah, would never have been. Henry Blackwater deserved his fate, thought Cole, but Sarah deserved a richer inheritance.

Sarah deserved far better.

He awoke to the smell of coffee.

Gord McSorlie stood over him, steaming cup in hand.

"Thought this might come in handy this morning."

Cole opened his eyes. He lay curled in the fetal position on the floor of the barn. He was cold, and his body ached terribly.

"I've never slept in this barn," said Gord, looking around him as if considering the possibility. "How was it?"

Cole groaned and pushed himself upright to lean on the pillar again. He accepted the cup of coffee and held it to warm his hands.

"That good, eh? Well, when you're ready, there's a hot shower and Peggy has breakfast ready for you too. I'm told you have a big day ahead of you. Better get cracking."

Cole looked up and offered a weak smile in thanks.

"You ran over one of Peggy's rock gardens last night, by the way."

Cole moaned under his breath. "Sorry," he said balefully.

"It will be fine. Better check the undercarriage of that truck of yours, though."

Half an hour later he sat at the McSorlie's long kitchen table drinking a third cup of coffee. He had showered and changed and felt surprisingly presentable.

"What happened to your chin?" asked Peggy as she served him breakfast.

He told her about Hank Henderson.

"You sure have a way with people, don't you? Have you ever met someone you didn't get in a fight with?" She chided him as she pushed a few more sausages onto his plate.

"You," he said. They shared a laugh and then he told her about the blood in the bathroom.

She sat down as he described what he thought had transpired in that fourth floor lavatory. Then he recounted his tour of the mine, and what Nancy had learned about the investigation's impasse on the murder weapon.

"You have to go to the RCMP with this new information," Peggy encouraged him.

"I know. Nancy said the same thing. I just thought that she wanted to scoop, so I was a bit of a crank with her."

"Scoop or not, it's important. I think they should know."

"I'll talk with Perry Gilbert first, and then go to the detachment to talk with Reimer. Which names have you got?"

"For the moles?"

Cole nodded and finished his sausages.

"I have three. James Preacher is a retired miner who worked

at the Buffalo Anthracite Mine for more than thirty years. When he retired he started coming to our monthly meetings, and has become more and more involved as this fight has heated up. He's been with us for about two years, and he seems pretty committed, though he'd never say so publicly. I know it's not very generous of me, but I just wonder if he's really on our side on this, you know, with his past and all."

Cole was nodding, making notes in his book.

"The second is Basilo Francesco. He owns one of the town's three hardware stores. He's been in Oracle most of his life, but only recently joined us. He tells me that he's worried about the direction the town is going in and wants to help create economic diversification. More than just mining and timber. He seems like he's on the up and up, but he's also a member of the Chamber of Commerce and that makes me wonder.

"The third is a girl named Anne Stanton. She's really new in town. Just moved here a month ago from Edmonton. She's graduated from the University of Alberta's Political Science program, and came to Oracle to work for the summer. Says she wanted to be closer to the mountains and to help with the Cardinal Divide fight. She says she took a class on activism at University where they talked about this campaign, and wanted to get involved. She seems pretty idealistic, but she's been a big help so far."

Cole sat back in his chair. "So what story are we going to give these people?"

They discussed it and Cole took notes to make sure he kept it straight.

"OK," he said, and stood up. "I better get cracking."

"I'd like to come along to these interviews," Peggy said.

"That's fine with me. I figure I'll be out all day. Why don't we take separate cars and I'll meet you at James Preacher's place around 11 AM?"

They agreed.

Cole called Perry Gilbert on his way into town. He filled him in on all the previous day's events. They decided to talk to Reimer together. It was nine-thirty when he arrived at the RCMP detachment. Perry was waiting for him.

"You look rough this morning."

"Thanks," said Cole as he walked toward the building. "I feel worse than I look."

"What happened to your chin?"

"It ran into Hank Henderson's fist."

"Nice work if you can get it."

"Can't beat the pay," Cole said and climbed the steps.

Sergeant Reimer came to the desk. "What can I do for you gentlemen?"

"Need a moment of your time this morning, Sergeant," said Gilbert. "Something has come up that I think you'll want to know about."

"My office," she said.

The followed her. She offered them two chairs opposite her and looked at them.

"Cole was at the mine site yesterday meeting with a few folks, and found something that we think will interest you."

"You were at the mine site?"

"Yes, I was."

"Didn't I tell you not to interfere with this investigation?"

Cole took a deep breath. "Are you interested in what I've found or not?"

Sergeant Reimer looked visibly angry. She said nothing.

"When I was using the washroom on the fourth floor, I happened to drop something from my pocket. I bent over to pick it up, and found blood splattered under the sink and on the walls beneath the counter. It looked to be about a week old."

Cole could see Sergeant Reimer processing this information.

"I don't think the blood came from some everyday kind of injury, you know, like a paper cut or what have you. There was a quite a lot of it."

"Will you reopen the investigation, Sergeant?" Perry Gilbert asked.

Reimer smiled thinly. "It's a bit too early for that, Mr. Gilbert. If anything this may be a case of changing the scene of the crime, not the perpetrator."

"But you'll send a team out to look at the room? Cole tells me there aren't any men working on the fourth floor now."

"That's what Mike Barnes' secretary told me," added Cole.

"So there shouldn't be too many prints on the door to the washroom."

"Assuming that the perpetrator didn't wear gloves," added Reimer.

"One way or another, it's worth looking into. You can at least match the blood types, and determine location. Maybe you'll get lucky and lift some prints too."

"I'll call Red Deer and have a forensics team sent in. Might take a day."

"Can you have the room sealed?"

"I don't have the manpower to put someone on the door, but I'll call the mine and ask that it be locked."

Perry smiled. "Good enough."

"Mr. Blackwater," said Sergeant Reimer. "Don't think that this information changes how I feel about your involvement in this case. This investigation is a matter for the police, not for a private citizen."

"Then it would be helpful, Sergeant," said Cole, failing to hide the contempt in his voice, "if the police actually investigated, instead of merely convicting a man based on a quote in a newspaper. If I hadn't found that blood, you'd still think the murder took place in the mill. What else don't you know? You still haven't established the murder weapon."

"Those results will be back tomorrow."

"And what will they show? That Mike Barnes hit his head on a drill bit? That could have happened after he was dead."

Sergeant Reimer stood up. "You gentlemen know your way out?"

Cole stood. "You've got an innocent man behind bars while the real killer is walking the streets of *this* town, Sergeant."

"That will be all, Mr. Blackwater."

"I have one more question, if you don't mind, Sergeant. Were Mike Barnes' keys found on his body when he died?" asked Perry.

Reimer shook her head, but she picked up the phone. "It's Reimer," she said into the handset. "Were there keys on the deceased when he was brought in? OK, thanks."

"Full set, including car keys, office keys, and the master key for the mine."

They left.

"That went well," said Perry Gilbert, stepping lightly down the entrance stairs.

Cole moved ponderously behind him. "'Bout as well as I expected. Can you get anybody to light a fire under her butt?"

"I'll call my supervisor and ask her to file a complaint. What are you up to for the rest of the day?"

"I'm going to ferret out the snitch inside ESCOG."

"You still think that's connected?"

"Who knows? But if nothing else, it will close up one hole in what is fast becoming a very leaky weir."

"Let me know if anything turns up."

They said goodbye and Cole drove across town to his meeting with Peggy McSorlie.

"You ready?" he asked her in front of James Preacher's house.

"I think so."

He rang the bell and a moment later James Preacher answered the door. Cole remembered him from the now-distant strategy session at Peggy's house. James Preacher stood under five foot ten and Cole pegged him as a welterweight. His narrow body was tucked into a pair of grey workpants that were clean, and a red and black chequered shirt that had been carefully pressed. He had thin, grey hair cut short and wore glasses. He greeted them and ushered them inside. "Come in, come in. Will you have coffee?"

"No thanks," said Cole, "not for me."

"Only if you're having some, James," said Peggy.

"I've got a pot on. Come on into the kitchen." The home was neat and clean, but showed signs of wear and age.

"How long have you lived here, James?"

"In this place, since 1967. In Oracle, all my life. I was born here. 1938."

Cole looked at the photos on the mantle of the fireplace. Two grown sons, with children of their own. "You're a grandfather, James?"

"I have four grandchildren. Three girls and a boy."

"Do you see them much?"

"Not as often as I'd like. The missus and I get out to Toronto about once a year; that's where our oldest son lives. Our other boy is in California, Silicon Valley, and we only get there every couple of years. It's just too expensive. But they all come here for Christmas every year, so that gives us a lot of time with the little ones."

They sat at the table. "What's this all about?" asked James.

"Well, we're trying to get the campaign started again, James," said Peggy.

"We're hoping for your input. Peggy and I are contemplating a new tack," said Cole, "and we want to see what you think. He explained the new direction that the campaign might take, watching the miner's face for any sign that might betray his intentions. He added the variation that he and Peggy had agreed on and then sat back. "What do you think?"

James folded his hands on his chest. "I don't know. It seems like a pretty big risk to take."

"We feel we need to get our side of the story out right now, James," said Peggy.

"But to publicly condemn Dale before he's gone to trial seems unnecessary."

Cole watched him. "Do you think the media will pick up on it?"

"Pick up on it? They'll eat Dale van Stempvort alive. I thought you two believe he's innocent."

"We do, James. But we're up against a wall."

James looked at his hands. "I trust you, Peggy. And you too, Cole. If this is what you have to do, I'll support you. I just feel bad for Dale is all. He's no killer. I don't think so, at least." The old man sighed. "So, when are you doing this?"

"Middle of next week," said Cole. That gave the story enough time to leak.

"Thanks for including me on this."

"We're going to try and meet with everybody today," said Cole.

James showed them to the door. When they were back at their vehicles Cole said, "That went well."

Peggy looked downcast, "I hate to set people up like that."

"Well, one of them is setting *us* up pretty good. And Dale too. They'll understand. Let's go and see Basilo."

They drove downtown and parked. Basilo was behind the counter at his hardware store when they walked in. He called for one of his store clerks to come, showed them into the small office behind the front desk, and closed the door.

"I know what you are thinking," he said after they shook hands and sat down. "You think I am the one who gave that information to that reporter. It's not so."

Cole and Peggy looked at each other. "That's not what this is about, Basilo," said Cole.

"Please, call me Basil. And it is OK. It makes sense, no? I am a business man, a member of the Chamber of Commerce. You think that because I run a business, because I take my lunch with people like David Smith, that I am only in favour of development. Of the mines. Of the mill. Well, it is not so. I came to Oracle because I wanted to make a better life for my family. We moved to the Crowsnest Pass when I was three years old." He held up three fingers to emphasis the point. "My father, he worked underground his whole life. He died when he was just sixty-two years old. Lung cancer. Breathed coal dust his whole life. My mother, she worked like a slave. Six kids. No running water until the 1950s. No telephone until 1961. We had nothing. That mine, they did nothing for us. Nothing, I tell you. When my father died, they did nothing for us. So I moved here. I knew mining was good for a town, but I see now that mining isn't what *this* town needs. Some day the mine will close. Maybe it will be next year. Maybe ten years from now. But what will be left after the mine closes? A hole in the ground. A bunch of rock in the creeks. What will the tourists want to see? A hole in the ground? I say no. I think they will want to see grizzly bears. So if the Cardinal Divide is turned into a hole in the ground, then in ten years there will be no Oracle. No town. No future. All the tourists, they will go someplace else. They will go to Banff. To Jasper. They will drive through here and not stop. They will not stop because there will be nothing to see."

Cole and Peggy watched him.

"So what do you think we should do?" asked Cole.

"Keep fighting. That's all we can do, no?"

"We were thinking about announcing our support for Dale van Stempvort in the newspapers next week," said Cole.

"I think that's nice, but I don't see how that stops the mine."

"We can use it as a hook to tell the story that the company only wants to build the haul road and rail line, and that Mike Barnes' murder is really just a diversion from the mine's plans."

Basilo looked at the two of them. "I would not do this. I would not say anything about Dale one way or another. Instead, I'd focus on the economics. What happens to a town after the mine closes? Then what? What about the independent businessmen like me?"

"You're taking a big risk being against the mine, aren't you?"

"Life is risk. To be alive is risk. My father taught me to stand up for what I believe. This I believe: if the mine is dug into Cardinal Divide and the McLeod River, then all will be lost for his region. We will have killed the goose that gave us the golden egg."

They left.

"We should put him on TV," said Cole as they walked out of the hardware store.

"We could, if the Chamber of Commerce doesn't first."

"Two down, one to go."

They drove back through the residential part of town and up the hill to the new homes and condos to find the building where Anne Stanton lived. It was a new building, three stories tall, with wide balconies that overlooked the forested foothills beyond the Portsmith River Valley.

Anne Stanton was twenty-two years old, a recent graduate with a degree in political science, and a poster child for the modern urban environmentalist. She wore her brown hair long and tied back in a pony tail, and wore black calf-length lululemon yoga pants and a matching shirt. She smiled when she greeted Cole and Peggy and welcomed them into the apartment. "I could have met you downtown," she said, "and saved you the trip to the 'burbs."

"We don't mind, Anne," said Peggy. "We're trying to stop in on everybody that was at last week's strategy session."

"Nice place," Cole said, looking at a print on the wall of a bull elk in rut.

"Thanks. I'm just subletting it for the summer," said Anne, looking at the print.

"Are you staying in Oracle after that?" asked Cole.

"We'll see about work," she said. "I might also head back to Edmonton to continue my Master's degree."

Cole moved around the apartment. It was sparsely furnished, with a couch and two overstuffed chairs in the living room facing the fireplace. There was no TV. Wildlife prints hung on the wall, most by local or amateur artists, Cole guessed. There was a cabinet of china in the dining room, along with some trophies for sporting events: curling, hockey, and skeet shooting.

"Who are you subletting the place from?" Cole called to Anne, who was in the kitchen making tea.

"Oh, a friend of mine from school. His family owns this place. They come out at Christmas. Otherwise it's mostly empty."

Funny place to have a Christmas retreat, through Cole. No skiing. No accounting for taste, though.

"So Anne, you know why we're here. We're trying to plot our course forward."

They talked for half an hour and when Cole and Peggy left, waterlogged with too much herbal tea, they stood by their vehicles and talked.

"Now what?" asked Peggy.

"We wait. See what happens."

"What did you think of Anne?"

"Idealistic," said Cole. "Too much school, not enough world."

Peggy smiled her agreement.

They parted ways. Peggy headed back to the farm and Cole drove downtown to find lunch and a bathroom to empty his bladder of herbal tea and think over the morning's conversations. There was something bothering him. Something that wasn't right. He couldn't put his finger on it. But it was there, in his brain. He needed more coffee to shake loose whatever it was that was needling him.

19

It was early afternoon when Cole parked the Toyota across the street from the Henderson residence. Next on his to-do list was to figure out if Hank Henderson had had the opportunity to kill Mike Barnes.

He sat in his truck for twenty minutes, working up the story he planned to give to Mrs. Henderson, if in fact she was home. He spent another ten minutes calculating how he would deal with Hank Henderson should he come home from work early. It was unlikely, but Cole wanted to have an escape plan etched clearly in his mind.

Cole grabbed his notebook, straightened himself as best he could, and examined his face in the Toyota's mirror. The cut on his chin was still covered with a bandage that Cole had forgotten to change that morning, and a little spot of blood showed through it. The wound on his cheek, now a week old, was healing, but the dark sutures still bristled, and had now begun to dig into the skin that they held fast. His eye was no longer discoloured from the beating in the bar, but both eyes were red and puffy from his night of drinking, and from his slumber on the barn floor. His hair was a curly mess. Really, he looked like someone who had just been released from prison, and he was not confident that anyone who answered the door at the Henderson residence would speak to him.

"What the hey," he said. Cole stepped out of the truck and heard his joints pop and protest as he called his body into action. He walked across the road and up the steps to the neat 1950s side-split that the telephone book said was the residence of H. Henderson, the only Henderson in the book.

He rang the bell and forced a pleasant smile onto his grisly face.

The door opened and a diminutive woman looked out through the screen door. "Yes?" she said.

"Mrs. Henderson?"

"Yes, I'm Emma Henderson."

"Ma'am, my name is Carey Blackstone. I'm with *Report on Business* magazine. I'm to meet Mr. Henderson here today."

"Oh, he didn't say anything to me."

"We were going to meet here and discuss a story I'm doing on

Oracle's economy, and the role that the mine plays in it. He didn't say anything to you?"

"No," she said, and looked a little worried.

"May I come in to wait for him?"

"I should give him a call."

"He's likely on his way home right now," said Cole quickly.

"I'll try him on his cell."

Cole held his breath. She closed the door and went to the kitchen to make the call. A minute later she came back.

"I couldn't reach him."

"Well, maybe I'll just forget it," said Cole calmly.

"Oh, no, Henry always keeps his word. He'll be here. Please, do come in."

Cole stepped inside.

"Don't worry about your shoes, Mr. Blackstone. Here, come sit in the kitchen while we wait for Henry."

"Thank you ma'am."

They sat at the Formica-topped kitchen table. Emma Henderson offered Cole coffee or tea, neither of which he accepted. "Just water please," he said.

She sat across from him.

"Have you lived here long?" he asked.

"Oh yes, both Henry and I were born in Oracle. And we've lived in this house all our married lives. Raised three children here, two boys and a girl."

Cole looked around the room. It was the picture of a well-kept home. Counters bare and orderly. Floor scrubbed. The CBC played low from a radio in the corner.

On the wall across from the kitchen table was a portrait taken in the early 1970s. It was easy for Cole to tell the photo's age; no other time in history presented such easily distinguished fashion. The image looked to be a Sears Portrait Studio picture. It showed a younger Hank Henderson surrounded by his family. The two sons and the daughter, all pre-teens, smiling, the boys flanking a grinning Hank Henderson. The boys resting their hands on their father's shoulder. The girl with her hand on Emma Henderson's arm. A loving family. The image startled Cole. It was not the one he had of Hank Henderson in his mind.

"What did you say your story was about?" asked Emma Henderson.

"Well, with all the news about the Buffalo Anthracite Mine these days, we thought we might look past, well, the unfortunate events of the past couple weeks and try to understand what makes Oracle, and the mine, tick."

Emma nodded.

"Your husband has been with the mine a long time?"

"Oh yes, he's been there for ..." She thought a moment. "For seventeen years now. He's been working his way up the ladder you know. He started on the shop floor at the mill here in town when he was just a young man, and now of course is the mine manager."

"You must be very proud of him."

"Oh my goodness, yes. He should have been manager long ago, but those fools in Toronto kept hiring men who didn't know the country, didn't know this town, and surely didn't know mining."

"Mike Barnes included?"

She looked down. "I know it's not Christian to speak ill of the dead, and I feel terrible for his widow and their little children, but Mike Barnes was nothing but trouble. He played around, you know. Was having an affair with some blonde that he met at his hotel. Can you imagine?"

"It's hard to believe," said Cole.

"It's shameful. My Henry is a family man. He runs the mine like it's his family. Those boys out there depend on him and he takes good care of them."

"Was Mr. Henderson unhappy when Mr. Barnes got the manager position?"

"Oh, he was pretty disappointed. Like I said, he should have had that job five years ago. But he waited his turn, and when the last manager left a year ago, he was certain that the job would be his. When they hired that Barnes fellow, well, he was beside himself." She looked away. Cole suspected that Hank Henderson had likely blown a gasket.

"Well, he must be very happy now."

"He never liked that man Barnes. Said that he was out to ruin the mine, ruin the town. It's sad what happened to him, but yes, I'd say that Henry is happy to be running things over there."

"It's just temporary, isn't it?"

"We'll see," said Emma.

"So his mood has been better since Mike Barnes was killed?"

"Oh my goodness, when you put it that way..." She drew in a quick breath.

"What I mean is, he's happy to be finally doing the job he wanted to?"

"Well, yes. He's happy to be helping the mine and the town."

"Listen, Mrs. Henderson, I don't mean to pry, but is Mr. Henderson pretty dependable?"

"My Henry is the most dependable man you'll ever meet."

"So he's usually on time for things."

"Oh, yes. Should I try him on his cellphone again?"

"No, no. I'm just wondering what time he usually gets home from work. Maybe I got my wires crossed and he thinks that he isn't meeting me until then."

"Henry comes home from work every night at six-thirty on the dot. You could set your clock by it."

"No exceptions?"

"What do you mean?"

"Well, he doesn't go bowling on Tuesdays or play cards on Fridays?"

"My Henry is a family man, and even with the kids grown and gone, he still comes home to me every night at six-thirty."

"Every night in the last two weeks?"

Emma Henderson looked at him closely. "What are you getting at, Mr. Blackstone?"

"Nothing at all. I'm thinking about profiling Mr. Henderson in my story and I'm just trying to learn more about his character."

"Well, he's been home every night the last two weeks at six-thirty sharp," she said. She sounded suspicious.

Cole stood up. "I think I must have mixed up the times. I'll call Mr. Henderson this evening after six-thirty and see about making arrangements to meet."

"You could come for dinner if you wish. I'm sure Henry would love to chat. We're having pot roast tonight."

"That's a lovely offer," said Cole, imagining the look on Hank Henderson's face should he come home to find Cole seated at the dinner table. "But I think I'll leave you two to enjoy your dinner and maybe catch up with him afterwards. Thank you for the chat, Mrs. Henderson. I enjoyed your company."

"No trouble," she said. She stood and wiped her hands on her apron, through they weren't wet. "I'll show you to the door."

When he was back in his truck he let out a long, deep sigh of relief. Emma Henderson had painted Hank – Henry – Henderson as a model husband, father, community member, and businessman. But her own scorn for Mike Barnes was palpable, no doubt a pale reflection of her husband's contempt. And she had grown suspicious when he had queried her about Hank Henderson's arrival home each night over the last couple of weeks. If Henderson had been late on the night Barnes was killed, it seemed pretty unlikely Emma Henderson would give that information up.

Cole looked around the neat neighbourhood of post-World War II side-splits and back-splits. He was willing to bet that these folks kept an eye out for one another. He was willing to bet that they kept an eye *on* one another.

He knocked on six doors before he found someone home, and then the elderly man couldn't hear him when he spoke. The man fumbled with his hearing aid and yelled "What?" at the top of his lungs. Cole apologized and beat a hasty retreat. Maybe he wouldn't find anybody who knew the comings and goings of the neighbourhood after all.

But two houses down the street a woman in her fifties answered the door.

"Hello, ma'am. My name is Casey Blackstone. I work for Citadel Insurance. One of our clients had a fender bender and we're investigating the claim before we pay out. Could I ask you a couple of quick questions?"

The woman looked up and down the street. "I don't see why not."

"Thank you. Do you know Henry and Emma Henderson?"

"Well, of course, they just live two doors up there." She pointed a long finger toward the Henderson home.

"Well, it seems that Mr. Henderson's truck was rear-ended and suffered a little damage."

"Oh, my goodness, I do hope Henry is OK. I didn't hear anything about this."

"Oh, he's just fine. Not even a scratch. They build vehicles so well these days," said Cole. "But there was some damage to his bumper, and with these new plastic alloys they use nowadays, replacing a bumper is very expensive. The accident was last Tuesday night, and I wonder if you remember Mr. Henderson's truck in the driveway that night, say after six-thirty or so?"

The woman thought about it for only a second and said, "You know, it's funny, but last Tuesday I noticed that Henry was late coming home. I mean, Mr. Henderson is always home for dinner. Emma is such a wonderful cook. But last Tuesday it was almost midnight before I saw the truck. I have such a terrible time falling asleep since my husband passed away, and so I was up watching a little television and was about to call Emma when I noticed the truck there."

"Do you remember what time you noticed it?"

"Well, I checked at midnight just as *The Price is Right* was coming on. It was a rerun, but I hadn't seen it so I thought I'd watch. I love that Bob Barker fellow. I noticed that Henry wasn't there then. I checked again about half way through the episode. Someone had just won a brand new car, and it made me think to look again. And there he was. I felt relieved that he was home."

"Thank you so very much. This has been very helpful," said Cole.

"Will Mr. Henderson get what's owed to him?" asked the neighbour.

"Oh, yes, he'll get what's coming to him," said Cole, walking down the path to his truck.

He pulled into the Tim Hortons parking lot when his cellphone rang. He snatched it up from the jumble of papers on the passenger seat.

"Blackwater."

"It's Jim Jones."

"Hiya Jim. Thanks for getting back to me."

"No trouble. Sorry it took so long."

"Did you find out who got advance copies of the report?"

"It took a little doing. I'm pretty deep in I-owe-you debt right now, but Jeremy Moon at Wild Rose Consulting gave me the list. It includes a bunch of government types in Edmonton which I'm guessing you don't really care about."

Cole locked the Toyota and walked into the doughnut shop for a coffee boost. "That's right. Just folks in this neck of the woods, really."

"Well, there's me, Mike Barnes, Hank Henderson, and somebody named Frans Lester at the mining company's head office in Toronto. He's one of their planners. A copy of the report was sent to the mayor of Oracle, but apparently she was out of town and hasn't even signed for it yet."

"I haven't met her," said Cole, standing in line. There was one person in front of him.

"And a fella named David Smith called and requested a copy, and received it last Monday by courier. I guess he's the head of the Chamber of Commerce. Powerful dude in Oracle. Wants to run for office or something."

Cole stood stock still.

"May I help you, sir?" said a young woman from behind the counter. Cole was silent. He didn't see the young woman. Instead his eyes visualized the information that Jim Jones had just presented him.

"May I help you?" she said again, her voice growing annoyed.

"You there, Cole?"

"Coffee, double cream, no sugar."

"What are you talking about?"

"Nothing, Jim. Just ordering a coffee."

"Do I sound like a drive through to you, Cole?" chuckled Jim Jones.

"I'm at Tim Hortons. Did you say last Monday?"

"Yeah, last Monday. He should have got it by about 4 PM, according to my man at Wild Rose. I guess he wasn't on the original list, and was pretty pissed. Called up and demanded a copy. I guess he figures that as head of the Chamber, he was owed one. Was talking about how he was going to be the next MP, and that he sure as hell would remember who was who when he got to Ottawa. Wild Rose sent him a copy after OKing it with the mine."

Cole was served his coffee. He fumbled, phone pressed between her ear and shoulder, to fish some change out of his pocket. He spilled some receipts, the cap from a ball point pen, and change on the floor and had to stoop, awkwardly, to collect them and present the change to the counter girl.

He took his coffee and stepped into the parking lot.

"Do you need anything else, Cole?"

"Not right now, Jim. That's really helpful information. Thanks."

Cole snapped the phone shut and jammed it into his pocket.

It was pretty clear where he would stop next. He sipped his coffee as he walked down the street, checked the time on his cell and found that it was almost four. My God, he thought, time sure flies when you're having fun. He didn't feel any closer to singling out a suspect.

George Cody had motive, means, and opportunity, but nothing conclusive pointed to him as the killer. The tarp in the back of his Pinto could be there to protect the seats and hatch from spilled beer when he was hauling bottles, or any number of things. Cole wondered if Nancy had turned anything up on George's past. If the man had a history of violence, then that might be something else altogether.

Hank Henderson had a clear motive: to stop Mike Barnes from shutting down the mine, and ascending to what must be in Henderson's mind his rightful place at the head of the operation. But surely Henderson must know that the company would send another flack to wind down operations, and that offing Barnes was only a temporary solution. Cole imagined that a man so possessed by anger and jealousy might conveniently overlook that sort of fact while in a murderous rage. Henderson's late arrival home on the night of the murder certainly established opportunity. A plethora of potential murder weapons in the man's office left no wiggle room for the establishment of means.

But there was a sticky loose end in all of this that festered in Cole Blackwater's mind. It was just too convenient that Dale van Stempvort had opened his mouth, inserted foot, and established such a clear motive to frame himself for the murder. Though it didn't make complete sense to Cole, he still believed that the mole was somehow tangled up in the murder of Mike Barnes. And the feeling that something from that morning held the key to both the mole and the murder still niggled in the back of his mind.

It niggled as he walked up the steps to the Chamber of Commerce offices.

"Is David Smith around?" he asked the woman at the reception desk. He didn't recognize her.

"Do you have an appointment?"

"No, but we're old friends."

"Who should I say is calling?"

"Cole Blackwater."

"Hold on a minute, Mr. Blackwater." She picked up the phone, punched a number, and told Smith that Cole Blackwater was there to see him. She listened a moment, then said, "Go on back. Do you know the way?"

"Sure do." He smiled and dropped his coffee cup into a trash can.

David Smith didn't rise when Cole entered his office. He sat with his back to the door, at work on his computer when Cole stepped in. "Still playing reporter, Mr. Blackwater?" he asked with an audible sneer.

"Still playing politician?"

"That's the difference between you and me, Mr. Blackwater," said Smith, turning around in his chair to face Cole. "I'm an up-and-comer, and you're a has-been. I learned everything I needed to know about you with just one little phone call. And I know you've been poking your nose into my business around these parts."

Cole shrugged. Although he appeared blasé on the outside, a fire kindled on the inside. He wanted to know, more than almost anything, who that phone call was directed to. "I haven't really been looking to learn anything about *you*. I have been poking around your town, though."

"Oh, and what have you learned?"

Cole helped himself to a seat. "Lots of interesting things. I've learned that Dale van Stempvort was set up."

"Dale van Stempvort is a lunatic and a killer," Smith insisted. "He's going to find life in a maximum security facility very difficult indeed."

"I bet that makes you plenty happy."

"Why shouldn't it? A man kills another man in cold blood. He should go to jail. That's the rule of law in this country. Maybe you bleeding-heart liberals think that he should be embraced by his community and spend some rejuvenating time on a tranquil gulf island to realign his what-have-you's, but here in Alberta, a man kills someone, he gets put away. If I had my way he'd hang. In fact, when I'm a Member of Parliament, I'll be pushing for a return to the noose."

"Might make for good politics here in Alberta, but good luck getting a government elected on that platform."

"I don't need political advice from a washed-up hack such as yourself, Blackwater," Smith said, smiling. "Save it for the environmentalists. They must have scraped the bottom of the barrel to hire you."

Cole had heard it all before. But still it rattled him.

"So how did you feel when you figured out that the mine was going to close, Smith?" Cole prodded.

Cole watched David Smith for any change in his expression. He had read that behavioural scientists using video recordings of subjects could slow the frames of the film down and see nearly imperceptible changes that projected emotions in a person's face. They could tell when a person was lying, or when, say, a couple having a seemingly innocent conversation actually hated each other's guts. These scientists got so good at this work that after a while they were able to do it without the video recordings and slow motion. Cole Blackwater didn't have that expertise. But he thought he saw a slight change in David Smith's ruddy face, despite a clear attempt to maintain equanimity. "That's just one of the options for the mine's future. I'm pretty sure it's not going to happen. I've talked with people in Toronto about it."

"But Mike Barnes was brought in with the sole purpose of wrapping up operations."

"Well, that was Mike's take on things, but it wasn't the only option."

"So you spoke to Mike about this?"

"We had words."

"When?"

"Oh, I learned about the possible closure some time ago. Mike and I had a long talk about it one night. Long talk. We didn't see eye to eye on the matter, but that's the way it goes. I'd say that the closure option is less than likely at this time. Mike Barnes was a fool. I knew that the day he arrived in this town. He was Bay Street and this is Main Street. He didn't know the first thing about how we do things here. And it cost him."

"That's not what you told me last week. You said he was a go-getter."

"And you said you were a reporter."

Cole remained implacable. "You think Barnes' being Bay Street got him killed?"

"I think that a man like Hank Henderson, for example, wouldn't have let anyone sneak up behind him and club him on the back of the head, that's what I think. But that's all said and done, isn't it? And I think the mine will stay in operation for some time to come."

"Why's that?"

"Well, I think the mining company has seen the error of their ways. They should never have sent Mike Barnes to do what he was here to do. It was the wrong approach to dealing with this mine. It was wrong for the mine. Wrong for the company. Wrong for the town."

"And wrong for you. For your political career."

"My job as Chamber president is to make sure this town flourishes. When I become MP, it will still be my job to safeguard the future of this town."

Cole watched the man carefully. His face was flushed, but no more so than Cole's. He sat back in his chair, trying to look relaxed. Cole imagined him sitting behind one of the looming mahogany desks in a Centre Block office on Parliament Hill. The image wasn't hard to conjure. David Smith looked every bit a Member of Parliament. Even a Cabinet Minister.

"Tough on crime, subsidies for the mining industry, to hell with regulations," said Cole, "That will be your campaign platform?"

"Something like that," grinned Smith. "Let's face it, in this riding, I don't have to worry about running against the Liberals or the NDP. All I have to worry about is winning the nomination battle. That's a ground game."

"Sell nominations. Turn out your vote."

"We speak the same language after all," said Smith.

"But if the mine closed, there would be a lot of people out of work in this town, wouldn't there? The economy of Oracle, and other towns in this area would hit the skids. That can't be allowed to happen, can it?"

David Smith laced his fingers behind his head and leaned back in his chair. It didn't take a boxer to know that David Smith was a heavyweight. He was big and not so much overweight as stout. Cole figured he weighed a solid 230 pounds, and while he might not be all muscle, he sure wasn't all blubber either. A wide grin came to David Smith's face. "So you're no longer masquerading as a reporter. Now you're a PI, is that it?"

"I'm just trying to save the Cardinal Divide is all."

"Well you can thank Dale van Stempvort for its destruction. He's turned the whole town against the environmentalists. Nobody's going to listen to their whining now."

"Dale van Stempvort didn't kill Mike Barnes."

"And you think I did?"

Cole was silent. He regarded the man opposite the desk, so effusive, so confident. "I'm not saying that," he finally said. "But I think that you set Dale up to say something stupid to that reporter. I think that you had one of your stooges from the Chamber of Commerce get inside the ESCOG and snitch on their goings on, and I think you got some Neanderthals from the mine to use me as a punching bag on the night Mike Barnes was killed."

Cole wasn't sure about the Neanderthals part. Hank Henderson could have easily set that up too. But he was on a roll.

Smith broke into laughter. "I'll admit that you don't look nearly as pretty as you did when you first waltzed into this office last week," he said, catching his breath, "but if I had wanted to give you a beating, I would have done it myself, son. That's how we do things around here. No, I didn't get those boys to lay some lumber to you. You'll have to go looking for another perpetrator for that one. And as for your conspiracy theory about a ferret in amongst the fish-kissers, you should probably know that Dale van Stempvort doesn't need anybody's assistance to put his foot in his mouth. That man was born with it there. He's been saying cockamamie things to the press for as long as he's been in this town. Looks like now he's finally fallen off the deep end and actually done something really awful."

Cole stood up. "I'm going to be doing some digging, Mr. Smith. You better hope I don't find whatever it is you're hiding behind that politician's smile." He turned to leave. Before he could step through the door, David Smith stopped him.

"Hold it there, pal. Hold it. You just better think twice about who you're threatening. You better think about it long and hard. I run this town. This town is mine. And no washed-up pecker-head like you is going to march in here and tell me what's what. I've been calling the shots here for a long time. I'm going to be calling them long after you leave. And if you don't watch yourself, watch that mouth of yours, and keep that busted-up nose of yours out of trouble, you're going to find yourself in way, way over your head."

Cole smiled. "Who's threatening who now, Mr. Smith?"

"Its not a threat, Mr. Blackwater. It's just the way things are. It's just the way things get done."

The two men regarded each other. David Smith leaned back in his chair, hands behind his head. "Blackwater," he said, leaning forward. "That's a funny name. What is it?"

"My father was black Irish. But the name comes from Scotland, where my great-great grandfather worked in the mines."

"That's what I thought," said Smith. "You know what black water is?"

Cole smiled. "Yeah. Mercenaries. In Iraq."

Now Smith grinned. "Hm," he said, "I hadn't thought of that one. You fancy yourself a mercenary, Blackwater?"

"This has been fun, but it's time for me to see about shutting your little plans for this town down now," Cole said and turned to go.

Smith stopped him again. "It's the water that forms at the bottom of the pit, or at the bottom of a stope in a coal mine. It's poison. It's deadly. Men in a mine know to avoid it like the plague. Better watch yourself, Mr. Blackwater. You'll find your name a fitting epitaph."

20 "Was Mike Barnes attacked from front or from behind?" Cole asked Perry Gilbert as he walked to his truck, cellphone in hand. Main Street smelled of wet pavement as raindrops spattered the street. The sun dogs of several days ago yielded their moisture.

"There were two wounds. A wound to the front of his head, which seems to have bled a great deal, and a wound to the back of his head, which fractured his skull."

"Which killed him?"

"I don't know. The RCMP still haven't released the results of their forensics, and because of that, the autopsy still hasn't been released."

"What about the bathroom?"

"I talked to Reimer this morning. She's lifted samples of the blood for a match with Barnes, and had the room sealed."

"They didn't happen to check the toilet, did they?"

"I didn't ask. Why?"

"Remember I told you that it was plugged?"

"I don't remember that, Cole, sorry."

"I might have forgotten to mention it. Getting hit in the head will do that to you."

Perry laughed, then sobered. "Sorry, I guess it's not funny."

"Go ahead and laugh; it feels pretty funny to me right now. Listen, I just got out of a meeting with a fellow named David Smith. Know him?"

"Should I?"

"He's president of the local Chamber of Commerce. Connected politically. Likes to play tough guy. I'm starting to think he might be the one who set the snitch up in the ESCOG, though I'm not one hundred percent certain who that snitch is. We've laid some bait and are waiting for the trap to be sprung. Anyway, this guy Smith came across pretty aggressive in a meeting just now. He's going on the suspects list."

"You're keeping a list?"

"You know what I mean. If I was a betting man, I'd still put my money on Henderson, but Smith is closing the gap on those odds."

"You have something new on Henderson?"

"Right, I almost forgot. I *am* losing my marbles. I cased Henderson's place this morning. I talked with his wife."

"You what? Are you trying to get yourself killed?"

"Look, just about everybody is threatening to kill me right now. Henderson had already made *that* list. Anyway, I talked to the wife this morning. Motherhood and apple pie, I tell you. Invited me to dinner."

Gilbert chuckled. Cole continued, "She tells me that our man Henry gets home from work every night by six-thirty."

"So?"

"So one of the nosey neighbours says that last Tuesday night Hank didn't make it home 'til after midnight."

"Man, you are really taking this PI bit seriously."

"I'm a serious guy."

"So maybe he was out with the boys?"

"Why would the old lady lie?"

"Got me."

"Me too."

"Now what?"

"I don't know now what," said Cole, arriving at his truck. "I need something to eat. Check in with Nancy. Try to make some sense of all this. Can you look into the head wound?"

"Yeah, what about it?"

"Something that Smith said. Said that if a good old boy had been running the shop he wouldn't have let someone sneak up behind him and club him."

"I'll look into it. Call you tomorrow."

Cole hung up.

He had no sooner hung up than his phone rang.

"Blackwater."

"It's me. Nancy."

"Hi."

"Listen, I'm sorry about last night. I really unloaded on you. It wasn't fair."

"I deserved it," he said, leaning against the passenger side door, looking up the street toward the Chamber of Commerce office.

"True, you do, but just the same, I went pretty rough on you."

"I can take it."

"Would you shut the fuck up and let me apologize?" He could tell she was smiling when she said it.

"OK," he said, and grinned.

"So, I'm sorry. Now, back to business. I got something on George."

"Things aren't getting any less complex, are they?"

"Why, what have you got?"

"Suspect number three."

"Who?"

"David Smith."

"Really?"

"Yeah, really."

"All right, let's compare notes. Can you come by?"

"Can't we go out?"

"Better not, Cole. I really can't be seen with you. You know the drill."

"OK," he said, and examined his boots. More sneaking around. It really was like old times. "I'll grab some food and come by."

"Get a bottle of wine, too, OK?"

"I'm still nursing a hangover."

"Hair of the dog that bit you," she said, and hung up.

It was seven o'clock before Cole arrived at Nancy Webber's room. He balanced a stack of take-out containers of Chinese food in one hand and a bottle of red wine and a six pack of Tsingtao beer in the other.

"Thank God you're here. I'm famished," Nancy said at the door.

They opened the boxes and arranged the food at the centre of the little round table. Nancy opened the wine and poured herself a glass. Cole opened a bottle of beer and took a sip.

"Where did you find that in this town?" Nancy asked.

"Ancient Chinese secret," replied Cole, and dug into the food.

"All right," announced Nancy when she had cleaned her first plate of food and heaped a second plate full. "Our man George has a record, and a history."

Cole took a sip of beer. "What's he done?"

"Well, he has one aggravated assault charge against him that was dropped when the victim refused to press charges. Looks like a bar-room fight. More interesting than that, he has a history of domestic violence. No charges, but I talked to some people in the community where he lived before he met Deborah, and they say the cops were always out at his place to break up fights between him and his old lady."

"That doesn't mean he's a killer."

"It gets better," said Nancy, and deftly guided chow mein noodles into her mouth with chopsticks.

"Do tell."

"When George Cody discovered his lady friend was having an affair, he slapped her around and went storming off in his Pinto to find the boyfriend. The lady called the cops and they had the wherewithal to intervene. They stopped George outside the bloke's house. Guess what he had with him?"

"Roses and a box of chocolates?"

"Funny. No, he had a baseball bat in the car."

"Ho ho!" said Cole, taking a pull on the beer.

"So old George has a history. When he found that note it must have been déjà vu all over again. I guess he figured, if at first you don't succeed try again. Picture this. He gets in his car, packs his trusty Louisville Slugger, drives out to the mine, gets into the building unseen, watches for his opportunity, and *whappo*, slugs Mike Barnes in the head. Then he carries him downstairs from the bathroom, loads him into the Pinto, drives him across the yard to the mill, carries him in through those double doors you've told me about, and walks right into the skid of bits and stuff, and knocks it over. Must have hurt like a bugger. Barnes falls onto the floor and his head hits one of the bits. That's when the night watchman opens the big bay doors at the far end and George beats a hasty retreat."

Cole opened another bottle of Tsingtao. "What about the Pinto?"

"Well, maybe he parked it somewhere out of sight."

"And what about the Day-Timer?"

"That bloody appointment book is a problem, isn't it? I doubt that George called ahead for a meeting. Maybe that appointment book has nothing to do with this. Maybe Barnes just lost it?"

"Between when I left him at seven and when he got killed?"

"You're right. Seems unlikely."

"Let me tell you about my day. That might help us sort out who's who."

279   Stephen Legault

He told her about his meetings with the three possible moles.

"This is so juicy!" Nancy said when he finished.

"You can't write about this!"

"Why the hell not?"

"Not yet."

"I've got to get a story out of this, Cole, or I'm going to get fired again."

"Never had a job so good I couldn't quit or get fired from it," he said, echoing Jim Jones.

"That's you, not me."

"At least let the mole surface. Then I'll talk it over with Peggy."

Nancy held up her hands in surrender.

"Things got more complex today, I'm afraid, not less. Let me tell you about Hank and about David."

He told her about his meeting with Emma Henderson, how he snooped around the neighbourhood, and what he learned as a result.

"You're taking one hell of a risk, Cole. When Henderson connects the dots, which," and she looked at her watch, "should be about now, he's going to be furious."

"No doubt, but I had to figure out if he was at home that night. And he wasn't."

Cole then told her about his run in with David Smith. "I went to see him because he got a copy of the environmental assessment. He would have figured out after one read that the company had no intention of digging the mine after putting in the rail line and the road to keep shareholders or trust unit owners satisfied. I doubt he would have been very pleased."

"You think he killed Mike Barnes because of it?"

"It's a possibility. Hear me out. Smith gets a copy of the report late on Monday night of last week. That's the day I was getting settled in with the ESCOG." Cole shook his head. "It seems like a year ago," he said, rubbing his face to feel for the various scars. "So he gets the report, and by Tuesday he's gone through it. Outraged, he calls Barnes and demands a meeting. Barnes tells him to come out to the mine in the evening, 'cause he's booked up with other meetings, including mine. Smith shows up and they get into a shouting match. Or maybe Smith goes berserk and Barnes keeps his cool—that seems more likely—and one thing leads to another and Smith finds something heavy and follows Barnes to the can and cracks him in the head. That makes sense, doesn't it?"

"So then he what? He drags the body downstairs and loads him into his *what*? What does he drive?"

"I don't know. I didn't think to check," said Cole and shook his head.

"So he loads him into his truck, a safe guess, right? And drives him across the yard to the mill," continued Nancy, "and brings him through the double doors into the little room."

"Right," said Cole. "Smith used to work in the mill, so he'd know his way around there in the dark. But he wasn't anticipating the mill doubling as storage now, so he smashes into the drill bits and down goes Mike Barnes. Splat! His head connects with a bit."

"That's when the night watchman arrives."

Cole frowned. "What I don't get is why none of these guys are limping. If I knocked over a pallet full of drill bits with my shanks I'd be hobbling around on crutches. Dale, David, and George are all just fine."

"You sure?"

"I think so." Cole thought about it. He tapped his bandaged chin with a finger. "Come to think of it, I haven't ever seen David Smith walk. He didn't get up when I was in his office today. He could be immobile for all I know."

"What about Smith's vehicle?" asked Nancy. "We've got the same problem with this story as George's. Why didn't the night watchman see his vehicle?"

"Maybe he parked it out of sight somewhere?"

"But how did he get the body from the office to the mill? It's a long walk, isn't it? Be a hell of a risk to just saunter across the yard like you were going for a quart of milk and a loaf of bread with a body over your shoulder."

"It's not that far, but Mike Barnes was a big man, and it would be a heck of a risk to take."

"Murder is a hell of a risk, period."

"Fair point," said Cole. He set his beer down and stood up.

"It all seems to come down to that appointment book," said Nancy. "If we could only get our hands on it. It's like the thing has been flushed down the toilet and out to sea."

Stephen Legault

Cole turned around so fast that Nancy started. "That's it!" he cried.

"What's it?"

"The toilet was plugged," said Cole, pacing like a tiger in a cage. "I bet anything that the Day-Timer is there."

"In the can?"

"Why not? Barnes goes to the washroom before heading home. He's got his Day-Timer with him. Whoever clubs him stuffs it in the toilet in a panic, but the toilet gets backed up. But he doesn't have time to deal with it, so he leaves it there and gets rid of the body."

"That's pretty thin. Even in a panic you'd think that whoever killed Barnes would know that a book like that isn't going to go down the toilet."

"It's worth checking out, don't you think?"

Nancy thought for a moment. "What about Henderson? What if he has the appointment book? Maybe he hid it. Or threw it out with the trash. We may never find this thing, you know."

"I know. But I'm going to give it one more try tomorrow."

"What are you going to do?"

"I'm going back to the mine and see if I can't get into that bathroom."

"That's a big risk, Cole. What if Henderson catches you?"

Cole rubbed his chin. "I can handle Henderson," he said, being cocky. But in his mind he wondered if he could.

They promised to be in touch first thing in the morning. Nancy would pester the RCMP about the forensics report and vowed to add the autopsy to her list of demands. She too was curious about which head wound killed Mike Barnes: the front or the back?

"And call me from the mine," she added, "I think you're out of your league going back there alone."

"There's no cell coverage there."

"Well, call me as soon as you have coverage."

"I'm touched that you're worried about me."

"I'm mostly worried about losing my source on this story," she said, but she smiled when she said it.

Cole was back at the McSorlie Ranch by 10 PM. He and Peggy sat in the kitchen and sipped herbal tea. "You going to sleep in the barn again tonight?" Peggy asked him, and smiled into her tea cup.

Cole grimaced. "Sorry about that. And sorry about your garden. I'll rebuild it for you just as soon as this mess with Dale is cleared up."

She laughed, "Don't worry about the garden. I hope your truck is OK."

"The truck is fine. It's a little out of alignment, but it's been through worse."

"Do you think the mess with Dale, as you call it, will be cleared up soon?"

"I don't know," said Cole, and rubbed his face wearily. "We've got more suspects at the end of the week than we had at the beginning. Dale gets shipped to Red Deer day after tomorrow. Nancy Webber, who has been very helpful, is likely to get recalled to Edmonton on the weekend. The good thing is that we should finally get some results on the forensics from the RCMP tomorrow. I don't know, Peggy. I think I might have bit off way more than I can chew here."

"You think?" Peggy rested her hand on Cole's shoulder. "I've told you how much I appreciate your work, haven't I?"

"You have. Thanks for that."

"I really mean it, Cole. You didn't have to stay."

"I came back, remember? First I left, and then I came back."

"Well, you didn't need to do that. But you did. You stuck to us."

"I did, didn't I?" he said, and smiled.

"I appreciate it. Now go get some sleep."

━━━━━━━━━━━━━━━━━━━━━━━━━━━━━━━━━━━

Friday morning started bright and sunny, but by breakfast dark clouds formed along the eastern slope west of Oracle, and rain threatened. It was cold, the temperature hovering just above freezing. Cole planned to meet with Perry Gilbert and Nancy Webber before he drove out to the mine in the afternoon to have a look in the washroom which was now considered the crime scene.

He drove the now-familiar gravel road and felt the Toyota grip the loose rock. Here and there he thought it drifted a little more than usual, but instead of assigning blame to his drunken drive, he attributed it to his auto-condriac tendency. To Cole, every little squeak and squeal that emanated from his trusty pickup foreboded a terminal illness, or at least a massive charge to his MasterCard. By the time he reached Oracle rain fell. To the west, over the Rockies, the clouds were dark and menacing. It was pouring, maybe even snowing, over the Front Ranges, and the weather was headed this way.

He met Perry Gilbert at 10 AM at Tim Hortons. They ordered coffee and sat in Gilbert's car as the rain pattered on the roof. "What's new?" Cole asked.

"I'm meeting with Sergeant Reimer at 2 PM this afternoon. I expect to get the forensics report and the autopsy at that time."

Cole filled Gilbert in on what he had learned about George Cody in the last twenty-four hours.

"It doesn't get any easier, does it?" said Gilbert.

"I thought we were supposed to eliminate suspects, not add them," said Cole as he sipped his coffee.

"Oh," said Gilbert. "You asked about the lights in the mill. To save money they turn them off at night. You know, turn off a light bulb, don't turn off a friend," he jingled.

Cole smiled. "So that means whoever lugged Mike Barnes into the mill would have been walking blind in that big room. They couldn't have seen where they were going. They would have walked right into those drill bits."

"Yeah, but it makes you wonder, doesn't it?"

"Why none of our three suspects are limping?"

"And why didn't Hank Henderson know the bits were there?"

"Good point. Maybe he knew, and forgot."

Perry shrugged.

"OK," said Cole, looking out the windshield as the rain fell harder. "I've got to see Nancy Webber and then I'm headed out to the mine."

"Now what?"

"I need to do some plumbing."

Perry Gilbert gave him a dumbfounded look.

"I've got to find that stupid Day-Timer. It could hold a vital piece of information. I'm going to check the toilet in the men's room where Barnes was clubbed."

"That's really sick," said Gilbert, and wrinkled his nose.

"I'll wear gloves," said Cole.

"Better wash your hands afterwards or you and me are through."

"Deal." Cole opened the door and made a dash for his Toyota through puddles dented with the falling rain. He drove to the Rim Rock and walked up to Nancy's room. She opened the door and admonished him to leave his dripping coat outside, under the awning.

"You're still going to the mine?"

"Yup," he said, and flopped down in one of the chairs at the little table. "What about you?"

"I'm going to do some digging on David Smith. See what I can turn up. I might wander over there and ask for an interview."

"Be careful," said Cole dourly.

"That's sweet. I'm a big girl. Plus, he hasn't the foggiest that we're in cahoots."

"Call me if you find anything."

"Thought you said there would be no cell service?"

"There isn't. But leave a message."

"Promise."

"OK," he said, leaving. He stopped at the door. "Nancy," he said.

She looked up at him. "What is it?"

For a moment he wanted to tell her that he too had been crushed. That in the four years since they had been torn apart by his stupidity, he hadn't found the gall to see anybody, anybody seriously at least. He felt something catch in his throat and realized that all the pain of the last three years — his exile from Ottawa, his estrangement from Sarah, and the thing with his father — was caught there in his throat, and he pushed it back down.

"What is it, Cole?" she asked, her held tilted to one side, her long dark hair falling loose over her shoulders.

"Nothing. We'll catch up when I get back from the mine. Talk to you later." And he dashed for his truck through the downpour.

The gravel road that lead out of town was slick with the rain. He had to face the fact that the misalignment in the truck's suspension, caused by driving over Peggy McSorlie's rock garden, didn't help his confidence on the winding road. He clutched the steering wheel and leaned ahead like an old man to peer through the rain-swept windshield. He even left the stereo off, to be less distracted. From time to time a gleaming white, red, or blue pickup truck appeared behind him and recklessly passed him on blind corners, throwing up mud and gravel and spray, forcing him to drive blindly for a few seconds while his worn windshield wipers cleared his view. He growled at them over the sound of the storm outside.

It took more than an hour and a quarter for Cole to make the drive normally done in forty-five minutes. He was exhausted when the mine finally came into view. The dark clouds pressed down on the sprawling complex, their weight giving the mine site an eastern-European feeling, as if it had been suddenly transplanted to a communist-era location. The rising wall of stone that was the eastern front of the Rockies, usually visible from the mine site, was eclipsed by the storm.

He stopped the truck and looked at his watch. It was one-thirty. He had been so focused on keeping his misaligned truck on the road that he hadn't considered how to get onto the mine property. He figured he could just wait until JP came on duty and drive through the gate. But he had to avoid being seen and reported.

What had JP told him about the property? He closed his eyes to try and remember. There were many ways on and off, he had said, though most access points were locked. Nevertheless, he set out to find his way around the property and into the mine site. He put the Toyota in gear and drove past the gate toward Cardinal Divide. When he came to the end of the mine site fence, he slowed and scanned the side of the gravel road for a track he could follow. There it was: a wide lane that wove away from the main road between the pines and ran parallel to the mine site fence. He checked to make sure he was in four-wheel-drive and turned onto the path. He zigged and zagged between trees and rocky outcrops for a few minutes and peered between the trees for glimpses of the mine site. He found a place where the trail split. One path continued parallel to the fence and the other veered toward it. He followed the right-hand track toward the fence.

The rain hadn't let up. When he reached the fence he sat for a moment, the truck's wipers slapping back and forth. He peered through the gloom at the mine. Parked within a stone's throw of the administration building, there was a gate in front of him. A heavy padlock hung from a length of chain. This was his way in, and he wondered if this, or some other gate, was where Mike Barnes' assailant had parked. If they had, it would suggest that the murder had been premeditated.

Cole took a deep breath. He gathered some things he thought he might need from the seat of the truck. He took his cellphone, even though it didn't work here. The digital camera function might come in handy. He stepped out of the truck into the deluge and made his way to the back of the truck, opened the tailgate, and flipped up the door to the canopy. He crawled inside, the rain drumming frantically on the roof. He found his Gore-tex raincoat in the canvas bag he had thrown into the back a lifetime ago. Was it really less than two weeks ago? He pulled it on awkwardly, sitting hunched over in the back of the truck. He pulled a baseball cap out too and fitted it over his dark, curly hair. Taking another deep breath, like a diver preparing to descend, he hopped out of the cab and into the rain.

He checked for signs of another vehicle but the torrent had erased all tracks that might have existed. Then he stepped to the gate. The padlock hung on the inside of the fence. He tried to fish it out from his side and found he could, with some difficulty. What did that tell him? The lock was very old but not rusty and it looked to be in decent condition. He hoped the keyhole might reveal something, but it didn't. Three lazy strands of barbed wire sagged above the fence. Cole mused that he should be able to press them together and climb over them.

"This ought to be fun," he thought as he started climbing. When he reached the wire above the fence he placed his fingers between the barbs and pulled the strands together, held them close to the top of the fence, and swung a leg over the top. His pants caught on the wire and he struggled to free himself. Finally he got his second foot atop the fence, stepped on the wire, and let himself drop to the ground on the other side. He landed heavily, grimacing. He tore a small hole on the inside of his jeans, but didn't leave any flesh behind. Squatting uncomfortably, he surveyed the scene. He was adjacent to the administration building. The parking lot was to his right, and he saw, for the first time, a smaller building perched low behind the admin building. Maintenance equipment leaned beside the door of that building: a couple of shovels, a rake, and a wheelbarrow. They'd

Stephen Legault

been left out in the rain and someone would be taken to task if Hank Henderson discovered the oversight.

Now, how to proceed? He couldn't very well waltz in the front door and wander the halls of the admin building. But what was the alternative? He walked briskly to the nearest wall of the office and inspected the back of the building, looking for another entrance. He found a fire exit, but it was locked. Muttering under his breath, rain dripping from the brim of his hat, he walked back to the front of the building and confidently strode up the steps. With luck he would be mistaken for someone who worked on site. He opened the door and walked inside.

He wiped his feet on a mat, tried to clean them of mud, and made his way to the stairs. He took a deep breath and started up, head down. Someone passed him on the stairs and he exhaled, preparing for whatever might happen, but the person muttered "afternoon" and kept walking. Cole passed the second floor, and the third, where Hank Henderson's office was, without incident. He wasn't even breathing hard. Progress. Onto the fourth floor.

He reached the top floor of the office building and met no one else in the stairs. He had come up the stairs closest the bathroom so he could avoid passing Tracey at Mike Barnes' office. He could hear her on the phone. He stood for a moment at the top of the stairs, eyes to the floor, his shaggy head of curls covered by his ball cap. He walked the few remaining feet and reached the washroom. The sign taped to the door read: "Closed. Crime Scene. Do not Cross." He tried the door and it was locked.

He muttered to himself. He hadn't considered this, then remembered that Perry Gilbert had asked that the washroom be put off limits. He leaned his head against the door and felt weary. He took a sharp breath, turned on his heels, and walked to Mike Barnes' office. He stopped before reaching the open reception area and checked for any sign of Hank Henderson. He saw and heard nothing, so he stepped in.

Tracey was on the phone, and when she looked up her eyes were as big as saucers. "I've got to go," she said and hung up the phone.

"Cole, what in God's name are you doing here? If Hank Henderson finds you he's going to have you arrested for trespassing."

Or worse, Cole thought. "Tracey, I need your help."

"Cole, he told me to call him if you showed up. He's my boss now."

"He's not inside Mike's office?"

"No, he still uses that rabbit warren downstairs, but he comes up here every hour or so to ask me for something. Cole, he said I should call him." He could see her hand poised to reach for the phone.

"Please don't Tracey. Please. I'm trying to find out who killed Mike, and I can't do that if you don't help me. Please."

"Cole, the police say they have Mike's killer."

"Well, they don't. You've got to trust me. Please."

She lowered her hand. "What do you need?"

"Keys to the men's washroom."

She looked at him. "Mike was killed in there, wasn't he?"

"Yes."

"And you figured that out?"

"Yes, and I told the RCMP. They've got the murder all wrong, Tracey."

"Why do you need to get in there?"

He explained quickly. She curled up her nose. Then she disappeared into Mike's office and returned with a key ring. "This is the master key," she said. "It opens every door in this building. And this is the master key for all the other buildings on the site."

"What's this one?" he asked taking the keys.

"Master key for all the padlocks."

"Who else has these?"

"Lots of people. Hank does for sure. People who work in different buildings have different keys. The padlock key is so old half the town of Oracle probably has it."

Cole smiled. "I'll get these back to you," and he trotted down the hallway, shoulder checking as he went. At the bathroom door he slipped the key in the lock and stepped inside.

The room was as he remembered. He flipped on the lights and looked under the sink. The speckles of blood were still there. He saw where the crime scene officers had lifted a sample. And there was a place on the floor where they had looked for the mark of boot prints, and Cole imagined they had dusted for fingerprints all around the room. What kind of killer, Cole wondered, didn't wear gloves? The kind that wasn't planning on doing any killing, Cole guessed.

He went to the stalls. The one that had been closed was no longer locked. He pushed it open with his elbow and looked inside. He couldn't tell if it was still plugged, so he got down on his knees to take a close look. Sure enough, something was wadded up in the drain of the toilet. The water was otherwise clear, for which Cole was deeply grateful. He took off his coat, rolled up his sleeve, and plunged his hand into the cold water.

21 The cold water stung his arm, but he ignored the discomfort and reached his hand down into the blockage at the bottom of the toilet. What did Mike Barnes' agenda look like? Eight inches by ten, with a plastic black cover, the kind any office supply store sold. He grabbed hold of whatever blocked the toilet and pulled. He extracted his hand and found it full of dark, wadded paper towels. He grumbled in disappointment. He dumped them on the floor and plunged his hand back in. He came up with more towels, and more. He emptied the drain. When he was done, a soggy mountain of towels oozed on the floor. The mess was darkly stained. Cole stared at the blood. Mike Barnes' blood.

Whoever clubbed Mike had cleaned up after himself and stuffed the towels in the toilet, flushing as he went. But he stuffed a few too many into the toilet and it backed up. Running out of time the assailant panicked. He'd tried to engineer a disappearance, rather than a murder. But he was sloppy, failed to dispose of the body at the mill, and left behind the blood that Cole had discovered here in the bathroom.

Despite these gaffs by the killer, Cole Blackwater was no closer to finding Mike Barnes' appointment book, and no closer to learning who met with Barnes after Cole on that fateful night.

Cole leaned against the side of the stall, his hand dripping, his arm numb from the cold water.

If George Cody had taken the agenda, it was likely long gone. George could have easily slipped it into a bag of garbage and hidden it among the trash from the Rim Rock and The Quarry.

If David Smith had taken the agenda, he might have hidden it in his office, but more than likely it was long buried in the landfill.

If Hank Henderson had taken the agenda, he might have thrown it out with the trash, or placed it on the conveyor at the mill, intending, perhaps, to pulverize the agenda in the mill's machinery along with the corpse. But JP foiled that plan, forcing the killer to stuff the agenda into his pocket for disposal later. If Hank killed Mike, he might have taken the agenda home for disposal, or he might have brought it back to his office. Hank Henderson was a pack rat. Maybe the agenda could be found in a filing cabinet or a drawer, rather than the trash. That was plausible, wasn't it? Cole

Stephen Legault

stood up and closed the stall door behind him, leaving the sodden towels on the floor.

He regarded himself in the mirror. He was pale and his face looked like he'd undergone plastic surgery that had failed miserably. The stitches should come out in the next few days. Otherwise they would start biting into his skin and leave small pock marks of their own. He took off his cap, ran his hands through his hair, and replaced the cap. He had peeled the bandage from his chin this morning; the cut there had begun to heal.

He intended to do something about this miserable shape he saw in the mirror. He would definitely do something about it. He washed his hands up to the elbow, dried them on his pants, rolled down his sleeves, and put his coat back on.

He peeked out of the bathroom to establish that the coast was clear. Cole locked the door behind him and listened intently to the sounds down the hall. Tracey was on the phone again, but no other voices were discernable.

He made his way to her office and stepped around the corner. Again she hung up. "Anything?"

"No Day-Timer."

"What did you find?" she asked, holding her breath.

"A lot of paper towels."

She stared at him, eyes pleading.

"With a lot of blood on them."

She put her face in her hands and began to cry again.

"Tracey, I have to get into Hank Henderson's office."

She looked up, tears smearing her mascara. "You think that Hank?..."

"I don't know. It's possible. I need to case his office for Mike's Day-Timer."

"Oh Cole, I don't know."

"I have to, Tracey."

"If he catches you ..."

"I know."

They formulated a plan. Cole would hide in the empty office next to Mike's. When Hank came upstairs next, Tracey would stall him as long as she could, while Cole slipped downstairs and into his office. When Hank left her office, she would call his extension, let it ring twice, and hang up. That would be Cole's signal to get out. He figured he'd have less than a minute to clear Hank's office and hide before the acting manager returned.

"It's a big risk," she said.

"I'm a big boy," he said. But his stomach turned over at the prospect.

He waited in the empty room beside Barnes' office for half an hour before he heard Hank's voice. That gave him a lot of time to think. It gave him *too much* time to think.

Things didn't turn out as planned very often in Cole Blackwater's life. If someone had predicted, during the heyday of his time in Ottawa, that in a few years he'd be trying to solve a murder at a mine in a backwoods town in the eastern slopes of Alberta, rather than end poverty or stop climate change, he would have laughed. If they had told him he'd be elbow deep in a toilet, he would have cried.

So he laughed. Eyes closed, shoulders moving up and down against the wall, belly contracting, he laughed silently. He sat with his back to the wall next to the closed door and laughed at the sheer stupidity of everything that had happened in the last four years. And the laughter turned to tears.

Before he knew it, tears rolled down his grisled cheeks, stained his face, and got caught in the scar on his chin. The laughter was now bittersweet. He never imagined being here. Even when things went completely sideways in Ottawa and then turned for the worse, far worse, on that dark night in the barn on the family ranch, even then, during his darkest moments, he never imagined he'd be trying to solve a murder.

It was half an hour before Hank Henderson left his office to snarl at Tracey. Cole bet that Mike Barnes never did that. Hank angrily demanded where College Boy filed the monthly financials. When Cole was certain Hank was out of the hall, he slipped out of the office and padded toward the stairs.

He checked his watch. Tracey had promised to keep Hank for five minutes at least, but he couldn't count on it. He reached the third floor and found that hallway clear. Luck was on his side. He slipped into Hank's office and shut the door. The room was dark and cluttered. First he cased Henderson's desk, opened the drawers and looked beneath stacks of paper. His heart skipped a beat when he found a Day-Timer, but it was Henderson's. On the off chance that Hank had marked down his appointment with Barnes, Cole scanned the previous week. He caught his breath when he read that Henderson indeed had an appointment for eight o'clock that night. It didn't say with whom; all it said was "Finalize E.A." Cole read that as finalize Environmental Assessment.

Cole returned the agenda and quickly moved to the row of filing cabinets on the opposite wall. They were ancient units, heavy and solid, the kind that would come in handy during a nuclear blast or some other apocalyptic event. They squealed when he opened the drawers. Cole looked quickly through the files and stacks of papers, desperately hoping that he would find what he was after.

The phone rang.

He froze.

It rang a second time.

His heart raced. He was about to slam the cabinet shut when it rang a third time.

It wasn't Tracey.

He hoped. They had agreed on two rings. What if she had forgotten?

Then his name was mud.

He continued his search. Nothing but paper. He removed a wad of files to search beneath and dropped one on the floor.

"Sweet mother of pearl," he muttered.

The phone rang.

He scooped up the file and jammed it back into the drawer.

The phone rang again.

His heart beat louder than the phone.

He waited for the next ring, but it never came.

He made a dash for the door, knocked the table as he went, upset several giant drill bits, and bruised his leg. He groaned. He reached for the door handle when he saw, through the opaque bevelled glass, movement down the hall. Henderson. Caught. The adrenaline coursed through his ears.

He searched for a place to hide in the room and spotted the windows with their dust-laden vertical blinds. He had only seconds.

Then he heard a female voice. "Mr. Henderson, I found them!"

He watched the doorknob slowly turn to open the door, and

then stop. He could see Henderson's outline through the glass. He wondered if he himself was as plainly visible.

"Mr. Henderson!" It was Tracey. The door remained closed. Cole scrambled through the drapes to the windows. He knocked a cloud of dust into the air as he pushed his way through, careful not to cough or sneeze or make a racket. He found the latch to the four-foot high window, pushed it open, and lifted himself out onto the sill.

The Buffalo Anthracite Mine's administration building was rectangular, four storeys high, and made of red brick, trimmed modestly with wide cement windowsills. Cole found himself twenty-five feet off the ground standing on such a sill. He closed the window behind him and prayed for the first time in his life, hoping that Hank Henderson had not seen him step out into this ledge.

The ledge in question was about eight inches wide, and the window was four feet tall. Cole's toes hung over the edge and he had to press his head into the brick above the window to balance. He took a deep breath. When he was younger he and his older brother Walter had often gone into the Highwood Range, west of the family ranch, to scramble in the mountains. He had been in a number of tricky situations in those days, and heights hadn't bothered him much then. But now, middle-aged and out of practice, Cole closed his eyes against the long drop to the ground below.

He forced himself to breathe. His lungs relaxed as moist air, still cloaked in cloud, still wet with rain, entered on a deep breath. He grew calm. And calmly he assessed the situation. I'm caught on a ledge three storeys above the ground, outside the office of a man who very likely killed his boss and took his job, a man who hates me. A man who threatened to kill me if I was seen on the mine property again. Cole suppressed a laugh. I'm in plain view of anybody who wanders by. This is not good.

Cole looked down. Behind the administration building was the two-storey-tall maintenance building that he had seen when he clambered over the fence. Below him were the wheelbarrow and other assorted tools, carelessly left in the rain.

He looked to his left. He could make his way along this ledge and, if he could turn around without falling, step to the next window, which he figured must also be one that looked into Hank

Henderson's office. Three feet of red brick separated the two windows. Could he turn around, and then make the awkward, off-balance step to the next window, somehow holding onto the brick as he did? And then what? Repeat it half a dozen more times to get to the end of the building. There was a stout-looking drain spout, not the cheap aluminium eavestroughs that were installed on homes today, but a solid iron affair that Cole thought might hold him. But he had to get to it. Then he could tackle the problem of what to do. Maybe his fleeting luck would hold and one of the empty offices would have an open window.

He looked in the other direction. Same situation. Half a dozen windows and corresponding ledges, and a drain spout at the corner.

He sighed and closed his eyes briefly to quell his fear.

What if he waited for Hank to leave? He looked at his watch. It was about two-thirty. He knew from Emma Henderson that Hank left for Oracle by five-thirty or quarter to six each night to make it home by six-thirty. Could Cole balance on this ledge for three hours or more? He doubted he could balance there for fifteen minutes. He looked at the gap between him and the next window. What if someone in one of the offices saw him as he shimmied along? Then the jig would be up, wouldn't it?

He looked at the maintenance shed. He guessed it was about a ten to fifteen-foot gap between the older admin building and the newer maintenance building. And about a fifteen-foot drop. He tried to do the math. Could he make that jump? He might be able to make ten feet. Any more, probably not.

His knees started to knock. He wanted to relieve the pressure on them, but there was no room to squat on the ledge. He had to choose. He decided to try and reach the drain spout.

He inched along the window ledge and when he got to the end of it, pressed a palm up against the brick above the window, and using that force, pivoted around on his right foot, swung his left foot around, and placed it on the sill. He pressed a second palm above him to steady himself. He took a calming breath. So far, so good. He was facing in now. Inching his right hand close to the end of the window opening, pressing hard on the brick, he began to reach his left foot out around the wall to the next windowsill.

Three feet is a long way. Even for a man as tall as Cole, three feet is a long way to reach with your foot when there is nothing but open space beneath you. He reached, tapped his toe along the wall, pressed harder and harder with his right hand, balanced the left hand on the brick wall, and searched for a gap in the bricks. After what seemed like a lifetime, but was more like five or ten seconds, Cole's left foot found the ledge. He settled it there, awkwardly, and pushed his left hand toward the next hold. He planned to grab the side of the window opening with his left hand, and with his right, do the same on the window opening he faced now, and use equal and opposite pressure to hold on as he transferred his weight. He risked a look at where he was going. He couldn't tell if the blinds were up or down. His eyes strayed and he saw the ground below.

He shifted his weight, breathing as slowly and consciously as he could.

He hadn't counted on the ledge being wet and he felt his left foot start to slip. He tried to press it more tightly to the concrete surface, but it continued to slide. He was going to fall. In the moment before he lost control he lunged, bending his right knee as deeply as he could, and pushed away from the wall with every ounce of strength in his body.

The gap between the administration building and the maintenance building was much closer to fifteen feet than ten. Even if it had been ten, Cole Blackwater, falling backward, could not have hoped to land on the roof of the shed. The only thought in his mind as he fell was that he didn't want to land on the tools by the door.

He hit the ground with a thud, his left foot first, then his left arm, and his back. He grunted loudly as he hit the ground, rolled backward in the mud, and collided with the wheelbarrow, which fell on top of him. He blacked out momentarily, the air forced from his lungs by the fall, and a sharp pain shot up his left leg. God, I've broken my leg, he thought as he lay in the mud by the door to the shed.

He lay there for a minute in a puddle of mud. Rain fell on him, getting in his eyes and nose and ears. The pain in his leg dulled. Maybe it wasn't broken. He moved his arms. His left elbow was very sore, but it worked. He tried his legs. The right leg was OK.

He moved the left. Some pain there, but bearable. He pushed the wheelbarrow off and it clattered to the ground. He tried to stand. As he put weight on his left leg a spasm of pain shot up his left side. He scanned the windows to see if he had been observed. He couldn't tell in the rain if anybody peered out at him.

He grabbed for the door handle to steady himself. He had to get off the mine property. How was he going to get back to his truck? He couldn't climb the fence.

Then he remembered that he still had the keys. Tracey would understand. She had, after all, bought him valuable seconds when he was in Henderson's office. He patted his pockets and felt the keys' reassuring weight.

The he bent down to pick up the wheelbarrow.

He stopped. He looked up from where he had fallen.

Mike Barnes was a heavy man.

It was a solid wheelbarrow.

If the murderer had known about a wheelbarrow behind the admin building, he might have used it to transport the body to the mill. That might also explain why none of the suspects limped from their collision with the bits and steel. The wheelbarrow had knocked over the pallet, dumping Mike Barnes to the floor.

Cole inspected the wheelbarrow for signs of blood. Nothing. He tried the door handle and found it locked. He fished the keys from his pockets, careful not to drop any of his trash, unlocked the door, and slipped inside. It was pitch black. He patted the wall, found a light switch, and flipped it on. There was a riding mower, a gas-powered push mower, a wall full of garden tools, a broad workbench, and three wheelbarrows on the opposite wall. Above the workbench there was an eye-wash station and a red plastic case with a familiar white cross on it. First aid. Hallelujah, thought Cole.

He hobbled to the wheelbarrows to inspect them. The first one in the stack of three revealed its dark secret. The hub over the wheel was speckled with blood. While the barrow itself was clean, the killer, as he had in the bathroom, had been in a rush and missed this. Cole smirked. Maybe the RCMP would get lucky and lift a set of prints from the barrow. He leaned it back against the wall and took a few pictures of it with his cellphone. Then he looked for the Day-Timer on the off chance that the killer had stashed it here. Nothing. Finally he took down the first aid kit and opened it.

He found a broad tensor bandage, a bottle of extra strength Tylenol, and an SAM splint. This would help. Sitting on the bench, he slowly removed his shoe, gritting his teeth and grimacing as the pain shot up his leg. The ankle was nearly black — a deep sprain, if not a small fracture — and he couldn't move it without pain. He wrapped the tensor bandage around it and then applied the splint. He left his sock off, but put his shoe back on. He still had to drive to Oracle. He swallowed two Tylenol, washing them down with water from the eye-wash station, and pocketed the bottle.

He put the first aid kit back on the wall. Time to get the heck out of Dodge, he thought.

He limped to the door, opened it slowly, and peeked out. The rain continued, and he stepped out into it and closed and locked the door behind him.

As quickly as his injury allowed, he hobbled to the fence, checking behind him for trouble. None appeared, and he unlocked the gate, let himself through, and locked it behind him. He discovered that the lock could easily be pushed back from the outside so it didn't reveal anybody's passage. He did so, and sloshed to his truck in the falling rain, wincing from the pain in his ankle.

He slumped in the seat, breathing hard from exertion and from the adrenaline that coursed through him. He took his hat off and his hair flopped across his forehead. He ran a hand through it and water ran down his face. He closed his eyes. He could hear his heart.

What am I doing here?

He opened his eyes with a start, realizing that he had fallen asleep. Pushing himself up with the palms of his hands on the seat, he winced at the pain in his left elbow. He'd have to have that looked at too. He wondered what Sarah would say when he returned home looking as if he'd been through combat. He had told her two weeks ago when she had implored him to be safe, that he was just going to do a little strategy work. Now he was falling out of third-storey windows.

Jumping out of third-storey windows.

He looked through the rain at the administration building and considered what he had learned in Henderson's office. His Day-Timer showed that Hank had a meeting to finalize the environmental assessment on the same night that Barnes was killed.

Cole had seen Hank leaving the admin building. Did Hank go home for an early dinner and return later to meet with Barnes? If so, had the meeting gone so badly that Henderson, already an angry and violent man, followed Barnes into the bathroom and bashed his head in? Cole shuddered. Some missing piece pestered him, something that he could not put his finger on. But despite all his snooping and risk-taking, he had found nothing to vindicate Dale van Stempvort and convict someone else. Despite great risk to his miserable life and limb, he was no farther ahead than he was that morning.

How, Cole thought, could this possibly be worth the peril he had put himself in?

He turned the truck's ignition over. He'd limp back to town, pay his second visit to the hospital, and reconsider the crazy notion that in one fell swoop he could solve the mystery of Mike Barnes' death, save Cardinal Divide, and purge himself of his anger, guilt, and sorrow for all that had happened in his downward-spiralling life. There were less demanding forms of therapy, mused Cole. Nobody in Vancouver took this sort of risk. They got their chakras realigned or went to Hollyhock and sat in supportive circles and ate vegetarian food; they didn't solve murders and confront killers.

The stereo started up with the truck and he turned up the volume on Ian Tyson, hoping the crooner's cowboy polkas and the lament of his ballads would vanquish Cole Blackwater's remorse. The Toyota in gear, he backed away from the gate, onto the track that paralleled the mine site, and toward Route 40. As he drove past the main gate he wished good riddance to the place. This was the last time he'd see it.

Rain continued to fall as he drove north. When the clouds parted, he saw snow dusting the crowns of the hills above. The long sweeping expanse of Cardinal Divide would be covered too. The grizzly bear family would be holed up in a day bed, in the hollow of a tree or maybe tucked under a ledge of stone, huddled together for warmth.

At that moment Cole Blackwater wanted very much to huddle together with someone for warmth. With his daughter. With Nancy Webber. With anybody. He brushed away a tear of self-pity.

The going was slow. It hurt his sprained ankle to work the

clutch and shift gears, so he stayed in fourth gear, in four-wheel drive, as much as possible. He lost power on the corners and nearly stalled a couple of times, but continued north, past Cadomin Mines and up through the hills cloaked with fir and spruce, their tops tipped with snow. If this keeps up, thought Cole, I'll be fighting a blizzard by the time I reach town. It certainly wouldn't be the first time the Eastern Slopes were snowed under in May. Happened nearly every year when he was a kid.

He was half an hour outside Oracle when he heard his cellphone jingle. It wasn't an incoming call; it was the little ditty it played when there were messages waiting for him.

He pushed some papers on the passenger seat aside, flipped the cellphone open, and hit the keys to dial his message service. He drove with his injured left arm while he held the phone to his right ear.

"Cole, it's Perry Gilbert. I just got out of my session with the RCMP. Holy shit, buddy, you're not going to believe this, but they are about this close to being convinced that Dale is innocent. They're getting heat from the Crown Prosecutor in Edmonton to reopen. They're not one hundred percent, but they are getting there. I talked with Reimer for more than two hours this afternoon. They have a positive on the blood in the bathroom, and that's not all.

"Listen, the autopsy shows that Mike Barnes was killed by the blow to the back of his head. The injury to the front on his head was caused later, likely when he was dropped on the floor of the mill. The forensics showed traces of orange paint in the wound to the rear of his head. The wounds to the front of his head showed traces of the oil used to lubricate drill bits. The forensics also showed that several of the bits found on the floor had Mike's hair and blood on them. So the RCMP are pretty convinced that he was hit from behind in the bathroom and transported to the mill. I've given them everything we have on Hank Henderson, George Cody, and David Smith. They're going to follow up. Good work, Cole. Call me when you get back into town, we'll have a drink."

The message ended. Cole felt a wave of elation. Finally, progress!

The next message began. He shifted the phone to his left hand so he could steer better on the slick roads. The truck slid awkwardly back and forth with its misaligned tires.

"Cole, it's Nancy. You're are never going to believe this. I got a call from David Smith today. Your buddy. He was all friendly on the phone, asked me to come and see him, so I arranged to meet at his office. Guess what he handed me?"

Cole guessed frantically.

"He told me that he learned ESCOG planned to give up on the fight to stop the mine. That's one of your stories!"

That was the story that Cole and Peggy had given suspected mole number three, Anne Stanton.

"You were right, Cole. It worked. So I called Peggy and got the name of the source, and I'm heading over to interview her now. Peggy told me I could. I'll call you when I've talked to her. She doesn't know I'm coming, so this should be interesting."

Cole's mind raced. Anne was the mole. She was connected to David Smith. After Peggy and he had been at her apartment, she had called David with the good news that the ESCOG was giving up on the Cardinal Divide. David waited a day, and then called the highest profile reporter in town, Nancy Webber. Nancy called Peggy, who gave up the mole, and Nancy was going to brace her.

Suddenly Cole realized what had been bothering him since the day that he and Peggy had interviewed the three possible moles. In Anne's apartment, rented from a friend of the family, were sports memorabilia, including a fair number of trap-shooting trophies. He hadn't looked closely enough at them to register the names on the engravings, but Cole guessed that they had been awarded to David Smith, a marksman, whose office was also adorned by trap-shooting awards. Anne and David were family friends. Or closer.

The message ended and Cole strained to hear the next message over static in the reception. His left arm ached and he stretched it to find some relief. As he was doing that he had to gear down, and he winced as he pressed in on the clutch.

When he got the phone back to his ear, the next message was already playing.

"...Cole, call me as soon as you get this message. It's David Smith! He's the one! He killed Mike Barnes!" The line went dead. Cole's heart jumped into his throat. He snapped the phone shut and guided the Toyota to the side of the road. He was breathing so hard that he had a hard time controlling the vehicle. Frantically, he dialled Nancy's number.

"Webber," she answered.

"Thank God you're OK."

"Cole, it's David! David Smith is the murderer!"

"How do you know?"

"I found Mike Barnes' agenda."

"Where? Where did you find it?"

"At Anne's place. You'll never believe where it was."

"Nancy, I don't have time for guessing games."

"It was in her recycling."

Cole coughed a laugh. "That is pretty ironic. What have you done with it?"

"I just found it half an hour ago. I spent the next twenty minutes putting the thumb screws to Anne. She told all. I'm on my way to the RCMP detachment right now."

Cole's mind was on a roller coaster ride. "It all makes perfect sense now that the missing piece has been found, Nancy. My God, this is good news."

"Where are you?"

"I'm about thirty minutes south of Oracle, on my way back into town."

"OK, well, come by the RCMP detachment when you get back. They will no doubt want to talk with you."

"Listen, Nancy, I've had a bit of an accident. I sort of fell out of a window."

"Christ, Cole, are you OK?"

"I can drive, but it's slow going."

"Do you want me to send some help?"

"No, but let Reimer know where I am, and that I'm on my way back."

"OK, Cole."

"And Nancy, steer clear of David Smith. You'll get your story without confronting him."

"I'm not an idiot, Cole," she said roughly, but then added, "Thanks for caring."

"Hold on," Cole said, "I'm parked at the side of the road and there's a truck slowing to see if I'm OK. I'm going to wave them off and then we'll finish this up."

Cole rolled down his window. Rain pelted the truck and splashed his face. He held the phone in his right hand while he leaned on the windowsill and watched the white Dodge Ram roll to a stop and saw the tinted driver-side window roll down. It was more than halfway down when Cole realized what was happening. He dropped the phone and grabbed at the gear shift, jammed it into reverse, and stepped on the accelerator as hard as he could, nearly popping the clutch with his injured left foot in the process. The Toyota jerked backward, and that's what saved him. The shotgun blast sprayed a tight pellet pattern across his windshield, cracked it in a dozen places, and punctured the hood in a dozen more. The shrubs at the side of the road suffered shredding by hundreds of pellets.

The Toyota's engine roared and the tachometer pushed into the red as he raced backward in reverse. A second blast from the shotgun missed the truck entirely, and Cole yanked on the wheel to turn the truck sideways in the road, jammed it into first gear and worked the clutch while howling in pain from the sprained ankle. He was in second gear before the third blast hit the back of the Toyota, shattering the taillights and breaking the glass on the back window of the canopy. He was doing sixty kilometres an hour before the white Dodge Ram took off after him. He fumbled for the phone on the floor, hoping that the connection hadn't been severed. He reached down, held the wheel with his injured left arm, and grabbed the phone.

"Nancy!"

"Cole, what the fuck was that!"

"It's David Smith," he said as calmly as he could. "He's shooting at me."

22 "Call the RCMP," Cole said. He held the phone with his left hand and shifted with his right, putting the truck into fourth gear. Behind him, David Smith gained quickly; the throaty roar of the Ram's V8 engine could be heard coming on fast.

"Cole!"

"Call Reimer. I'm heading south!"

The Ram collided with the Toyota and Cole lurched forward. His injured left arm jerked wildly, the left hand hit the front of the passenger door window, and the cellphone clattered away into the rain to smash on the road.

"Fuck!" Cole grimaced and put both hands on the wheel to steer his truck into the road. The Ram was more powerful by far and pressed on his bumper, guiding him toward the shoulder. Cole geared down into third, groaning, and stepped on the accelerator. The Toyota lurched wildly forward. He power shifted into fourth again and pulled ahead of the larger truck.

The rain fell in torrents now, was turning to sleet and sticking to the windshield. He pressed the Toyota, stayed just ahead of Smith, and raced along the gravel road at a hundred kilometres per hour. He checked the rear-view mirror, saw the Dodge Ram a few metres back, but could not see David Smith through the tinted windshield.

He had turned his radio on while driving back from the mine, and the music still blared. For the rest of his life he would think of this day when he listened to Ian Tyson. That is, he thought, if I live for the rest of my life.

The road straightened and he shifted into fifth gear, pushing the Toyota too hard for four-wheel drive. But it was the four-wheel drive that kept him on the road, which was slick with sleet and dotted with puddles that made his light truck hydroplane. He steered into some of the smaller puddles, hoping to kick up some spray to obscure Smith's vision, but he only managed to slow himself down.

He rolled the driver-side window up halfway and Smith rammed him again. Cole looked in the rear-view mirror and saw nothing but the behemoth's grill behind him. If he lived through this, he would start a campaign to outlaw V8 gas-guzzling redneck trucks like the Dodge Ram 2500. If he lived through this.

Cole jerked the wheel to the right and suddenly the Dodge was alongside of him. Before David Smith could do it, Cole jerked the wheel violently to the left and the two trucks collided. Cole snapped against the seatbelt, his left arm crushed between himself and the door. But the force of the impact was enough to send the Ram onto the shoulder, and in a second Cole was more than a hundred metres ahead of Smith.

He pressed the accelerator down and raced along the gravel road. In a few minutes he would pass through Cadomin, and he wondered if he might stop and find a refuge in one of the homes there. But before he could consider it, the Ram was behind him again, pressing him. "Christ, that truck has guts," spat Cole, and floored the Toyota's accelerator. They raced through Cadomin doing over 120 kilometres per hour, the Toyota's engine whining.

Cole now aimed for the mine. He figured he had about five minutes to get into a position where he could make the sharp right-hand turn off the gravel road into the mine site. He would shoot for the admin building, use the keys in his pocket to let himself in, find a phone, and call for help. It was a faint hope, Cole knew, but he had no other.

Trees whizzed past in a foggy, green-grey blur. David Smith drove out to meet Mike Barnes late the same night that Cole met with the mine manager. Smith must have read the environmental assessment, put two and two together, and called Barnes for a meeting. Barnes, never imagining that David Smith's ambition made him so dangerous, invited the Chamber of Commerce president to his office for a chat. Smith drove to the mine and parked at the admin building. Murder had not been on his mind then. Only forceful persuasion. But something went wrong during their conversation. Maybe Barnes got under David Smith's skin the same way he got under Hank Henderson's. Whatever transpired between the two men set David Smith on a homicidal path. He found something sufficiently heavy to bludgeon Mike Barnes with, waited for the man to leave his office, followed him into the bathroom, and bashed the back of his head in. The body hit the ground like a tonne of bricks and sprayed blood around the room. Smith cleaned up the blood as best as he could, hoping to create the impression that Barnes had disappeared rather than been killed.

But he made two mistakes. He hadn't cleaned under the counter, and he plugged the toilet when he flushed too many blood-soaked paper towels down at once.

He then carried Barnes' body out the admin building and, rather than risk having his truck seen across the yard at the mill, he retrieved a wheelbarrow from the maintenance building, maybe using Barnes' own keys to do so. He wheeled Barnes' corpse across the wide yard, the head hanging over the front of the wheelbarrow and dripping blood on the hub of the wheel, and entered the mill through the side entrance. Cole remembered that David Smith had worked in the mill years ago, and was familiar with its layout. But some things had changed, and as he left the side storage room for the main mill itself, he crashed the wheelbarrow into a pallet of bits. He spilled Barnes' carcass onto the floor and knocked some of the head-sized bits down with him. That's when JP had opened the far door to the mill.

Cole imagined David Smith saw the giant door opening. Carefully he backtracked the wheelbarrow through the double doors into the storage area and patiently waited for the security guard to leave.

He might have waited on the other side of the door to club JP if the watchman had come prowling around the storage area. Luck, prudence, or divine intervention saved the man's life that night, and prevented the disappearance of Mike Barnes' body.

Once JP left to call the RCMP, Smith quickly returned the wheelbarrow and drove his truck through the side gate. Maybe he used a key kept from his stint at the mine. After all, half the town had a copy of that key, Tracey said.

Cole steered the truck in a straight line, the Ram pressing him from behind.

Soon the mine would come into view. Cole knew he must slow down to make the turn through the mine gate and avoid side swiping the tiny entrance booth. With luck, JP or the other night watchman would see the chase and call the RCMP. With luck.

He rounded a tight bend in the road, moaning in pain as he geared down into fourth grinding the gears, and the Dodge Ram pulled alongside him. Again Cole swung the wheel wildly; the box of his truck hit the front wheel cover of Smith's truck. The force of the blow and the momentum of Smith's vehicle twisted Cole's

Stephen Legault

smaller Toyota, and for a moment, he slipped side-on to Smith. He jerked the wheel back, geared down again and gunned the engine, lurching violently forward.

He remembered a few years back when he had been stuck in the mud along a logging road in the Chilcotin Mountains north of Vancouver. A logging crew had stopped to give him a hand. When Cole was unable to drive the truck out of the gumbo that entombed it, one of the loggers attached a winch and the other guy slipped in behind the wheel. While the winch pulled, the fellow deftly guided the truck in compound low out of the goo. "You just got to drive it like they do in the commercials!" the man laughed, and popped the truck out onto the road.

If they could see him now. He raced ahead of David Smith, hugged the right side of the road, and tried to prevent the Dodge Ram from cutting off his possible escape into the mine yard.

Cole looked in the mirror. The Ram was right on his tail. He looked again and it was gone. Suddenly it was on his left side. It raced up beside him. He pounded his foot into the floor and the Toyota evened out with the Ram. Then Smith's truck was against his, pushing the Toyota toward the rough shoulder of the road. Cole pushed back but the Dodge was much larger than his own vehicle, and his wobbly alignment made the manoeuvre more difficult. His vehicle started to slide to the right as his wheels grabbed at the loose rock along the ditch. If he hit that ditch at this speed he'd be done for.

The mine came into view. He was driving much too fast. He hit the brake and the clutch at the same time and pain shot up his left leg and made him roar. As the Dodge flew out in front of him, he steered to the left to regain the centre of the road. The Dodge veered wildly to the right.

The Dodge Ram smashed through the chain link fence at eighty kilometres per hour, Smith steering madly to avoid the tiny gate-house. He spun out to the left, compensating for the turn to keep his vehicle from rolling, and kicked up a plume of gravel and sand and muddy water as he did so. Cole pressed harder on the brakes and turned the wheel so that the Toyota came to rest twenty metres past the gatehouse, parked across the road. He pushed in the clutch to keep the truck from stalling. The Dodge was between him and the mine yard. He looked at the fence. Between him and the fence was a ditch deep enough, Cole figured, that he would bottom out in it. He'd be a sitting duck for David Smith. He looked north along the road that he and Smith had raced over. He guessed that if he drove in that direction, Smith could T-bone him before he made it past the mine.

There was only one choice. He put the truck into first gear, spun the tires in the loose gravel, and drove south, the sleet pelting his windshield. The big white Ram roared after him.

This stretch of road was largely unknown to him. He'd driven it once during the day, the afternoon that he had visited Mike Barnes at the mine. But its twists and turns came much more quickly than along the road between the mine and the town. The shoulders were narrower and the trees leaned much closer to the road. He found third gear and fourth, and pressed the Toyota to negotiate the narrow turns, kicking up gravel and bits of snow as he climbed higher toward Cardinal Divide.

Smith gained on him, and though Cole thought himself the better driver, Smith's truck had over a hundred horsepower more than his aging Toyota. He wouldn't be far behind for long. To what end this mad race, thought Cole? Was he going to keep driving until he ran out of gas or Smith overtook him? Then what? Smith was armed, and Cole, with a sprained left ankle and bruised elbow, wouldn't provide much of a contest.

Suddenly, as Cole rounded a sharp corner on the north side of Cardinal Divide, a downed tree appeared in the middle of the road. In the dim light Cole saw that the tree had fallen from the right side of the road. Cole jerked the wheel left and ran over the top five feet of the pine. He checked his mirror and to his delight watched David Smith take the foot-thick tree head on in the Ram, spinning wildly in the road as he did.

Cole kept up his pace, twisting and turning his way up to the crest of the Divide, checking his mirror often. Even if Smith was stopped, Cole's only option was to drive on.

Highway 40 wound south from Oracle to Cochrane north of Highway One, but crossed Highway 16, the David Thompson Highway, somewhere in between. The long, narrow, winding road snaked along river valleys and over low saddles between foothills. On the south side of the Trans Canada Highway, 40 re-emerged to weave its way through Kananaskis Country, and finally exited the mountains west of Longview. From there it was another hour south to the Porcupine Hills and his family's ranch. If he had to he'd drive all the way there, but Cole knew that between him and the Porcupine Hills there were towns and police stations and hopefully salvation. He checked his gas. He'd had the presence of mind to keep the truck topped up these days in Oracle, so he had nearly a full tank. The Toyota could get 500 kilometres on that. He'd easily make Rocky Mountain House. He felt relief. He relaxed a little, and eased his white knuckles off the wheel to flex his hands.

He didn't see the next downed tree until it was too late. Its dark hulk emerged across the road from the blowing snow like an iceberg looming out of the fog. He locked the brakes, then let up a little to try to steer the truck to safety, but couldn't. The right side of the truck hit the tree and the Toyota flipped on its side, catapulting over the fallen giant, and rolled into the ditch, horn blaring. The world went black, then light, then black again as the truck flipped over. Cole could not tell which way was up. He felt something hot on his face, and then a rush of cold air, and realized that the windshield had smashed and sprayed him with flying glass. The world went dim as the truck came to a stop.

He awoke to sadness. A sadness that seemed to fill his head beyond reason. His first thought was of Sarah. God, she would be sad. He had promised her. Promised her that he would be careful. Promised her that he would call. He'd broken all his promises again.

He thought of his mother, alone on the ranch, waiting for visits from Walter, who came every few weeks from his posting at Waterton Lakes National Park, and from her errant son, Cole, who lived in a world full of anger and hatred, fuelled by the very thought of his father and his father's final moments. Even his end hadn't cooled Cole's hatred, Cole's rage, and now there was nothing left that Cole could do to cool those flames.

He realized that Ian Tyson was still singing on the stereo. It was a sad ballad. *"There's a pay phone in paradise, out on the edge of town, big cottonwood trees, golden leaves coming down. I'll wait a little longer, give it one more try, please try your call later means cowboy, goodbye."*

Cole groped to switch the stereo off. Sometimes that song helped and sometimes it didn't.

His face burned. He opened his eyes and tried to blink, but he couldn't see.

He was right side up. He tried to move and found that he could. His right arm was fine. He reached up to wipe his face and came away with bloody fingers.

"Good Christ," he muttered. He wiped the blood away from his eyes and tried to open them again. He could see, though his eyes stung as blood dripped into them from his forehead.

He reached and undid the seat belt. No doubt another life saved by the belt, he thought. Maybe they'd put him in a commercial.

With his right arm he reached across himself and tried to open the door, but couldn't. The door was pushed in against his left arm and would not budge. So he leaned across the bench seat and tried the other door, and this he was able to open. He crawled out of the truck, taking the keys and his hat, and popped open the glove box to find a heavy flashlight there. He limped around to the north side of the truck to look at the tree that had been his undoing. Fifty feet back down the road he found it, blocking the road entirely. Where the Toyota had hit it, all the branches, some as big as his leg, had been severed. He had sideswiped it, and the truck had flipped and rolled – how many times? – and he had walked away, some cuts from the broken glass his only apparent injury. He looked at his watch. The chase lasted more than twenty minutes. If he was lucky, the RCMP would be on their way and would pick up David Smith a few miles back on the road within the next fifteen or twenty minutes. Then they would find him. Cole would find a place in the trees, out of the snow, now six inches deep on the ground and still falling, and wait.

He walked toward the trees, dark and heavy with snow. The snow muffled all sound. Whereas before he swam in bird song on Cardinal Divide, now there was only a gummy silence. But something made him stop. He listened. He looked at his watch again. There was no way. He took a breath and held it, strained to hear. It grew slowly, then it became clear. There was no mistaking the roar of the Dodge Ram's V8 racing up the crest of the Cardinal Divide toward him.

23 How long could he keep this up? Cole had been plodding up the forested slope of Cardinal Divide for what seemed a very long time, but when he looked at his watch he realized that it had been less than five minutes. With every step his ankle shot a fiery jolt up his left leg, through his hips, and into the rest of his body. He envisioned the ankle inside the splint and tensor bandage, the damaged tendons and ligaments slowly succumbing to the repeated strain of his demands on them, and finally giving way entirely. The pain, and that image, blotted out all sense of time.

He clutched the flashlight and pushed on through the trees. Branches whipping him in the face added to the already bloody mess there. His Gore-tex jacket protected him some from the branches and from the snow that dropped on him as he pushed through the forest.

Cole tried, in vain, to run along a course that camouflaged his footprints. The snow was six inches deep and very wet, and every time he stepped in it a tell-tale sign of his passage remained. So he jumped from the shadow of one tree where there was no snow to the next, groaning as he did so.

Cole had no idea what kind of shape David Smith was in. He still hadn't seen the man's face, except briefly when Smith pulled alongside him and fired three rounds from the shotgun at him. Since that time, Smith's truck had collided with a tree, but Cole guessed that the man had suffered little injury. The Dodge Ram fared well enough to run him down while the Toyota had finally expired.

He didn't have long to wonder about David Smith's well-being. As the trees thinned, Cole faced a dilemma: run out into the open toward the crest of Cardinal Divide, or double back through the trees toward the road and try to evade his pursuer. The trees grew shorter as he climbed higher up the ridge; in a few more seconds he would be in the open. He stopped and listened and heard nothing. His own heart beat so loudly, and his breathing was so laborious, that he imagined a bulldozer could sneak up behind him. Doubling back might allow him to get to Smith's truck, or better still, meet the RCMP at the road before Smith realized where he was going. That was, if the RCMP were coming. He could only hope.

Taking the ridge meant he would be exposed, at least until he crested the top, but he might also be able to lose Smith in the rocks. He couldn't hear Smith, but he could feel him coming through the trees below him — he could feel the white hot anger, the rage — and so he made a split-second decision and limped toward the crest of the Cardinal Divide.

When he had hiked along the ridge on the day Mike Barnes was killed, it didn't take him more than a couple of minutes to gain the apogee after he left the trees. But now, injured and bone-weary, Cole Blackwater realized he would be exposed to David Smith's field of view as soon as Smith broke the cover of the trees. His mind raced as he reviewed the possibilities, of which there were very few. Duck and cover? There was nowhere to hide, not until he reached the crest. Keep running was all he could think to do. Every step became more painful. Every step brought a new experience in agony. He began to wonder if he would make it to the ridge.

That was when he heard the gunshot, a clean, violent crack that echoed its sharp retort through the hills. Now there was no question whether or not Cole Blackwater could keep running. Gunfire was a powerful motivator.

The shot that had been fired was not from a shotgun. Cole knew it was from a high-calibre hunting rifle. He pushed himself harder, his whole left side suffused with pain. If David Smith had a scope on that weapon ...

A bullet ricocheted off a rock, and at that very moment he heard a second shot. Smith had spotted him and was zeroing in. The crest of the ridge was near, and Cole felt hot tears running down his face as he winced with pain, pushing for the relative safety of the crest. A third shot rang out as he gained the crest and loped toward the sharp drop-off point. Here he was shielded from view by the swell of the land, but he once again had to choose which way to go. The ground, slippery with snow, made the choice difficult. He stopped, keeled over, and vomited. He wiped blood from his eyes and sucked breath into his lungs. He could not outrun David Smith. That much was obvious. There was enough daylight left that Smith could track him easily for the next hour. Cole figured he had less than five minutes before Smith was over the top of the ridge.

The Cardinal Divide was a broad, sweeping foothill ridge that ran roughly east and west, against the grain of the mostly north-south trending hills. Its western terminus was tucked into the wall of Front Range peaks that guarded the flank of Jasper National Park. To the east, it extended into the foothills and fingered toward the prairie. Along its crest it was devoid of trees except where the road crossed it at a low point. The ridge itself sloped gently, but fell off sharply to the north. A rocky band maybe fifty feet thick crowned the ridge there. Below the rocky outcrop the ridge fell away at a steep angle in a grass-covered slope.

With sudden clarity, Cole knew what to do. Determined, he ran along the ridge line to the east, dragging his feet in the snow, pushing as much of it as he could while covering as much ground as possible. He ran right along the rocky drop off, his head dizzy as the earth slipped away to his left and disappeared into the fog below. He came to the place where he had sat and watched the grizzly sow and her cubs and pressed farther down the slope, and then quickly turned back. He counted on the fading light and the wet snow to cover his tracks. He struggled back a few hundred feet and then, fearing he would meet David Smith running down the slope, found a crevice in the rock and, flashlight tucked under one arm, lowered himself in. He wedged himself there, feet on tiny knobs of stone, his head a few feet below the top of the rocks. He had chosen a place where his tracks had come close to the rock, and he took pains to step from those broad tracks to the stone without disturbing any snow.

And he waited, his heart beating so loudly that he worried David Smith might hear it. He closed his eyes and calmed his breath. He felt the searing pain reach from his ankle up his leg and into his torso. He breathed slowly.

Two minutes is a long time to wait for death. In two minutes there is plenty of opportunity for every bad decision you've ever made to play itself out in the theatre of your mind. So it was with Cole Blackwater. He even had time to re-run some of the really colossally bad mistakes he'd made. The moment of indiscretion when he had met Nancy Webber that turned into a marriage-ending affair. The lie that he told to preserve his ego, and the life path that it cost him. Had cost Nancy. The foolish belief that by returning to the family ranch something good might come. He pressed his eyes shut and tried to block out the awful sound, the roar of the shotgun in the barn that always ended that dark memory.

The only good decision he made was to follow Sarah to Vancouver. He pressed his mind to hold onto that choice. He had, over the last three years, worked hard every day to be a good father, a loving, if not completely dependable, father to his daughter.

That was what he was thinking when he heard David Smith's laboured breathing above him. In the crepuscular light he saw Smith not fifteen feet away, walking along his tracks. The man appeared to favour his right leg. He too had been injured, but not as badly as Cole. He wore a grey-green canvas coat and a camouflage ball cap, and in his arms, held at the ready, was a short-barrelled hunting rifle with a scope mounted on top, the type that Cole had used as a young man hunting deer in the Eastern Slopes. Cole held his breath as David Smith moved above him, studying the tracks. He made up his mind to jump backward if Smith spotted him as he had at the admin building only a few hours before. He would take his chances with the fifty-foot drop, loose stone, and what would certainly be a long, bone-crushing roll down the steep northing slope of the Cardinal Divide.

Cole watched as Smith stepped carefully past his hiding place. Now, thought Cole, was the moment to make his move. He guessed that Smith would come to the end of his tracks, where Cole had turned around, in less than a minute. Left elbow aching, Cole hoisted himself up the narrow crevice. He put the flashlight down in the snow and pulled himself up to the crest. He grabbed the heavy flashlight. His adrenaline surging, his temples pounding, he began to slowly close the gap between himself and David Smith.

Snow obliterates most sound, and so it was that Cole could get behind David Smith without being heard. Smith stepped onto the rock that Cole sat on to watch the grizzly family, and looked down to see Cole's tracks end twenty feet down the ridge.

Smith stopped.

Cole stepped onto the rock.

He brought the flashlight back behind him with his right arm and swung.

At that moment Smith turned, realizing that his quarry had doubled back, and saw Cole looming right behind him. Smith gasped. His eyes bulged and his mouth opened as if to speak. Cole

Stephen Legault

arced the flashlight down at Smith's head. But Smith was able to raise his left arm and the barrel of the rifle as Cole swung the heavy flashlight toward him. The blow caught the gun barrel first, knocked the rifle from Smith's hands, and then hit Smith in the side of the head with an audible crack. The man went down on one knee, the gun falling into the snow on the edge of the drop off.

Cole winced in pain as he completed the swing, his left ankle giving out under the force of his blow. The two men knelt in front of each other in the snow. Smith put his right hand down to steady himself. His eyes lacked focus. Cole blinked back tears and raised the flashlight again. As he struck, Smith lunged at him and the blow hit the man's back. Smith and Cole were locked in each other's arms, Cole beating at the man with the light and Smith punching at Cole with left and right jabs to his sides and kidneys. They rolled on the rocks and in the snow this way, pummelled each other with blows to the body, back, and arms, each man protecting his head. Cole pushed Smith away with his right foot and managed to land two quick punches to David Smith's face so that a spray of blood erupted from his nose. But Smith then found Cole's weakness. As the two men rolled, Smith's knee connected with Cole's ankle, and he roared in pain. Smith brought his foot down on the ankle and Cole blacked out. He felt a fist connect with his face and the world went momentarily white. He hit the rocks and felt the cold of the snow on his neck but he did not make any sound.

"This has gone far enough." David Smith spat blood as he spoke. "Far enough."

He struggled to his feet. Cole saw Smith through clouds of blood and the dizzying pain that obscured his vision.

"You fucking people come in here and try to fuck everything up. You try to destroy my town, and ruin my career. I own this fucking town," Smith ranted. He moved backward, turned around, and searched the ground.

"And no Goddamn pointy head or some two-bit has-been is going to stop me."

Cole struggled to sit up. He felt like puking and his left arm didn't want to work so he kept falling over.

"I'm going to make things right again. Now things will be back to normal around here."

He's looking for the rifle, thought Cole. If he finds it, I'll never see Sarah again. He steadied himself with his left hand and tried to make his legs work. He was nauseated and couldn't see anything but dim outlines. But he knew Smith neared the gun in the snow. He could see, through the miasma of pain and blood and memory, Smith bend over.

"Now, Mr. Blackwater ..."

The retort a pistol shot makes when heard in the open is so much quieter than one might expect, especially after hearing the blast from a rifle or shotgun. So it was that Cole heard the pop and then a voice yell through the snow: "Don't make another move!"

It was a female voice, and Cole's brain tried to connect it with a face. Why did Nancy Webber have a gun?

"Don't touch the rifle!" the voice called again. Cole tried to turn to see who spoke, but he fell sideways instead, his burning face cooled by the heavy, wet snow.

So it was that he didn't see what happened next, but heard four quick pops, and then nothing more.

24 Alberta could break your heart. It was a place of paradox. The way the prairie grasses rose to the undulating swell of the Porcupine Hills and gave way to the twisted pines and clutching aspens at their summit. The way the land plunged again, down into valley after valley, the rise and fall of ridges of rough fescue along the corrugated spine of the Whaleback. Finally, the perpendicular thrust of the Front Range Mountains, peaks dragging their ragged edges along the basement of heaven. It was heartbreakingly beautiful. But what could break your heart without remorse was how little regard some had for its majesty. Torn and ripped by off-highway vehicles. Plundered by logging and oil and gas companies. The guts ripped out of the land by mining. That left your heart in pieces.

And there was the weather, impervious to people's will. Winter and summer failed to obey even the most basic rules of their respective seasons. In the Eastern Slopes, some of the most vicious storms happened late in the spring, on the solstice's door step, dumping a foot of snow or more as the winds shifted and twisted and curled. These storms didn't come from the west as winter weather did, but from the south, and from the east. As high-pressure systems formed in the Rockies and on the Great Plains south of the Medicine Line, they pushed moist Pacific air back toward the eastern edge of the mountains. These "up slope" storms could make May feel like January, and June feel like March.

Then in November and December, summer often found its redemption, as autumn ushered in days so sunny, and skies so blue, that a walk in the woods, with the golden leaves crisp underfoot from a light frost the night before, seemed like heaven on earth.

It could break your heart.

Cole Blackwater dreamed of such things. He dreamed of a twisted patch of aspen tucked in along the banks of a tiny creek that emerged from the eastern side of the Porcupine Hills. It was a place he knew well, not far from the family ranch, but far enough that he could pretend not to hear his father's angry yelling or his mother's invitation to dinner. In the shortening days of autumn he could run along an ancient trail that wove through those trees, their grey bark dull against the copper-coloured ground. He could run until his legs gave up as he reached the top of the rise, find a place alone on the crown of the hill, and rest against a twisted pine to watch the final rays of sunlight be eclipsed by the Rocky Mountains. The sky would fade from blue to indigo, and finally grey, like the aspens. In that half-light of autumn he would make his way home.

He opened his eyes slowly. The room was dim, but even the soft light hurt so he closed his eyes again.

"Cole?"

He opened his eyes more slowly. They adjusted to the light and he blinked several times and drew the room into focus.

"Hi Cole."

He tried to turn his head to see who was speaking. But his neck and shoulders ached and he closed his eyes instead.

"Cole, it's Nancy."

He opened his eyes for a third time. "I'm in the hospital?" he croaked.

"Yes," she said, and reached for a bottle of water with a bent straw and handed it to him.

He took it and sipped. The water was cool in his throat, and the image of water tumbling from a glacier onto sun-parched rock came to his mind. "What day is it?"

"Sunday."

Two weeks. A lifetime.

"How do I look?" he asked, remembering the accident.

"Like shit," she said. "But the doctor says it won't be any worse than you normally look in a couple of weeks."

He smiled thinly. His lips felt dry. "That's a relief."

"David Smith is dead," she said.

His brow furrowed, trying to remember. He remembered climbing down the crevice of rock, but couldn't remember climbing back out.

"Sergeant Reimer and one of her constables shot him. Four times."

Pop, pop, pop, pop, he remembered, the individual sounds merging into one.

"I remember now," he said, then, "You called me?"

"Yeah, I called you," she smiled. "I called you from Anne's place. Right after I found Mike Barnes' appointment book. After Peggy gave me the name of the people you figured to be moles and their

Stephen Legault

stories, I went to Anne's apartment and confronted her, you know, just hoping for the story. Totally self-serving. But she cracked and said she didn't know what her uncle was up to."

"Uncle." It was a statement, not a question.

"Yeah, David Smith's sister is Anne's mother. Anyway, she just cracked, told me that she didn't mean for anybody to get hurt. She was just trying to help her uncle save the town. She cried and cried. I called the RCMP but by the time they got to the Chamber, Smith was gone. I guess he was headed back to the mine to destroy evidence or something. We'll never know. I found the Day-Timer in Anne's recycling. She said she'd found it in the trash one night after her uncle had been over and thinking that it must have been a mistake, put it in her blue box."

"I can't believe how ironic that is," said Cole, smiling.

"Recycling really does pay," said Nancy.

They sat in silence for a moment, then Cole asked, "What happened to Dale?"

"He's been released. I got a front-page story with him saying he planned to sue the RCMP and the town and the mine and anybody else he could think of. He came by yesterday to see you, but you were asleep. Peggy McSorlie has been here a few times, and so has Perry Gilbert."

"That's nice, isn't it?" asked Cole.

"It is," she said. She put her hand on his, and he held her fingers.

"What about Sarah?"

"Peggy called her. Talked to your ex. They know you're fine. Sarah called here yesterday evening, and I told her you would call her when you were awake."

"Sounds like you've been here a lot."

"I've left to sleep," she said, "but otherwise, someone's got to be here to make sure you don't do anything stupid."

Cole smiled. "Thank you," he said. He managed to turn his head to look at her. She smiled at him.

"It's OK," she finally said, her smile wide, showing her lovely teeth. "But you better start talking, buddy. I'm just waiting around here to get a story out of this."

Epilogue

They rode together across the open meadows, the first wildflowers of summer touching the bellies of the horses. The May blizzard had dumped more than a foot of wet snow all up and down the foothills, and that moisture, when the sun finally emerged at the beginning of June, created a riot of colour. From the meadow at the crest of the gently sloping hill, Cole pointed the nose of his horse west and the other followed, so they could sit side by side and look out over the vast sweep of hills and valleys.

Far below, to the west, ran Highway 22. Every now and again a truck was heard labouring up the grade heading south, but aside from that intrusion there was no sound save the wind, the cacophony of bird song, and the buzzing of the season's first insects.

In the late afternoon light the row upon row of hills that climbed and fell between their perch on top of the Porcupine Hills and the great, breaking wave of stone that formed the eastern wall of the Rocky Mountains were painted in receding tones of green and blue. Then at the base of the great mountains grey, and finally black. A cloud scudded overhead and its shadow followed it, as if pulled by a string, slipping easy across the folded earth below.

"This is the most beautiful place in the world," said Sarah, her eyes wide.

"It is God's country," agreed Cole.

"I can't believe you've never taken me here!"

"We're here now. Enjoy it."

"You grew up here," she said, as if that somehow that made him different than everybody else.

"I did," he said, knowing that even this place couldn't mask the other forces that shaped his life.

"It's so beautiful."

"It's so beautiful," he said, turning from the vista to look at his daughter, "that it breaks my heart."

"I won't let that happen," she said.

Cole turned away and pushed the tears across his cheek with his knuckles.

They turned their horses and Cole led her down through the aspens and picked their way along the faint trail of his youthful exploits. The new leaves unfurled, so green and so fragrant, that

Stephen Legault

the eyes ached for seeing them and the mind reeled to know that the fight between winter and spring had finally been settled.

Cole had stayed in the hospital for three more days. He had suffered a serious concussion and a host of other maladies that required medical attention, including a broken ankle, a sprained wrist and a cracked bone in his cheek. When he was finally released, Peggy McSorlie wheeled him to her car and drove him to her ranch, where he spent another two weeks nursing his wounds, and once again wrapping up loose ends.

There were many to be wrapped.

Perry Gilbert came to the McSorlie Ranch one afternoon. Cole sat on a lawn chair with his foot resting on a pillow on a stump under a cottonwood when Gilbert drove up. He motioned him over.

"How's the foot?" Gilbert asked. He pulled up another stump and sat down on it.

"Doc says I'll be back walking in another week. But I won't be able to pole vault anymore."

"Life's tough."

"Yeah, but I never was good at it anyway. Kept spearing myself with the pole."

Gilbert told him that Dale had been cleared of all charges and the RCMP had issued an apology. "He's still going to sue," said Gilbert.

"Does he have a chance?"

"Who knows? But when was the last time Dale did anything because he thought he could win?"

Cole nodded.

"So they found the murder weapon in the back of Smith's truck," Gilbert said flatly.

Cole raised an eyebrow. His face still had a number of small bandages on it, and it was pocked with tiny cuts from the shattered glass. One longer cut dissected his left eyebrow. He had been lucky not to lose that eye, the doctor told him. He raised it now.

"Pipe wrench. Orange. About two feet long. He had washed it, but the forensics people can pick up even the faintest traces of blood. It was a match with Mike Barnes."

Cole exhaled slowly. "What about the story that Dale's truck was seen at the mine?" he asked.

Perry shrugged. "Now that Dale's been cleared, we'll never know. There are three or four similar vehicles registered to men who work at the mine." The two men watched a woodpecker at work on a tree at the edge of the farm. Then Perry said, "I looked into Hank Henderson's whereabouts on the night of the murder like you asked. Boy, he was pretty sour about you messing around at his place. He nearly turfed me on my butt when I went there to talk with him. But I told him it was official business and he told me where he had been at. Made a trip to Red Deer that night to meet with a dude named Jeremy Moon. You know him?"

Cole nodded.

"So he and Moon finished up the final version of the Environmental Assessment that night. Henderson didn't get back 'til after midnight."

"I wonder why Emma Henderson lied to me?"

"I think you must have spooked her. She panicked. It happens. We're under pressure, someone we love is being threatened. We do stupid things. We lie."

Cole took a deep breath and let it out. He understood.

"And one last thing," Perry Gilbert said. "I ran into your friend Nancy this morning. She had just checked out of the Rim Rock and was on her way back to Edmonton. She said that she asked Deborah Cody about her hand. I guess she hit that gorilla George and busted a couple of bones. Nancy said that they were 'making up' after their big fight and that's why George wasn't at the bar that night."

"All neat and tidy."

"Seems like."

Cole stayed with the McSorlies for another week after that. He tried to write a strategy for saving the Cardinal Divide, but in the end it seemed futile. Finally, one night, he, Gord and Peggy McSorlie, and a couple of others from the East Slopes Conservation Group were having dinner at the McSorlie place when Peggy said, "I think we've got to change course entirely. We've got to win over this community. They don't trust us. We don't trust them. We're at each other's throats. We say we're doing this to save this town, and to save Cardinal Divide, but we're hardly even a part of this community."

"What do you propose, darling?" asked Gord.

"Go underground for a few months. Maybe a year. Build some bridges. Turn down the heat a little. Win some friends. Work on some things that the local community people want to see done, not just our own priorities, but the priorities of our neighbours. Show them that we're real people, not zealots."

"How's that going to stop the McLeod River project?" asked Cole.

"Maybe it won't. But what we're doing now isn't stopping it either. We need to get organized in this town so that it's not just twenty of us opposing the mine because it's bad for bears. It needs to be two hundred, or two thousand of us opposing it because it's just plain bad, period. Bad for our future, bad for business, bad for our kids."

Cole sat up all night that night, writing. In the morning he handed Peggy a fifteen-page strategy paper, and by the end of the next day they'd polished it.

"We might not win in the short-term with this strategy," said Cole, "but we just might pull this off over the long-term."

Peggy flipped through the pages and smiled. She looked up at him. "I like the fact that you said we."

He saw Nancy again before he left. "Did you ever figure out who put the goons on you in the bar?" she asked.

He shook his head. "Likely never will, but my money is on Henderson."

"Sounds like a good guess. You going to ask him?"

Cole just grinned.

"Where are you headed?" she asked.

"Home," he said, leaning against the bumper of a rental car he had been issued by his insurance company.

"Vancouver?" she asked.

He smiled. Where was home? "I'm going to Calgary first to pick up Sarah at the airport, and then I'm going to see my mom and my brother. What about you?"

"Back to Edmonton I guess."

"You don't sound too thrilled by the prospect."

"It's OK. The *Journal* isn't really my cup of tea."

"The *Vancouver Sun* is a much better paper." Cole smirked through his bandages.

Cole and Sarah Blackwater reached the ranch just as Cole's stomach began to rumble. He smiled. "You hungry?"

"Sure am!"

"Why don't you go and wash up and help Grandma set the table while I brush Mac and Sally here?"

"That sounds good," she said, pulling gently on the reins as they came to the barn.

He stepped from Mac and helped her down off Sally. "Off you go," he said, patting her arm. She ran to the house. When the screen door had slammed shut behind her he turned to face the barn.

"OK, you two, time for a handful of oats and then some dinner."

He led the two horses around the back of the barn and gave them each its oats and a pail of water. He unsaddled them and felt the hot, wet flesh under each saddle with his hands. Then he patted their withers and their muscles twitched. He brushed them down and scratched their ears and rubbed their forelocks and led them into the darkness under the barn. "Thanks for taking good care of Sarah," he said to Sally as he stowed her in her stall. "And thanks for taking it easy on me, Mac," he said when the other horse was stowed inside.

He put the saddles and tack away, washed his hands in a bucket of water, and stepped into the yard, breathing in the rich scent of the horses and of spring.

He didn't plan to, but as he walked around the barn, he was drawn to its double front doors. Without thinking he walked up the grade toward them. When he stood before their weathered boards he reached up and flipped the latch and swung them both wide open. They creaked. The smell of hay flavoured the air. The barn was dark except for the sunlight that seeped through the big doors and found its way through the chinks in the walls. But there was enough illumination to see the boxing ring at the barn's centre. The four lights still swayed overhead, moving slightly in the breeze that swept through the open doors. It looked so much smaller than when he was a child. So much smaller than just three years ago.

He could see in the middle of the ring the dark stain that reached back angrily toward the sagging hemp ropes. He could see the fingers of that stain reach out, red and unforgiving.

"Thinking about making a comeback?" The voice behind

made him start. He turned slowly on his sore ankle and saw his brother walk up the grade to the barn.

He grinned tightly. "I don't think so," he said and turned back to the ring.

Walter stood beside him. He was an inch shorter than Cole, his shoulders wide and body still muscular and compact. He was wearing his sweat-stained Stetson; the hat was an old Park Service issue, the badge removed from the leather strap that circled it. Cole looked at his brother. He wore a canvas coat and blue Wranglers and a pair of brown boots. He looked every bit the cowboy.

"When are you going to stop dressing like a cowpoke?" Cole asked.

"When I stop being one, I guess," said Walter, and winked. Then, "This is where it happened, ain't it?"

Cole caught his breath. He was silent for a full minute. "You know it is. We talked about it after the funeral."

"I know," said Walter, peering into the darkness of the barn. "Just never really had time to talk with you about it after that. You headed off to BC so quick afterwards. Like you were running from something or somebody. Thing is, Cole, nobody would blame you for it, if they knew what really went down here. As they say, the old man had it coming."

Cole shrugged and was silent. Finally he said, "Yeah, they would. It's not about blame. It's not even about right or wrong. It's about responsibility. He never took responsibility for what he did to me. To us. To mom."

"So you're going to fix that somehow? By taking responsibility yourself? How's that going to help?"

Cole stood still for a long time, thinking of Sarah. Then he shook his head.

The two brothers stared at the ring.

"Maybe we should go a few rounds before we take this thing apart tomorrow. What do you say?" said Walter. He turned to Cole, put his hands in front of his face, and danced side to side in the dust.

"I don't think so, Walt," Cole said quietly.

"Body not up to it yet?"

"Body is fine, Walt. It's my heart that isn't up to it."

Walter put his hand on his brother's shoulder. "Let's go and get some dinner, Cole. Mom's been in the kitchen all day. And Sarah's got the table set. Don't want to keep them waiting."

They turned and closed the barn doors and walked back across the yard side by side.

The Cardinal Divide: Final Environmental Assessment
Stephen Legault on writing the Cole Blackwater series

The beginning

The Cardinal Divide was born of too much beer and not enough sun during a two-week vacation in Costa Rica in 2003. It was November and it rained nearly every day I was there. The lawn surrounding my tiny *cabina* became a shin-deep lake and red ants by the thousands invaded the airy hut, giving me something to do with my vacation time. Between bouts of fruitless struggle to prevent the *formicidae* invasion and mopping up after storm surges, I sat on the deck, drank *cervaza* Imperial, and read half a dozen damp and worn paperback mystery novels bought or traded from local vendors.

It wasn't my first foray into the mystery genre. Tony Hillerman's *Skinwalkers* was a gift from my colleagues at Grand Canyon National Park in 1994, and I read it on the inhumanly long journey home from the southwest that spring. For years I associated long cross-continental plane trips with Tony Hillerman books: stories just long enough to get me from Calgary to Toronto or back. My friend Paul Novitski gave me a Nevada Barr mystery in 2001, and I read a bunch of her excellent Anna Pigeon mysteries that year as well. I love James Lee Burke's Dave Robicheaux series. But on the Costa Rica trip, I read *The First Deadly Sin* by Lawrence Saunders and became hooked on the genre.

I started to think about what I might have to contribute to the mass of murder mysteries crowding the shelves of used bookstores. I've been writing since 1988, seriously trying to get published since 1993 or so. I always imagined myself as a composer of literary essays on the relationship between people and nature, or the writer of a desperately sad, tragic work of fiction in which the protagonist reveals something core to the nature of the human condition before succumbing to a broken heart.

While I didn't see myself penning a mystery about a mine, I have been trying to *stop* mines from being dug in beautiful wilderness areas for the last twenty years. In 2003 the effort to stop the Cheviot Coal Mine from being dug on the northern side of the Cardinal Divide, just east of Jasper National Park, was one of the most important environmental challenges in Alberta. I had first become involved in this fight in 1995 when, as a freshman member of the Board of Directors of the Alberta Wilderness Association, I heard Ben Gadd and Dianne Pachal talk about the new plans for the mine. The Cardinal Divide had been much on my mind since I had first walked along its gently sloping, sinuous summit some years back.

Sitting on the porch of my *cabina* in Costa Rica in 2003, knocking back Imperials, I started to piece some thoughts together: Could I find a way to tell a story about a cherished, beautiful place in a way that might appeal to someone other than an armchair activist or closet environmentalist? Could I do it so that the novel didn't simply rant against coal mining, but actually told a good story?

I remember something my friend and fellow writer Greer Chesher once told me when I worked for her at Grand Canyon National Park: "You have to have a plot." Fiction can't simply be a new, shiny vessel in which to carry around my polemic. As an activist, I'm always searching for new ways to interest the public in an important issue. As a writer, I'm always looking for a new story to tell while delivering a poignant message.

As I sat there, watching the Caribbean Sea, I let the issue, the landscape, and the story slowly congeal in my head.

The flight back was long and, late at night on the silent plane, I sat with a tiny notebook and jotted down the names of the characters: Cole Blackwater, Nancy Webber, Dale van Stempvort, Mike Barnes.... I wrote down the events of the fictional opening crime, and then I crafted the story around the truth that would make the book a mystery. By the time I had defrosted my aging Toyota pickup at the Calgary airport at 2 AM, *The Cardinal Divide* filled two dozen pages in my little notebook. It would occupy my mind, and keep my fingers moving, for the next five years.

Substantive form

While *The Cardinal Divide* had taken shape in a few days late in 2003, it was several years before it found any substantive form. During the winter of 2004 I managed to pen the first six chapters of the book, but I lost my momentum and the book languished for a while. I didn't stop writing, I just stopped typing. I do a lot of "writing" in my head, playing with the characters and mapping out story ideas while I'm running or walking in the mountains.

An injury in the summer of 2004 was a boon for the book. I pinched my sciatic nerve (playing with Lego with my nephew) and had to bail halfway through a 250-kilometre backpacking trip. I swallowed a fist full of Advil, found a bottle of gin in the freezer, and drove to the Columbia Valley to hide out at my friend Mark Holmes' place. I used the remaining six days of my down time to write an outline of the entire book.

Which then sat untouched for more than a year and a half.

In April 2006 my first book, *Carry Tiger to Mountain: the Tao of Activism and Leadership,* was published by Arsenal Pulp Press. The year previous was consumed with the writing, editing, and marketing of that work, so Cole Blackwater was again put on the backburner. When *Carry Tiger* was set loose on the unsuspecting public, I found new energy for Cole Blackwater. In just over a month I penned 17 chapters, 75,000 words, and 278 pages. My one-day record was over the May long weekend, when on Sunday I wrote 31 pages and almost 8,000 words. Many, many tea bags were sacrificed to accomplish this feat.

I like writing first drafts, but to me this is a mechanical process. The detailed chapter outline written at Mark Holmes' place two years before made the first draft easy to compose. With a detailed outline, the first draft is just a process of adding the filler to the plot. Much good narrative emerges and the general gist of the story forms, and from time to time I experience the pure bliss of creativity. But it's the second draft where I find the real magic of writing. Here I can concentrate on the subtleties of character development and add prose to landscape descriptions. The second draft is my favourite part of the writing process. It's the next seven or eight drafts I could do without....

Facts and fiction about the real Cardinal Divide

While most of the places and all of the people in *The Cardinal Divide* are figments of my imagination, the rocky buttress of the Cardinal Divide is not. It is very real, and for thirty years it has been threatened by development in one form or another. As this book goes to print, much of the landscape around the Cardinal Divide has been lost to coal mining.

The Divide is in fact a north-south height of land. On the north side of the Cardinal Divide, the waters flow to the Arctic Ocean via a circuitous route, following the Athabasca River, which flows into Lake Athabasca and then empties, via the Slave River and Great Slave Lake, into one of Canada's greatest waterways: the McKenzie.

To the south, the waters drain into the South Saskatchewan River and find their way into the Saskatchewan River, then empty into Lake Winnipeg and drain north into Hudson's Bay via the mighty Nelson River.

When I was introduced to the Cardinal Divide in 1995 by Ben Gadd and Dianne Pachal, various factions were conspiring to dig a twenty-two kilometre long open-pit mine along the north side of the Divide, back toward Jasper National Park. I went there on an Alberta Wilderness Association field trip and fell in love with its sensuous curve.

Battles have been fought and won, and lost, over the Cardinal Divide. While the Divide itself is protected from development in the Whitehorse Wildland Provincial Park, the area immediately to the north and west of the Cardinal Divide is not. In the book, Cole looks out at the Cardinal Divide in the direction that has recently been destroyed by road building and open-pit mining for the real Cheviot mining operations. Five open pits are planned by Elk River Coal for the region, with two already complete. Massive road building operations have been underway for several years. Updates on the mine can be found at www.thecardinaldivide.com.

Names

I have a hard time with character names, so I poach them from my friends.

Finding a name for the book's protagonist was my first task. In 1996 I met three brothers who own an outfitting company in Moab, Utah called Tex's Riverways. Darren, Dirk, and Devon helped my friends and me on various multi-week river trips down the serpentine Green River, and we became friends. I think it was Dirk who started referring to me as Glint Longshadow. It was a stupid name, but for some reason Dirk had this image of me striding across the Utah landscape, fighting evil developers with a glint in my eye. It's hard *not* to get attached to that image of oneself. When searching for a name for Cole I first thought of Glint, and then let my imagination run wild. Blackwater somehow emerged from my cerebral morass, and it stuck.

I stole "Cole" from Cormac McCarthy's *All the Pretty Horses,* which is my favourite book of all time (I was pretty damn unimpressed with the movie). John Grady Cole is, in my opinion, the best character ever drawn.

My original intent was to simply name this book "Blackwater" and call it a day. But then the US invaded Iraq, which brought to light the world's largest private army of mercenaries staffed by Blackwater USA, and my plans were shot to hell. *The Cardinal Divide* came into being after NeWest agreed to publish the book.

Some folks I know may find their names in the book. A word of warning: don't think that because a character bares your name that I have attributed your characteristics to that fictional personality. I'm always bereft of ideas for names and find myself picking them randomly from the ether and saying, "I'll just use this name until I come up with something different." And then suddenly the book is in print and it's too late.

Oh, and there is no Oracle in Alberta. Really, there isn't.

What's next for Cole?

From the very start of my scribbling, I've intended to use the Cole Blackwater series to tell more than one story. It might have been on that same flight from Costa Rica that I mapped out a phalanx of possible plots. These environmental and social justice stories are all important to me, ones I know about given my work over the last twenty years in the environmental movement in Canada. But as I've said, the books need to be more than just polemics. So there are subplots – other conflicts to be resolved – that form a narrative thread throughout the Cole Blackwater series.

Two more Cole Blackwater mysteries are in production, and NeWest has agreed to publish the next book in the series, *The Darkening Archipelago.* Set in the Broughton Archipelago, a wild, beautiful, and rugged region of coastal British Columbia that is being strangled by the development of salmon farms, the book finds Cole in the remote fishing village of Port Lostcoast at the funeral of his friend and native activist Archie Ravenwing, who disappeared in a violent storm. In *The Darkening Archipelago*, Cole helps to tie up loose ends in his friend's work and discovers that Archie was unravelling a complex plot involving provincial and local band politicians, anti-native bigots, and a salmon farming company with deep pockets, its operations spreading like sea lice across the troubled Broughton. What had Archie Ravenwing discovered on his last voyage to the mysterious Humphrey Rock? Was his death really an accident, or was it murder?

In the third book, *The Lucky Strike Manifesto*, Cole teams up with his best friend and homelessness advocate Denman Scott to help stop the least fortunate of Vancouver's residents from being evicted from their low-rent hotels to make way for upscale condominiums. Soon they learn that one by one, the homeless of Vancouver's troubled Downtown Eastside are disappearing without a trace. Cole and Denman venture into the dark corners of the city's underworld and into political corruption at City Hall to unravel the mystery behind one of the city's landmark hotels – the Lucky Strike – before more homeless people vanish from its shadow.

Stitched through the plots of these books is Cole's violent, tragic relationship with his father. What happened between Cole and his father remains a mystery throughout the second book, but its impact on Cole becomes increasingly apparent: the brutal end of Cole's father's life haunts him. How he will resolve the role he played in his father's death, if any, forms a narrative thread throughout the first three books in the series.

I have a dozen more ideas for Cole, his friends, and for the myriad social and environmental issues, landscapes, and people stretching across North America (I have one book I want to set in Costa Rica, and another in Baja) that I believe are important. Climate change, bulk water exports, resort development, the Great Plains, the Rocky Mountains, Utah's canyonous desert. But, one book at a time....

The Darkening Archipelago

Cole Blackwater Mystery #2 by Stephen Legault

Chapter One

The rain began suddenly. From the west, skipping like a flat stone over the broad waters that separate Vancouver Island from the convoluted knot of smaller islands at the mouth of Knight Inlet, the storm raced toward the steep slopes of the Coast Mountains. When it reached them, it ricocheted up their slopes, and back and forth across the narrow passage at the mouth of the fjord. With the rain came wind. At first it moved the water into small waves, but within an hour it was pushing hard on the sea, churning it into ten-foot swells. The rain hit hard on the water, pounding it with machine gun bursts. The sky pressed downward. The tops of the densely forested mountains that rose straight up from the water disappeared, and a tattered blackness settled against the sea.

Archie Ravenwing felt the storm approaching before he saw it, before it soaked him through. He could feel it coming for most of the day. Maybe someone had done the weather dance last night, their blankets twisting as they rapidly moved back and forth to the chorus of voices, to the beating of drums. Maybe he should have paid closer attention to that morning's marine weather forecast.

Ravenwing felt the storm in his hands. Twisted and corded like the ropes he had spent his sixty years working with, his joints always ached when a storm loomed. From November to March, and sometimes well into April, his hands always seemed to ache. There was no denying it—he was past his prime. But he still had work to do.

Ravenwing had set off from Port Lostcoast on the *Inlet Dancer* before dawn. Lostcoast was on the north shore of Parish Island where he had been born, and where he had spent most of his life. But he wasn't fishing today. The salmon season wasn't set to open for another two months, if it opened at all. For thousands of years people along the wild, ragged west coast of British Columbia had guided their boats into the heaving waters of the Pacific, harvesting the fish for food and ceremony. Among the tribes of the west coast, salmon was the most important animal in the world. Life turned on salmon seasons. But in the last twenty years, so much had changed. Ravenwing thought of this as he powered up the inlet that morning, intent on his destination but aware of the shifting day around him.

Salmon smolts had been running for nearly two weeks, and Ravenwing had spent every day on the water since they had started. These silvery darts had spent as much as three years living in the tiny headwater tributaries of Knight Inlet. Most of the salmon born there were eaten or died of natural causes. Only ten percent survived to grow large enough to migrate down river and out into the salty water at the mouth of the creeks, and then into the inlet itself.

The morning had been bright enough, with nothing more menacing than bunched up pillows of clouds hanging over the mountains of Vancouver Island, far to the west. But Ravenwing suspected that by day's end there would be rain. He flexed his thick, burled hands as he lightly played the wheel of his thirty-two troller, heading east up the inlet.

By the time the day had started to warm, Ravenwing had arrived at Minstrel Island and the narrow mouth to Clio Channel, the ideal place for a couple of hours of dip net sampling before he turned his attention to the small bays and coves that marked the jigsaw puzzle shore. Archie shut down the *Inlet Dancer*'s powerful Cummins 130-horsepower inboard motor and let the silence of the morning wash over him. He stepped from the wheelhouse onto the aft deck of the boat with a thermos of coffee; he stretched and yawned. Thermos in hand, he deftly walked the high, narrow gunwale and sat down on the raised fish box, which doubled as a table. He unscrewed the cap of the thermos and caught the first scent of the hot, rich coffee, closing his eyes to savour the aroma. The smell of the coffee mingled with other scents. The tang of the ocean, salty and spiced with the yin and yang of life and decay, and the pungent fragrance of the woods, the thick Sitka spruce and red cedar forest rising up along the towering cliffs just a hundred metres off his port side. Archie Ravenwing smiled broadly as these fragrances perfumed the air he drew deeply into his lungs.

He poured the coffee into the thermos cap and blew on it gently, the steam rising up and disappearing on the breeze. Later, Archie guessed, that breeze would turn into a squall. But for the moment the morning was warm and gentle, and he savoured it. He sipped at his coffee and looked around him.

Born into the Lostcoast Band of the North Salish First Nation, Archie Ravenwing had been fishing, guiding, hunting, and exploring the coastal estuaries, inlets, reaches, and straits from as far away as Puget Sound in the south to the Queen Charlotte Islands in the north since he was old enough to stand. As he let his eyes roll over the massive sweep of land and water and sky before him that morning, he was happy that this reach of the Broughton Archipelago still seemed very much as it had for generations. The hills jutted steeply from the rich waters, their shoulders cloaked in spruce and fir. Beneath those giant trees, tangles of salmon berries and alders gripped the soil. Between them walked another totem species for the Lostcoast people – the grizzly bear.

Bears and salmon and the ancient forests that surrounded them had always been a holy trinity for Archie and his people. Grizzly bears fed on the salmon as the fish beat and bashed their way up through the ankle-deep waters of the tiny tributaries to their spawning grounds each fall. The grizzly bears grew fat on the fish, often eating only their brains, rich in nutrients they would need for their winter hibernation. The dead fish, left to rot in the woods, nourished the stalwart trees, which in turn held the entire ecosystem together with their wide, spreading roots. The trees sheltered and cooled the salmon rivers, and fed the many smaller creatures that made their homes among them. When the trees fell into the streams, downed logs created places for the spawning salmon to hide and rest as, exhausted and crazed, they struggled back to the source of life.

Archie sipped his coffee, thinking about this cycle of existence. He pushed back the sadness that approached whenever he thought this way. There was some question as to whether there would be enough wild salmon in this year's run to allow for a commercial fishery. Talk in the provincial capital, Victoria, and among senior federal officials responsible for the fishery suggested that a complete ban might be necessary to allow decimated salmon runs to recover.

The people of the Lostcoast Band had been fishing for thousands of years but had never contributed to the decimation of the salmon fishery the way the modern industrial fishery had. Now Archie

Ravenwing's people would pay the price incurred by the greed and myopic short-sightedness of the commercial fishing industry and its protectors and proponents in government.

In the years since the new BC Liberal government had lifted the moratorium on new salmon farms in the province, there had been an explosion of interest in new aquaculture developments all along BC's knotted west coast. In the Broughton Archipelago, where Archie Ravenwing fished and lived, there were nearly thirty salmon farms in operation. Many of these open-net farms were located on the migration routes of native wild salmon. And though industry advocates argued that the two were unrelated, along with the development of salmon farms came a corresponding decline in the number of wild salmon. Archie knew that, in a recent count, only 150,000 wild salmon returned to the Broughton, down from the historical three and a half million. In 2002 the wild pink salmon stock collapsed, with only five percent of the native wild fish returning to spawn. Archie knew the numbers by rote.

For Ravenwing, it was as if part of his own body, his own soul, had vanished. The part of his heart that swam through the waters of Tribune Channel to the north, and up the mouth of Knight Inlet, was gone.

Archie tried to keep that darkening sadness at bay. How could it have come to this? he wondered. After a thousand years, his family wouldn't be allowed to fish their ancestral waters? He turned his face toward the sky. A throaty call greeted him, and he opened his eyes to see a jet-black shape cruise overhead. The husky chortled again. Archie raised a hand in greeting. "Good morning, Grandpa!" he said quietly, waving at the raven, a smile creasing his face.

"U'melth, Raven, who brought us the moon, fire, salmon, sun, and the tides," he recited. "Trickster, grandfather of a thousand pranks. OK! I'll lighten up!" he added, draining his mug and slinging the dregs into the water. Then he said: "Time to get to work."

Archie rose lightly and walked back to the wheelhouse, where he opened a large Rubbermaid bin and removed the tools he would need for his morning work. He put the long, flexible net together on its pole and readied half a dozen plastic sample jars. These he put on the fish box on the deck of the boat. Without ceremony he began his sampling, drawing forth the tiny salmon fry to be funnelled into the jars. So few, so few. Ravenwing shook his head as he dipped again into the waters.

His work that morning lasted until almost noon. By then he had filled the jars with juvenile salmon, their tiny, finger-sized bodies being consumed by sea lice. This was what Archie Raven-wing was seeking – the irrefutable evidence that the wild salmon stocks of Knight Inlet, and the Broughton Archipelago, were being parasitized by sea lice.

Archie considered the tiny pink salmon smolts in the sample jars. He held one up to the light and counted the lice clinging to it. On one smolt he counted four of the parasites from two different species. Adults might succumb when they had six or seven sea lice on their fins, gills, or skin. Smolts like those in Archie's sampling jars would die with only a few sea lice feeding on them. Archie regarded his unfortunate catch. "Not doing so good, are you little friend?" He was finding more and more smolts with more and more sea lice. And he had yet to reach his day's destination: Jeopardy Rock. There he expected to find the epicentre of sea lice contamination.

"Not so good...." he said again, his voice trailing off.

Ravenwing knew that sea lice were a natural parasite that preyed on wild salmon along British Columbia's wild coast, and elsewhere across North America. But in the last ten years, there had been a shocking rise in the number of lice infesting wild salmon. Where before the numbers had been low, and very few salmon actually died as a result of playing host to the lice, now entire runs of wild pink and other salmon were being devastated by them. Despite protests from the salmon farming industry, ir-refutable evidence pointed to the rash of farmed Atlantic salmon as the source of the outbreak. The Atlantic salmon could survive with many more sea lice than the native pink, chum, and Coho.

Archie took a sharp, black felt pen from his shirt pocket and labelled the jars. He would return these to Dr. Cassandra Petrel for her study.

Archie flexed his big hands and looked at the sky. "Starting to crowd in," he said aloud to nobody in particular. "Fixing to churn up pretty good, I think."

He knew he should head back down the inlet toward Port Lost-coast before the storm set upon him, but he had one more thing to do that day. Something had been eating Archie Ravenwing that he had to set straight. So instead of turning the *Inlet Dancer* for home, he powered across the inlet toward the mouth of Tribune Channel, skipping the heavy boat across the small waves already being formed by the wind.

* * *

Now the rain fell in torrents, churning the waves like so many knives thrust into the sea. The *Inlet Dancer* bounced and rocked, nose into the waves, powering past the fish farms at Doctor Islets and into the main body of Knight Inlet, making for home. Archie stood in the pilothouse near the stern of the boat, one hand locked on the wheel, the other clenching the throttle. This blow was bigger than he had foreseen and, though he was prepared to moor and wait out the storm, this stretch of water had few safe harbours.

And after what he had seen at Jeopardy Rock, a new urgency filled Archie Ravenwing that made him push for home against what seemed prudent for the weather.

A wave crashed over the bow of the *Inlet Dancer* and the boat dipped into the trough behind it, rising up the side of another stack of water. The swells topped fifteen feet now and came in irregular patterns, every fourth, fifth, or sixth wave taller than the rest, coming on faster than the others. Ravenwing held the wheel firmly, keeping the boat head on to the storm, not wanting the narrow vessel to get punched side-to by one of the rogue waves.

He had suspected for some time that what was happening at Jeopardy Rock was more than just simple salmon farming. He had suspected for some time that the company was doing more than just breeding Atlantic salmon. Now he was certain. Now he would make his calls when he got back to Port Lostcoast and begin to set the record straight. He would begin to make amends. Did Archie Ravenwing believe in redemption? He believed in justice, even if his own actions hadn't always seemed just. He believed that a man's motivation sometimes compelled behaviour that appeared inconsistent with his espoused values. But we are complex creatures, reasoned Ravenwing.

Another wave rocked the *Inlet Dancer* and Archie pitched forward. He patted the wheel and reminisced that she had survived worse.

It was growing dark, the day slipping from the sky, and the clouds pressed down so low that the tops of the trees on mighty Gilford Island were hardly visible. Ravenwing switched on his running lights, not so he could see, but so he could be seen. Sonar and radar would guide him down the inlet, through the darkness and the storm, but he worried about small pleasure crafts caught in the weather with no such second sight.

Ravenwing counted the waves, counted the minutes. Half an hour passed and the hulk of Gilford Island started to recede. The waves still crashed on the *Inlet Dancer*'s bow, and now he was moving across the channel toward the eastern tip of Turnour Island. At his pace of seven or eight knots per hour, it would be another two hours or more before he would be abreast of Parish Island, and home.

The VHF marine radio in the pilothouse crackled and, intuitively, Ravenwing set it to scan. Static filled the wheelhouse, the white noise being engulfed by the sound of the storm that darkened the archipelago around Ravenwing. Then a voice, clear as a bell: "Any craft in the vicinity of Deep Water Cove, this is the *Rising Moon*. I've lost my primary and am taking on water."

Ravenwing snatched the handset for the marine radio and spoke over the howl of the storm. "*Rising Moon*, this is the *Inlet Dancer*. I'm passing Ship Rock now, about to make the crossing. What is your position?"

"Glad to hear your voice, *Inlet Dancer*. I'm about one mile west of Deep Water, but I'm getting pushed toward the rocks on Deep Water Bluff."

"Do you have secondary?"

"I'm running on my little Evinrude 25, *Inlet Dancer*."

"OK, hold on, I'll circle back for you."

"I'm glad to find you out here," came the static-filled response.

"I'm not," Ravenwing said over the VHF and set the handset back on the radio.

For a moment he would be side to the brunt of the storm, so Ravenwing determined to make that quick. He throttled up, pushing over the breaking waves, and counted. The big waves were pushing a wall of water over the boat's bow onto the deck, momentarily flooding it until the water drained away through the breaks in the gunwales. He counted. A wave crested, ebbed, and Ravenwing

Stephen Legault

throttled back, spun the wheel, and turned to lee, then powered back up again as the stern of the boat was engulfed in the next white breaker. The ocean flooded into the wheelhouse, washing Ravenwing to his ankles in icy water.

In ten minutes he was adjacent to Deep Water Cove, the massive bluffs that guarded the opening black through the shadowless night.

"*Rising Moon*, this is *Inlet Dancer*. Can you see my running lights?" Ravenwing spoke calmly into the handset.

There was no response. He peered at his sonar and radar, watching the rocky coast weave its white line along the left side of the screen, searching for rocks and logs in his path, scanning for the tell-tale shape of a boat to emerge from the black.

"*Rising Moon*, this is *Inlet Dancer*...."

"I see you, Archie," came the voice, clear through the radio.

"What's your location?"

"I'm right behind you."

Archie turned in the pilothouse and saw the *Rising Moon*'s running lights emerge from the cove.

"I found some shelter to wait in. Can you come along side of me?"

"Yup," Archie said, turning again in the roiling channel waters. Another wave broke over his boat and Archie was slammed hard into the fibreglass wall of the pilothouse. He stayed standing, his fingers locked on the wheel and the throttle.

The *Rising Moon* was a small pleasure craft, not twenty feet in length, which had seen better days. Archie cut his throttle as much as he dared so close to the shore, and eased toward the smaller boat. The canopy was up, the pilot eclipsed by the windshield and the rain that drove down on the inlet like an angry fist.

"Do you want me to tow you into the cove, *Rising Moon*?" Archie asked into the handset.

"Can you come alongside, and we'll talk it through?"

Archie cursed. It was always this way with this guy, it seemed. "Sure, but let's make it quick, as it's fixing to blow pretty good and I don't want to be out longer than need be." He put the handset down again and guided the *Inlet Dancer* along side the drifting *Rising Moon*.

When the two boats were just ten feet apart, Archie killed his motor and stepped from the pilothouse, grabbing a gaff hook from the wall. He stepped onto the narrow deck of the boat and peered through the storm, holding onto the gunwale for support. Jesus Christ, man, come on deck and let's get this over with, Archie cursed into the howling night.

Finally a shape emerged from beneath the canopy of the *Rising Moon*. The man waved and moved to the stern of his vessel, holding on for dear life. Over the clamour of the storm he yelled, "Imagine *me* needing help from *you*."

"Imagine," mocked Ravenwing. "So what exactly are you doing out on a night like this? And in that little tub?"

"I could ask you the same question," replied the man, who was using a gaff of his own to hook the stern gunwale of Ravenwing's boat. Ravenwing used his tool to reach for the *Rising Moon*'s fore cleats.

The boats rose and fell, waves raging against them, and they came together with a crash of the *Inlet Dancer*'s sturdy, fibreglass-covered wood against the *Rising Moon*'s aging hull.

"Your boat is going to be crushed if we stay out like this," Ravenwing yelled. "Let's hook a line and I'll tow you into the cove. We can find a place to secure this tub and we'll motor back to Lostcoast on the *Dancer*."

The man on the *Rising Moon* gave the thumbs up and manoeuvred to the bow of his boat on hands and knees, clinging to the craft lest he be washed into the sea. He tossed his bow line to Archie. Ravenwing then secured the line from the *Rising Moon* to a cleat on the port side of the *Inlet Dancer*'s stern. The man on the *Rising Moon* held onto his line firmly in his right hand, the three-foot gaff in his right, and made it fast on the bow cleat, then turning and clambering for the safety of the stern of his boat.

"Permission to come aboard, *Captain*," he barked to Ravenwing, who had stepped back into the pilothouse to crank up the fishing boat's powerful inboard motors.

"You know the way," Ravenwing yelled, shaking his head.

The man, gaff still clenched in his hands, stepped onto the *Inlet Dancer* and grabbed the handrail on the side of the pilothouse for stability. Ravenwing engaged the throttle and the boats began to cut into the cresting waves again.

　Stephen Legault

"What the hell were you doing out on a night like this?" Raven-wing said, his voice disappearing into the storm.

"I have my reasons."

"They must have been good ones. Only a fool would venture out on a night like this."

"Well, you're out."

"I am. But everybody around here knows I'm a fool."

The two men stood next to one another as the *Inlet Dancer* began west toward the mouth of Deep Water Cove.

"You said you took shelter. Where?

"I just set the throttle to keep abreast of the cove and waited for you."

"I didn't see you."

"I was there."

"What happened to that nice E-Tec 115 you bought last year?"

"Don't know. Think I took on too much water. Washed it out. Maybe water in the fuel line. I couldn't get that thing going."

Ravenwing looked at the man, who looked straight ahead, his face hidden by the bill of his cap, his body snug in an orange float coat.

"But you could use the 25 to keep abreast of this storm?"

"You're not the only one in this country who can pilot a boat, Archie."

"Who's towing who?" Ravenwing spat. Then he sighed and said, "OK, let's see if we can't find a place to leave this tub for the night and make for home." He looked at his sonar for the depth of the water beneath him and at his radar to read the shore for a safe harbour.

"You're still pissed at me," the man said through the pelting rain.

"You done anything that would change my mind otherwise?"

"That's the thing with you, Archie. You hold everybody to such a high standard, we can never live up to your expectations."

"That isn't true and you know it. But I do expect some common sense. And what you've done is beyond the pale. You know it, so don't play dumb with me. I know you got plenty of brains in that thick head of yours. You've got a responsibility."

"You can be a real jackass, Archie."

"Don't I know it? But at least I know when I've done something wrong. I aim to fix it. You? I just never figured this sort of thing from you. But then I should have guessed this was coming."

The man turned to regard Archie Ravenwing, who was watching his sonar, the VHF still crackling. He said, "Don't you think that your people deserve better? Don't you think that I deserve better?"

"Of course we do. Of course you do!" Archie's voice was coarse over the din. "So act that way. Act like you deserve better. Stop waiting around for someone to hand you things. Go out and get what you want."

The man stepped back a few feet from Archie. "I'm goin' to."

"Well, I'm glad to hear you say it...."

But Archie didn't finish the sentence. The gaff hook caught him in the side of his head, just above the ear, behind the softness of the temple. There was no sound to the blow over the din of the storm. The curved hook pierced Ravenwing's skull and he fell sideways and down, hard onto the pilothouse floor. There he lay as the water washed into the pilothouse. In the darkness the deep pool of blood from where the gaff pierced Ravenwing's skull was indiscernible from the dark water that sluiced on the deck of the *Inlet Dancer*.

The assailant dropped the gaff on top of the body and took control of the fishing boat. He pulled back on the throttle, easing the boat's speed, and turned off its running lights so it could not be seen. He set the wheel so the boat would veer into the inlet, toward more open water. He flipped open the seat top in the pilothouse and found what he was looking for – a short, stout bungee cord. He used it to secure the wheel of the boat so that it maintained its current course. There was no time to set the boat's autopilot.

The killer dropped to one knee, looked at the body of Archie Ravenwing on the deck of the boat – his eyes open, lifeless – and then dragged Ravenwing from the pilothouse onto the narrow aft deck, pulling him to the lee side gunnels and heaving him into the ocean. He threw the gaff hook overboard next.

The man took hold of the rope that connected the *Inlet Dancer* to the *Rising Moon* and reeled in the smaller craft. When the pleasure boat was close enough, he tied a clove hitch in the rope that connected the boats and fastened it to the aft cleat. Then he lowered himself onto the bow of his own craft, holding on again for dear life to the boat's safety rail. He turned and tried to untie the ropes from the cleat on the stern of the *Inlet Dancer.*

His clove hitch came loose, but the second knot wouldn't come free with the weight of both boats on it. Cursing against the storm he struggled to free his boat from the other but to no avail.

He slid on his belly down the length of the bow for the *Rising Moon* and scrambled under the canopy. Moments later he emerged with a hatchet in his right hand and felt his way, the boats roiling in the waves, back toward the bow. As he reached the tip of his boat, he pulled again so that the two boats were bow to stern, and where Archie had made the rope fast around a metal cleat began to chop. A giant wave broke over the bow of the *Inlet Dancer* and then the *Rising Moon,* sending a wall of white foam and black ocean into the man's face, washing him down the slick nose of his boat. He managed to grab the safety rail with his left hand, his right hand still clinging to the hatchet. The water streamed from the bow of the pleasure craft, pushing the man's legs over the port side as he scrambled to hold onto the boat. Eyes wild with panic, he heaved himself back onto the bow and slid back to the fore of the craft. He pulled the boats together again, raised his right hand, and hacked at the rope on the stern cleat — once, twice, three times he brought the axe down on it — and then he was free. He threw the remnant tatters of the rope into the ocean and slid back to the cockpit, under the canopy. Then he fired up the boat's 115 outboard motor, switched on the craft's running lights, and made for home.

Acknowledgements

Frances Thorsen of Chronicles of Crime, Victoria for her extraordinary support, and for reading a late draft of the book, making excellent recommendations, and suggesting NeWest Press as a home for the manuscript.

Kat Wiebe for making this book immeasurably better through numerous edits, suggestions, and tremendous support.

Joe Wiebe and Alison Yauk for support during early phases of the writing.

Greer Chesher and the Ranger Naturalists at Grand Canyon National Park for introducing me to the genre with a gift of Tony Hillerman's *Skinwalkers* in 1994.

Connor Sharpe for being the biggest little fan of Cole Blackwater.

Josh Slatkoff for his friendship and for reading the manuscript and providing feedback.

Ben Gadd for his insight into the coal industry and the coking coal process.

Joel Solomon and the Hollyhock Retreat Centre for providing time and space to work on this book.

The Alberta Wilderness Association, for its more than thirty-five years of tireless defence of the Cardinal Divide; to all of those in Alberta's conservation community who have spent the last decade fighting to keep that magnificent landscape wild and free.

Stephen Legault has been a social and political activist for twenty years. He has worked with local, national, and international conservation organizations to protect Canada's endangered species and wilderness, and to combat climate change. In July 2005 he launched HighWater Mark Strategy and Communications to work with ethically driven businesses, the labour movement, political parties, and cultural organizations. He is Senior Development Officer for Sustainability at the Royal Roads University Foundation. An avid cross-country runner, skier, hiker, and paddler, Stephen has an intimate knowledge of places like Alberta's breathtaking Cardinal Divide.

His first book, *Carry Tiger to Mountain: The Tao of Activism and Leadership*, was published in April 2006. He is the father of two boys, Rio Bergen and Silas Morgen. He and his partner Jenn split their time between Victoria, BC and Canmore, AB.

For details about Stephen Legault's consulting work, visit www.highwatermark.ca. For more information on his Cole Blackwater mystery series, visit www.thecardinaldivide.com.

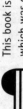

This book is set in the Rotis typeface family, which was developed by Otl Aicher in 1988.